The
Mounted Police
Novels
Volume 4

The Mounted Police Novels Volume 4

The Flaming Forest and Five Short Stories

James Oliver Curwood

LEONAUR

The
Mounted Police
Novels
Volume 4
The Flaming Forest
and Five Short Stories
by James Oliver Curwood

First published under the titles
The Flaming Forest
The Fiddling Man
The Match
The Yellow-Back
The Case of Beauvais
and
The Mouse
Leonaur is an imprint
of Oakpast Ltd

ISBN: 978-0-85706-098-3 (hardcover)
ISBN: 978-0-85706-097-6 (softcover)

http://www.leonaur.com

Publisher's Notes

In the interests of authenticity, the spellings, grammar and place names used have been retained from the original editions.

The opinions of the authors represent a view of events in which he was a participant related from his own perspective, as such the text is relevant as an historical document.

The views expressed in this book are not necessarily those of the publisher.

Contents

The Flaming Forest

1

An hour ago, under the marvellous canopy of the blue northern sky, David Carrigan, Sergeant in His Most Excellent Majesty's Royal Northwest Mounted Police, had hummed softly to himself, and had thanked God that he was alive. He had blessed McVane, superintendent of "N" Division at Athabasca Landing, for detailing him to the mission on which he was bent. He was glad that he was travelling alone, and in the deep forest, and that for many weeks his adventure would carry him deeper and deeper into his beloved north. Making his noonday tea over a fire at the edge of the river, with the green forest crowding like an inundation on three sides of him, he had come to the conclusion—for the hundredth time, perhaps—that it was a nice thing to be alone in the world, for he was on what his comrades at the Landing called a "bad assignment."

"If anything happens to me," Carrigan had said to McVane, "there isn't anybody in particular to notify. I lost out in the matter of family a long time ago."

He was not a man who talked much about himself, even to the superintendent of "N" Division, yet there were a thousand who loved Dave Carrigan, and many who placed their confidences in him. Superintendent McVane had one story which he might have told, but he kept it to himself, instinctively sensing the sacredness of it. Even Carrigan did not know that the one thing which never passed his lips was known to McVane.

Of that, too, he had been thinking an hour ago. It was the thing which, first of all, had driven him into the north. And though it had twisted and disrupted the earth under his feet for a time, it had brought its compensation. For he had come to love the north with a

7

passionate devotion. It was, in a way, his God. It seemed to him that the time had never been when he had lived any other life than this under the open skies. He was thirty-seven now. A bit of a philosopher, as philosophy comes to one in a sun-cleaned and unpolluted air, A good-humoured brother of humanity, even when he put manacles on other men's wrists; graying a little over the temples—and a lover of life. Above all else he was that. A lover of life. A worshiper at the shrine of God's Country.

So he sat, that hour ago, deep in the wilderness eighty miles north of Athabasca Landing, congratulating himself on the present conditions of his existence. A hundred and eighty miles farther on was Fort McMurray, and another two hundred beyond that was Chipewyan, and still beyond that the Mackenzie and its fifteen-hundred-mile trail to the northern sea. He was glad there was no end to this world of his. He was glad there were few people in it. But these people he loved. That hour ago he had looked out on the river as two York boats had forged up against the stream, craft like the long, slim galleys of old, brought over through the Churchill and Clearwater countries from Hudson's Bay.

There were eight rowers in each boat. They were singing. Their voices rolled between the walls of the forests. Their naked arms and shoulders glistened in the sun. They rowed like Vikings, and to him they were symbols of the freedom of the world. He had watched them until they were gone up-stream, but it was a long time before the chanting of their voices had died away. And then he had risen from beside his tiny fire, and had stretched himself until his muscles cracked. It was good to feel the blood running red and strong in one's veins at the age of thirty-seven. For Carrigan felt the thrill of these days when strong men were coming out of the north—days when the glory of June hung over the land, when out of the deep wilderness threaded by the Three Rivers came romance and courage and red-blooded men and women of an almost forgotten people to laugh and sing and barter for a time with the outpost guardians of a younger and more progressive world.

It was north of Fifty-Four, and the waters of a continent flowed toward the Arctic Sea. Yet soon would the strawberries be crushing red underfoot; the forest road was in bloom, scarlet fire-flowers reddened the trail, wild hyacinths and golden-freckled violets played hide-and-seek with the forget-me-nots in the meadows, and the sky was a great splash of velvety blue. It was the north triumphant—at the edge of civilization; the north triumphant, and yet paying its tribute. For at the other end were waiting the royal Upper Ten Thousand and the smart Four Hundred with all the *beau monde* behind them, coveting and demanding that tribute to their sex—the silken furs of a far country, the life's blood and labour of a land infinitely beyond the pale of drawing-rooms and the whims of fashion.

Carrigan had thought of these things that hour ago, as he sat at the edge of the first of the Three Rivers, the great Athabasca. From down the other two, the Slave and the Mackenzie, the fur fleets of the unmapped country had been toiling since the first breakups of ice. Steadily, week after week, the north had been emptying itself of its picturesque tide of life and voice, of muscle and brawn, of laughter and song—and wealth. Through, long months of deep winter, in ten thousand shacks and tepees and cabins, the story of this June had been written as fate had written it each winter for a hundred years or more. A story of the triumph of the fittest. A story of tears, of happiness here and there, of hunger and plenty, of new life and quick death; a story of strong men and strong women, living in the faith of their forefathers, with the best blood of old England and France still surviving in their veins.

Through those same months of winter, the great captains of trade in the city of Edmonton had been preparing for the coming of the river brigades. The hundred and fifty miles of trail between that last city outpost of civilization and Athabasca Landing, the door that opened into the North, were packed hard by team and dog-sledge and packer bringing up the freight that for another year was to last the forest people of the Three River country—a domain reaching from the Landing to the Arctic Ocean. In competition fought the drivers of Revillon Brothers and Hudson's Bay, of free trader and independent adventurer. Freight that grew more precious with each mile it advanced must reach the beginning of the waterway. It started with the early snows. The tide was at full by midwinter. In temperature that nipped men's lungs it did not cease. There was no let-up in the whip-hands of the masters of trade at Edmonton, Winnipeg, Montreal, and London across the sea.

It was not a work of philanthropy. These men cared not whether Jean and Jacqueline and Pierre and Marie were well-fed or hungry, whether they lived or died, so far as humanity was concerned. But Paris, Vienna, London, and the great capitals of the earth must have their furs—and unless that freight went north, there would be no velvety offerings for the white shoulders of the world. Christmas windows two years hence would be bare. A feminine wail of grief would rise to the skies. For woman must have her furs, and in return for those furs Jean and Jacqueline and Pierre and Marie must have their freight. So the pendulum swung, as it had swung for a century or two, touching, on the one side, luxury, warmth, wealth, and beauty; on the other, cold and hardship, deep snows and open skies—with that precious freight the thing between.

And now, in this year before rail and steamboat, the glory of early summer was at hand, and the wilderness people were coming up to meet the freight. The Three Rivers—the Athabasca, the Slave, and the Mackenzie, all joining in one great two-thousand-mile waterway to the northern sea—were athrill with the wild impulse and beat of life as the forest people lived it. The Great Father had sent in his treaty money, and Cree song and Chipewyan chant joined the age-old melodies of French and half-breed. Countless canoes drove past the slower and mightier scow brigades; huge York boats with two rows of oars heaved up and down like the ancient galleys of Rome; tightly woven cribs of timber, and giant rafts made tip of many cribs were ready for their long drift into a timberless country. On this two-thousand-mile waterway a world had gathered. It was the Nile of the northland, and each post and gathering place along its length was turned into a metropolis, half savage, archaic, splendid with the strength of red blood, clear eyes, and souls that read the word of God in wind and tree.

And up and down this mighty waterway of wilderness trade ran the whispering spirit of song, like the voice of a mighty god heard under the stars and in the winds.

But it was an hour ago that David Carrigan had vividly pictured these things to himself close to the big river, and many things may happen in the sixty minutes that follow any given minute in a man's life. That hour ago his one great purpose had been to bring in Black Roger Audemard, alive or dead—Black Roger, the forest fiend who had destroyed half a dozen lives in a blind passion of vengeance nearly fifteen years ago. For ten of those fifteen years it had been thought that Black Roger was dead. But mysterious rumours had lately come out of the North. He was alive. People had seen him. Fact followed rumour. His existence became certainty. The Law took up once more his hazardous trail, and David Carrigan was the messenger it sent.

"Bring him back, alive or dead," were Superintendent McVane's last words.

And now, thinking of that parting injunction, Carrigan grinned, even as the sweat of death dampened his face in the heat of the afternoon sun. For at the end of those sixty minutes that had passed since his midday pot of tea, the grimly, atrociously unexpected had happened, like a thunderbolt out of the azure of the sky.

2

Huddled behind a rock which was scarcely larger than his body, grovelling in the white, soft sand like a turtle making a nest for its eggs, Carrigan told himself this without any reservation. He was, as he kept repeating to himself for the comfort of his soul, in a deuce of a fix. His head was bare—simply because a bullet had taken his hat away. His blond hair was filled with sand. His face was sweating. But his blue eyes were alight with a grim sort of humour, though he knew that unless the other fellow's ammunition ran out he was going to die.

For the twentieth time in as many minutes he looked about him. He was in the centre of a flat area of sand. Fifty feet from him the river murmured gently over yellow bars and a carpet of pebbles. Fifty feet on the opposite side of him was the cool, green wall of the forest. The sunshine playing in it seemed like laughter to him now, a whimsical sort of merriment roused by the sheer effrontery of the joke which fate had inflicted upon him.

Between the river and the balsam and spruce was only the rock behind which he was cringing like a rabbit afraid to take to the open. And his rock was a mere up-jutting of the solid floor of shale that was under him. The wash sand that covered it like a carpet was not more than four or five inches deep. He could not dig in. There was not enough of it within reach to scrape up as a protection. And his enemy, a hundred yards or so away, was a determined wretch—and the deadliest shot he had ever known.

Three times Carrigan had made experiments to prove this, for he had in mind a sudden rush to the shelter of the timber. Three times he had raised the crown of his hat slightly above the top of the rock, and three times the marksmanship of the other had perforated it with neatness and dispatch. The third bullet had carried his hat a dozen feet away. Whenever he showed a patch of his clothing, a bullet replied with unerring precision. Twice they had drawn blood. And the humour faded out of Carrigan's eyes.

Not long ago he had exulted in the bigness and glory of this country of his, where strong men met hand to hand and eye to eye. There were the other kind in it, the sort that made his profession of man-hunting a thing of reality and danger, but he expected these—forgot them—when the wilderness itself filled his vision. But his present situation was something unlike anything that had ever happened in his previous experience with the outlawed. He had faced dangers. He had fought. There were times when he had almost died. Fanchet, the half-breed who had robbed a dozen wilderness mail sledges, had come nearest to trapping him and putting him out of business.

Fanchet was a desperate man and had few scruples. But even Fanchet—before he was caught—would not have cornered a man with such bloodthirsty unfairness as Carrigan found himself cornered now. He no longer had a doubt as to what was in the other's mind. It was not to wound and make merely helpless. It was to kill. It was not difficult to prove this. Careful not to expose a part of his arm or shoulder, he drew a white handkerchief from his pocket, fastened it to the end of his rifle, and held the flag of surrender three feet above the rock. And then, with equal caution, he slowly thrust up a flat piece of shale, which at a distance of a hundred yards might appear as his shoulder or even his head. Scarcely was it four inches above the top of the rock before there came the report of a rifle, and the shale was splintered into a hundred bits.

Carrigan lowered his flag and gathered himself in tighter. The accuracy of the other's marksmanship was appalling. He knew that if he exposed himself for an instant to use his own rifle or the heavy automatic in his holster, he would be a dead man before he could press a trigger. And that time, he felt equally sure, would come sooner or later. His muscles were growing cramped. He could not forever double himself up like a four-bladed jack-knife behind the altogether inefficient shelter of the rock.

His executioner was hidden in the edge of the timber, not directly opposite him, but nearly a hundred yards downstream. Twenty times he had wondered why the fiend with the rifle did not creep up through that timber and take a good, open pot-shot at him from the vantage point which lay at the end of a straight line between his rock and the nearest spruce and balsam. From that angle he could not completely shelter himself. But the man a hundred yards below had not moved a foot from his ambush since he had fired his first shot. That had come when Carrigan was crossing the open space of soft, white sand. It had left a burning sensation at his temple—half an inch to the right and it would have killed him. Swift as the shot itself, he dropped behind the one protection at hand, the up-jutting shoulder of shale.

For a quarter of an hour he had been making efforts to wriggle himself free from his bulky shoulder-pack without exposing himself to a coup-de-grace. At last he had the thing off. It was a tremendous relief when he thrust it out beside the rock, almost doubling the size of his shelter. Instantly there came the crash of a bullet in it, and then another. He heard the rattle of pans, and wondered if his skillet would be any good after today.

For the first time he could wipe the sweat from his face and stretch himself. And also he could think. Carrigan possessed an unalterable faith in the infallibility of the mind. "You can do anything with the mind," was his code. "It is better than a good gun."

Now that he was physically more at ease, he began reassembling his scattered mental faculties. Who was this stranger who was pot-shotting at him with such deadly animosity from the ambush below? Who—

Another crash of lead in tin-ware and steel put an unpleasant emphasis to the question. It was so close to his head that it made him wince, and now—with a wide area within reach about him—he began scraping up the sand for an added protection. There came a long silence after that third clatter of distress from his cooking utensils. To David Carrigan, even in his hour of deadly peril, there was something about it that for an instant brought back the glow of humour in his eyes. It was hot, swelteringly hot, in that packet of sand with the unclouded sun almost straight overhead. He could have tossed a pebble to where a bright-eyed sandpiper was cocking itself backward and forward, its jerky movements accompanied by friendly little tittering noises. Everything about him seemed friendly.

The river rippled and murmured in cooling song just beyond the sandpiper. On the other side the still cooler forest was a paradise of shade and contentment, astir with subdued and hidden life. It was nesting season. He heard the twitter of birds. A tiny, brown wood warbler fluttered out to the end of a silvery birch limb, and it seemed to David that its throat must surely burst with the burden of its song. The little fellow's brown body, scarcely larger than a butternut, was swelling up like a round ball in his effort to vanquish all other song.

"Go to it, old man," chuckled Carrigan. "Go to it!"

The little warbler, that he might have crushed between thumb and forefinger, gave him a lot of courage.

Then the tiny chorister stopped for breath. In that interval Carrigan listened to the wrangling of two vivid-coloured Canada jays deeper in the timber. Chronic scolds they were, never without a grouch. They were like some people Carrigan had known, born pessimists, always finding something to complain about, even in their love days.

And these were love days. That was the odd thought that came to Carrigan as he lay half on his face, his fingers slowly and cautiously working a loophole between his shoulder-pack and the rock. They were love days all up and down the big rivers, where men and women sang for joy, and children played, forgetful of the long, hard days of winter. And in forest, plain, and swamp was this spirit of love also triumphant over the land. It was the mating season of all feathered things. In countless nests were the peeps and twitters of new life; mothers of first-born were teaching their children to swim and fly; from end to end of the forest world the little children of the silent places, furred and feathered, clawed and hoofed, were learning the ways of life. Nature's yearly birthday was half-way gone, and the doors of nature's school wide open. And the tiny brown songster at the end of his birch twig proclaimed the joy of it again, and challenged all the world to beat him in his adulation.

Carrigan found that he could peer between his pack and the rock to where the other warbler was singing—and where his enemy lay watching for the opportunity to kill. It was taking a chance. If a movement betrayed his loophole, his minutes were numbered. But he had worked cautiously, an inch at a time, and was confident that the beginning of his effort to fight back was, up to the present moment, undiscovered. He believed that he knew about where the ambushed man was concealed. In the edge of a low-hanging mass of balsam was a fallen cedar. From behind the butt of that cedar he was sure the shots had come.

And now, even more cautiously than he had made the tiny opening, he began to work the muzzle of his rifle through the loophole. As he did this he was thinking of Black Roger Audemard. And yet, almost as quickly as suspicion leaped into his mind, he told himself that the thing was impossible. It could not be Black Roger, or one of Black Roger's friends, behind the cedar log. The idea was inconceivable, when he considered how carefully the secret of his mission had been kept at the Landing. He had not even said goodbye to his best friends. And because Black Roger had won through all the preceding years, Carrigan was stalking his prey out of uniform. There had been nothing to betray him. Besides, Black Roger Audemard must be at least a thousand miles north, unless something had tempted him to come up the rivers with the spring brigades. If he used logic at all, there was but one conclusion for him to arrive at. The man in ambush was some rascally half-breed who coveted his outfit and whatever valuables he might have about his person.

A fourth smashing eruption among his comestibles and culinary possessions came to drive home the fact that even that analysis of the situation was absurd. Whoever was behind the rifle fire had small respect for the contents of his pack, and he was surely not in grievous need of a good gun or ammunition. A sticky mess of condensed cream was running over Carrigan's hand. He doubted if there was a whole tin in his kit.

For a few moments he lay quietly on his face after the fourth shot. His eyes were turned toward the river, and on the far side, a quarter of a mile away, three canoes were moving swiftly up the slow current of the stream. The sunlight flashed on their wet sides. The gleam of dripping paddles was like the flutter of silvery birds' wings, and across the water came an unintelligible shout in response to the rifle shot. It occurred to David that he might make a trumpet of his hands and shout back, but the distance was too great for his voice to carry its message for help. Besides, now that he had the added protection of the pack, he felt a certain sense of humiliation at the thought of showing the white feather. A few minutes more, if all went well, and he would settle for the man behind the log.

He continued again the slow operation of worming his rifle barrel between the pack and the rock. The near-sighted little sandpiper had discovered him and seemed interested in the operation. It had come a dozen feet nearer, and was perking its head and seesawing on its long legs as it watched with inquisitive inspection the unusual manifestation of life behind the rock. Its twittering note had changed to an occasional sharp and querulous cry. Carrigan wanted to wring its neck. That cry told the other fellow that he was still alive and moving.

It seemed an age before his rifle was through, and every moment he expected another shot. He flattened himself out, Indian fashion, and sighted along the barrel. He was positive that his enemy was watching, yet he could make out nothing that looked like a head anywhere along the log. At one end was a clump of deeper foliage. He was sure he saw a sudden slight movement there, and in the thrill of the moment was tempted to send a bullet into the heart of it. But he saved his cartridge. He felt the mighty importance of certainty. If he fired once—and missed—the advantage of his unsuspected loophole would be gone. It would be transformed into a deadly menace. Even as it was, if his enemy's next bullet should enter that way—

He felt the discomfort of the thought, and in spite of himself a tremor of apprehension ran up his spine. He felt an even greater desire to wring the neck of the inquisitive little sandpiper. The creature had circled round squarely in front of him and stood there tilting its tail and bobbing its head as if its one insane desire was to look down the length of his rifle barrel. The bird was giving him away. If the other fellow was only half as clever as his marksmanship was good—

Suddenly every nerve in Carrigan's body tightened. He was positive that he had caught the outline of a human head and shoulders in the foliage. His finger pressed gently against the trigger of his Winchester. Before he breathed again he would have fired. But a shot from the foliage beat him out by the fraction of a second. In that precious time lost, his enemy's bullet entered the edge of his kit—and came through. He felt the shock of it, and in the infinitesimal space between the physical impact and the mental effect of shock his brain told him the horrible thing had happened. It was his head—his face. It was as if he had plunged them suddenly into hot water, and what was left of his skull was filled with the rushing and roaring of a flood. He staggered up, clutching his face with both hands. The world about him was twisted and black, a dizzily revolving thing—yet his still fighting mental vision pictured clearly for him a monstrous, bulging-eyed sandpiper as big as a house. Then he toppled back on the white sand, his arms flung out limply, his face turned to the ambush wherein his murderer lay.

His body was clear of the rock and the pack, but there came no other shot from the thick clump of balsam. Nor, for a time, was there movement. The wood warbler was cheeping inquiringly at this sudden change in the deportment of his friend behind the shoulder of shale. The sandpiper, a bit startled, had gone back to the edge of the river and was running a race with himself along the wet sand. And the two quarrelsome jays had brought their family squabble to the edge of the timber.

It was their wrangling that roused Carrigan to the fact that he was not dead. It was a thrilling discovery—that and the fact that he made out clearly a patch of sunlight in the sand. He did not move, but opened his eyes wider. He could see the timber. On a straight line with his vision was the thick clump of balsam. And as he looked, the boughs parted and a figure came out. Carrigan drew a deep breath. He found that it did not hurt him. He gripped the fingers of the hand that was under his body, and they closed on the butt of his service automatic. He would win yet, if God gave him life a few minutes longer.

His enemy advanced. As he drew nearer, Carrigan closed his eyes more and more. They must be shut, and he must appear as if dead, when the other came up. Then, when the scoundrel put down his gun, as he naturally would—his chance would be at hand. If a quiver of his eyes betrayed him—

He closed them tight. Dizziness began to creep over him, and the fire in his brain grew hot again. He heard footsteps, and they stopped in the sand close beside him. Then he heard a human voice. It did not speak in words, but gave utterance to a strange and unnatural cry. With a mighty effort Carrigan assembled his last strength. It seemed to him that he brought himself up quickly, but his movement was slow, painful—the effort of a man who might be dying. The automatic hung limply in his hand, its muzzle pointing to the sand. He looked up, trying to swing into action that mighty weight of his weapon. And then from his own lips, even in his utter physical impotence, fell a cry of wonder and amazement.

His enemy stood there in the sunlight, staring down at him with big, dark eyes that were filled with horror. They were not the eyes of a man. David Carrigan, in this most astounding moment of his life, found himself looking up into the face of a woman.

3

For a matter of twenty seconds—even longer it seemed to Carrigan—the life of these two was expressed in a vivid and unforgettable tableau. One half of it David saw—the blue sky, the dazzling sun, the girl in between. The pistol dropped from his limp hand, and the weight of his body tottered on the crook of his under-elbow. Mentally and physically he was on the point of collapse, and yet in those few moments every detail of the picture was painted with a brush of fire in his brain. The girl was bareheaded. Her face was as white as any face he had ever seen, living or dead; her eyes were like pools that had caught the reflection of fire; he saw the sheen of her hair, the poise of her slender body—its shock, stupefaction, horror. He sensed these things even as his brain wobbled dizzily, and the larger part of the picture began to fade out of his vision. But her face remained to the last. It grew clearer, like a cameo framed in an iris—a beautiful, staring, horrified face with shimmering tresses of jet-black hair blowing about it like a veil. He noticed the hair, that was partly undone as if she had been in a struggle of some sort, or had been running fast against the breeze that came up the river.

He fought with himself to hold that picture of her, to utter some word, make some movement. But the power to see and to live died out of him. He sank back with a queer sound in his throat. He did not hear the answering cry from the girl as she flung herself, with a quick little prayer for help, on her knees in the soft, white sand beside him. He felt no movement when she raised his head in her arm and with her bare hand brushed back his sand-littered hair, revealing where the bullet had struck him. He did not know when she ran back to the river.

His first sensation was of a cool and comforting something trickling over his burning temples and his face. It was water. Subconsciously he knew that, and in the same way he began to think. But it was hard to pull his thoughts together. They persisted in hopping about, like a lot of sand-fleas in a dance, and just as he got hold of one and reached for another, the first would slip away from him. He began to get the best of them after a time, and he had an uncontrollable desire to say something. But his eyes and his lips were sealed tight, and to open them, a little army of gnomes came out of the darkness in the back of his head, each of them armed with a lever, and began prying with all their might. After that came the beginning of light and a flash of consciousness.

The girl was working over him. He could feel her and hear her movement. Water was trickling over his face. Then he heard a voice, close over him, saying something in a sobbing monotone which he could not understand.

With a mighty effort he opened his eyes.

"Thank *le bon dieu*, you live, *m'sieu*," he heard the voice say, as if coming from a long distance away. "You live, you live—"

"Tryin' to," he mumbled thickly, feeling suddenly a sense of great elation. "Tryin'—"

He wanted to curse the gnomes for deserting him, for as soon as they were gone with their levers, his eyes and his lips shut tight again, or at least he thought they did. But he began to sense things in a curious sort of way. Someone was dragging him. He could feel the grind of sand under his body. There were intervals when the dragging operation paused. And then, after a long time, he seemed to hear more than one voice. There were two—sometimes a murmur of them. And odd visions came to him. He seemed to see the girl with shining black hair and dark eyes, and then swiftly she would change into a girl with hair like blazing gold. This was a different girl. She was not like Pretty Eyes, as his twisted mind called the other. This second vision that he saw was like a radiant bit of the sun, her hair all aflame with the fire of it and her face a different sort of face. He was always glad when she went away and Pretty Eyes came back.

To David Carrigan this interesting experience in his life might have covered an hour, a day, or a month. Or a year for that matter, for he seemed to have had an indefinite association with Pretty Eyes. He had known her for a long time and very intimately, it seemed. Yet he had no memory of the long fight in the hot sun, or of the river, or of the singing warblers, or of the inquisitive sandpiper that had marked out the line which his enemy's last bullet had travelled. He had entered into a new world in which everything was vague and unreal except that vision of dark hair, dark eyes, and pale, beautiful face. Several times he saw it with marvellous clearness, and each time he drifted away into darkness again with the sound of a voice growing fainter and fainter in his ears.

Then came a time of utter chaos and soundless gloom. He was in a pit, where even his subconscious self was almost dead under a crushing oppression. At last a star began to glimmer in this pit, a star pale and indistinct and a vast distance away. But it crept steadily up through the eternity of darkness, and the nearer it came, the less there was of the blackness of night. From a star it grew into a sun, and with the sun came dawn. In that dawn he heard the singing of a bird, and the bird was just over his head. When Carrigan opened his eyes, and understanding came to him, he found himself under the silver birch that belonged to the wood warbler.

For a space he did not ask himself how he had come there. He was looking at the river and the white strip of sand. Out there were the rock and his dunnage pack. Also his rifle. Instinctively his eyes turned to the balsam ambush farther down. That, too, was in a blaze of sunlight now. But where he lay, or sat, or stood—he was not sure what he was doing at that moment—it was shady and deliciously cool. The green of the cedar and spruce and balsam was close about him, inset with the silver and gold of the thickly-leaved birch. He discovered that he was bolstered up partly against the trunk of this birch and partly against a spruce sapling. Between these two, where his head rested, was a pile of soft moss freshly torn from the earth. And within reach of him was his own kit pail filled with water.

He moved himself cautiously and raised a hand to his head. His fingers came in contact with a bandage.

For a minute or two after that he sat without moving while his amazed senses seized upon the significance of it all. In the first place he was alive. But even this fact of living was less remarkable than the other things that had happened. He remembered the final moments of the unequal duel. His enemy had got him. And that enemy was a woman! Moreover, after she had blown away a part of his head and had him helpless in the sand, she had—in place of finishing him there—dragged him to this cool nook and tied up his wound. It was hard for him to believe, but the pail of water, the moss behind his shoulders, the bandage, and certain visions that were reforming themselves in his brain convinced him. A woman had shot him. She had worked like the very devil to kill him. And afterward she had saved him! He grinned. It was final proof that his mind hadn't been playing tricks on him. No one but a woman would have been quite so unreasonable. A man would have completed the job.

He began to look for her up and down the white strip of sand. And in looking he saw the gray and silver flash of the hard-working sandpiper. He chuckled, for he was exceedingly comfortable, and also exhilaratingly happy to know that the thing was over and he was not dead. If the sandpiper had been a man, he would have called him up to shake hands with him. For if it hadn't been for the bird getting squarely in front of him and giving him away, there might have been a more horrible end to it all. He shuddered as he thought of the mighty effort he had made to fire a shot into the heart of the balsam ambush—and perhaps into the heart of a woman!

He reached for the pail and drank deeply of the water in it. He felt no pain. His dizziness was gone. His mind had grown suddenly clear and alert. The warmth of the water told him almost instantly that it had been taken from the river some time ago. He observed the change in sun and shadows. With the instinct of a man trained to note details, he pulled out his watch. It was almost six o'clock. More than three hours had passed since the sandpiper had got in front of his gun. He did not attempt to rise to his feet, but scanned with slower and more careful scrutiny the edge of the forest and the river. He had been mystified while cringing for his life behind the rock, but he was infinitely more so now.

Greater desire he had never had than this which thrilled him in these present minutes of his readjustment—desire to look upon the woman again. And then, all at once, there came back to him a mental flash of the other. He remembered, as if something was coming back to him out of a dream, how the whimsical twistings of his sick brain had made him see two faces instead of one. Yet he knew that the first picture of his mysterious assailant, the picture painted in his brain when he had tried to raise his pistol, was the right one. He had seen her dark eyes aglow; he had seen the sunlit sheen of her black hair rippling in the wind; he had seen the white pallor in her face, the slimness of her as she stood over him in horror—he remembered even the clutch of her white hand at her throat. A moment before she had tried to kill him. And then he had looked up and had seen her like that! It must have been some unaccountable trick in his brain that had flooded her hair with golden fire at times.

His eyes followed a furrow in the white sand which led from where

22

he sat bolstered against the tree down to his pack and the rock. It was the trail made by his body when she had dragged him up to the shelter and coolness of the timber. One of his laws of physical care was to keep himself trained down to a hundred and sixty, but he wondered how she had dragged up even so much as that of dead weight. It had taken a great deal of effort. He could see distinctly three different places in the sand where she had stopped to rest.

Carrigan had earned a reputation as the expert analyst of "N" Division. In delicate matters it was seldom that McVane did not take him into consultation. He possessed an almost uncanny grip on the working processes of a criminal mind, and the first rule he had set down for himself was to regard the acts of omission rather than the one outstanding act of commission. But when he proved to himself that the chief actor in a drama possessed a normal rather than a criminal mind, he found himself in the position of checkmate. It was a thrilling game. And he was frankly puzzled now, until—one after another—he added up the sum total of what had been omitted in this instance of his own personal adventure. Hidden in her ambush, the woman who had shot him had been in both purpose and act an assassin. Her determination had been to kill him. She had disregarded the white flag with which he had pleaded for mercy. Her marksmanship was of fiendish cleverness. Up to her last shot she had been, to all intent and purpose, a murderess.

The change had come when she looked down upon him, bleeding and helpless, in the sand. Undoubtedly she had thought he was dying. But why, when she saw his eyes open a little later, had she cried out her gratitude to God? What had worked the sudden transformation in her? Why had she laboured to save the life she had so atrociously coveted a minute before?

If his assailant had been a man, Carrigan would have found an answer. For he was not robbed, and therefore robbery was not a motif. "A case of mistaken identity," he would have told himself. "An error in visual judgment."

But the fact that in his analysis he was dealing with a woman made his answer only partly satisfying. He could not disassociate himself from her eyes—their beauty, their horror, the way they had looked at him. It was as if a sudden revulsion had come over her; as if, looking down upon her bleeding handiwork, the woman's soul in her had revolted, and with that revulsion had come repentance—repentance and pity.

"That," thought Carrigan, "would be just like a woman—and especially a woman with eyes like hers."

This left him but two conclusions to choose from. Either there had been a mistake, and the woman had shown both horror and desire to amend when she discovered it, or a too tender-hearted agent of Black Roger Audemard had waylaid him in the heart of the white strip of sand.

The sun was another hour lower in the sky when Carrigan assured himself in a series of cautious experiments that he was not in a condition to stand upon his feet. In his pack were a number of things he wanted—his blankets, for instance, a steel mirror, and the thermometer in his medical kit. He was beginning to feel a bit anxious about himself. There were sharp pains back of his eyes. His face was hot, and he was developing an unhealthy appetite for water. It was fever and he knew what fever meant in this sort of thing, when one was alone. He had given up hope of the woman's return. It was not reasonable to expect her to come back after her furious attempt to kill him. She had bandaged him, bolstered him up, placed water beside him, and had then left him to work out the rest of his salvation alone. But why the deuce hadn't she brought up his pack?

On his hands and knees he began to work himself toward it slowly. He found that the movement caused him pain, and that with this pain, if he persisted in movement, there was a synchronous rise of nausea. The two seemed to work in a sort of unity. But his medicine case was important now, and his blankets, and his rifle if he hoped to signal help that might chance to pass on the river. A foot at a time, a yard at a time, he made his way down into the sand. His fingers dug into the footprints of the mysterious gun-woman. He approved of their size. They were small and narrow, scarcely longer than the palm and fingers of his hand—and they were made by shoes instead of moccasins.

It seemed an interminable time to him before he reached his pack. When he got there, a pendulum seemed swinging back and forth inside his head, beating against his skull. He lay down with his pack for a pillow, intending to rest for a spell. But the minutes added themselves one on top of another. The sun slipped behind clouds banking in the west. It grew cooler, while within him he was consumed by a burning thirst. He could hear the ripple of running water, the laughter of it among pebbles a few yards away. And the river itself became even more desirable than his medicine case, or his blankets, or his rifle. The song of it, inviting and tempting him, blotted thought of the other things out of his mind. And he continued his journey, the swing of the pendulum in his head becoming harder, but the sound of the river growing nearer. At last he came to the wet sand, and fell on his face, and drank.

After this he had no great desire to go back. He rolled himself over, so that his face was turned up to the sky. Under him the wet sand was soft, and it was comfortingly cool. The fire in his head died out. He could hear new sounds in the edge of the forest evening sounds. Only weak little twitters came from the wood warblers, driven to silence by thickening gloom in the densely canopied balsams and cedars, and frightened by the first low hoots of the owls. There was a crash not far distant, probably a porcupine waddling through brush on his way for a drink; or perhaps it was a thirsty deer, or a bear coming out in the hope of finding a dead fish.

Carrigan loved that sort of sound, even when a pendulum was beating back and forth in his head. It was like medicine to him, and he lay with wide-open eyes, his ears picking up one after another the voices that marked the change from day to night. He heard the cry of a loon, its softer, chuckling note of honeymoon days. From across the river came a cry that was half howl, half bark. Carrigan knew that it was coyote, and not wolf, a coyote whose breed had wandered hundreds of miles north of the prairie country.

The gloom gathered in, and yet it was not darkness as the darkness of night is known a thousand miles south. It was the dusky twilight of day where the sun rises at three o'clock in the morning and still throws its ruddy light in the western sky at nine o'clock at night; where the poplar buds unfold themselves into leaf before one's very eyes; where strawberries are green in the morning and red in the afternoon; where, a little later, one could read newspaper print until midnight by the glow of the sun—and between the rising and the setting of that sun there would be from eighteen to twenty hours of day. It was evening time in the wonderland of the north, a wonderland hard and frozen and ridden by pain and death in winter, but a paradise upon earth in this month of June.

The beauty of it filled Carrigan's soul, even as he lay on his back in the damp sand. Far south of him steam and steel were coming, and the world would soon know that it was easy to grow wheat at the Arctic Circle, that cucumbers grew to half the size of a man's arm, that flowers smothered the land and berries turned it scarlet and black. He had dreaded these days—days of what he called "the great discovery"-

the time when a crowded civilization would at last understand how the fruits of the earth leaped up to the call of twenty hours of sun each day, even though that earth itself was eternally frozen if one went down under its surface four feet with a pick and shovel.

Tonight the gloom came earlier because of the clouds in the west. It was very still. Even the breeze had ceased to come from up the river. And as Carrigan listened, exulting in the thought that the coolness of the wet sand was drawing the fever from him, he heard another sound. At first he thought it was the splashing of a fish. But after that it came again, and still again, and he knew that it was the steady and rhythmic dip of paddles.

A thrill shot through him, and he raised himself to his elbow. Dusk covered the river, and he could not see. But he heard low voices as the paddles dipped. And after a little he knew that one of these was the voice of a woman.

His heart gave a big jump. "She is coming back," he whispered to himself. "She is coming back!"

4

Carrigan's first impulse, sudden as the thrill that leaped through him, was to cry out to the occupants of the unseen canoe. Words were on his lips, but he forced them back. They could not miss him, could not get beyond the reach of his voice—and he waited. After all, there might be profit in a reasonable degree of caution. He crept back toward his rifle, sensing the fact that movement no longer gave him very great distress. At the same time he lost no sound from the river. The voices were silent, and the dip, dip, dip of paddles was approaching softly and with extreme caution. At last he could barely hear the trickle of them, yet he knew the canoe was coming steadily nearer. There was a suspicious secretiveness in its approach. Perhaps the lady with the beautiful eyes and the glistening hair had changed her mind again and was returning to put an end to him.

The thought sharpened his vision. He saw a thin shadow a little darker than the gloom of the river; it grew into shape; something grated lightly upon sand and pebbles, and then he heard the guarded plash of feet in shallow water and saw someone pulling the canoe up higher. A second figure joined the first. They advanced a few paces and stopped. In a moment a voice called softly,

"*M'sieu*! M'sieu Carrigan!"

There was an anxious note in the voice, but Carrigan held his tongue. And then he heard the woman say,

"It was here, Bateese! I am sure of it!"

There was more than anxiety in her voice now. Her words trembled with distress. "Bateese—if he is dead—he is up there close to the trees."

"But he isn't dead," said Carrigan, raising himself a little. "He is here, behind the rock again!"

In a moment she had run to where he was lying, his hand clutching the cold barrel of the pistol which he had found in the sand, his white face looking up at her. Again he found himself staring into the glow of her eyes, and in that pale light which precedes the coming of stars and moon the fancy struck him that she was lovelier than in the full radiance of the sun. He heard a throbbing note in her throat. And then she was down on her knees at his side, leaning close over him, her hands groping at his shoulders, her quick breath betraying how swiftly her heart was beating.

"You are not hurt—badly?" she cried.

"I don't know," replied David. "You made a perfect shot. I think a part of my head is gone. At least you've shot away my balance, because I can't stand on my feet!"

Her hand touched his face, remaining there for an instant, and the palm of it pressed his forehead. It was like the touch of cool velvet, he thought. Then she called to the man named Bateese. He made Carrigan think of a huge chimpanzee as he came near, because of the shortness of his body and the length of his arms. In the half light he might have been a huge animal, a hulking creature of some sort walking upright. Carrigan's fingers closed more tightly on the butt of his automatic. The woman began to talk swiftly in a patois of French and Cree. David caught the gist of it. She was telling Bateese to carry him to the canoe, and to be very careful, because *m'sieu* was badly hurt. It was his head, she emphasized. Bateese must be careful of his head.

David slipped his pistol into its holster as Bateese bent over him. He tried to smile at the woman to thank her for her solicitude—after having nearly killed him. There was an increasing glow in the night, and he began to see her more plainly. Out on the middle of the river was a silvery bar of light. The moon was coming up, a little pale as yet, but triumphant in the fact that clouds had blotted out the sun an hour before his time. Between this bar of light and himself he saw the head of Bateese. It was a wild, savage-looking head, bound pirate-fashion round the forehead with a huge Hudson's Bay kerchief. Bateese might have been old Jack Ketch himself bending over to give the final twist to a victim's neck. His long arms slipped under David. Gently and without effort he raised him to his feet. And then, as easily as he might have lifted a child, he trundled him up in his arms and walked off with him over the sand.

Carrigan had not expected this. He was a little shocked and felt also the impropriety of the thing. The idea of being lugged off like a baby was embarrassing, even in the presence of the one who had deliberately put him in his present condition. Bateese did the thing with such beastly ease. It was as if he was no more than a small boy, a runt with no weight whatever, and Bateese was a man. He would have preferred to stagger along on his own feet or creep on his hands and knees, and he grunted as much to Bateese on the way to the canoe. He felt, at the same time, that the situation owed him something more of discussion and explanation.

Even now, after half killing him, the woman was taking a rather high-handed advantage of him. She might at least have assured him that she had made a mistake and was sorry. But she did not speak to him again. She said nothing more to Bateese, and when the half-breed deposited him in the midship part of the canoe, facing the bow, she stood back in silence. Then Bateese brought his pack and rifle, and wedged the pack in behind him so that he could sit upright. After that, without pausing to ask permission, he picked up the woman and carried her through the shallow water to the bow, saving her the wetting of her feet.

As she turned to find her paddle her face was toward David, and for a moment she was looking at him.

"Do you mind telling me who you are, and where we are going?" he asked.

"I am Jeanne Marie-Anne Boulain," she said. "My brigade is down the river, M'sieu Carrigan."

He was amazed at the promptness of her confession, for as one of the working factors of the long arm of the police he accepted it as that. He had scarcely expected her to divulge her name after the cold-blooded way in which she had attempted to kill him. And she had spoken quite calmly of "my brigade." He had heard of the Boulain Brigade. It was a name associated with Chipewyan, as he remembered it—or Fort McMurray. He was not sure just where the Boulain scows had traded freight with the upper-river craft. Until this year he was positive they had not come as far south as Athabasca Landing. Boulain—Boulain—The name repeated itself over and over in his mind. Bateese shoved off the canoe, and the woman's paddle dipped in and out of the water beginning to shimmer in moonlight.

But he could not, for a time, get himself beyond the pounding of that name in his brain. It was not merely that he had heard the name before. There was something significant about it. Something that made him grope back in his memory of things. Boulain! He whispered it to himself, his eyes on the slender figure of the woman ahead of him, swaying gently to the steady sweep of the paddle in her hands. Yet he could think of nothing. A feeling of irritation swept over him, disgust at his own mental impotency. And the dizzying sickness was brewing in his head again.

"I have heard that name—somewhere—before," he said. There was a space of only five or six feet between them, and he spoke with studied distinctness.

"Possibly you have, *m'sieu*."

Her voice was exquisite, clear as the note of a bird, yet so soft and low that she seemed scarcely to have spoken. And it was, Carrigan thought, criminally evasive—under the circumstances. He wanted her to turn round and say something. He wanted, first of all, to ask her why she had tried to kill him. It was his right to demand an explanation. And it was his duty to get her back to the Landing, where the law would ask an accounting of her. She must know that. There was only one way in which she could have learned his name, and that was by prying into his identification papers while he was unconscious. Therefore she not only knew his name, but also that he was Sergeant Carrigan of the Royal Northwest Mounted Police. In spite of all this she was apparently not very deeply concerned. She was not frightened, and she did not appear to be even slightly excited.

He leaned nearer to her, the movement sending a sharp pain between his eyes. It almost drew a cry from him, but he forced himself to speak without betraying it.

"You tried to murder me—and almost succeeded. Haven't you anything to say?"

"Not now, *m'sieu*—except that it was a mistake, and I am sorry. But you must not talk. You must remain quiet. I am afraid your skull is fractured."

Afraid his skull was fractured! And she expressed her fear in the casual way she might have spoken of a toothache. He leaned back against his dunnage sack and closed his eyes. Probably she was right. These fits of dizziness and nausea were suspicious. They made him top-heavy and filled him with a desire to crumple up somewhere. He was clear-mindedly conscious of this and of his fight against the weakness. But in those moments when he felt better and his head was clear of pain, he had not seriously thought of a fractured skull. If she believed it, why did she not treat him a bit more considerately? Bateese, with that strength of an ox in his arms, had no use for her assistance with the paddle. She might at least have sat facing him, even if she refused to explain matters more definitely.

A mistake, she called it. And she was sorry for him! She had made those statements in a matter-of-fact way, but with a voice that was like music. She had spoken perfect English, but in her words were the inflection and velvety softness of the French blood which must be running red in her veins. And her name was Jeanne Marie-Anne Boulain!

With eyes closed, Carrigan called himself an idiot for thinking of these things at the present time. Primarily he was a man-hunter out on important duty, and here was duty right at hand, a thousand miles south of Black Roger Audemard, the wholesale murderer he was after. He would have sworn on his life that Black Roger had never gone at a killing more deliberately than this same Jeanne Marie-Anne Boulain had gone after him behind the rock!

Now that it was all over, and he was alive, she was taking him somewhere as coolly and as unexcitedly as though they were returning from a picnic. Carrigan shut his eyes tighter and wondered if he was thinking straight. He believed he was badly hurt, but he was as strongly convinced that his mind was clear. And he lay quietly with his head against the pack, his eyes closed, waiting for the coolness of the river to drive his nausea away again.

He sensed rather than felt the swift movement of the canoe. There was no perceptible tremor to its progress. The current and a perfect craftsmanship with the paddles were carrying it along at six or seven miles an hour. He heard the rippling of water that at times was almost like the tinkling of tiny bells, and more and more bell-like became that sound as he listened to it. It struck a certain note for him. And to that note another added itself, until in the purling rhythm of the river he caught the murmuring monotone of a name Boulain—Boulain— Boulain. The name became an obsession. It meant something. And he knew what it meant—if he could only whip his memory back into harness again. But that was impossible now. When he tried to concentrate his mental faculties, his head ached terrifically.

He dipped his hand into the water and held it over his eyes. For half an hour after that he did not raise his head. In that time not a word was spoken by Bateese or Jeanne Marie-Anne Boulain. For the forest people it was not an hour in which to talk. The moon had risen swiftly, and the stars were out. Where there had been gloom, the world was now a flood of gold and silver light. At first Carrigan allowed this to filter between his fingers; then he opened his eyes. He felt more evenly balanced again.

Straight in front of him was Jeanne Marie-Anne Boulain. The curtain of dusk had risen from between them, and she was full in the radiance of the moon. She was no longer paddling, but was looking straight ahead. To Cardigan her figure was exquisitely girlish as he saw it now. She was bareheaded, as he had seen tier first, and her hair hung down her back like a shimmering mass of velvety sable in the star-and-moon glow. Something told Carrigan she was going to turn her face in his direction, and he dropped his hand over his eyes again, leaving a space between the fingers. He was right in his guess. She fronted the moon, looking at him closely—rather anxiously, he thought. She even leaned a little toward him that she might see more clearly. Then she turned and resumed her paddling.

Carrigan was a bit elated. Probably she had looked at him a number of times like that during the past half-hour. And she was disturbed. She was worrying about him. The thought of being a murderess was beginning to frighten her. In spite of the beauty of her eyes and hair and the slim witchery of her body he had no sympathy for her. He told himself that he would give a year of his life to have her down at Barracks this minute. He would never forget that three-quarters of an hour behind the rock, not if he lived to be a hundred.

And if he did live, she was going to pay, even if she was lovelier than Venus and all the Graces combined. He felt irritated with himself that he should have observed in such a silly way the sable glow of her hair in the moonlight. And her eyes. What the deuce did prettiness matter in the present situation? The sister of Fanchet, the mail robber, was beautiful, but her beauty had failed to save Fanchet. The Law had taken him in spite of the tears in Carmin Fanchet's big black eyes, and in that particular instance he was the Law. And Carmin Fanchet was pretty—deucedly pretty. Even the Old Man's heart had been stirred by her loveliness.

"A shame!" he had said to Carrigan. "A shame!" But the rascally Fanchet was hung by the neck until he was dead.

Carrigan drew himself up slowly until he was sitting erect. He wondered what Jeanne Marie-Anne Boulain would say if he told her about Carmin. But there was a big gulf between the names Fanchet and Boulain. The Fanchets had come from the dance halls of Alaska. They were bad, both of them. At least, so they had judged Carmin Fanchet—along with her brother. And Boulain—

His hand, in dropping to his side, fell upon the butt of his pistol.

Neither Bateese nor the girl had thought of disarming him. It was careless of them, unless Bateese was keeping a good eye on him from behind.

A new sort of thrill crept into Carrigan's blood. He began to see where he had made a huge error in not playing his part more cleverly. It was this girl Jeanne who had shot him. It was Jeanne who had stood over him in that last moment when he had made an effort to use his pistol. It was she who had tried to murder him and who had turned faint-hearted when it came to finishing the job. But his knowledge of these things he should have kept from her. Then, when the proper moment came, he would have been in a position to act. Even now it might be possible to cover his blunder. He leaned toward her again, determined to make the effort.

"I want to ask your pardon," he said. "May I?"

His voice startled her. It was as if the stinging tip of a whip-lash had touched her bare neck. He was smiling when she turned. In her face and eyes was a relief which she made no effort to repress.

"You thought I might be dead," he laughed softly. "I'm not, Miss Jeanne. I'm very much alive again. It was that accursed fever—and I want to ask your pardon! I think—I know—that I accused you of shooting me. It's impossible. I couldn't think of it—In my clear mind. I am quite sure that I know the rascally half-breed who pot-shotted me like that. And it was you who came in time, and frightened him away, and saved my life. Will you forgive me—and accept my gratitude?"

There came into the glowing eyes of the girl a reflection of his own smile. It seemed to him that he saw the corners of her mouth tremble a little before she answered him.

"I am glad you are feeling better, m'sieu."

"And you will forgive me for—for saying such beastly things to you?"

She was lovely when she smiled, and she was smiling at him now. "If you want to be forgiven for lying, yes," she said. "I forgive you that, because it is sometimes your business to lie. It was I who tried to kill you, m'sieu. And you know it."

"But—"

"You must not talk, m'sieu. It is not good for you: Bateese, will you tell m'sieu not to talk?"

Carrigan heard a movement behind him.

"M'sieu, you will stop ze talk or I brak hees head wit' ze paddle in my han'!" came the voice of Bateese close to his shoulder. "Do I mak'

33

ze word plain so *m'sieu compren'*?"

"I get you, old man," grunted Carrigan. "I get you—both!"

And he leaned back against his dunnage-sack, staring again at the witching slimness of the lovely Jeanne Marie-Anne Boulain as she calmly resumed her paddling in the bow of the canoe.

5

In the few minutes following the efficient and unexpected warning of Bateese an entirely new element of interest entered into the situation for David Carrigan. He had more than once assured himself that he had made a success of his profession of man-hunting not because he was brighter than the other fellow, but largely because he possessed a sense of humour and no vanities to prick. He was in the game because he loved the adventure of it. He was loyal to his duty, but he was not a worshipper of the law, nor did he covet the small monthly stipend of dollars and cents that came of his allegiance to it. As a member of the Scarlet Police, and especially of "N" Division, he felt the pulse and thrill of life as he loved to live it. And the greatest of all thrills came when he was after a man as clever as himself, or cleverer.

This time it was a woman—or a girl! He had not yet made up his mind which she was. Her voice, low and musical, her poise, and the tranquil and unexcitable loveliness of her face had made him, at first, register her as a woman. Yet as he looked at the slim girlishness of her figure in the bow of the canoe, accentuated by the soft sheen of her partly unbraided hair, he wondered if she were eighteen or thirty. It would take the clear light of day to tell him. But whether a girl or a woman, she had handled him so cleverly that the unpleasantness of his earlier experience began to give way slowly to an admiration for her capability.

He wondered what the superintendent of "N" Division would say if he could see Black Roger Audemard's latest trailer propped up here in the centre of the canoe, the prisoner of a velvety-haired but dangerously efficient bit of feminine loveliness—and a bull-necked, chimpanzee-armed half-breed!

Bateese had confirmed the suspicion that he was a prisoner, even though this mysterious pair were bent on saving his life. Why it was their desire to keep life in him when only a few hours ago one of them had tried to kill him was a question which only the future could answer. He did not bother himself with that problem now. The present was altogether too interesting, and there was but little doubt that other developments equally important were close at hand. The attitude of both Jeanne Marie-Anne Boulain and her piratical-looking henchman was sufficient evidence of that. Bateese had threatened to knock his head off, and he could have sworn that the girl—or woman—had smiled her approbation of the threat. Yet he held no grudge against Bateese. An odd sort of liking for the man began to possess him, just as he found himself powerless to resist an ingrowing admiration for Marie-Anne. The existence of Black Roger Audemard became with him a sort of indefinite reality. Black Roger was a long way off. Marie-Anne and Bateese were very near. He began thinking of her as Marie-Anne. He liked the name. It was the Boulain part of it that worked in him with an irritating insistence.

For the first time since the canoe journey had begun, he looked beyond the darkly glowing head and the slender figure in the bow. It was a splendid night. Ahead of him the river was like a rippling sheet of molten silver. On both sides, a quarter of a mile apart, rose the walls of the forest, like low-hung, oriental tapestries. The sky seemed near, loaded with stars, and the moon, rising with almost perceptible movement toward the zenith, had changed from red to a mellow gold. Carrigan's soul always rose to this glory of the northern light. Youth and vigor, he told himself, must always exist under those unpolluted lights of the upper worlds, the unspeaking things which had told him more than he had ever learned from the mouths of other men. They stood for his religion, his faith, his belief in the existence of things greater than the insignificant spark which animated his own body.

He appreciated them most when there was stillness. And tonight it was still. It was so quiet that the trickling of the paddles was like subdued music. From the forest there came no sound. Yet he knew there was life there, wide-eyed, questing life, life that moved on velvety wing and padded foot, just as he and Marie-Anne and the half-breed Bateese were moving in the canoe. To have called out in this hour would have taken an effort, for a supreme and invisible Hand seemed to have commanded stillness upon the earth.

And then there came droning upon his ears a break in the stillness, and as he listened, the shores closed slowly in, narrowing the channel until he saw giant masses of gray rock replacing the thick verdure of balsam, spruce, and cedar. The moaning grew louder, and the rocks climbed skyward until they hung in great cliffs. There could be but one meaning to this sudden change. They were close *to le Saint-Esprit Rapide*—the Holy Ghost Rapids. Carrigan was astonished. That day at noon he had believed the Holy Ghost to be twenty or thirty miles below him. Now they were at its mouth, and he saw that Bateese and Jeanne Marie-Anne Boulain were quietly and unexcitedly preparing to run that vicious stretch of water.

Unconsciously he gripped the gunwales of the canoe with both hands as the sound of the rapids grew into low and sullen thunder. In the moonlight ahead he could see the rock walls closing in until the channel was crushed between two precipitous ramparts, and the moon and stars, sending their glow between those walls, lighted up a frothing path of water that made Carrigan hold his breath. He would have portaged this place even in broad day.

He looked at the girl in the bow. The slender figure Was a little more erect, the glowing head held a little higher. In those moments he would have liked to see her face, the wonderful something that must be in her eyes as she rode fearlessly into the teeth of the menace ahead. For he could see that she was not afraid, that she was facing this thing with a sort of exultation, that there was something about it which thrilled her until every drop of blood in her body was racing with the impetus of the stream itself. Eddies of wind puffing out from between the chasm walls tossed her loose hair about her back in a glistening veil. He saw a long strand of it trailing over the edge of the canoe into the water. It made him shiver, and he wanted to cry out to Bateese that he was a fool for risking her life like this. He forgot that he was the one helpless individual in the canoe, and that an upset would mean the end for him, while Bateese and his companion might still fight on. His thought and his vision were focused on the girl— and what lay straight ahead.

A mass of froth, like a windrow of snow, rose up before them, and the canoe plunged into it with the swiftness of a shot. It spattered in his face, and blinded him for an instant. Then they were out of it, and he fancied he heard a note of laughter from the girl in the bow. In the next breath he called himself a fool for imagining that. For the run was dead ahead, and the girl became vibrant with life, her paddle flashing in and out, while from her lips came sharp, clear cries which brought from Eateese frog-like bellows of response. The walls shot past; inundations rose and plunged under them; black rocks whipped with caps of foam raced up-stream with the speed of living things; the roar became a drowning voice, and then—as if outreached by the wings of a swifter thing—dropped suddenly behind them. Smoother water lay ahead. The channel broadened. Moonlight filled it with a clearer radiance, and Carrigan saw the girl's hair glistening wet, and her arms dripping.

For the first time he turned about and faced Bateese. The half-breed was grinning like a Cheshire cat!

"You're a confoundedly queer pair!" grunted Carrigan, and he turned about again to find Jeanne Marie-Anne Boulain as uncon-cerned as though running the Holy Ghost Rapids in the glow of the moon was nothing more than a matter of play.

It was impossible for him to keep his heart from beating a little faster as he watched her, even though he was trying to regard her in a most professional sort of way. He reminded himself that she was an iniquitous little Jezebel who had almost murdered him. Carmin Fanchet had been like her, an *ame damnee*—a fallen angel—but his business was not sympathy in such matters as these. At the same time he could not resist the lure of both her audacity and her courage, and he found himself all at once asking himself the amazing question as to what her relationship might be to Bateese. It occurred to him rather unpleasantly that there had been something distinctly proprietary in the way the half-breed had picked her up on the sand, and that Ba-teese had shown no hesitation a little later in threatening to knock his head off unless he stopped talking to her. He wondered if Bateese was a Boulain.

The two or three minutes of excitement in the boiling waters of the Holy Ghost had acted like medicine on Carrigan. It seemed to him that something had given way in his head, relieving him of an oppression that had been like an iron hoop drawn tightly about his skull. He did not want Bateese to suspect this change in him, and he slouched lower against the dunnage-pack with his eyes still on the girl. He was finding it increasingly difficult to keep from looking at her. She had resumed her paddling, and Bateese was putting mighty efforts in his strokes now, so that the narrow, birchbark canoe shot like an arrow with the down-sweeping current of the river. A few hun-dred yards below was a twist in the channel, and as the canoe rounded this, taking the shoreward curve with dizzying swiftness, a wide, still straight-water lay ahead. And far down this Carrigan saw the glow of fires.

The forest had drawn back from the river, leaving in its place a broken tundra of rock and shale and a wide strip of black sand along the edge of the stream itself. Carrigan knew what it was—an upheaval of the tar-sand country so common still farther north, the beginning of that treasure of the earth which would someday make the top of the American continent one of the Eldorados of the world. The fires drew nearer, and suddenly the still night was broken by the wild chanting of men. David heard behind him a choking note in the throat of Bateese. A soft word came from the lips of the girl, and it seemed to Carrigan that her head was held higher in the moon glow. The chant increased in volume, a rhythmic, throbbing, savage music that for a hundred and fifty years had come from the throats of men along the Three Rivers.

It thrilled Carrigan as they bore down upon it. It was not song as civilization would have counted song. It was like an explosion, an exultation of human voice unchained, ebullient with the love of life, savage in its good-humor. It was *le gaite de coeur* of the rivermen, who thought and sang as their forefathers did in the days of Radisson and good Prince Rupert; it was their merriment, their exhilaration, their freedom and optimism, reaching up to the farthest stars. In that song men were straining their vocal muscles, shouting to beat out their nearest neighbour, bellowing like bulls in a frenzy of sudden fun. And then, as suddenly as it had risen in the night, the clamour of voices died away. A single shout came up the river. Carrigan thought he heard a low rumble of laughter. A tin pan banged against another. A dog howled. The flat of an oar played a tattoo for a moment on the bottom of a boat. Then one last yell from a single throat—and the night was silent again.

And that was the Boulain Brigade—singing at this hour of the night, when men should have been sleeping if they expected to be up with the sun. Carrigan stared ahead. Shortly his adventure would take a new twist. Something was bound to happen when they got ashore. The peculiar glow of the fires had puzzled him. Now he began to understand. Jeanne Marie-Anne Boulain's men were camped in the edge of the tar-sands and had lighted a number of natural gas-jets that came up out of the earth. Many times he had seen fires like these burning up and down the Three Rivers. He had lighted fires of his own; he had cooked over them and had afterward had the fun and excitement of extinguishing them with pails of water. But he had never seen anything quite like this that was unfolding itself before his eyes now.

There were seven of the fires over an area of half an acre—spouts of yellowish flame burning like giant torches ten or fifteen feet in the air. And between them he very soon made out great bustle and activity. Many figures were moving about. They looked like dwarfs at first, gnomes at play in a little world made out of witchcraft. But Bateese was sending the canoe nearer with powerful strokes, and the figures grew taller, and the spouts of flame higher. Then he knew what was happening. The Boulain men were taking advantage of the cool hours of the night and were tarring up.

He could smell the tar, and he could see the big York boats drawn up in the circle of yellowish light. There were half a dozen of them, and men stripped to the waist were smearing the bottoms of the boats with boiling tar and pitch. In the centre was a big, black cauldron steaming over a gas-jet, and between this cauldron and the boats men were running back and forth with pails. Still nearer to the huge kettle other men were filling a row of kegs with the precious black *goudron* that oozed up from the bowels of the earth, forming here and there jet-black pools that Carrigan could see glistening in the flare of the gas-lamps. He figured there were thirty men at work. Six big York boats were turned keel up in the black sand. Close inshore, just outside the circle of light, was a single scow.

Toward this scow Bateese sent the canoe. And as they drew nearer, until the labouring men ashore were scarcely a stone's throw away, the weirdness of the scene impressed itself more upon Carrigan. Never had he seen such a crew. There were no Indians among them. Lithe, quick-moving, bare-headed, their naked arms and shoulders gleaming in the ghostly illumination, they were racing against time with the boiling tar and pitch in the cauldron. They did not see the approach of the canoe, and Bateese did not draw their attention to it. Quietly he drove the birchbark under the shadow of the big *bateau*. Hands were waiting to seize and steady it. Carrigan caught but a glimpse of the faces.

In another instant the girl was aboard the scow, and Bateese was bending over him. A second time he was picked up like a child in the chimpanzee-like arms of the half-breed. The moonlight showed him a scow bigger than he had ever seen on the upper river, and two-thirds of it seemed to be cabin. Into this cabin Bateese carried him, and in darkness laid him upon what Carrigan thought must be a cot built against the wall. He made no sound, but let himself fall limply upon it. He listened to Bateese as he moved about, and closed his eyes

40

when Bateese struck a match. A moment later he heard the door of the cabin close behind the half-breed. Not until then did he open his eyes and sit up.

He was alone. And what he saw in the next few moments drew an exclamation of amazement from him. Never had he seen a cabin like this on the Three Rivers. It was thirty feet long if an inch, and at least eight feet wide. The walls and ceiling were of polished cedar; the floor was of cedar closely matched. It was the exquisite finish and craftsmanship of the woodwork that caught his eyes first. Then his astonished senses seized upon the other things. Under his feet was a soft rug of dark green velvet. Two magnificent white bearskins lay between him and the end of the room. The walls were hung with pictures, and at the four windows were curtains of ivory lace draped with damask. The lamp which Bateese had lighted was fastened to the wall close to him. It was of polished silver and threw a brilliant light softened by a shade of old gold. There were three other lamps like this, unlighted.

The far end of the room was in deep shadow, but Carrigan made out the thing he was staring at—a piano. He rose to his feet, disbelieving his eyes, and made his way toward it. He passed between chairs. Near the piano was another door, and a wide divan of the same soft, green upholstery. Looking back, he saw that what he had been lying upon was another divan. And close to this were book-shelves, and a table on which were magazines and papers and a woman's workbasket, and in the workbasket—sound asleep—a cat!

And then, over the table and the sleeping cat, his eyes rested upon a triangular banner fastened to the wall. In white against a background of black was a mighty polar bear holding at bay a horde of Arctic wolves. And suddenly the thing he had been fighting to recall came to Carrigan—the great bear—the fighting wolves—the crest of St. Pierre Boulain!

He took a quick step toward the table—then caught at the back of a chair. Confound his head! Or was it the big *bateau* rocking under his feet? The cat seemed to be turning round in its basket. There were half a dozen banners instead of one; the lamp was shaking in its bracket; the floor was tilting, everything was becoming hideously contorted and out of place. A shroud of darkness gathered about him, and through that darkness Carrigan staggered blindly toward the divan. He reached it just in time to fall upon it like a dead man.

6

For what seemed to be an interminable time after the final break-
down of his physical strength David Carrigan lived in a black world
where a horde of unseen little devils were shooting red-hot arrows
into his brain. He did not sense the fact of human presence; nor that
the divan had been changed into a bed and the four lamps lighted, and
that wrinkled, brown hands with talon-like fingers were performing
a miracle of wilderness surgery upon him. He did not see the age-
old face of Nepapinas—"The Wandering Bolt of Lightning"—as the
bent and tottering Cree called upon all his eighty years of experience
to bring him back to life. And he did not see Bateese, stolid-faced,
silent, nor the dead-white face and wide-open, staring eyes of Jeanne
Marie-Anne Boulain as her slim, white fingers worked with the old
medicine man's. He was in a gulf of blackness that writhed with the
spirits of torment. He fought them and cried out against them, and
his fighting and his cries brought the look of death itself into the eyes
of the girl who was over him. He did not hear her voice nor feel the
soothing of her hands, nor the powerful grip of Bateese as he held him
when the critical moments came. And Nepapinas, like a machine that
had looked upon death a thousand times, gave no rest to his claw-like
fingers until the work was done—and it was then that something
came to drive the arrow-shooting devils out of the darkness that was
smothering Carrigan.

After that Carrigan lived through an eternity of unrest, a life in
which he seemed powerless and yet was always struggling for suprem-
acy over things that were holding him down. There were lapses in it,
like the hours of oblivion that come with sleep, and there were other
times when he seemed keenly alive, yet unable to move or act. The
darkness gave way to flashes of light, and in these flashes he began to
see things, curiously twisted, fleeting, and yet fighting themselves in-

sistently upon his senses. He was back in the hot sand again, and this time he heard the voices of Jeanne Marie-Anne and Golden-Hair, and Golden-Hair flaunted a banner in his face, a triangular pennon of black on which a huge bear was fighting white Arctic wolves, and then she would run away from him, crying out—"St. Pierre Boulain—St. Pierre Boulain—" and the last he could see of her was her hair flaming like fire in the sun. But it was always the other—the dark hair and dark eyes—that came to him when the little devils returned to assault him with their arrows. From somewhere she would come out of darkness and frighten them away. He could hear her voice like a whisper in his ears, and the touch of her hands comforted him and quieted his pain. After a time he grew to be afraid when the darkness swallowed her up, and in that darkness he would call for her, and always he heard her voice in answer.

Then came a long oblivion. He floated through cool space away from the imps of torment; his bed was of downy clouds, and on these clouds he drifted with a great shining river under him; and at last the cloud he was in began to shape itself into walls and on these walls were pictures, and a window through which the sun was shining, and a black pennon—and he heard a soft, wonderful music that seemed to come to him faintly from another world. Other creatures were at work in his brain now. They were building up and putting together the loose ends of things. Carrigan became one of them, working so hard that frequently a pair of dark eyes came out of the dawning of things to stop him, and quieting hands and a voice soothed him to rest. The hands and the voice became very intimate. He missed them when they were not near, especially the hands, and he was always groping for them to make sure they had not gone away.

Only once after the floating cloud transformed itself into the walls of the *bateau* cabin did the chaotic darkness of the sands fully possess him again. In that darkness he heard a voice. It was not the voice of Golden-Hair, or of Bateese, or of Jeanne Marie-Anne. It was close to his ears. And in that darkness that smothered him there was something terrible about it as it droned slowly the words—"Has-any-one-seen-Black-Roger-Audemard?" He tried to answer, to call back to it, and the voice came again, repeating the words, emotionless, hollow, as if echoing up out of a grave. And still harder he struggled to reply to it, to say that he was David Carrigan, and that he was out on the trail of Black Roger Audemard, and that Black Roger was far north.

And suddenly it seemed to him that the voice changed into the flesh and blood of Black Roger himself, though he could not see in the darkness—and he reached out, gripping fiercely at the warm substance of flesh, until he heard another voice, the voice of Jeanne Marie-Anne Boulain, entreating him to let his victim go. It was this time that his eyes shot open, wide and seeing, and straight over him was the face of Jeanne Marie-Anne, nearer him than it had been even in the visionings of his feverish mind. His fingers were clutching her shoulders, gripping like steel hooks.

"*M'sieu*—M'sieu David!" she was crying.

For a moment he stared; then his hands and fingers relaxed, and his arms dropped limply. "Pardon—I—I was dreaming," he struggled weakly. "I thought—"

He had seen the pain in her face. Now, changing swiftly, it lighted up with relief and gladness. His vision, cleared by long darkness, saw the change come in an instant like a flash of sunshine. And then—so near that he could have touched her—she was smiling down into his eyes. He smiled back. It took an effort, for his face felt stiff and unnatural.

"I was dreaming—of a man—named Roger Audemard," he continued to apologize. "Did I—hurt you?"

The smile on her lips was gone as swiftly as it had come. "A little, *m'sieu*. I am glad you are better. You have been very sick."

He raised a hand to his face. The bandage was there, and also a stubble of beard on his cheeks. He was puzzled. This morning he had fastened his steel mirror to the side of a tree and shaved.

"It was three days ago you were hurt," she said quietly. "This is the afternoon of the third day. You have been in a great fever. Nepapinas, my Indian doctor, saved your life. You must lie quietly now. You have been talking a great deal."

"About—Black Roger?" he said.

She nodded.

"And—Golden—Hair?"

"Yes, of Golden—Hair."

"And—someone else—with dark hair—and dark eyes—"

"It may be, *m'sieu*."

"And of little devils with bows and arrows, and of polar bears, and white wolves, and of a great lord of the north who calls himself St. Pierre Boulain?"

"Yes, of all those."

"Then I haven't anything more to tell you," grunted David. "I

44

guess I've told you all I know. You shot me, back there. And here I am. What are you going to do next?"

"Call Bateese," she answered promptly, and she rose swiftly from beside him and moved toward the door.

He made no effort to call her back. His wits were working slowly, readjusting themselves after a carnival in chaos, and he scarcely sensed that she was gone until the cabin door closed behind her. Then again he raised a hand to his face and felt his beard. Three days! He turned his head so that he could take in the length of the cabin. It was filled with subdued sunlight now, a western sun that glowed softly, giving depth and richness to the colours on the floor and walls, lighting up the piano keys, suffusing the pictures with a warmth of life. David's eyes travelled slowly to his own feet. The divan had been opened and transformed into a bed. He was undressed. He had on somebody's white nightgown. And there was a big bunch of wild roses on the table where three days ago the cat had been sleeping in the work-basket. His head cleared swiftly, and he raised himself a little on one elbow, with extreme caution, and listened. The big *bateau* was not moving. It was still tied up, but he could hear no voices out where the tar-sands were.

He dropped back on his pillow, and his eyes rested on the black pennon. His blood stirred again as he looked at the white bear and the fighting wolves. Wherever men rode the waters of the Three Rivers that pennon was known. Yet it was not common. Seldom was it seen, and never had it come south of Chipewyan. Many things came to Carrigan now, things that he had heard at the Landing and up and down the rivers. Once he had read the tail-end of a report the Superintendent of "N" Division had sent in to headquarters.

"We do not know this St. Pierre. Few men have seen him out of his own country, the far headwaters of the Yellowknife, where he rules like a great overlord. Both the Yellowknives and the Dog Ribs call him *Kicheoo Kimow*, or King, and the same rumours say there is never starvation or plague in his regions; and it is fact that neither the Hudson's Bay nor Revillon Brothers in their cleverest generalship and trade have been able to uproot his almost dynastic jurisdiction. The Police have had no reason to investigate or interfere."

At least that was the gist of what Carrigan had read in McVane's report. But he had never associated it with the name of Boulain. It was of St. Pierre that he had heard stories, St. Pierre and his black pennon with its white bear and fighting wolves. And so—it was St. Pierre

BOULAIN!

He closed his eyes and thought of the long winter weeks he had passed at Hay River Post, watching for Fanchet, the mail robber. It was there he had heard most about this St. Pierre, and yet no one he had talked with had ever seen him; no one knew whether he was old or young, a pigmy or a giant. Some stories said that he was strong, that he could twist a gun-barrel double in his hands; others said that he was old, very old, so that he never set forth with his brigades that brought down each year a treasure of furs to be exchanged for freight. And never did a Dog Rib or a Yellowknife open his mouth about *Kicheoo Kimow* St. Pierre, the master of their unmapped domains. In that great country north and west of the Great Slave he remained an enigma and a sphinx.

If he ever came out with his brigades, he did not disclose his identity, so that if one saw a fleet of boats or canoes with the St. Pierre pennon, one had to make his own guess whether St. Pierre himself was there or not. But these things were known—that the keenest, quickest, and strongest men in the northland ran the St. Pierre brigades, that they brought out the richest cargoes of furs, and that they carried back with them into the secret fastnesses of their wilderness the greatest cargoes of freight that treasure could buy. So much the name St. Pierre dragged out of Carrigan's memory. It came to him now why the name "Boulain" had pounded so insistently in his brain. He had seen this pennon with its white bear and fighting wolves only once before, and that had been over a Boulain scow at Chipewyan. But his memory had lost its grip on that incident while retaining vividly its hold on the stories and rumours of the mystery-man, St. Pierre.

Carrigan pulled himself a little higher on his pillow and with a new interest scanned the cabin. He had never heard of Boulain women. Yet here was the proof of their existence and of the greatness that ran in the red blood of their veins. The history of the great northland, hidden in the dust-dry tomes and guarded documents of the great company, had always been of absorbing interest to him. He wondered why it was that the outside world knew so little about it and believed so little of what it heard. A long time ago he had penned an article telling briefly the story of this half of a great continent in which for two hundred years romance and tragedy and strife for mastery had gone on in a way to thrill the hearts of men. He had told of huge forts with thirty-foot stone bastions, of fierce wars, of great warships that had fired their broadsides in battle in the ice-filled waters of Hudson's

Bay.

He had described the coming into this northern world of thousands and tens of thousands of the bravest and best-blooded men of England and France, and how these thousands had continued to come, bringing with them the names of kings, of princes, and of great lords, until out of the savagery of the north rose an aristocracy of race built up of the strongest men of the earth. And these men of later days he had called Lords of the North—men who had held power of life and death in the hollow of their hands until the great company yielded up its suzerainty to the Government of the Dominion in 1870; men who were kings in their domains, whose word was law, who were more powerful in their wilderness castles than their mistress over the sea, the Queen of Britain.

And Carrigan, after writing of these things, had stuffed his manuscript away in the bottom of his chest at barracks, for he believed that it was not in his power to do justice to the people of this wilderness world that he loved. The powerful old lords were gone. Like dethroned monarchs, stripped to the level of other men, they lived in the memories of what had been. Their might now lay in trade. No more could they set out to wage war upon their rivals with powder and ball. Keen wit, swift dogs, and the politics of barter had taken the place of deadlier things. *Le facteur* could no longer slay or command that others be slain. A mightier hand than his now ruled the destinies of the northern people—the hand of the Royal Northwest Mounted Police.

It was this thought, the thought that Law and one of the powerful forces of the wilderness had met in this cabin of the big *bateau*, that came to Carrigan as he drew himself still higher against his pillow. A greater thrill possessed him than the thrill of his hunt for Black Roger Audemard. Black Roger was a murderer, a wholesale murderer and a fiend, a Moloch for whom there could be no pity. Of all men the Law wanted Black Roger most, and he, David Carrigan, was the chosen one to consummate its desire. Yet in spite of that he felt upon him the strange unrest of a greater adventure than the quest for Black Roger. It was like an impending thing that could not be seen, urging him, rousing his faculties from the slough into which they had fallen because of his wound and sickness.

It was, after all, the most vital of all things, a matter of his own life. Jeanne Marie-Anne Boulain had tried to kill him deliberately, with malice and intent. That she had saved him afterward only added to the necessity of an explanation, and he was determined that he would have that explanation and settle the present matter before he allowed another thought of Black Roger to enter his head.

This resolution reiterated itself in his mind as the machine-like voice of duty. He was not thinking of the Law, and yet the consciousness of his accountability to that Law kept repeating itself. In the very face of it Carrigan knew that something besides the moral obligation of the thing was urging him, something that was becoming deeply and dangerously personal. At least—he tried to think of it as dangerous. And that danger was his unbecoming interest in the girl herself. It was an interest distinctly removed from any ethical code that might have governed him in his experience with Carmin Fanchet, for instance. Comparatively, if they had stood together, Carmin would have been the lovelier. But he would have looked longer at Jeanne Marie-Anne Boulain.

He conceded the point, smiling a bit grimly as he continued to study that part of the cabin which he could see from his pillow. He had lost interest—temporarily at least—in Black Roger Audemard. Not long ago the one question to which, above all others, he had desired an answer was, why had Jeanne Marie-Anne Boulain worked so desperately to kill him and so hard to save him afterward? Now, as he looked about him, the question which repeated itself insistently was, what relationship did she bear to this mysterious lord of the north, St. Pierre?

Undoubtedly she was his daughter, for whom St. Pierre had built this luxurious barge of state. A fierce-blooded offspring, he thought, one like Cleopatra herself, not afraid to kill—and equally quick to make amends when there was a mistake.

There came the quiet opening of the cabin door to break in upon his thought. He hoped it was Jeanne Marie-Anne returning to him. It was Nepapinas. The old Indian stood over him for a moment and put a cold, claw-like hand to his forehead. He grunted and nodded his head, his little sunken eyes gleaming with satisfaction. Then he put his hands under David's arms and lifted him until he was sitting upright, with three or four pillows at his back.

"Thanks," said Carrigan. "That makes me feel better. And—if you don't mind—my last lunch was three days ago, boiled prunes and a piece of bannock—"

"I have brought you something to eat, M'sieu David," broke in a soft voice behind him.

Nepapinas slipped away, and Jeanne Marie-Anne stood in his place. David stared up at her, speechless. He heard the door close behind the old Indian. Then Jeanne Marie-Anne drew up a chair, so that for the first time he could see her clear eyes with the light of day full upon her.

He forgot that a few days ago she had been his deadliest enemy. He forgot the existence of a man named Black Roger Audemard. Her slimness was as it had pictured itself to him in the hot sands. Her hair was as he had seen it there. It was coiled upon her head like ropes of spun silk, jet-black, glowing softly. But it was her eyes he stared at, and so fixed was his look that the red lips trembled a bit on the verge of a smile. She was not embarrassed. There was no colour in the clear whiteness of her skin, except that redness of her lips.

"I thought you had black eyes," he said bluntly. "I'm glad you haven't. I don't like them. Yours are as brown as—as—"

"Please, *m'sieu*," she interrupted him, sitting down close beside him. "Will you eat—now?"

A spoon was at his mouth, and he was forced to take it in or have its contents spilled over him. The spoon continued to move quickly between the bowl and his mouth. He was robbed of speech. And the girl's eyes, as surely as he was alive, were beginning to laugh at him. They were a wonderful brown, with little, golden specks in them, like the freckles he had seen in wood-violets. Her lips parted. Between their bewitching redness he saw the gleam of her white teeth. In a crowd, with her glorious hair covered and her eyes looking straight ahead, one would not have picked her out. But close, like this, with her eyes smiling at him, she was adorable.

Something of Carrigan's thoughts must have shown in his face, for suddenly the girl's lips tightened a little, and the warmth went out of her eyes, leaving them cold and distant. He finished the soup, and she rose again to her feet.

"Please don't go," he said. "If you do, I think I shall get up and follow. I am quite sure I am entitled to a little something more than soup."

"Nepapinas says that you may have a bit of boiled fish for supper," she assured him.

"You know I don't mean that. I want to know why you shot me, and what you think you are going to do with me."

"I shot you by mistake—and—I don't know just what to do with you," she said, looking at him tranquilly, but with what he thought was

49

a growing shadow of perplexity in her eyes. "Bateese says to fasten a big stone to your neck and throw you in the river. But Bateese doesn't always mean what he says. I don't think he is quite as bloodthirsty—"

"—As the young lady who tried to murder me behind the rock," Carrigan interjected.

"Exactly, *m'sieu*. I don't think he would throw you into the river-unless I told him to. And I don't believe I am going to ask him to do that," she added, the soft glow flashing back into her eyes for an instant. "Not after the splendid work Nepapinas has done on your head. St. Pierre must see that. And then, if St. Pierre wishes to finish you, why—" She shrugged her slim shoulders and made a little gesture with her hands.

In that same moment there came over her a change as sudden as the passing of light itself. It was as if a thing she was hiding had broken beyond her control for an instant and had betrayed her. The gesture died. The glow went out of her eyes, and in its place came a light that was almost fear—or pain. She came nearer to Carrigan again, and somehow, looking up at her, he thought of the little brush warbler singing at the end of its birch twig to give him courage. It must have been because of her throat, white and soft, which he saw pulsing like a beating heart before she spoke to him.

"I have made a terrible mistake, M'sieu David," she said, her voice barely rising above a whisper. "I'm sorry I hurt you. I thought it was someone else behind the rock. But I cannot tell you more than that-ever. And I know it is impossible for us to be friends." She paused, one of her hands creeping to her bare throat, as if to cover the throbbing he had seen there.

"Why is it impossible?" he demanded, leaning away from his pillows so that he might bring himself nearer to her.

"Because—you are of the police, *m'sieu*."

"The police, yes," he said, his heart thrumming inside his breast. "I am Sergeant Carrigan. I am out after Roger Audemard, a murderer. But my commission has nothing to do with the daughter of St. Pierre Boulain. Please—let's be friends—"

He held out his hand; and in that moment David Carrigan placed another thing higher than duty—and in his eyes was the confession of it, like the glow of a subdued fire. The girl's fingers drew more closely at her throat, and she made no movement to accept his hand.

"Friends," he repeated. "Friends—in spite of the police."

Slowly the girl's eyes had widened, as if she saw that new-born thing riding over all other things in his swiftly beating heart. And afraid of it, she drew a step away from him.

"I am not St. Pierre Boulain's daughter," she said, forcing the words out one by one. "I am—his wife."

7

Afterward Carrigan wondered to what depths he had fallen in the first moments of his disillusionment. Something like shock, perhaps even more than that, must have betrayed itself in his face. He did not speak. Slowly his outstretched arm dropped to the white counterpane. Later he called himself a fool for allowing it to happen, for it was as if he had measured his proffered friendship by what its future might hold for him. In a low, quiet voice Jeanne Marie-Anne Boulain was saying again that she was St. Pierre's wife. She was not excited, yet he understood now why it was he had thought her eyes were very dark. They had changed swiftly. The violet freckles in them were like little flecks of gold. They were almost liquid in their glow, neither brown nor black now, and with that threat of gathering lightning in them.

For the first time he saw the slightest flush of colour in her cheeks. It deepened even as he held out his hand again. He knew that it was not embarrassment. It was the heat of the fire back of her eyes. "It's-funny," he said, making an effort to redeem himself with a lie and smiling. "You rather amaze me. You see, I have been told this St. Pierre is an old, old man—so old that he can't stand on his feet or go with his brigades, and if that is the truth, it is hard for me to picture you as his wife. But that isn't a reason why we should not be friends. Is it?"

He felt that he was himself again, except for the three days' growth of beard on his face. He tried to laugh, but it was rather a poor attempt. And St. Pierre's wife did not seem to hear him. She was looking at him, looking into and through him with those wide-open glowing eyes. Then she sat down, out of reach of the hand which he had held toward her.

"You are a sergeant of the police," she said, the softness gone suddenly out of her voice. "You are an honorable man, *m'sieu*. Your hand is against all wrong. Is it not so?" It was the voice of an inquisitor. She was demanding an answer of him.

He nodded. "Yes, it is so."

The fire in her eyes deepened. "And yet you say you want to be the friend of a stranger who has tried to kill you. WHY, *m'sieu*?"

He was cornered. He sensed the humiliation of it, the impossibility of confessing to her the wild impulse that had moved him before he knew she was St. Pierre's wife. And she did not wait for him to answer.

"This—this Roger Audemard—if you catch him—what will you do with him?" she asked.

"He will be hanged," said David. "He is a murderer."

"And one who tries to kill—who almost succeeds—what is the penalty for that?" She leaned toward him, waiting. Her hands were clasped tightly in her lap, the spots were brighter in her cheeks.

"From ten to twenty years," he acknowledged. "But, of course, there may be circumstances—"

"If so, you do not know them," she interrupted him. "You say Roger Audemard is a murderer. You know I tried to kill you. Then why is it you would be my friend and Roger Audemard's enemy? Why, *m'sieu*?"

Carrigan shrugged his shoulders hopelessly. "I shouldn't," he confessed. "I guess you are proving I was wrong in what I said. I ought to arrest you and take you back to the Landing as soon as I can. But, you see, it strikes me there is a big personal element in this. I was the man almost killed. There was a mistake,—must have been, for as soon as you put me out of business you began nursing me back to life again. And—"

"But that doesn't change it," insisted St. Pierre's wife. "If there had been no mistake, there would have been a murder. Do you understand, *m'sieu*? If it had been someone else behind that rock, I am quite certain he would have died. The Law, at least, would have called it murder. If Roger Audemard is a criminal, then I also am a criminal. And an honourable man would not make a distinction because one of them is a woman!"

"But—Black Roger was a fiend. He deserves no mercy. He—"

"Perhaps, *m'sieu*!"

She was on her feet, her eyes flaming down upon him. In that moment her beauty was like the beauty of Carmin Fanchet. The poise of her slender body, her glowing cheeks, her lustrous hair, her gold-flecked eyes with the light of diamonds in them, held him speechless.

53

"I was sorry and went back for you," she said. "I wanted you to live, after I saw you like that on the sand. Bateese says I was indiscreet, that I should have left you there to die. Perhaps he is right. And yet—even Roger Audemard might have had that pity for you."

She turned quickly, and he heard her moving away from him. Then, from the door, she said,

"Bateese will make you comfortable, *m'sieu*."

The door opened and closed. She was gone. And he was alone in the cabin again.

The swiftness of the change in her amazed him. It was as if he had suddenly touched fire to an explosive. There had been the flare, but no violence. She had not raised her voice, yet he heard in it the tremble of an emotion that was consuming her. He had seen the flame of it in her face and eyes. Something he had said, or had done, had tremendously upset her, changing in an instant her attitude toward him. The thought that came to him made his face burn under its scrub of beard. Did she think he was a scoundrel? The dropping of his hand, the shock that must have betrayed itself in his face when she said she was St. Pierre's wife—had those things warned her against him? The heat went slowly out of his face. It was impossible. She could not think that of him. It must have been a sudden giving way under terrific strain. She had compared herself to Roger Audemard, and she was beginning to realize her peril—that Bateese was right—that she should have left him to die in the sand!

The thought pressed itself heavily upon Carrigan. It brought him suddenly back to a realization of how small a part he had played in this last half hour in the cabin. He had offered to Pierre's wife a friendship which he had no right to offer and which she knew he had no right to offer. He was the Law. And she, like Roger Audemard, was a criminal. Her quick woman's instinct had told her there could be no distinction between them, unless there was a reason. And now Carrigan confessed to himself that there had been a reason.

That reason had come to him with the first glimpse of her as he lay in the hot sand. He had fought against it in the canoe; it had mastered him in those thrilling moments when he had beheld this slim, beautiful creature riding fearlessly into the boiling waters of the Holy Ghost. Her eyes, her hair, the sweet, low voice that had been with him in his fever, had become a definite and unalterable part of him. And this must have shown in his eyes and face when he dropped his hand—when she told him she was St. Pierre's wife.

And now she was afraid of him! She was regretting that she had not left him to die. She had misunderstood what she had seen betraying itself during those few seconds of his proffered friendship. She saw only a man whom she had nearly killed, a man who represented the Law, a man whose power held her in the hollow of his hand. And she had stepped back from him, startled, and had told him that she was not St. Pierre's daughter, but his wife!

In the science of criminal analysis Carrigan always placed himself in the position of the other man. And he was beginning to see the present situation from the view-point of Jeanne Marie-Anne Boulain. He was satisfied that she had made a desperate mistake and that until the last moment she had believed it was another man behind the rock. Yet she had shown no inclination to explain away her error. She had definitely refused to make an explanation. And it was simply a matter of common sense to concede that there must be a powerful motive for her refusal. There was but one conclusion for him to arrive at—the error which St. Pierre's wife had made in shooting the wrong man was less important to her than keeping the secret of why she had wanted to kill some other man.

David was not unconscious of the breach in his own armour. He had weakened, just as the Superintendent of "N" Division had weakened that day four years ago when they had almost quarrelled over Carmin Fanchet.

"I'll swear to Heaven she isn't bad, no matter what her brother has been," McVane had said. "I'll gamble my life on that, Carrigan!"

And because the Chief of Division with sixty years of experience behind him, had believed that, Carmin Fanchet had not been held as an accomplice in her brother's evildoing, but had gone back into her wilderness uncrucified by the law that had demanded the life of her brother. He would never forget the last time he had seen Carmin Fanchet's eyes—great, black, glorious pools of gratitude as they looked at grizzled old McVane; blazing fires of venomous hatred when they turned on him. And he had said to McVane,

"The man pays, the woman goes—justice indeed is blind!"

McVane, not being a stickler on regulations when it came to Carrigan, had made no answer.

The incident came back vividly to David as he waited for the promised coming of Bateese. He began to appreciate McVane's point of view, and it was comforting, because he realized that his own logic was assailable. If McVane had been comparing the two women now, he knew what his argument would be. There had been no absolute proof of crime against Carmin Fanchet, unless to fight desperately for the life of her brother was a crime. In the case of Jeanne Marie-Anne Boulain there was proof. She had tried to kill. Therefore, of the two, Carmin Fanchet would have been the better woman in the eyes of McVane.

In spite of the legal force of the argument which he was bringing against himself, David felt unconvinced. Carmin Fanchet, had she been in the place of St. Pierre's wife, would have finished him there in the sand. She would have realized the menace of letting him live and would probably have commanded Bateese to dump him in the river. St. Pierre's wife had gone to the other extreme. She was not only repentant, but was making restitution, for her mistake, and in making that restitution had crossed far beyond the dead-line of caution. She had frankly told him who she was; she had brought him into the privacy of what was undeniably her own home; in her desire to undo what she had done she had hopelessly enmeshed herself in the net of the Law—if that Law saw fit to act. She had done these things with courage and conviction. And of such a woman, Carrigan thought, St. Pierre must be very proud.

He looked slowly about the cabin again and each thing that he saw was a living voice breaking up a dream for him. These voices told him that he was in a temple built because of a man's worship for a woman—and that man was St. Pierre. Through the two western windows came the last glow of the western sun, like a golden benediction finding its way into a sacred place. Here there was—or had been—a great happiness, for only a great pride and a great happiness could have made it as it was. Nothing that wealth and toil could drag up out of a civilization a thousand miles away had been too good for St. Pierre's wife. And about him, looking more closely, David saw the undisturbed evidences of a woman's contentment. On the table were embroidery materials with which she had been working, and a lamp-shade half finished.

A woman's magazine printed in a city four thousand miles away lay open at the fashion plates. There were other magazines, and many books, and open music above the white keyboard of the piano, and vases glowing red and yellow with wild-flowers and silver birch leaves. He could smell the faint perfume of the fire-glow blossoms, red as blood. In a pool of sunlight on one of the big white bear rugs lay the sleeping cat. And then, at the far end of the cabin, an ivory-white

Cross of Christ glowed for a few moments in a last homage of the sinking sun.

Uneasiness stole upon him. This was the woman's holy ground, her sanctuary and her home, and for three days his presence had driven her from it. There was no other room. In making restitution she had given up to him her most sacred of all things. And again there rose up in him that new-born thing which had set strange fires stirring in his heart, and which from this hour on he knew he must fight until it was dead.

For an hour after the last of the sun was obliterated by the western mountains he lay in the gloom of coming darkness. Only the lapping of water under the *bateau* broke the strange stillness of the evening. He heard no sound of life, no voice, no tread of feet, and he wondered where the woman and her men had gone and if the scow was still tied up at the edge of the tar-sands. And for the first time he asked himself another question, Where was the man, St. Pierre?

8

It was utterly dark in the cabin, when the stillness was broken by low voices outside. The door opened, and someone came in. A moment later a match flared up, and in the shifting glow of it Carrigan saw the dark face of Bateese, the half-breed. One after another he lighted the four lamps. Not until he had finished did he turn toward the bed. It was then that David had his first good impression of the man. He was not tall, but built with the strength of a giant. His arms were long. His shoulders were stooped. His head was like the head of a stone gargoyle come to life. Wide-eyed, heavy-lipped, with the high cheek-bones of an Indian and uncut black hair bound with the knotted red *mouchoir*, he looked more than ever like a pirate and a cut-throat to David. Such a man, he thought, might make play out of the business of murder. And yet, in spite of his ugliness, David felt again the mysterious inclination to like the man.

Bateese grinned. It was a huge grin, for his mouth was big. "You ver' lucky fellow," he announced. "You sleep lak that in nice sof' bed an' not back on san'-bar, dead lak ze feesh I bring you, *m'sieu*. That ees wan beeg mistake. Bateese say, 'Tie ze stone roun' hees neck an' mak' heem wan *ange de mer*. Chuck heem in ze river, *ma belle* Jeanne!' An' she say no, mak heem well, an' feed heem feesh. So I bring ze feesh which she promise, an' when you have eat, I tell you somet'ing!"

He returned to the door and brought back with him a wicker basket. Then he drew up the table beside Carrigan and proceeded to lay out before him the boiled fish which St. Pierre's wife had promised him. With it was bread and an earthen pot of hot tea.

"She say that ees all you have because of ze fever. Bateese say, 'Stuff heem wit' much so that he die queek!'"

"You want to see me dead. Is that it, Bateese?"

"*OUI*. You mak' wan ver' good dead man, *m'sieu*!" Bateese was no longer grinning. He stood back and pointed at the food. "You eat-queek. An' when you have finish' I tell you somet'ing!"

Now that he saw the luscious bit of whitefish before him, Carrigan was possessed of the hungering emptiness of three days and nights. As he ate, he observed that Bateese was performing curious duties. He straightened a couple of rugs, ran fresh water into the flower vases, picked up half a dozen scattered magazines, and then, to David's increasing interest, produced a dust-cloth from somewhere and began to dust. David finished his fish, the one slice of bread, and his cup of tea. He felt tremendously good. The hot tea was like a trickle of new life through every vein in his body, and he had the desire to get up and try out his legs. Suddenly Bateese discovered that his patient was laughing at him.

"*Que diable!*" he demanded, coming up ferociously with the cloth in his great hand. "You see somet'ing ver' fonny, *m'sieu?*"

"No, nothing funny, Bateese," grinned Carrigan. "I was just thinking what a handsome chambermaid you make. You are so gentle, so nice to look at, so—"

"*Diable!*" exploded Bateese, dropping his dust cloth and bringing his huge hands down upon the table with a smash that almost wrecked the dishes. "You have eat, an' now you lissen. You have never hear' before of Concombre Bateese. An' zat ees me. See! Wit' these two hands I have choke' ze polar bear to deat'. I am strongest man w'at ees in all nort' countree. I pack four hundre' pound ovair portage. I crack ze caribou bones wit' my teeth, lak a dog. I run sixt' or hundre' miles wit'out stop for rest. I pull down trees w'at oder man cut wit' axe. I am not 'fraid of not'ing. You lissen? You hear w'at I say?"

"I hear you."

"*Bien!* Then I tell you w'at Concombre Bateese ees goin' do wit' you, M'sieu Sergent de Police! *Ma belle* Jeanne she mak' wan gran' meestake. She too much leetle bird heart, too much pity for want you to die. Bateese say, 'Keel him, so no wan know w'at happen t'ree day ago behin' ze rock.' But *ma belle* Jeanne, she say, 'No, Bateese, he ees meestake for oder man, an' we mus' let heem live.' An' then she tell me to come an' bring you feesh, an' tell you w'at is goin' happen if you try go away from thees *bateau*. You *compren'?* If you try run away, Bateese ees goin' keel you! See—wit' thees han's I br'ak your neck an' t'row you in river. *Ma belle* Jeanne say do zat, an' she tell oder mans—twent', thirt', almos' hundre' *garçons*—to keel you if you try run away. She tell me bring zat word to you wit' ze feesh. You listen hard w'at I say?"

If ever a worker of iniquity lived on earth, Carrigan might have judged Bateese as that man in these moments. The half-breed had worked himself up to a ferocious pitch. His eyes rolled. His wide mouth snarled in the virulence of its speech. His thick neck grew corded, and his huge hands clenched menacingly upon the table. Yet David had no fear. He wanted to laugh, but he knew laughter would be the deadliest of insults to Bateese just now. He remembered that the half-breed, fierce as a pirate, had a touch as gentle as a woman's. This man, who could choke an ox with his monstrous hands, had a moment before petted a cat, straightened out rugs, watered the woman's flowers, and had dusted. He was harmless—now. And yet in the same breath David sensed the fact that a single word from St. Pierre's wife would be sufficient to fire his brute strength into a blazing volcano of action. Such a henchman was priceless—under certain conditions! And he had brought a warning straight from the woman.

"I think I understand what you mean, Bateese," he said. "She says that I am to make no effort to leave this *bateau*—that I am to be killed if I try to escape? Are you sure she said that?"

"*Par les mille cornes du diable*, you t'ink Bateese lie, *m'sieu*? Concombre Bateese, who choke ze w'ite bear wit' hees two ban', who pull down ze tree—"

"No, no, I don't think you lie. But I am wondering why she didn't tell me that when she was here."

"Becaus' she have too much leetle bird heart, zat ees w'y. She say: 'Bateese, you tell heem he mus' wait for St. Pierre. An' you tell heem good an' hard, lak you choke ze w'ite bear an' lak you pull down ze tree, so he mak' no meestake an' try get away.' An' she tell zat before all ze *bateliers*—all ze St. Pierre mans gathered 'bout a beeg fire—an' they shout up lak wan gargon that they watch an' keel you if you try get away."

Carrigan reached out a hand. "Let's shake, Bateese. I'll give you my word that I won't try to escape—not until you and I have a good stand-up fight with the earth under our feet, and I've whipped you. Is it a go?"

Bateese stared for a moment, and then his face broke into a wide grin. "You lak ze fight, *m'sieu*?"

"Yes. I love a scrap with a good man like you."

One of Bateese's huge hands crawled slowly over the table and engulfed David's. Joy shone on his face.

"An' you promise give me zat fight, w'en you are strong?"

"If I don't, I'll let you tie a stone around my neck and drop me into the river."

"You are brave *garcon*," cried the delighted Bateese. "Up an' down ze rivers ees no man w'at can whip Concombre Bateese!" Suddenly his face grew clouded. "But ze head, m'sieu?" he added anxiously.

"It will get well quickly if you will help me, Bateese. Right now I want to get up. I want to stretch my legs. Was my head bad?"

"*Non*. Ze bullet scrape ze ha'r off—so—so—an' turn ze brain seek. I t'ink you be good fighting man in week!"

"And you will help me up?"

Bateese was a changed man. Again David felt that mighty but gentle strength of his arms as he helped him to his feet. He was a trifle unsteady for a moment. Then, with the half-breed close at his side, ready to catch him if his legs gave way, he walked to one of the windows and looked out. Across the river, fully half a mile away, he saw the glow of fires.

"Her camp?" he asked.

"*Oui, m'sieu.*"

"We have moved from the tar-sands?"

"Yes, two days down ze river."

"Why are they not camping over here with us?"

Bateese gave a disgusted grunt. "Becaus' *ma belle* Jeanne have such leetle bird heart, m'sieu. She say you mus' not have noise near, lak ze talk an' laugh an' *ze chansons*. She say it disturb, an' zat it mak you worse wit' ze fever. She ees mak you lak de baby, Bateese say to her. But she on'y laugh at zat an' snap her leetle w'ite finger. Wait St. Pierre come! He brak yo'r head wit' hees two fists. I hope we have ze fight before then, *m'sieu!*"

"We'll have it anyway, Bateese. Where is St. Pierre, and when shall we see him?"

Bateese shrugged his shoulders. "Mebby week, mebby more. He long way off."

"Is he an old man?"

Slowly Bateese turned David about until he was facing him. "You ask not'ing more about St. Pierre," he warned. "No mans talk 'bout St. Pierre. Only wan—*ma belle* Jeanne. You ask her, an' she tell you shut up. W'en you don't shut up she call Bateese to brak your head."

"You're a—a sort of all-round head-breaker, as I understand it," grunted David, walking slowly back to his bed. "Will you bring me my pack and clothes in the morning? I want to shave and dress."

Bateese was ahead of him, smoothing the pillows and straightening out the rumpled bed-clothes. His huge hands were quick and capable as a woman's, and David could not keep himself from chuckling at this feminine ingeniousness of the powerful half-breed. Once in the crush of those gorilla-like arms that were working over his bed now, he thought, and it would be all over with the strongest man in "N" Division. Bateese heard the chuckle and looked up.

"Somet'ing ver' funny once more, is eet—w'at?" he demanded.

"I was thinking, Bateese—what will happen to me if you get me in those arms when we fight? But it isn't going to happen. I fight with my fists, and I'm going to batter you up so badly that nobody will recognize you for a long time."

"You wait!" exploded Bateese, making a horrible grimace. "I choke you lak w'ite bear, I t'row you ovair my should'r, I mash you lak leetle strawberr', I—" He paused in his task to advance with a formidable gesture.

"Not now," warned Carrigan. "I'm still a bit groggy, Bateese." He pointed down at the bed. "I'm driving HER from that," he said. "I don't like it. Is she sleepin' over there—in the camp?"

"Mebby—an' mebby not, m'sieu," growled Bateese. "You mak' guess, eh?"

He began extinguishing the lights, until only the one nearest the door was left burning. He did not turn toward Carrigan or speak to him again. When he went out, David heard the click of a lock in the door. Bateese had not exaggerated. It was the intention of St. Pierre's wife that he should consider himself a prisoner—at least for tonight.

He had no desire to lie down again. There was an unsteadiness in his legs, but outside of that the evil of his sickness no longer oppressed him. The staff doctor at the Landing would probably have called him a fool for not convalescing in the usual prescribed way, but Carrigan was already beginning to feel the demand for action. In spite of what physical effort he had made, his head did not hurt him, and his mind was keenly alive. He returned to the window through which he could see the fires on the western shore, and found no difficulty in opening it.

A strong screen netting kept him from thrusting out his head and shoulders. Through it came the cool night breeze of the river. It seemed good to fill his lungs with it again and smell the fresh aroma of the forest. It was very dark, and the fires across the river were brighter because of the deep gloom. There was no promise of the moon in the sky. He could not see a star. From far in the west he caught the low intonation of thunder.

Carrigan turned from the window to the end of the cabin in which the piano stood. Here, too, was the second divan, and he saw the meaning now of two close-tied curtains, one at each side of the cabin. Drawn together on a taut wire stretched two inches under the ceiling, they shut off this end of the *bateau* and turned at least a third of the cabin into the privacy of the woman's bedroom. With growing uneasiness David saw the evidences that this had been her sleeping apartment. At each side of the piano was a small door, and he opened one of these just enough to discover that it was a wardrobe closet. A third door opened on the shore side of the *bateau*, but this was locked. Shut out from the view of the lower end of the cabin by a Japanese screen were a small dresser and a mirror. In the dim illumination that came from the distant lamp David bent over the open sheet of music on the piano. It was Mascagni's *Ave Maria*.

His blood tingled. His brain was stirred by a new emotion, a growing thing that made him uneasy and filled him with a strange restlessness. He felt as though he had come suddenly to the edge of a great danger; somewhere within him an intelligence seized upon it and understood. Yet it was not physical enough for him to fight. It was a danger which crept up and about him, something which he could not see or touch and yet which made his heart beat faster and the blood come into his face. It drew him, triumphed over him, dragged his hand forth until his fingers closed upon a lacy, crumpled bit of a handkerchief that lay on the edge of the piano keys. It was the woman's handkerchief, and like a thief he raised it slowly. It smelled faintly of crushed violets; it was as if she were bending over him in his sickness again, and it was her breath that came to him. He was not thinking of her as St. Pierre's wife. And then sharply he caught himself and placed the handkerchief back on the piano keys. He tried to laugh at himself, but there was an emptiness where a moment before there had been that thrill of which he was now ashamed.

He turned back to the window. The thunder had come nearer. It was coming up fast out of the west, and with it a darkness that was like the blackness of a pit. A dead stillness was preceding it now, and in that stillness it seemed to Carrigan that he could hear the soapy, slitting sound of the streaming flashes of electrical fire that blazoned the advance of the storm. The camp-fires across the river were dying down. One of them went out as he looked at it, and he stared into the darkness as if trying to pierce distance and gloom to see what sort of a shelter it was that St. Pierre's wife had over there. And there came over him in these moments a desire that was almost cowardly. It was the desire to escape, to leave behind him the memory of the rock and of St. Pierre's wife, and to pursue once more his own great adventure, the quest of Black Roger Audemard.

He heard the rain coming. At first the sound of it was like the pattering of ten million tiny feet in dry leaves; then, suddenly, it was like the roar of an avalanche. It was an inundation, and with it came crash after crash of thunder, and the black skies were illumined by an almost uninterrupted glare of lightning. It had been a long time since Carrigan had felt the shock of such a storm. He closed the window to keep the rain out, and after that stood with his face flattened against the glass, staring over the river. The camp-fires were all gone now, blotted out like so many candles snuffed between thumb and forefinger, and he shuddered.

No canvas ever made would keep that deluge out. And now there was growing up a wind with it. The tents on the other side would be beaten down like pegged sheets of paper, ripped up and torn to pieces. He imagined St. Pierre's wife in that tumult and distress—the breath blown out of her, half drowned, blinded by deluge and lightning, broken and beaten because of him. Thought of her companions did not ease his mind. Human hands were entirely inadequate to cope with a storm like this that was rocking the earth about him.

Suddenly he went to the door, determined that if Bateese was outside he would get some satisfaction out of him or challenge him to a fight right there. He beat against it, first with one fist and then with both. He shouted. There was no response. Then he exerted his strength and his weight against the door. It was solid.

He was half turned when his eyes discovered, in a corner where the lamplight struck dimly, his pack and clothes. In thirty seconds he had his pipe and tobacco. After that for half an hour he paced up and down the cabin, while the storm crashed and thundered as if bent upon destroying all life off the face of the earth.

Comforted by the company of his pipe, Carrigan did not beat at the door again. He waited, and at the end of another half-hour the storm had softened down into a steady patter of rain. The thunder had travelled east, and the lightning had gone with it. David opened the window again. The air that came in was rain-sweet, soft, and warm. He puffed out a cloud of smoke and smiled. His pipe always brought his

64

good humor to the surface, even in the worst places. St. Pierre's wife had certainly had a good soaking. And in a way the whole thing was a bit funny. He was thinking now of a poor little golden-plumaged partridge, soaked to the skin, with its tail-feathers dragging pathetically.

Grinning, he told himself that it was an insult to think of her and a half-drowned partridge in the same breath. But the simile still remained, and he chuckled. Probably she was wringing out her clothes now, and the men were cursing under their breath while trying to light a fire. He watched for the fire. It failed to appear. Probably she was hating him for bringing all this discomfort and humiliation upon her. It was not impossible that tomorrow she would give Bateese permission to brain him. And St. Pierre? What would this man, her husband, think and do if he knew that his wife had given up her bedroom to this stranger? What complications might arise IF HE KNEW!

It was late—past midnight—when Carrigan went to bed. Even then he did not sleep for a long time. The patter of the rain grew less and less on the roof of the *bateau*, and as the sound of it droned itself off into nothingness, slumber came. David was conscious of the moment when the rain ceased entirely. Then he slept. At least he must have been very close to sleep, or had been asleep and was returning for a moment close to consciousness, when he heard a voice. It came several times before he was roused enough to realize that it was a voice. And then, suddenly, piercing his slowly wakening brain almost with the shock of one of the thunder crashes, it came to him so distinctly that he found himself sitting up straight, his hands clenched, eyes staring in the darkness, waiting for it to come again.

Somewhere very near him, in his room, within the reach of his hands, a strange and indescribable voice had cried out in the darkness the words which twice before had beat themselves mysteriously into David Carrigan's brain—"HAS ANY ONE SEEN BLACK ROGER AUDEMARD? HAS ANY ONE SEEN BLACK ROGER AUDEMARD?"

And David, holding his breath, listened for the sound of another breath which he knew was in that room.

9

For perhaps a minute Carrigan made no sound that could have been heard three feet away from him. It was not fear that held him quiet. It was something which he could not explain afterward, the sensation, perhaps, of one who feels himself confronted for a moment by a presence more potent than that of flesh and blood. BLACK ROGER AUDEMARD! Three times, twice in his sickness, someone had cried out that name in his ears since the hour when St. Pierre's wife had ambushed him on the white carpet of sand. And the voice was now in his room!

Was it Bateese, inspired by some sort of malformed humour? Carrigan listened. Another minute passed. He reached out a hand and groped about him, very careful not to make a sound, urged by the feeling that someone was almost within reach of him. He flung back his blanket and stood out in the middle of the floor.

Still he heard no movement, no soft footfalls of retreat or advance. He lighted a match and held it high above his head. In its yellow illumination he could see nothing alive. He lighted a lamp. The cabin was empty. He drew a deep breath and went to the window. It was still open. The voice had undoubtedly come to him through that window, and he fancied he could see where the screen netting was crushed a bit inward, as though a face had pressed heavily against it. Outside the night was beautifully calm. The sky, washed by storm, was bright with stars. But there was not a ripple of movement that he could hear.

After that he looked at his watch. He must have been sleeping for some time when the voice roused him, for it was nearly three o'clock. In spite of the stars, dawn was close at hand. When he looked out of the window again they were paler and more distant. He had no intention of going back to bed. He was restless and felt himself surrendering more and more to the grip of presentiment.

It was still early, not later than six o'clock, when Bateese came in with his breakfast. He was surprised, as he had heard no movement or sound of voices to give evidence of life anywhere near the *bateau*. Instantly he made up his mind that it was not Bateese who had uttered the mysterious words of a few hours ago, for the half-breed had evidently experienced a most uncomfortable night. He was like a rat recently pulled out of water. His clothes hung upon him sodden and heavy, his head kerchief dripped, and his lank hair was wet. He slammed the breakfast things down on the table and went out again without so much as nodding at his prisoner.

Again a sense of discomfort and shame swept over David, as he sat down to breakfast. Here he was comfortably, even luxuriously, housed, while out there somewhere St. Pierre's lovely wife was drenched and even more miserable than Bateese. And the breakfast amazed him. It was not so much the caribou tenderloin, rich in its own red juice, or the potato, or the pot of coffee that was filling the cabin with its aroma, that roused his wonder, but the hot, brown muffins that accompanied the other things. Muffins! And after a deluge that had drowned every square inch of the earth! How had Bateese turned the trick?

Bateese did not return immediately for the dishes, and for half an hour after he had finished breakfast Carrigan smoked his pipe and watched the blue haze of fires on the far side of the river. The world was a blaze of sunlit glory. His imagination carried him across the river. Somewhere over there, in an open spot where the sun was blazing, Jeanne Marie-Anne was probably drying herself after the night of storm. There was but little doubt in his mind that she was already heaping the ignominy of blame upon him. That was the woman of it.

A knock at his door drew him about. It was a light, quick TAP, TAP, TAP—not like the fist of either Bateese or Nepapinas. In another moment the door swung open, and in the flood of sunlight that poured into the cabin stood St. Pierre's wife!

It was not her presence, but the beauty of her, that held him spellbound. It was a sort of shock after the vivid imaginings of his mind in which he had seen her beaten and tortured by storm. Her hair, glowing in the sun and piled up in shining coils on the crown of her head, was not wet. She was not the rain-beaten little partridge that had passed in tragic bedragglement through his mind. Storm had not touched her. Her cheeks were soft with the warm flush of long hours of sleep. When she came in, her lips greeting him with a little smile, all that he had built up for himself in the hours of the night crumbled away in dust. Again he forgot for a moment that she was St. Pierre's wife. She was woman, and as he looked upon her now, the most adorable woman in all the world.

"You are better this morning," she said. Real pleasure shone in her eyes. She had left the door open, so that the sun filled the room. "I think the storm helped you. Wasn't it splendid?"

David swallowed hard. "Quite splendid," he managed to say. "Have you seen Bateese this morning?"

A little note of laughter came into her throat. "Yes. I don't think he liked it. He doesn't understand why I love storms. Did you sleep well, M'sieu Carrigan?"

"An hour or two, I think. I was worrying about you. I didn't like the thought that I had turned you out into the storm. But it doesn't seem to have touched you."

"No. I was there—quite comfortable." She nodded to the forward bulkhead of the cabin, beyond the wardrobe closets and the piano. "There is a little dining-room and kitchenette ahead," she explained. "Didn't Bateese tell you that?"

"No, he didn't. I asked him where you were, and I think he told me to shut up."

"Bateese is very odd," said St. Pierre's wife. "He is exceedingly jealous of me, M'sieu David. Even when I was a baby and he carried me about in his arms, he was just that way. Bateese, you know, is older than he appears. He is fifty-one."

She was moving about, quite as if his presence was in no way going to disturb her usual duties of the day. She rearranged the damask curtains which he had crumpled with his hands, placed two or three chairs in their usual places, and moved from this to that with the air of a housewife who is in the habit of brushing up a bit in the morning.

She seemed not at all embarrassed because he was her prisoner, nor uncomfortably restrained because of the message she had sent to him by Bateese. She was warmly and gloriously human. In her apparent unconcern at his presence he found himself sweating inwardly. A bit nervously he struck a match to light his pipe, then extinguished it.

She noticed what he had done. "You may smoke," she said, with that little note in her throat which he loved to hear, like the faintest melody of laughter that did not quite reach her lips. "St. Pierre smokes a great deal, and I like it."

She opened a drawer in the dressing-table and came to him with a box half filled with cigars.

"St. Pierre prefers these—on occasions," she said, "Do you?"

His fingers seemed all thumbs as he took a cigar from the proffered box. He cursed himself because his tongue felt thick. Perhaps it was his silence, betraying something of his mental clumsiness, that brought a faint flush of colour into her cheeks. He noted that; and also that the top of her shining head came just about to his chin, and that her mouth and throat, looking down on them, were bewitchingly soft and sweet.

And what she said, when her eyes opened wide and beautiful on him again, was like a knife cutting suddenly into the heart of his thoughts.

"In the evening I love to sit at St. Pierre's feet and watch him smoke," she said. "I am glad it doesn't annoy you, because—I like to smoke," he replied lamely.

She placed the box on the little reading table and looked at his breakfast things. "You like muffins, too. I was up early this morning, making them for you!"

"You made them?" he demanded, as if her words were a most amazing revelation to him.

"Surely, M'sieu David. I make them every morning for St. Pierre. He is very fond of them. He says the third nicest thing about me is my muffins!"

"And the other two?" asked David.

"Are St. Pierre's little secrets, *m'sieu*," she laughed softly, the colour deepening in her cheeks. "It wouldn't be fair to tell you, would it?"

"Perhaps it wouldn't," he said slowly. "But there are one or two other things, Mrs.—Mrs. Boulain—"

"You may call me Jeanne, or Marie-Anne, if you care to," she interrupted him. "It will be quite all right."

She was picking up the breakfast dishes, not at all perturbed by the fact that she was offering him a privilege which had the effect of quickening his pulse for a moment or two.

"Thank you," he said. "I don't mind telling you it is going to be difficult for me to do that—because—well, this is a most unusual situation, isn't it? In spite of all your kindness, including what was probably your good-intentioned endeavour to put an end to my earthly miseries behind the rock, I believe it is necessary for you to give me some kind of explanation. Don't you?"

"Didn't Bateese explain to you last night?" she asked, facing him.

"He brought a message from you to the effect that I was a prisoner, that I must make no attempt to escape, and that if I did try to escape, you had given your men instructions to kill me."

She nodded, quite seriously. "That is right, M'sieu David."

His face flamed. "Then I am a prisoner? You threaten me with death?"

"I shall treat you very nicely if you make no attempt to escape, M'sieu David. Isn't that fair?"

"Fair!" he cried, choking back an explosion that would have vented itself on a man. "Don't you realize what has happened? Don't you know that according to every law of God and man I should arrest you and give you over to the Law? Is it possible that you don't comprehend my own duty? What I must do?"

If he had noticed, he would have seen that there was no longer the flush of colour in her cheeks. But her eyes, looking straight at him, were tranquil and unexcited. She nodded.

"That is why you must remain a prisoner, M'sieu David, It is because I do realize, I shall not tell you why that happened behind the rock, and if you ask me, I shall refuse to talk to you. If I let you go now, you would probably have me arrested and put in jail. So I must keep you until St. Pierre comes. I don't know what to do—except to keep you, and not let you escape until then. What would you do?"

The question was so honest, so like a question that might have been asked by a puzzled child, that his argument for the Law was struck dead. He stared into the pale face, the beautiful, waiting eyes, saw the pathetic intertwining of her slim fingers, and suddenly he was grinning in that big, honest way which made people love Dave Carrigan.

"You're—doing—absolutely—right," he said.

A swift change came in her face. Her cheeks flushed. Her eyes filled with a sudden glow that made the little violet-freckles in them dance like tiny flecks of gold.

"From your point of view you are right," he repeated, "and I shall make no attempt to escape until I have talked with St. Pierre. But I can't quite see—just now—how he is going to help the situation."

"He will," she assured him confidently.

"You seem to have an unlimited faith in St. Pierre," he replied a little grimly.

"Yes, M'sieu David. He is the most wonderful man in the world. And he will know what to do."

David shrugged his shoulders. "Perhaps, in some nice, quiet place, he will follow the advice Bateese gave you—tie a stone round my neck and sink me to the bottom of the river."

"Perhaps. But I don't think he will do that I should object to it."

"Oh, you would!"

"Yes. St. Pierre is big and strong, afraid of nothing in the world, but he will do anything for me. I don't think he would kill you if I asked him not to." She turned to resume her task of cleaning up the breakfast things.

With a sudden movement David swung one of the big chairs close to her. "Please sit down," he commanded. "I can talk to you better that way. As an officer of the law it is my duty to ask you a few questions. It rests in your power to answer all of them or none of them. I have given you my word not to act until I have seen St. Pierre, and I shall keep that promise. But when we do meet I shall act largely on the strength of what you tell me during the next tea minutes. Please sit down!"

10

In that big, deep chair which must have been St. Pierre's own, Marie-Anne sat facing Carrigan. Between its great arms her slim little figure seemed diminutive and out of place. Her brown eyes were level and clear, waiting. They were not warm or nervous, but so coolly and calmly beautiful that they disturbed Carrigan. She raised her hands, her slim fingers crumpling for a moment in the soft, thick coils of her hair. That little movement, the unconscious feminism of it, the way she folded her hands in her lap afterward, disturbed Carrigan even more. What a glory on earth it must be to possess a woman like that! The thought made him uneasy. And she sat waiting, a vivid, softly-breathing question-mark against the warm colouring of the uphol-stered chair.

"When you shot me," he began, "I saw you, first, standing over me. I thought you had come to finish me. It was then that I saw something in your face—horror, amazement, as though you had done something you did not know you were doing. You see, I want to be charitable. I want to understand. I want to excuse you if I can. Won't you tell me why you shot me, and why that change came over you when you saw me lying there?"

"No, M'sieu David, I shall not tell." She was not antagonistic or de-fiant. Her voice was not raised, nor did it betray an unusual emotion. It was simply decisive, and the unflinching steadiness of her eyes and the way in which she sat with her hands folded gave to it an unquali-fied definiteness.

"You mean that I must make my own guess?"

She nodded.

"Or get it out of St. Pierre?"

"If St. Pierre wishes to tell you, yes."

"Well—" He leaned a little toward her. "After that you dragged me up into the shade, dressed my wound and made me comfortable. In a hazy sort of way I knew what was going on. And a curious thing happened. At times—" he leaned still a little nearer to her—"at times there seemed to be two of you!"

He was not looking at her hands, or he would have seen her fingers slowly tighten in her lap.

"You were badly hurt," she said. "It is not strange that you should have imagined things, M'sieu David."

"And I seemed to hear two voices," he went on.

She made no answer, but continued to look at him steadily.

"And the other had hair that was like copper and gold fire in the sun. I would see your face and then hers, again and again—and—since then—I have thought I was a heavy load for your hands to drag up through that sand to the shade alone."

She held up her two hands, looking at them. "They are strong," she said.

"They are small," he insisted, "and I doubt if they could drag me across this floor."

For the first time the quiet of her eyes gave way to a warm fire. "It was hard work," she said, and the note in her voice gave him warning that he was approaching the dead-line again. "Bateese says I was a fool for doing it. And if you saw two of me, or three or four, it doesn't matter. Are you through questioning me, M'sieu David? If so, I have a number of things to do."

He made a gesture of despair. "No, I am not through. But why ask you questions if you won't answer them?"

"I simply cannot. You must wait."

"For your husband?"

"Yes, for St. Pierre."

He was silent for a moment, then said, "I raved about a number of things when I was sick, didn't I?"

"You did, and especially about what you thought happened in the sand. You called this—this other person—the Fire Goddess. You were so near dying that of course it wasn't amusing. Otherwise it would have been. You see MY hair is black, almost!" Again, in a quick movement, her fingers were crumpling the lustrous coils on the crown of her head.

"Why do you say 'almost'?" he asked.

"Because St. Pierre has often told me that when I am in the sun there are red fires in it. And the sun was very bright that afternoon in

73

the sand, M'sieu David."

"I think I understand," he nodded. "And I'm rather glad, too. I like to know that it was you who dragged me up into the shade after trying to kill me. It proves you aren't quite so savage as—"

"Carmin Fanchet," she interrupted him softly. "You talked about her in your sickness, M'sieu David. It made me terribly afraid of you-so much so that at times I almost wondered if Bateese wasn't right. It made me understand what would happen to me if I should let you go. What terrible thing did she do to you? What could she have done more terrible than I have done?"

"Is that why you have given your men orders to kill me if I try to escape?" he asked. "Because I talked about this woman, Carmin Fanchet?"

"Yes, it is because of Carmin Fanchet that I am keeping you for St. Pierre," she acknowledged. "If you had no mercy for her, you could have none for me. What terrible thing did she do to you, *M'sieu?*"

"Nothing—to me," he said, feeling that she was putting him where the earth was unsteady under his feet again. "But her brother was a criminal of the worst sort. And I was convinced then, and am convinced now, that his sister was a partner in his crimes. She was very beautiful. And that, I think, was what saved her."

He was fingering his unlighted cigar as he spoke. When he looked up, he was surprised at the swift change that had come into the face of St. Pierre's wife. Her cheeks were flaming, and there were burning fires screened behind the long lashes of her eyes. But her voice was unchanged. It was without a quiver that betrayed the emotion which had sent the hot flush into her face.

"Then—you judged her without absolute knowledge of fact? You judged her—as you hinted in your fever—because she fought so desperately to save a brother who had gone wrong?"

"I believe she was bad."

The long lashes fell lower, like fringes of velvet closing over the fires in her eyes. "But you didn't know!"

"Not absolutely," he conceded. "But investigations—"

"Might have shown her to be one of the most wonderful women that ever lived, M'sieu David. It is not hard to fight for a good brother—but if he is bad, it may take an angel to do it!"

He stared, thoughts tangling themselves in his head. A slow shame crept over him. She had cornered him. She had convicted him of unfairness to the one creature on earth his strength and his manhood were bound to protect—a woman. She had convicted him of judging without fact. And in his head a voice seemed to cry out to him, "What did Carmin Fanchet ever do to you?"

He rose suddenly to his feet and stood at the back of his chair, his hands gripping the top of it. "Maybe you are right," he said. "Maybe I was wrong. I remember now that when I got Fanchet I manacled him, and she sat beside him all through that first night. I didn't intend to sleep, but I was tired—and did. I must have slept for an hour, and SHE roused me—trying to get the key to the handcuffs. She had the opportunity then—to kill me."

Triumph swept over the face that was looking up at him. "Yes, she could have killed you—while you slept. But she didn't. WHY?"

"I don't know. Perhaps she had the idea of getting the key and letting her brother do the job. Two or three days later I am convinced she would not have hesitated. I caught her twice trying to steal my gun. And a third time, late at night, when we were within a day or two of Athabasca Landing, she almost got me with a club. So I concede that she never did anything very terrible to me. But I am sure that she tried, especially toward the last."

"And because she failed, she hated you; and because she hated you, something was warped inside you, and you made up your mind she should be punished along with her brother. You didn't look at it from a woman's viewpoint. A woman will fight, and kill, to save one she loves. She tried, perhaps, and failed. The result was that her brother was killed by the Law. Was not that enough? Was it fair or honest to destroy her simply because you thought she might be a partner in her brother's crimes?"

"It is rather strange," he replied, a moment of indecision in his voice. "McVane, the superintendent, asked me that same question. I thought he was touched by her beauty. And I'm sorry—very sorry-that I talked about her when I was sick. I don't want you to think I am a bad sort—that way. I'm going to think about it. I'm going over the whole thing again, from the time I manacled Fanchet, and if I find that I was wrong—and I ever meet Carmin Fanchet again—I shall not be ashamed to get down on my knees and ask her pardon, Marie-Anne!"

For the first time he spoke the name which she had given him permission to use. And she noticed it. He could not help seeing that—a flashing instant in which the indefinable confession of it was in her face, as though his use of it had surprised her, or pleased her, or both.

Then it was gone.

She did not answer, but rose from the big chair, and went to the window, and stood with her back toward him, looking out over the river. And then, suddenly, they heard a voice. It was the voice he had heard twice in his sickness, the voice that had roused him from his sleep last night, crying out in his room for Black Roger Audemard. It came to him distinctly through the open door in a low and moaning monotone. He had not taken his eyes from the slim figure of St. Pierre's wife, and he saw a little tremor pass through her now.

"I heard that voice—again—last night," said David. "It was in this cabin, asking for Black Roger Audemard."

She did not seem to hear him, and he also turned so that he was looking at the open door of the cabin.

The sun, pouring through in a golden flood, was all at once darkened, and in the doorway—framed vividly against the day—was the figure of a man. A tense breath came to Carrigan's lips. At first he felt a shock, then an overwhelming sense of curiosity and of pity. The man was terribly deformed. His back and massive shoulders were so twisted and bent that he stood no higher than a twelve-year-old boy; yet standing straight, he would have been six feet tall if an inch, and splendidly proportioned. And in that same breath with which shock and pity came to him, David knew that it was accident and not birth that had malformed the great body that stood like a crouching animal in the open door.

At first he saw only the grotesqueness of it—the long arms that almost touched the floor, the broken back, the twisted shoulders—and then, with a deeper thrill, he saw nothing of these things but only the face and the head of the man. There was something god-like about them, fastened there between the crippled shoulders. It was not beauty, but strength—the strength of rock, of carven granite, as if each feature had been chiselled out of something imperishable and everlasting, yet lacking strangely and mysteriously the warm illumination that comes from a living soul. The man was not old, nor was he young. And he did not seem to see Carrigan, who stood nearest to him. He was looking at St. Pierre's wife.

The look which David saw in her face was infinitely tender. She was smiling at the misshapen hulk in the door as she might have smiled at a little child. And David, looking back at the wide, deep-set eyes of the man, saw the slumbering fire of a dog-like worship in them. They shifted slowly, taking in the cabin, questing, seeking, searching for something which they could not find. The lips moved, and again he heard that weird and mysterious monotone, as if the plaintive voice of a child were coming out of the huge frame of the man, crying out as it had cried last night, "HAS-ANYONE-SEEN-BLACK-ROGER-AUDEMARD?"

In another moment St. Pierre's wife was at the deformed giant's side. She seemed tall beside him. She put her hands to his head and brushed back the grizzled black hair, laughing softly into his upturned face, her eyes shining and a strange glow in her cheeks. Carrigan, looking at them, felt his heart stand still. WAS THIS MAN ST. PIERRE? The thought came like a lightning flash—and went as quickly; it was impossible and inconceivable. And yet there was something more than pity in the voice of the woman who was speaking now.

"No, no, we have not seen him, Andre—we have not seen Black Roger Audemard. If he comes, I will call you. I promise, *Michiwan*. I will call you!"

She was stroking his bearded cheek, and then she put an arm about his twisted shoulders, and slowly she turned so that in a moment or two they were facing the sun—and it seemed to Carrigan that she was talking and sobbing and laughing in the same breath, as that great, broken hulk of a man moved out slowly from under the caress of her arm and went on his way. For a space she looked after him. Then in a swift movement she closed the door and faced Carrigan. She did not speak, but waited. Her head was high. She was breathing quickly. The tenderness that a moment before had filled her face was gone, and in her eyes was the blaze of fighting fires as she waited for him to speak—to give voice to what she knew was passing in his mind.

11

For a space there was silence between Carrigan and St. Pierre's wife. He knew what she was thinking as she stood with her back to the door, waiting half defiantly, her cheeks still flushed, her eyes bright with the anticipation of battle. She was ready to fight for the broken creature on the other side of the door. She expected him to give no quarter in his questioning of her, to corner her if he could, to demand of her why the deformed giant had spoken the name of the man he was after, Black Roger Audemard. The truth hammered in David's brain. It had not been a delusion of his fevered mind after all; it was not a possible deception of the half-breed's, as he had thought last night. Chance had brought him face to face with the mystery of Black Roger. St. Pierre's wife, waiting for him to speak, was in some way associated with that mystery, and the cripple was asking for the man McVane had told him to bring in dead or alive! Yet he did not question her. He turned to the window and looked out from where Marie-Anne had stood a few moments before.

The day was glorious. On the far shore he saw life where last night's camp had been. Men were moving about close to the water, and a York boat was putting out slowly into the stream. Close under the window moved a canoe with a single occupant. It was Andre, the Broken Man. With powerful strokes he was paddling across the river. His deformity was scarcely noticeable in the canoe. His bare head and black beard shone in the sun, and between his great shoulders his head looked more than ever to Carrigan like the head of a carven god. And this man, like a mighty tree stricken by lightning, his mind gone, was yet a thing that was more than mere flesh and blood to Marie-Anne Boulain!

David turned toward her. Her attitude was changed. It was no longer one of proud defiance. She had expected to defend herself from something, and he had given her no occasion for defence. She did not try to hide the fact from him, and he nodded toward the window.

"He is going away in a canoe. I am afraid you didn't want me to see him, and I am sorry I happened to be here when he came."

"I made no effort to keep him away, M'sieu David. Perhaps I wanted you to see him. And I thought, when you did—" She hesitated.

"You expected me to crucify you, if necessary, to learn the truth of what he knows about Roger Audemard," he said. "And you were ready to fight back. But I am not going to question you unless you give me permission."

"I am glad," she said in a low voice. "I am beginning to have faith in you, M'sieu David. You have promised not to try to escape, and I believe you. Will you also promise not to ask me questions, which I cannot answer—until St. Pierre comes?"

"I will try."

She came up to him slowly and stood facing him, so near that she could have reached out and put her hands on his shoulders.

"St. Pierre has told me a great deal about the Scarlet Police," she said, looking at him quietly and steadily. "He says that the men who wear the red jackets never play low tricks, and that they come after a man squarely and openly. He says they are men, and many times he has told me wonderful stories of the things they have done. He calls it 'playing the game.' And I'm going to ask you, M'sieu David, will you play square with me? If I give you the freedom of the *bateau*, of the boats, even of the shore, will you wait for St. Pierre and play the rest of the game out with him, man to man?"

Carrigan bowed his head slightly. "Yes, I will wait and finish the game with St. Pierre."

He saw a quick throb come and go in her white throat, and with a sudden, impulsive movement she held out her hand to him. For a moment he held it close. Her little fingers tightened about his own, and the warm thrill of them set his blood leaping with the thing he was fighting down. She was so near that he could feel the throb of her body. For an instant she bowed her head, and the sweet perfume of her hair was in his nostrils, the lustrous beauty of it close under his lips.

Gently she withdrew her hand and stood back from him. To Carrigan she was like a young girl now. It was the loveliness of girlhood he saw in the flush of her face and in the gladness that was flaming unashamed in her eyes.

79

"I am not frightened anymore," she exclaimed, her voice trembling a bit. "When St. Pierre comes, I shall tell him everything. And then you may ask the questions, and he will answer. And he will not cheat! He will play square. You will love St. Pierre, and you will forgive me for what happened behind the rock!"

She made a little gesture toward the door. "Everything is free to you out there now," she added. "I shall tell Bateese and the others. When we are tied up, you may go ashore. And we will forget all that has happened, M'sieu David. We will forget until St. Pierre comes."

"St. Pierre!" he groaned. "If there were no St. Pierre!"

"I should be lost," she broke in quickly. "I should want to die!"

Through the open window came the sound of a voice. It was the weird monotone of Andre, the Broken Man. Marie-Anne went to the window. And David, following her, looked over her head, again so near that his lips almost touched her hair. Andre had come back. He was watching two York boats that were heading for the *bateau.*

"You heard him asking for Black Roger Audemard," she said. "It is strange. I know how it must have shocked you when he stood like that in the door. His mind, like his body, is a wreck, M'sieu David. Years ago, after a great storm, St. Pierre found him in the forest. A tree had fallen on him. St. Pierre carried him in on his shoulders. He lived, but he has always been like that. St. Pierre loves him, and poor Andre worships St. Pierre and follows him about like a dog. His brain is gone. He does not know what his name is, and we call him Andre. And always, day and night, he is asking that same question, 'Has any one seen Black Roger Audemard?' Sometime—if you will, M'sieu David—I should like to have you tell me what it is so terrible that you know about Roger Audemard."

The York boats were half-way across the river, and from them came a sudden burst of wild song. David could make out six men in each boat, their oars flashing in the morning sun to the rhythm of their chant. Marie-Anne looked up at him suddenly, and in her face and eyes he saw what the starry gloom of evening had half hidden from him in those thrilling moments when they shot through the rapids of the Holy Ghost. She was girl now. He did not think of her as woman. He did not think of her as St. Pierre's wife. In that upward glance of her eyes was something that thrilled him to the depth of his soul. She seemed, for a moment, to have dropped a curtain from between herself and him.

Her red lips trembled, she smiled at him, and then she faced the river again, and he leaned a little forward, so that a breath of wind floated a shimmering tress of her hair against his cheek. An irresistible impulse seized upon him. He leaned still nearer to her, holding his breath, until his lips softly touched one of the velvety coils of her hair. And then he stepped back. Shame swept over him. His heart rose and choked him, and his fists were clenched at his side. She had not noticed what he had done, and she seemed to him like a bird yearning to fly out through the window, throbbing with the desire to answer the chanting song that came over the water. And then she was smiling up again into his face hardened with the struggle which he was making with himself.

"My people are happy," she cried. "Even in storm they laugh and sing. Listen, m'sieu. They are singing *La Derniere Domaine*. That is our song. It is what we call our home, away up there in the lost wilderness where people never come—the Last Domain. Their wives and sweethearts and families are up there, and they are happy in knowing that today we shall travel a few miles nearer to them. They are not like your people in Montreal and Ottawa and Quebec, M'sieu David. They are like children. And yet they are glorious children!"

She ran to the wall and took down the banner of St. Pierre Boulain. "St. Pierre is behind us," she explained. "He is coming down with a raft of timber such as we cannot get in our country, and we are waiting for him. But each day we must float down with the stream a few miles nearer the homes of my people. It makes them happier, even though it is but a few miles. They are coming now for my *bateau*. We shall travel slowly, and it will be wonderful on a day like this. It will do you good to come outside, M'sieu David—with me. Would you care for that? Or would you rather be alone?"

In her face there was no longer the old restraint. On her lips was the witchery of a half-smile; in her eyes a glow that flamed the blood in his veins. It was not a flash of coquetry. It was something deeper and warmer than that, something real—a new Marie-Anne Boulain telling him plainly that she wanted him to come. He did not know that his hands were still clenched at his side. Perhaps she knew. But her eyes did not leave his face, eyes that were repeating the invitation of her lips, openly asking him not to refuse.

"I shall be happy to come," he said.

The words fell out of him numbly. He scarcely heard them or knew what he was saying, yet he was conscious of the unnatural note in his voice. He did not know he was betraying himself beyond that, did not see the deepening of the wild-rose flush in the cheeks of St. Pierre's wife. He picked up his pipe from the table and moved to accompany her.

"You must wait a little while," she said, and her hand rested for an instant upon his arm. Its touch was as light as the touch of his lips had been against her shining hair, but he felt it in every nerve of his body. "Nepapinas is making a special lotion for your hurt. I will send him in, and then you may come."

The wild chant of the rivermen was near as she turned to the door. From it she looked back at him swiftly.

"They are happy, M'sieu David," she repeated softly. "And I, too, am happy. I am no longer afraid. And the world is beautiful again. Can you guess why? It is because you have given me your promise, M'sieu David, and because I believe you!"

And then she was gone.

For many minutes he did not move. The chanting of the rivermen, a sudden wilder shout, the voices of men, and after that the grating of something alongside the *bateau* came to him like sounds from another world. Within himself there was a crash greater than that of physical things. It was the truth breaking upon him, truth surging over him like the waves of a sea, breaking down the barriers he had set up, inundating him with a force that was mightier than his own will. A voice in his soul was crying out the truth—that above all else in the world he wanted to reach out his arms to this glorious creature who was the wife of St. Pierre, this woman who had tried to kill him and was sorry. He knew that it was not desire for beauty. It was the worship which St. Pierre himself must have for this woman who was his wife.

And the shock of it was like a conflagration sweeping through him, leaving him dead and shriven, like the crucified trees standing in the wake of a fire. A breath that was almost a cry came from him, and his fists knotted until they were purple. She was St. Pierre's wife! And he, David Carrigan, proud of his honour, proud of the strength that made him man, had dared covet her in this hour when her husband was gone! He stared at the closed door, beginning to cry out against himself, and over him there swept slowly and terribly another thing—the shame of his weakness, the hopelessness of the thing that for a space had eaten into him and consumed him.

And as he stared, the door opened, and Nepapinas came in.

12

During the next quarter of an hour David was as silent as the old Indian doctor. He was conscious of no pain when Nepapinas took off his bandage and bathed his head in the lotion he had brought. Before a fresh bandage was put on, he looked at himself for a moment in the mirror. It was the first time he had seen his wound, and he expected to find himself marked with a disfiguring scar. To his surprise there was no sign of his hurt except a slightly inflamed spot above his temple. He stared at Nepapinas, and there was no need of the question that was in his mind.

The old Indian understood, and his dried-up face cracked and crinkled in a grin. "Bullet hit a piece of rock, an' rock, not bullet, hit um head," he explained. "Make skull almost break—bend um in—but Nepapinas straighten again with fingers, so-so." He shrugged his thin shoulders with a cackling laugh of pride as he worked his claw-like fingers to show how the operation had been done.

David shook hands with him in silence; then Nepapinas put on the fresh bandage, and after that went out, chuckling again in his weird way, as though he had played a great joke on the white man whom his wizardry had snatched out of the jaws of death.

For some time there had been a subdued activity outside. The singing of the boatmen had ceased, a low voice was giving commands, and looking through the window, David saw that the *bateau* was slowly swinging away from the shore. He turned from the window to the table and lighted the cigar St. Pierre's wife had given him.

In spite of the mental struggle he had made during the presence of Nepapinas, he had failed to get a grip on himself. For a time he had ceased to be David Carrigan, the man-hunter. A few days ago his blood had run to that almost savage thrill of the great game of one against one, the game in which Law sat on one side of the board and

Lawlessness on the other, with the cards between.

It was the great gamble. The cards meant life or death; there was never a checkmate—one or the other had to lose. Had someone told him then that soon he would meet the broken and twisted hulk of a man who had known Black Roger Audemard, every nerve in him would have thrilled in anticipation of that hour. He realized this as he paced back and forth over the thick rugs of the *bateau* floor. And he knew, even as he struggled to bring them back, that the old thrill and the old desire were gone. It was impossible to lie to himself. St. Pierre, in this moment, was of more importance to him than Roger Audemard. And St. Pierre's wife, Marie-Anne—

His eyes fell on the crumpled handkerchief on the piano keys. Again he was crushing it in the palm of his hand, and again the flood of humiliation and shame swept over him. He dropped the handkerchief, and the great law of his own life seemed to rise up in his face and taunt him. He was clean. That had been his greatest pride. He hated the man who was unclean. It was his instinct to kill the man who desecrated another man's home. And here, in the sacredness of St. Pierre's paradise, he found himself at last face to face with that greatest fight of all the ages.

He faced the door. He threw back his shoulders until they snapped, and he laughed, as if at the thing that had risen up to point its finger at him. After all, it did not hurt a man to go through a bit of fire—if he came out of it unburned. And deep in his heart he knew it was not a sin to love, even as he loved, if he kept that love to himself. What he had done when Marie-Anne stood at the window he could not undo. St. Pierre would probably have killed him for touching her hair with his lips, and he would not have blamed St. Pierre. But she had not felt that stolen caress. No one knew—but himself. And he was happier because of it. It was a sort of sacred thing, even though it brought the heat of shame into his face.

He went to the door, opened it, and stood out in the sunshine. It was good to feel the warmth of the sun in his face again and the sweet air of the open day in his lungs. The *bateau* was free of the shore and drifting steadily towards midstream. Bateese was at the great birchwood rudder sweep, and to David's surprise he nodded in a friendly way, and his wide mouth broke into a grin.

"Ah, it is coming soon, that fight of ours, little *coq de bruyere!*" he chuckled gloatingly. "An' ze fight will be jus' lak that, *m'sieu*—you ze little fool-hen's rooster, ze partridge, an' I, Concombre Bateese, ze eagle!"

The anticipation in the half-breed's eyes reflected itself for an instant in David's. He turned back into the cabin, bent over his pack, and found among his clothes two pairs of boxing gloves. He fondled them with the loving touch of a brother and comrade, and their velvety smoothness was more soothing to his nerves than the cigar he was smoking. His one passion above all others was boxing, and wherever he went, either on pleasure or adventure, the gloves went with him. In many a cabin and shack of the far hinterland he had taught white men and Indians how to use them, so that he might have the pleasure of feeling the thrill of them on his hands. And now here was Concombre Bateese inviting him on, waiting for him to get well!

He went out and dangled the clumsy-looking mittens under the half-breed's nose.

Bateese looked at them curiously. "*Mitaines*," he nodded. "Does ze little partridge rooster keep his claws warm in those in ze winter? They are clumsy, *m'sieu*. I can make a better mitten of caribou skin." Putting on one of the gloves, David doubled up his fist. "Do you see that, Concombre Bateese?" he asked. "Well, I will tell you this, that they are not mittens to keep your hands warm. I am going to fight you in them when our time comes. With these mittens I will fight you and your naked fists. Why? Because I do not want to hurt you too badly, friend Bateese! I do not want to break your face all to pieces, which I would surely do if I did not put on these soft mittens. Then, when you have really learned to fight—"

The bull neck of Concombre Bateese looked as if it were about to burst. His eyes seemed ready to pop out of their sockets, and suddenly he let out a roar. "What!—You dare talk lak that to Concombre Bateese, w'at is great'st fightin' man on all T'ree River? You talk lak that to me, Concombre Bateese, who will kill ze bear wit' hees han's, who pull down ze tree, who—who—"

The word-flood of his outraged dignity sprang to his lips; emotion choked him, and then, looking suddenly over Carrigan's shoulder—he stopped. Something in his look made David turn. Three paces behind him stood Marie-Anne, and he knew that from the corner of the cabin she had heard what had passed between them. She was biting her lips, and behind the flash of her eyes he saw laughter.

"You must not quarrel, children," she said. "Bateese, you are steering badly."

She reached out her hands, and without a word David gave her the gloves. With her palm and fingers she caressed them softly, yet David saw little lines of doubt come into her white forehead.

"They are pretty—and soft, M'sieu David. Surely they cannot hurt much! Some day when St. Pierre comes, will you teach me how to use them?"

"Always it is 'When St. Pierre comes,'" he replied. "Shall we be waiting long?"

"Two or three days, perhaps a little longer. Are you coming with me to the proue, *m'sieu*?"

She did not wait for his answer, but went ahead of him, dangling the two pairs of gloves at her side. David caught a last glimpse of the half-breed's face as he followed Marie-Anne around the end of the cabin. Bateese was making a frightful grimace and shaking his huge fist, but scarcely were they out of sight on the narrow footway that ran between the cabin and the outer timbers of the scow when a huge roar of laughter followed them. Bateese had not done laughing when they reached the proue, or bow-nest, a deck fully ten feet in length by eight in width, sheltered above by an awning, and comfortably arranged with chairs, several rugs, a small table, and, to David's amazement, a hammock. He had never seen anything like this on the Three Rivers, nor had he ever heard of a scow so large or so luxuriously appointed.

Over his head, at the tip of a flagstaff attached to the forward end of the cabin, floated the black and white pennant of St. Pierre Boulain. And under this staff was a screened door which undoubtedly opened into the kitchenette which Marie-Anne had told him about. He made no effort to hide his surprise. But St. Pierre's wife seemed not to notice it. The puckery little lines were still in her forehead, and the laughter had faded out of her eyes. The tiny lines deepened as there came another wild roar of laughter from Bateese in the stern.

"Is it true that you have given your word to fight Bateese?" she asked.

"It is true, Marie-Anne. And I feel that Bateese is looking ahead joyously to the occasion."

"He is," she affirmed. "Last night he spread the news among all my people. Those who left to join St. Pierre this morning have taken the news with them, and there is a great deal of excitement and much betting. I am afraid you have made a bad promise. No man has offered to fight Bateese in three years—not even my great St. Pierre, who says that Concombre is more than a match for him."

"And yet they must have a little doubt, as there is betting, and it takes two to make a bet," chuckled David.

The lines went out of Marie-Anne's forehead, and a half-smile trembled on her red lips. "Yes, there is betting. But those who are for you are offering next autumn's muskrat skins and frozen fish against lynx and fisher and marten. The odds are about thirty to one against you, M'sieu David!"

The look of pity which was clearly in her eyes brought a rush of blood to David's face. "If only I had something to wager!" he groaned.

"You must not fight. I shall forbid it!"

"Then Bateese and I will steal off into the forest and have it out by ourselves."

"He will hurt you badly. He is terrible, like a great beast, when he fights. He loves to fight and is always asking if there is not someone who will stand up to him. I think he would desert even me for a good fight. But you, M'sieu David—"

"I also love a fight," he admitted, unashamed.

St. Pierre's wife studied him thoughtfully for a moment. "With these?" she asked then, holding up the gloves.

"Yes, with those. Bateese may use his fists, but I shall use those, so that I shall not disfigure him permanently. His face is none too handsome as it is."

For another flash her lips trembled on the edge of a smile. Then she gave him the gloves, a bit troubled, and nodded to a chair with a deep, cushioned seat and wide arms. "Please make yourself comfortable, M'sieu David. I have something to do in the cabin and will return in a little while."

He wondered if she had gone back to settle the matter with Bateese at once, for it was clear that she did not regard with favour the promised bout between himself and the half-breed. It was on the spur of a careless moment that he had promised to fight Bateese, and with little thought that it was likely to be carried out or that it would become a matter of importance with all of St. Pierre's brigade. He was evidently in for it, he told himself, and as a fighting man it looked as though Concombre Bateese was at least the equal of his braggadocio. He was glad of that. He grinned as he watched the bending backs of St. Pierre's men. So they were betting thirty to one against him! Even St. Pierre might be induced to bet—with HIM. And if he did—

The hot blood leaped for a moment in Carrigan's veins. The thrill went to the tips of his fingers. He stared out over the river, unseeing, as the possibilities of the thing that had come into his mind made him for a moment oblivious of the world. He possessed one thing against which St. Pierre and St. Pierre's wife would wager a half of all they owned in the world! And if he should gamble that one thing, which had come to him like an inspiration, and should whip Bateese—

He began to pace back and forth over the narrow deck, no longer watching the rowers or the shore. The thought grew, and his mind was consumed by it. Thus far, from the moment the first shot was fired at him from the ambush, he had been playing with adventure in the dark. But fate had at last dealt him a trump card. That something which he possessed was more precious than furs or gold to St. Pierre, and St. Pierre would not refuse the wager when it was offered. He would not dare refuse. More than that, he would accept eagerly, strong in the faith that Bateese would whip him as he had whipped all other fighters who had come up against him along the Three Rivers. And when Marie-Anne knew what that wager was to be, she, too, would pray for the gods of chance to be with Concombre Bateese!

He did not hear the light footsteps behind him, and when he turned suddenly in his pacing, he found himself facing Marie-Anne, who carried in her hands the little basket he had seen on the cabin table. She seated herself in the hammock and took from the basket a bit of lace work. For a moment he watched her fingers flashing in and out with the needles.

Perhaps his thought went to her. He was almost frightened as he saw her cheeks colouring under the long, dark lashes. He faced the rivermen again, and while he gripped at his own weakness, he tried to count the flashings of their oars. And behind him, the beautiful eyes of St. Pierre's wife were looking at him with a strange glow in their depths.

"Do you know," he said, speaking slowly and still looking toward the flashing of the oars, "something tells me that unexpected things are going to happen when St. Pierre returns. I am going to make a bet with him that I can whip Bateese. He will not refuse. He will accept. And St. Pierre will lose, because I shall whip Bateese. It is then that these unexpected things will begin to happen. And I am wondering-after they do happen—if you will care so very much?"

There was a moment of silence. And then, "I don't want you to fight Bateese," she said.

The needles were working swiftly when he turned toward her

again, and a second time the long lashes shadowed what a moment before he might have seen in her eyes.

13

The morning passed like a dream to Carrigan. He permitted himself to live and breathe it as one who finds himself for a space in the heart of a golden mirage. He was sitting so near Marie-Anne that now and then the faint perfume of her came to him like the delicate scent of a flower. It was a breath of crushed violets, sweet as the air he was breathing, violets gathered in the deep cool of the forest, a whisper of sweetness about her, as if on her bosom she wore always the living flowers. He fancied her gathering them last bloom-time, a year ago, alone, her feet seeking out the damp mosses, her little fingers plucking the smiling and laughing faces of the violet flowers to be treasured away in fragrant sachets, as gentle as the wood-thrush's note, compared with the bottled aromas fifteen hundred miles south. It seemed to be a physical part of her, a thing born of the glow in her cheeks, a living exhalation of her soft red lips—and yet only when he was near, very near, did the life of it reach him.

She did not know he was thinking these things. There was nothing in his voice, he thought, to betray him. He was sure she was unconscious of the fight he was making. Her eyes smiled and laughed with him, she counted her stitches, her fingers worked, and she talked to him as she might have talked to a friend of St. Pierre's. She told him how St. Pierre had made the barge, the largest that had ever been on the river, and that he had built it entirely of dry cedar, so that it floated like a feather wherever there was water enough to run a York boat.

She told him how St. Pierre had brought the piano down from Edmonton, and how he had saved it from pitching in the river by carrying the full weight of it on his shoulders when they met with an accident in running through a dangerous rapids bringing it down. St. Pierre was a very strong man, she said, a note of pride in her voice. And then she added,

"Sometimes, when he picks me up in his arms, I feel that he is going to squeeze the life out of me!"

Her words were like a sharp thrust into his heart. For an instant they painted a vision for him, a picture of that slim and adorable creature crushed close in the great arms of St. Pierre, so close that she could not breathe. In that mad moment of his hurt it was almost a living, breathing reality for him there on the golden fore-deck of the scow. He turned his face toward the far shore, where the wilderness seemed to reach off into eternity. What a glory it was—the green seas of spruce and cedar and balsam, the ridges of poplar and birch rising like silvery spume above the darker billows, and afar off, mellowed in the sun-mists, the guardian crests of Trout Mountains sentineling the country beyond! Into that mystery-land on the farther side of the Wabiskaw waterways Carrigan would have loved to set his foot four days ago.

It was that mystery of the unpeopled places that he most desired, their silence, the comradeship of spaces untrod by the feet of man. And now, what a fool he was! Through vast distances the forests he loved seemed to whisper it to him, and ahead of him the river seemed to look back, nodding over its shoulder, beckoning to him, telling him the word of the forests was true. It streamed on lazily, half a mile wide, as if resting for the splashing and roaring rush it would make among the rocks of the next rapids, and in its indolence it sang the low and everlasting song of deep and slowly passing water. In that song David heard the same whisper, that he was a fool! And the lure of the wilderness shores crept in on him and gripped him as of old. He looked at the rowers in the two York boats, and then his eyes came back to the end of the barge and to St. Pierre's wife.

Her little toes were tapping the floor of the deck. She, too, was looking out over the wilderness. And again it seemed to him that she was like a bird that wanted to fly.

"I should like to go into those hills," she said, without looking at him. "Away off yonder!"

"And I—I should like to go with you."

"You love all that, m'sieu?" she asked.

"Yes, madame!"

"Why 'madame,' when I have given you permission to call me 'Marie-Anne'?" she demanded.

"Because you call me 'm'sieu'."

"But you—you have not given me permission—"

"Then I do now," he interrupted quickly.

"*Merci*! I have wondered why you did not return the courtesy," she laughed softly. "I do not like the *m'sieu*. I shall call you 'David'!"

She rose out of the hammock suddenly and dropped her needles and lace work into the little basket. "I have forgotten something. It is for you to eat when it comes dinner-time, *m'sieu*—I mean David. So I must turn *fille de cuisine* for a little while. That is what St. Pierre sometimes calls me, because I love to play at cooking. I am going to bake a pie!"

The dark-screened door of the kitchenette closed behind her, and Carrigan walked out from under the awning, so that the sun beat down upon him. There was no longer a doubt in his mind. He was more than fool. He envied St. Pierre, and he coveted that which St. Pierre possessed. And yet, before he would take what did not belong to him, he knew he would put a pistol to his head and blow his life out. He was confident of himself there. Yet he had fallen, and out of the mire into which he had sunk he knew also that he must drag himself, and quickly, or be everlastingly lowered in his own esteem. He stripped himself naked and did not lie to that other and greater thing of life that was in him.

He was not only a fool, but a coward. Only a coward would have touched the hair of St. Pierre's wife with his lips; only a coward would have let live the thoughts that burned in his brain. She was St. Pierre's wife—and he was anxious now for the quick homecoming of the chief of the Boulains. After that everything would happen quickly. He thanked God that the inspiration of the wager had come to him. After the fight, after he had won, then once more would he be the old Dave Carrigan, holding the trump hand in a thrilling game.

Loud voices from the York boats ahead and answering cries from Bateese in the stern drew him to the open deck. The *bateau* was close to shore, and the half-breed was working the long stern sweep as if the power of a steam-engine was in his mighty arms. The York boats had shortened their towline and were pulling at right angles within a few yards of a gravelly beach. A few strokes more, and men who were bare to the knees jumped out into shallow water and began tugging at the tow rope with their hands. David looked at his watch. It was ten o'clock. Never in his life had time passed so swiftly as that morning on the forward deck of the barge. And now they were tying up, after a drop of six or eight miles down the river, and he wondered how swiftly St. Pierre was overtaking them with his raft.

He was filled with the desire to feel the soft crush of the earth under his feet again, and not waiting for the long plank that Bateese was already swinging from the scow to the shore, he made a leap that put him on the sandy beach, St. Pierre's wife had given him this permission, and he looked to see what effect his act had on the half-breed. The face of Concombre Bateese was like sullen stone. Not a sound came from his thick lips, but in his eyes was a deep and dangerous fire as he looked at Carrigan. There was no need for words. In them were suspicion, warning, the deadly threat of what would happen if he did not come back when it was time to return.

David nodded. He understood. Even though St. Pierre's wife had faith in him, Bateese had not. He passed between the men, and to a man their faces turned on him, and in their quiet and watchful eyes he saw again that warning and suspicion, the unspoken threat of what would happen if he forgot his promise to Marie-Anne Boulain. Never, in a single outfit, had he seen such splendid men. They were not a mongrel assortment of the lower country. Slim, tall, clean-cut, sinewy—they were stock of the old voyageurs of a hundred years ago, and all of them were young. The older men had gone to St. Pierre. The reason for this dawned upon Carrigan. Not one of these twelve but could beat him in a race through the forest; not one that could not outrun him and cut him off though he had hours the start!

Passing beyond them, he paused and looked back at the *bateau*. On the forward deck stood Marie-Anne, and she, too, was looking at him now. Even at that distance he saw that her face was quiet and troubled with anxiety. She did not smile when he lifted his hat to her, but gave only a little nod. Then he turned and buried himself in the green balsams that grew within fifty paces of the river. The old joy of life leaped into him as his feet crushed in the soft moss of the shaded places where the sun did not break through. He went on, passing through a vast and silent cathedral of spruce and cedar so dense that the sky was hidden, and came then to higher ground, where the evergreen was sprinkled with birch and poplar.

About him was an invisible choir of voices, the low twittering of timid little gray-backs, the song of hidden—warblers, the scolding of distant jays. Big-eyed moose-birds stared at him as he passed, fluttering so close to his face that they almost touched his shoulders in their foolish inquisitiveness. A porcupine crashed within a dozen feet of his trail. And then he came to a beaten path, and other paths worn deep in the cool, damp earth by the hoofs of moose and caribou. Half a mile from the *bateau* he sat down on a rotting log and filled his pipe with fresh tobacco, while he listened to catch the subdued voice of the life in this land that he loved.

It was then that the curious feeling came over him that he was not alone, that other eyes than those of beast and bird were watching him. It was an impression that grew on him. He seemed to feel their stare, seeking him out from the darkest coverts, waiting for him to shove on, dogging him like a ghost. Within him the hound-like instincts of the man-hunter rose swiftly to the suspicion of invisible presence.

He began to note the changes in the cries of certain birds. A hundred yards on his right a jay, most talkative of all the forest things, was screeching with a new note in its voice. On the other side of him, in a dense pocket of poplar and spruce, a warbler suddenly brought its song to a jerky end. He heard the excited Pe-wee—Pe-wee—Pe-wee of a startled little gray-back giving warning of an unwelcome intruder near its nest. And he rose to his feet, laughing softly as he thumbed down the tobacco in his pipe. Jeanne Marie-Anne Boulain might believe in him, but Bateese and her wary henchmen had ways of their own of strengthening their faith.

It was close to noon when he turned back, and he did not return by the moose path. Deliberately he struck out a hundred yards on either side of it, travelling where the moss grew thick and the earth was damp and soft. And five times he found the moccasin-prints of men.

Bateese, with his sleeves up, was scrubbing the deck of the *bateau* when David came over the plank.

"There are moose and caribou in there, but I fear I disturbed your hunters," said Carrigan, grinning at the half-breed. "They are too clumsy to hunt well, so clumsy that even the birds give them away. I am afraid we shall go without fresh meat tomorrow!"

Concombre Bateese stared as if someone had stunned him with a blow, and he spoke no word as David went on to the forward deck. Marie-Anne had come out under the awning. She gave a little cry of relief and pleasure.

"I am glad you have come back, M'sieu David!"

"So am I, *madame*," he replied. "I think the woods are unhealthful to travel in!"

Out of the earth he felt that a part of the old strength had returned to him. Alone they sat at dinner, and Marie-Anne waited on him and called him David again—and he found it easier now to call her Marie-Anne and look into her eyes without fear that he was betraying himself. A part of the afternoon he spent in her company, and it was not difficult for him to tell her something of his adventuring in the north, and how, body and soul, the northland had claimed him, and that he hoped to die in it when his time came. Her eyes glowed at that. She told him of two years she had spent in Montreal and Quebec, of her homesickness, her joy when she returned to her forests. It seemed, for a time, that they had forgotten St. Pierre. They did not speak of him. Twice they saw Andre, the Broken Man, but the name of Roger Audemard was not spoken. And a little at a time she told him of the hidden paradise of the Boulains away up in the unmapped wildernesses of the Yellowknife beyond the Great Bear, and of the great log *château* that was her home.

A part of the afternoon he spent on shore. He filled a moosehide bag full of sand and suspended it from the limb of a tree, and for three-quarters of an hour pommeled it with his fists, much to the curiosity and amusement of St. Pierre's men, who could see nothing of man-fighting in these antics. But the exercise assured David that he had lost but little of his strength and that he would be in form to meet Bateese when the time came. Toward evening Marie-Anne joined him, and they walked for half an hour up and down the beach. It was Bateese who got supper. And after that Carrigan sat with Marie-Anne on the foredeck of the barge and smoked another of St. Pierre's cigars.

The camp of the rivermen was two hundred yards below the *bateau*, screened between by a finger of hardwood, so that except when they broke into a chorus of laughter or strengthened their throats with snatches of song, there was no sound of their voices. But Bateese was in the stern, and Nepapinas was forever flitting in and out among the shadows on the shore, like a shadow himself, and Andre, the Broken Man, hovered near as night came on. At last he sat down in the edge of the white sand of the beach, and there he remained, a silent and lonely figure, as the twilight deepened. Over the world hovered a sleepy quiet. Out of the forest came the droning of the wood-crickets, the last twitterings of the day birds, and the beginning of night sounds.

A great shadow floated out over the river close to the *bateau*, the first of the questing, blood-seeking owls adventuring out like pirates from their hiding-places of the day. One after another, as the darkness thickened, the different tribes of the people of the night answered the summons of the first stars. A mile down the river a loon gave its harsh love-cry; far out of the west came the faint trail-song of a wolf; in the river the night-feeding trout splashed like the tails of beaver; over the roof of the wilderness came the coughing, moaning challenge of a bull moose that yearned for battle. And over these same forest tops rose the moon, the stars grew thicker and brighter, and through the finger of hardwood glowed the fire of St. Pierre Boulain's men—while close beside him, silent in these hours of silence, David felt growing nearer and still nearer to him the presence of St. Pierre's wife.

On the strip of sand Andre, the Broken Man, rose and stood like the stub of a misshapen tree. And then slowly he moved on and was swallowed up in the mellow glow of the night.

"It is at night that he seeks," said St. Pierre's wife, for it was as if David had spoken the thought that was in his mind.

David, for a moment, was silent. And then he said, "You asked me to tell you about Black Roger Audemard. I will, if you care to have me. Do you?"

He saw the nodding of her head, though the moon and star-mist veiled her face.

"Yes. What do the Police say about Roger Audemard?"

He told her. And not once in the telling of the story did she speak or move. It was a terrible story at best, he thought, but he did not weaken it by smoothing over the details. This was his opportunity. He wanted her to know why he must possess the body of Roger Audemard, if not alive, then dead, and he wanted her to understand how important it was that he learn more about Andre, the Broken Man.

"He was a fiend, this Roger Audemard," he began. "A devil in man shape, afterward called 'Black Roger' because of the colour of his soul."

Then he went on. He described Hatchet River Post, where the tragedy had happened; then told of the fight that came about one day between Roger Audemard and the factor of the post and his two sons. It was an unfair fight; he conceded that—three to one was cowardly in a fight. But it could not excuse what happened afterward. Audemard was beaten. He crept off into the forest, almost dead. Then he came back one stormy night in the winter with three strange friends. Who the friends were the Police never learned. There was a fight, but all through the fight Black Roger Audemard cried out not to kill the factor and his sons. In spite of that one of the sons was killed.

Then the terrible thing happened. The father and his remaining son were bound hand and foot and fastened in the ancient dungeon room under the Post building. Then Black Roger set the building on fire, and stood outside in the storm and laughed like a madman at the dying shrieks of his victims. It was the season when the trappers were on their lines, and there were but few people at the post. The company clerk and one other attempted to interfere, and Black Roger killed them with his own hands. Five deaths that night—two of them horrible beyond description!

Resting for a moment, Carrigan went on to tell of the long years of unavailing search made by the Police after that; how Black Roger was caught once and killed his captor. Then came the rumour that he was dead, and rumour grew into official belief, and the Police no longer hunted for his trails. Then, not long ago, came the discovery that Black Roger was still living, and he, Dave Carrigan, was after him.

For a time there was silence after he had finished. Then St. Pierre's wife rose to her feet. "I wonder," she said in a low voice, "what Roger Audemard's own story might be if he were here to tell it?"

She stepped out from under the awning, and in the full radiance of the moon he saw the pale beauty of her face and the crowning lustre of her hair.

"Goodnight!" she whispered.

"Goodnight!" said David.

He listened until her retreating footsteps died away, and for hours after that he had no thought of sleep. He had insisted that she take possession of her cabin again, and Bateese had brought out a bundle of blankets. These he spread under the awning, and when he drowsed off, it was to dream of the lovely face he had seen last in the glow of the moon.

It was in the afternoon of the fourth day that two things happened—one that he had prepared himself for, and another so unexpected that for a space it sent his world crashing out of its orbit. With St. Pierre's wife he had gone again to the ridge-line for flowers, half a mile back from the river. Returning a new way, they came to a shallow stream, and Marie-Anne stood at the edge of it, and there was laughter in her shining eyes as she looked to the other side of it. She had twined flowers into her hair. Her cheeks were rich with colour. Her slim figure was exquisite in its wild pulse of life.

Suddenly she turned on him, her red lips smiling their witchery in his face. "You must carry me across," she said.

He did not answer. He was a-tremble as he drew near her. She raised her arms a little, waiting. And then he picked her up. She was against his breast. Her two hands went to his shoulders as he waded into the stream; he slipped, and they clung a little tighter. The soft note of laughter was in her throat when the current came to his knees out in the middle of the stream. He held her tighter; and then stupidly, he slipped again, and the movement brought her lower in his arms, so that for a space her head was against his breast and his face was crushed in the soft masses of her hair. He came with her that way to the opposite shore and stood her on her feet again, standing back quickly so that she would not hear the pounding of his heart. Her face was radiantly beautiful, and she did not look at David, but away from him.

"Thank you," she said.

And then, suddenly, they heard running feet behind them, and in another moment one of the brigade men came dashing through the stream. At the same time there came from the river a quarter of a mile away a thunderous burst of voice. It was not the voice of a dozen men, but of half a hundred, and Marie-Anne grew tense, listening, her eyes on fire even before the messenger could get the words out of his mouth.

"It is St. Pierre!" he cried then. "He has come with the great raft, and you must hurry if you would reach the *bateau* before he lands!"

In that moment it seemed to David that Marie-Anne forgot he was alive. A little cry came to her lips, and then she left him, running swiftly, saying no word to him, flying with the speed of a fawn to St. Pierre Boulain! And when David turned to the man who had come up behind them, there was a strange smile on the lips of the lithe-limbed forest-runner as his eyes followed the hurrying figure of St. Pierre's wife.

Until she was out of sight he stood in silence and then he said:

"Come, *m'sieu*. We, also, must meet St. Pierre!"

14

David moved slowly behind the brigade man. He had no desire to hurry. He did not wish to see what happened when Marie-Anne met St. Pierre Boulain. Only a moment ago she had been in his arms; her hair had smothered his face; her hands had clung to his shoulders; her flushed cheeks and long lashes had for an instant lain close against his breast. And now, swiftly, without a word of apology, she was running away from him to meet her husband.

He almost spoke that word aloud as he saw the last of her slim figure among the silver birches. She was going to the man to whom she belonged, and there was no hesitation in the manner of her going. She was glad. And she was entirely forgetful of him, Dave Carrigan, in that gladness.

He quickened his steps, narrowing the distance between him and the hurrying brigade man. Only the diseased thoughts in his brain had made the happening in the creek anything but an accident. It was all an accident, he told himself. Marie-Anne had asked him to carry her across just as she would have asked any one of her rivermen. It was his fault, and not hers, that he had slipped in mid-stream, and that his arms had closed tighter about her, and that her hair had brushed his face. He remembered she had laughed, when it seemed for a moment that they were going to fall into the stream together. Probably she would tell St. Pierre all about it. Surely she would never guess it had been nearer tragedy than comedy for him.

Once more he was convinced he had proved himself a weakling and a fool. His business now was with St. Pierre, and the hour was at hand when the game had ceased to be a woman's game. He had looked ahead to this hour. He had prepared himself for it and had promised himself action that would be both quick and decisive. And yet, as he went on, his heart was still thumping unsteadily, and in his arms and against his face remained still the sweet, warm thrill of his contact with Marie-Anne. He could not drive that from him. It would never completely go.

As long as he lived, what had happened in the creek would live with him. He did not deny that crying voice inside him. It was easy for his mouth to make words. He could call himself a fool and a weakling, but those words were purely mechanical, hollow, meaningless. The truth remained. It was a blazing fire in his breast, a conflagration that might easily get the best of him, a thing which he must fight and triumph over for his own salvation. He did not think of danger for Marie-Anne, for such a thought was inconceivable. The tragedy was one-sided. It was his own folly, his own danger. For just as he loved Marie-Anne, so did she love her husband, St. Pierre.

He came to the low ridge close to the river and climbed up through the thick birches and poplars. At the top was a bald knob of sandstone, over which the riverman had already passed. David paused there and looked down on the broad sweep of the Athabasca.

What he saw was like a picture spread out on the great breast of the river and the white strip of shoreline. Still a quarter of a mile upstream, floating down slowly with the current, was a mighty raft, and for a space his eyes took in nothing else. On the Mackenzie, the Athabasca, the Saskatchewan, and the Peace he had seen many rafts, but never a raft like this of St. Pierre Boulain. It was a hundred feet in width and twice and a half times as long, and with the sun blazing down upon it from out of a cloudless sky it looked to him like a little city swept up from out of some archaic and savage desert land to be transplanted to the river. It was dotted with tents and canvas shelters.

Some of these were gray, and some were white, and two or three were striped with broad bands of yellow and red. Behind all these was a cabin, and over this there rose a slender staff from which floated the black and white pennant of St. Pierre. The raft was alive. Men were running between the tents. The long rudder sweeps were flashing in the sun. Rowers with naked arms and shoulders were straining their muscles in four York boats that were pulling like ants at the giant mass of timber. And to David's ears came a deep monotone of human voices, the chanting of the men as they worked.

Nearer to him a louder response suddenly made answer to it. A dozen steps carried him round a projecting thumb of brush, and he could see the open shore where the *bateau* was tied. Marie-Anne had crossed the strip of sand, and Bateese was helping her into a waiting

York boat. Then Bateese shoved it off, and the four men in it began to row. Two canoes were already half-way to the raft, and David recognized the occupant of one of them as Andre, the Broken Man. Then he saw Marie-Anne rise in the York boat and wave something white in her hand.

He looked again toward the raft. The current and the sweeps and the tugging boats were drawing it steadily nearer. Standing at the very edge of it he saw now a solitary figure, and in the clear sunlight the man stood out clean-cut as a carven statue. He was a giant in size. His head and arms were bare, and he was looking steadily toward the *bateau* and the approaching York boat. He raised an arm, and a moment later the movement was followed by a voice that rose above all other voices. It boomed over the river like the rumble of a gun. In response to it Marie-Anne waved the white thing in her hand, and David thought he heard her voice in an answering cry. He stared again at the solitary figure of the man, seeing nothing else, hearing no other sound but the booming of the deep cry that came again over the river. His heart was thumping. In his eyes was a gathering fire. His body grew tense. For he knew that at last he was looking at St. Pierre, chief of the Boulains, and husband of the woman he loved.

As the significance of the situation grew upon him, a flash of his old humour returned. It was the same grim humour that had possessed him behind the rock, when he had thought he was going to die. Fate had played him a dishonest turn then, and it was doing the same thing by him now. Unless he deliberately turned his face away, he was going to see the reunion of Marie-Anne and St. Pierre.

Yesterday he had strapped his binoculars to his belt. Today Marie-Anne had looked through them a dozen times. They had been a source of pleasure and thrill to her. Now, David thought, they would be good medicine for him. He would see the whole thing through, and at close range. He would leave himself no room for doubt. He had laughed behind the rock, when bullets were zipping close to his head, and the same grim smile came to his lips now as he focused his glasses on the solitary figure at the head of the raft.

The smile died away when he saw St. Pierre. It was as if he could reach out and touch him with his hand. And never, he thought, had he seen such a man. A moment before, a flashing vision had come to him from out of an Arabian desert; the multitude of coloured tents, the half-naked men, the great raft floating almost without perceptible motion on the placid breast of the river had stirred his imagination until he saw a strange picture. But there was nothing Arabic, nothing desert-like, in this man his binoculars brought within a few feet of his eyes. He was more like a Viking pirate who had roved the sea a few centuries ago. One great, bare arm was raised as David looked, and his booming voice was rolling over the river again. His hair was shaggy, and untrimmed, and red; he wore a short beard that glistened in the sun—he was laughing as he waved and shouted to Marie-Anne—a joyous, splendid giant of a man who seemed almost on the point of leaping into the water in his eagerness to clasp in his naked arms the woman who was coming to him.

David drew a deep breath, and there came an unconscious tightening at his heart as he turned his glasses upon Marie-Anne. She was still standing in the bow of the York boat, and her back was toward him. He could see the glisten of the sun in her hair. She was waving her handkerchief, and the poise of her slim body told him that in her eagerness she would have darted from the bow of the boat had she possessed wings.

Again he looked at St. Pierre. And this was the man who was no match for Concombre Bateese! It was inconceivable. Yet he heard Marie-Anne's voice repeating those very words in his ear. But she had surely been joking with him. She had been storing up this little surprise for him. She had wanted him to discover with his own eyes what a splendid man was this chief of the Boulains. And yet, as David stared, there came to him an unpleasant thought of the incongruity of this thing he was looking upon. It struck upon him like a clashing discord, the fact of matehood between these two—a condition inconsistent and out of tune with the beautiful things he had built up in his mind about the woman.

In his soul he had enshrined her as a lovely wildflower, easily crushed, easily destroyed, a sweet treasure to be guarded from all that was rough and savage, a little violet-goddess as fragile as she was brave and loyal. And St. Pierre, standing there at the edge of his raft, looked as if he had come up out of the caves of a million years ago! There was something barbaric about him. He needed only a club and a shield and the skin of a beast about his loins to transform him into prehistoric man. At least these were his first impressions—impressions roused by thought of Marie-Anne's slim, beautiful body crushed close in the embrace of that laughing, powerful-lunged giant.

Then the reaction swept over him. St. Pierre was not a monster, even though his disturbed mind unconsciously made an effort to conceive him as such. There were gladness and laughter in his face. There was the contagion of joy and good cheer in the voice that boomed over the water. Laughter and shouts answered it from the shore. The rowers in Marie-Anne's York boat burst into a wild and exultant snatch of song and made their oars fairly crack. There came a solitary yell from Andre, the Broken Man, who was close to the head of the raft now. And from the raft itself came a slowly swelling volume of sound, the urge and voice and exultation of red-blooded men a-thrill with the glory of this day and the wild freedom of their world. The truth came to David. St. Pierre Boulain was the beloved Big Brother of his people.

He waited, his muscles tense, his jaws set tight. Good medicine, he called it again, a righteous sort of punishment set upon him for the moral cowardice he had betrayed in falling down in worship at the feet of another man's wife. The York boat was very close to the head of the raft now. He saw Marie-Anne herself fling a rope to St. Pierre. Then the boat swung alongside. In another moment St. Pierre had leaned over, and Marie-Anne was with him on the raft. For a space everything else in the world was obliterated for David. He saw St. Pierre's arms gather the slim form into their embrace. He saw Marie-Anne's hands go up fondly to the bearded face. And then—

Carrigan cut the picture there. He turned his shoulder to the raft and snapped the binoculars in the case at his belt. Someone was coming in his direction from the *bateau*. It was the riverman who had brought to Marie-Anne the news of St. Pierre's arrival. David went down to meet him. From the foot of the ridge he again turned his eyes in the direction of the raft. St. Pierre and Marie-Anne were just about to enter the little cabin built in the centre of the drifting mass of timber.

15

It was easy for Carrigan to guess why the riverman had turned back for him. Men were busy about the *bateau*, and Concombre Bateese stood in the stern, a long pole in his hands, giving commands to the others. The *bateau* was beginning to swing out into the stream when he leaped aboard. A wide grin spread over the half-breed's face. He eyed David keenly and laughed in his deep chest, an unmistakable suggestiveness in the note of it.

"You look seek, m'sieu," he said in an undertone, for David's ears alone, "You look ver' unhappy, an' pale lak leetle boy! Wat happen w'en you look t'rough ze glass up there, eh? Or ees it zat you grow frighten because ver' soon you stan' up an' fight Concombre Bateese? Eh, *coq de bruyere*? Ees it zat?"

A quick thought came to David. "Is it true that St. Pierre cannot whip you, Bateese?"

Bateese threw out his chest with a mighty intake of breath. Then he exploded: "No man on all T'ree River can w'ip Concombre Bateese."

"And St. Pierre is a powerful man," mused David, letting his eyes travel slowly from the half-breed's moccasined feet to the top of his head. "I measured him well through the glasses, Bateese. It will be a great fight. But I shall whip you!"

He did not wait for the half-breed to reply, but went into the cabin and closed the door behind him. He did not like the taunting note of suggestiveness in the other's words. Was it possible that Bateese suspected the true state of his mind, that he was in love with the wife of St. Pierre, and that his heart was sick because of what he had seen aboard the raft? He flushed hotly. It made him uncomfortable to feel that even the half-breed might have guessed his humiliation.

David looked through the window toward the raft. The *bateau* was drifting downstream, possibly a hundred feet from the shore, but it was quite evident that Concombre Bateese was making no effort to bring it close to the floating mass of timber, which had made no change in its course down the river. David's mind painted swiftly what was happening in the cabin into which Marie-Anne and St. Pierre had disappeared. At this moment Marie-Anne was telling of him, of the adventure in the hot patch of sand. He fancied the suppressed excitement in her voice as she unburdened herself. He saw St. Pierre's face darken, his muscles tighten—and crouching in silence, he seemed to see the misshapen hulk of Andre, the Broken Man, listening to what was passing between the other two. And he heard again the mad monotone of Andre's voice, crying plaintively, "HAS ANY ONE SEEN BLACK ROGER AUDEMARD?"

His blood ran a little faster, and his old craft was a dominantly living thing within him once more. Love had dulled both his ingenuity and his desire. For a space a thing had risen before him that was mightier than the majesty of the Law, and he had TRIED to miss the bull's-eye—because of his love for the wife of St. Pierre Boulain. Now he shot squarely for it, and the bell rang in his brain. Two times two again made four. Facts assembled themselves like arguments in flesh and blood. Those facts would have convinced Superintendent McVane, and they now convinced David. He had set out to get Black Roger Audemard, alive or dead. And Black Roger, wholesale murderer, a monster who had painted the blackest page of crime known in the history of Canadian law, was closely and vitally associated with Marie-Anne and St. Pierre Boulain!

The thing was a shock, but Carrigan no longer tried to evade the point. His business was no longer with a man supposed to be a thousand or fifteen hundred miles farther north. It was with Marie-Anne, St. Pierre, and Andre, the Broken Man. And also with Concombre Bateese.

He smiled a little grimly as he thought of his approaching battle with the half-breed. St. Pierre would be astounded at the proposition he had in store for him. But he was sure that St. Pierre would accept. And then, if he won the fight with Bateese—

The smile faded from his lips. His face grew older as he looked slowly about the *bateau* cabin, with its sweet and lingering whispers of a woman's presence. It was a part of her. It breathed of her fragrance and her beauty; it seemed to be waiting for her, crying softly for her return. Yet once had there been another woman even lovelier than the wife of St. Pierre. He had not hesitated then. Without great effort he had triumphed over the loveliness of Carmin Fanchet and had sent her brother to the hangman. And now, as he recalled those days, the truth came to him that even in the darkest hour Carmin Fanchet had made not the slightest effort to buy him off with her beauty. She had not tried to lure him. She had fought proudly and defiantly. And had Marie-Anne done that?

His fingers clenched slowly, and a thickening came in his throat. Would she tell St. Pierre of the many hours they had spent together? Would she confess to him the secret of that precious moment when she had lain close against his breast, her arms about him, her face pressed to his? Would she speak to him of secret hours, of warm flushes that had come to her face, of glowing fires that at times had burned in her eyes when he had been very near to her? Would she reveal EVE-RYTHING to St. Pierre—her husband? He was powerless to combat the voice that told him no. Carmin Fanchet had fought him openly as an enemy and had not employed her beauty as a weapon. Marie-Anne had put in his way a great temptation. What he was thinking seemed to him like a sacrilege, yet he knew there could be no discriminating distinctions between weapons, now that he was determined to play the game to the end, for the Law.

When Carrigan went out on deck, the half-breed was sweating from his exertion at the stern sweep. He looked at the *agent de police* who was going to fight him, perhaps tomorrow or the next day. There was a change in Carrigan. He was not the same man who had gone into the cabin an hour before, and the fact impressed itself upon Bateese. There was something in his appearance that held back the loose talk at the end of Concombre's tongue. And so it was Carrigan himself who spoke first.

"When will this man St. Pierre come to see me?" he demanded. "If he doesn't come soon, I shall go to him."

For an instant Concombre's face darkened. Then, as he bent over the sweep with his great back to David, he chuckled audibly, and said:

"Would you go, *m'sieu*? Ah—it is *le malade d'amour* over there in the cabin. Surely you would not break in upon their love-making?"

Bateese did not look over his shoulder, and so he did not see the hot flush that gathered in David's face. But David was sure he knew it was there and that Concombre had guessed the truth of matters. There was a sly note in his voice, as if he could not quite keep to himself his exultation that beauty and bright eyes had played a clever trick on this man who, if his own judgment had been followed, would now be resting peacefully at the bottom of the river. It was the final stab to Carrigan. His muscles tensed. For the first time he felt the desire to shoot a naked fist into the grinning mouth of Concombre Bateese. He laid a hand on the half-breed's shoulder, and Bateese turned about slowly. He saw what was in the other's eyes.

"Until this moment I have not known what a great pleasure it will be to fight you, Bateese," said David quietly. "Make it tomorrow—in the morning, if you wish. Take word to St. Pierre that I will make him a great wager that I win, a gamble so large that I think he will be afraid to cover it. For I don't think much of this St. Pierre of yours, Bateese. I believe him to be a big-winded bluff, like yourself. And also a coward. Mark my word, he will be so much afraid that he will not accept my wager!"

Bateese did not answer. He was looking over David's shoulder. He seemed not to have heard what the other had said, yet there had come a sudden gleam of exultation in his eyes, and he replied, still gazing toward the raft,

"*Diantre, m'sieu coq de bruyere* may keep ze beeg word in hees mout'! See!—St. Pierre, he ees comin' to answer for himself. *Mon Dieu,* I hope he does not wring ze leetle rooster's neck, for zat would spoil wan great, gran' fight tomorrow!"

David turned toward the big raft. At the distance which separated them he could make out the giant figure of St. Pierre Boulain getting into a canoe. The humped-up form already in that canoe he knew was the Broken Man. He could not see Marie-Anne.

Very lightly Bateese touched his arm. "*M'sieu* will go into ze cabin," he suggested softly. "If somet'ing happens, it ees bes' too many eyes do not see it. You understan', *m'sieu agent de police?*"

Carrigan nodded. "I understand," he said.

16

In the cabin David waited. He did not look through the window to watch St. Pierre's approach. He sat down and picked up a magazine from the table upon which Marie-Anne's work-basket lay. He was cool as ice now. His blood flowed evenly and his pulse beat unhurriedly. Never had he felt himself more his own master, more like grappling with a situation. St. Pierre was coming to fight. He had no doubt of that. Perhaps not physically, at first. But, one way or another, something dynamic was bound to happen in the *bateau* cabin within the next half-hour. Now that the impending drama was close at hand, Carrigan's scheme of luring St. Pierre into the making of a stupendous wager seemed to him rather ridiculous. With calculating coldness he was forced to concede that St. Pierre would be somewhat of a fool to accept the wager he had in mind, when he was so completely in St. Pierre's power. For Marie-Anne and the chief of the Boulains, the bottom of the river would undoubtedly be the best and easiest solution, and the half-breed's suggestion might be acted upon after all.

As his mind charged itself for the approaching struggle, David found himself staring at a double page in the magazine, given up entirely to impossibly slim young creatures exhibiting certain bits of illusive and mysterious feminine apparel. Marie-Anne had expressed her approbation in the form of pencil notes under several of them. Under a cobwebby affair that wreathed one of the slim figures he read, "St. Pierre will love this!" There were two exclamation points after that particular notation!

David replaced the magazine on the table and looked toward the door. No, St. Pierre would not hesitate to put him at the bottom of the river, for her. Not if he, Dave Carrigan, made the solution of the matter a necessity. There were times, he told himself, when it was confoundedly embarrassing to force the letter of the law. And this was one of them. He was not afraid of the river bottom. He was thinking again of Marie-Anne.

The scraping of a canoe against the side of the *bateau* recalled him suddenly to the moment at hand. He heard low voices, and one of them, he knew, was St. Pierre's. For an interval the voices continued, frequently so low that he could not distinguish them at all. For ten minutes he waited impatiently. Then the door swung open, and St. Pierre came in.

Slowly and coolly David rose to meet him, and at the same moment the chief of the Boulains closed the door behind him. There was no greeting in Carrigan's manner. He was the Law, waiting, unexcited, sure of himself, impassive as a thing of steel. He was ready to fight. He expected to fight. It only remained for St. Pierre to show what sort of fight it was to be. And he was amazed at St. Pierre, without betraying that amazement. In the vivid light that shot through the western windows the chief of the Boulains stood looking at David. He wore a gray flannel shirt open at the throat, and it was a splendid throat David saw, and a splendid head above it, with its reddish beard and hair.

But what he saw chiefly were St. Pierre's eyes. They were the sort of eyes he disliked to find in an enemy—a grayish, steely blue that reflected sunlight like polished flint. But there was no flash of battle-glow in them now. St. Pierre was neither excited nor in a bad humour. Nor did Carrigan's attitude appear to disturb him in the least. He was smiling; his eyes glowed with almost boyish curiosity as he stared appraisingly at David—and then, slowly, a low chuckle of laughter rose in his deep chest, and he advanced with an outstretched hand.

"I am St. Pierre Boulain," he said. "I have heard a great deal about you, Sergeant Carrigan. You have had an unfortunate time!"

Had the man advanced menacingly, David would have felt more comfortable. It was disturbing to have this giant come to him with an extended hand of apparent friendship when he had anticipated an entirely different sort of meeting. And St. Pierre was laughing at him! There was no doubt of that. And he had the colossal nerve to tell him that he had been unfortunate, as though being shot up by somebody's wife was a fairly decent joke!

Carrigan's attitude did not change. He did not reach out a hand to meet the other. There was no responsive glimmer of humour in his eyes or on his lips. And seeing these things, St. Pierre turned his extended hand to the open box of cigars, so that he stood for a moment with his back toward him.

"It's funny," he said, as if speaking to himself, and with only a drawling note of the French *patois* in his voice. "I come home, find my Jeanne in a terrible mix-up, a stranger in her room—and the stranger refuses to let me laugh or shake hands with him. *Tonnerre*, I say it is funny! And my Jeanne saved his life, and made him muffins, and gave him my own bed, and walked with him in the forest! Ah, the ungrateful *cochon*!"

He turned, laughing openly, so that his deep voice filled the cabin. "*Vous aves de la corde de pendu, m'sieu*—yes, you are a lucky dog! For only one other man in the world would my Jeanne have done that. You are lucky because you were not ended behind the rock; you are lucky because you are not at the bottom of the river; you are lucky—"

He shrugged his big shoulders hopelessly. "And now, after all our kindness and your good luck, you wait for me like an enemy, *m'sieu*. *Diable*, I cannot understand!"

For the life of him Carrigan could not, in these few moments, measure up his man. He had said nothing. He had let St. Pierre talk. And now St. Pierre stood there, one of the finest men he had ever looked upon, as if honestly overcome by a great wonder. And yet behind that apparent incredulity in his voice and manner David sensed the deep underflow of another thing. St. Pierre was all that Marie-Anne had claimed for him, and more. She had given him assurance of her unlimited confidence that her husband could adjust any situation in the world, and Carrigan conceded that St. Pierre measured up splendidly to that particular type of man. The smile had not left his face; the good humour was still in his eyes.

David smiled back at him coldly. He recognized the cleverness of the other's play. St. Pierre was a man who would smile like that even as he fought, and Carrigan loved a smiling fighter, even when he had to slip steel bracelets over his wrists.

"I am Sergeant Carrigan, of 'N' Division, Royal Northwest Mounted Police," he said, repeating the formula of the law. "Sit down, St. Pierre, and I will tell you a few things that have happened. And then—"

"*Non, non*, it is not necessary, m'sieu. I have already listened for an hour, and I do not like to hear a story twice. You are of the Police. I love the Police. They are brave men, and brave men are my brothers. You are out after Roger Audemard, the rascal! Is it not so? And you were shot at behind the rock back there. You were almost killed. *Ma foi*, and it was my Jeanne who did the shooting! Yes, she thought you were another man." The chuckling, drum-like note of laughter came again out of St. Pierre's great chest. "It was bad shooting. I have taught her better, but the sun was blinding there in the hot, white sand. And after that—I know everything that has happened. Bateese was wrong. I shall scold him for wanting to put you at the bottom of the river—perhaps.

"*Oui, ce que femme veut, Dieu le veut*—that is it. A woman must have her way, and my Jeanne's gentle heart was touched because you were a brave and handsome man, M'sieu Carrigan. But I am not jealous. Jealousy is a worm that does not make friendship! And we shall be friends. Only as a friend could I take you to the Chateau Boulain, far up on the Yellowknife. And we are going there."

In spite of what might have been the entirely proper thing to do at this particular moment, Carrigan's face broke into a smile as he drew a second chair up close to the table. He was swift to readjust himself. It came suddenly back to him how he had grinned behind the rock, when death seemed close at hand. And St. Pierre was like that now. David measured him again as the chief of the Boulains sat down opposite him. Such a man could not be afraid of anything on the face of the earth, even of the Law. The gleam that lay in his eyes told David that as they met his own over the table. "We are smiling now because it happens to please us," David read in them. "But in a moment, if it is necessary, we shall fight."

Carrigan leaned a little over the table. "You know we are not going to the Chateau Boulain, St. Pierre," he said. "We are going to stop at Fort McMurray, and there you and your wife must answer for a number of things that have happened. There is one way out—possibly. That is largely up to you. Why did your wife try to kill me behind the rock? And what did you know about Black Roger Audemard?"

St. Pierre's eyes did not for an instant leave Carrigan's face. Slowly a change came into them; the smile faded, the blue went out, and up from behind seemed to come another pair of eyes that were hard as steel and cold as ice. Yet they were not eyes that threatened, nor eyes that betrayed excitement or passion. And St. Pierre's voice, when he spoke, lacked the deep and vibrant note that had been in it. It was as if he had placed upon it the force of a mighty will, chaining it back, just as something hidden and terrible lay chained behind his eyes.

"Why play like little children, M'sieu Carrigan?" he asked. "Why not come out squarely, honestly, like men? I know what has happened. *Mon Dieu*, it was bad! You were almost killed, and you heard that poor wreck, Andre, call for Roger Audemard. My Jeanne has told you about that—how I found him in the forest with his broken mind and body. And about my Jeanne—" St. Pierre's fists grew into knotted lumps on the table. "*Non*, I will die—I will kill you—before I will tell you why she shot at you behind the rock! We are men, both of us. We are not afraid. And you—in my place—what would YOU do, *m'sieu?*"

In the moment's silence each man looked steadily at the other.

"I would—fight," said David slowly. "If it was for her, I am pretty sure I would fight."

He believed that he was drawing the net in now, that it would catch St. Pierre. He leaned a little farther over the table.

"And I, too, must fight," he added. "You know our law, St. Pierre. We don't go back without our man—unless we happen to die. And I would be stupid if I did not understand the situation here. It would be quite easy for you to get rid of me. But I don't believe you are a murderer, even if your Jeanne tried to be." A flicker of a smile crossed his lips. "And Marie-Anne—I beg pardon!—your wife—"

St. Pierre interrupted him. "It will please me to have you call her Marie-Anne. And it will please her also, *m'sieu. Dieu*, if we only had eyes that could see what is in a woman's heart! Life is funny, *m'sieu*. It is a great joke, I swear it on my soul!"

He shrugged his shoulders, smiling again straight into David's eyes. "See what has happened! You set out for a murderer. My Jeanne makes a great mistake and shoots you. Then she pities you, saves your life, brings you here, and—*ma foi!* it is true—learns to care for you more than she should! But that does not make me want to kill you. *Non*, her happiness is mine. Dead men tell no tales, *m'sieu*, but there are times when living men also keep tales to themselves. And that is what you are going to do, M'sieu Carrigan. You are going to keep to yourself the thing that happened behind the rock. You are going to keep to yourself the mumblings of our poor mad Andre. Never will they pass your lips. I know. I swear it. I stake my life on it!" St. Pierre was talking slowly and unexcitedly. There was an immeasurable confidence in his deep voice. It did not imply a threat or a warning. He was sure of himself. And his eyes had deepened into blue again and were almost friendly.

"You would stake your life?" repeated Carrigan questioningly. "You would do that?"

St. Pierre rose to his feet and looked about the cabin with a shining light in his eyes that was both pride and exaltation. He moved toward the end of the room, where the piano stood, and for a moment his big fingers touched the keys; then, seeing the lacy bit of handkerchief that lay there, he picked it up—and placed it back again. Carrigan did not urge his question, but waited. In spite of his effort to fight it down he found himself in the grip of a mysterious and growing thrill as he watched St. Pierre. Never had the presence of another man had the same effect upon him, and strangely the thought came to him that he was matched—even overmatched.

It was as if St. Pierre had brought with him into the cabin something more than the splendid strength of his body, a thing that reached out in the interval of silence between them, warning Carrigan that all the law in the world would not swerve the chief of the Boulains from what was already in his mind. For a moment the thought passed from David that fate had placed him up against the hazard of enmity with St. Pierre. His vision centred in the man alone. And as he, too, rose to his feet, an unconscious smile came to his lips as he recalled the boastings of Bateese.

"I ask you," said he, "if you would really stake your life in a matter such as that? Of course, if your words were merely accidental, and meant nothing—"

"If I had a dozen lives, I would stake them, one on top of the other, as I have said," interrupted St. Pierre. Suddenly his laugh boomed out and his voice became louder. "M'sieu Carrigan, I have come to offer you just that test! *Oui*, I could kill you now. I could put you at the bottom of the river, as Bateese thinks is right. *Mon Dieu*, how completely I could make you disappear! And then my Jeanne would be safe. She would not go behind prison bars. She would go on living, and laughing, and singing in the big forests, where she belongs. And Black Roger Audemard, the rascal, would be safe for a time! But that would be like destroying a little child. You are so helpless now. So you are going on to the Chateau Boulain with us, and if at the end of the second month from today you do not willingly say I have won my wager—why—*m'sieu*—I will go with you into the forest, and you may shoot out of me the life which is my end of the gamble. Is that not fair? Can you suggest a better way—between men like you and me?"

"I can at least suggest a way that has the virtue of saving time," replied David. "First, however, I must understand my position here. I am, I take it, a prisoner."

"A guest, with certain restrictions placed upon you, *m'sieu*," corrected St. Pierre.

The eyes of the two men met on a dead level.

"Tomorrow morning I am going to fight Bateese," said David. "It is a little sporting event we have fixed up between us for the amusement of—your men. I have heard that Bateese is the best fighting man along the Three Rivers. And I—I do not like to have any other man claim that distinction when I am around."

For the first time St. Pierre's placidity seemed to leave him. His brow became clouded, a moment's frown grew in his face, and there was a certain disconsolate hopelessness in the shrug of his shoulders. It was as if Carrigan's words had suddenly robbed the day of all its sunshine for the chief of the Boulains. His voice, too, carried an unhappy and disappointed note as he made a gesture toward the window.

"*M'sieu*, on that raft out there are many of my men, and they have scarcely rested or slept since word was brought to them that a stranger was to fight Concombre Bateese. *Tonnerre*, they have gambled without ever seeing you until the clothes on their backs are in the hazard, and they have cracked their muscles in labour to overtake you! They have prayed away their very souls that it would be a good fight, and that Bateese would not eat you up too quickly. It has been a long time since we have seen a good fight, a long time since the last man dared to stand up against the half-breed. Ugh, it tears out my heart to tell you that the fight cannot be!"

St. Pierre made no effort to suppress his emotion. He was like a huge, disappointed boy. He walked to the window, peered forth at the raft, and as he shrugged his big shoulders again something like a groan came from him.

The thrill of approaching triumph swept through David's blood. The flame of it was in his eyes when St. Pierre turned from the window.

"And you are disappointed, St. Pierre? You would like to see that fight!"

The blue steel in St. Pierre's eyes flashed back. "If the price were a year of my life, I would give it—if Bateese did not eat you up too quickly. I love to look upon a good fight, where there is no venom of hatred in the blows!"

"Then you shall see a good fight, St. Pierre."

"Bateese would kill you, *m'sieu*. You are not big. You are not his match."

"I shall whip him, St. Pierre—whip him until he avows me his master."

"You do not know the half-breed, *m'sieu*. Twice I have tried him in friendly combat myself and have been beaten."

"But I shall whip him," repeated Carrigan. "I will wager you anything—anything in the world—even life against life—that I whip him!"

The gloom had faded from the face of St. Pierre Boulain. But in a moment it clouded again.

"My Jeanne has made me promise that I will stop the fight," he said.

"And why—why should she insist in a matter such as this, which properly should be settled among men?" asked David.

Again St. Pierre laughed; with an effort, it seemed, "She is gentle-hearted, *m'sieu*. She laughed and thought it quite a joke when Bateese humbled me. 'What! My great St. Pierre, with the blood of old France in his veins, beaten by a man who has been named after a vegetable!' she cried. I tell you she was merry over it, *m'sieu*! She laughed until the tears came into her eyes. But with you it is different. She was white when she entreated me not to let you fight Bateese. Yes, she is afraid you will be badly hurt. And she does not want to see you hurt again. But I tell you that I am not jealous, *m'sieu*! She does not try to hide things from me. She tells me everything, like a little child. And so—"

"I am going to fight Bateese," said David. He wondered if St. Pierre could hear the thumping of his heart, or if his face gave betrayal of the hot flood it was pumping through his body. "Bateese and I have pledged ourselves. We shall fight, unless you tie one of us hand and foot. And as for a wager—"

"Yes—what have you to wager?" demanded St. Pierre eagerly.

"You know the odds are great," temporized Carrigan.

"That I concede, *m'sieu*."

"But a fight without a wager would be like a pipe without tobacco, St. Pierre."

"You speak truly, *m'sieu*."

David came nearer and laid a hand on the other's arm. "St. Pierre, I hope you—and your Jeanne—will understand what I am about to offer. It is this. If Bateese whips me, I will disappear into the forests, and no word shall ever pass my lips of what has passed since that hour behind the rock—and this. No whisper of it will ever reach the Law. I will forget the attempted murder and the suspicious mumblings of your Broken Man. You will be safe. Your Jeanne will be safe—if Bateese whips me."

115

He paused, and waited. St. Pierre made no answer, but amazement came into his face, and after that a slow and burning fire in his eyes which told how deeply and vitally Carrigan's words had struck into his soul.

"And if I should happen to win," continued David, turning a bit carelessly toward the window, "why, I should expect as large a payment from you. If I win, your fulfilment of the wager will be to tell me in every detail why your wife tried to kill me behind the rock, and you will also tell me all that you know about the man I am after, Black Roger Audemard. That is all. I am asking for no odds, though you concede the handicap is great."

He did not look at St. Pierre. Behind him he heard the other's deep breathing. For a space neither spoke. Outside they could hear the soft swish of water, the low voices of men in the stern, and a shout and the barking of a dog coming from the raft far out on the river. For David the moment was one of suspense. He turned again, a bit carelessly, as if his proposition were a matter of but little significance to him. St. Pierre was not looking at him. He was staring toward the door, as if through it he could see the powerful form of Bateese bending over the stern sweep. And Carrigan could see that his face was flaming with a great desire, and that the blood in his body was pounding to the mighty urge of it.

Suddenly he faced Carrigan.

"*M'sieu*, listen to me," he said. "You are a brave man. You are a man of honour, and I know you will bury sacredly in your heart what I am going to tell you now, and never let a word of it escape—even to my Jeanne. I do not blame you for loving her. *Non!* You could not help that. You have fought well to keep it within yourself, and for that I honour you. How do I know? *Mon Dieu*, she has told me! A woman's heart understands, and a woman's ears are quick to hear, *m'sieu*. When you were sick, and your mind was wandering, you told her again and again that you loved her—and when she brought you back to life, her eyes saw more than once the truth of what your lips had betrayed, though you tried to keep it to yourself.

"Even more, *m'sieu*—she felt the touch of your lips on her hair that day. She understands. She has told me everything, openly, innocently—yet her heart thrills with that sympathy of a woman who knows she is loved. *M'sieu*, if you could have seen the light in her eyes and the glow in her cheeks as she told me these secrets. But I am not jealous! *Non!* It is only because you are a brave man, and one of honour, that I tell you all this. She would die of shame did she know I had betrayed her confidence. Yet it is necessary that I tell you, because if we make the big wager we must drop my Jeanne from the gamble. Do you comprehend me, *m'sieu*?

"We are two men, strong men, fighting men. I—Pierre Boulain-cannot feel the shame of jealousy where a woman's heart is pure and sweet, and where a man has fought against love with honour as you have fought. And you, *m'sieu*—David Carrigan, of the Police—cannot strike with your hard man's hand that tender heart, that is like a flower, and which this moment is beating faster than it should with the fear that some harm is going to befall you. Is it not so, *m'sieu*? We will make the wager, yes. But if you whip Bateese—and you cannot do that in a hundred years of fighting—I will not tell you why my Jeanne shot at you behind the rock. *Non*, never! Yet I swear I will tell you the other. If you win, I will tell you all I know about Roger Audemard, and that is considerable, *m'sieu*. Do you agree?"

Slowly David held out a hand. St. Pierre's gripped it. The fingers of the two men met like bands of steel.

"Tomorrow you will fight," said St. Pierre. "You will fight and be beaten so terribly that you may always show the marks of it. I am sorry. Such a man as you I would rather have as a brother than an enemy. And she will never forgive me. She will always remember it. The thought will never die out of her heart that I was a beast to let you fight Bateese. But it is best for all. And my men? Ah! *Diable*, but it will be great sport for them, *m'sieu*!"

His hand unclasped. He turned to the door. A moment later it closed behind him, and David was alone. He had not spoken. He had not replied to the engulfing truths that had fallen quietly and without a betrayal of passion from St. Pierre's lips. Inwardly he was crushed. Yet his face was like stone, hiding his shame. And then, suddenly, there came a sound from outside that sent the blood through his cold veins again. It was laughter, the great, booming laughter of St. Pierre! It was not the merriment of a man whose heart was bleeding, or into whose life had come an unexpected pain or grief. It was wild and free, and filled with the joy of the sun-filled day.

And David, listening to it, felt something that was more than admiration for this man growing within him. And unconsciously his lips repeated St. Pierre's words.

"Tomorrow—you will fight."

17

For many minutes David stood at the *bateau* window and watched the canoe that carried St. Pierre Boulain and the Broken Man back to the raft. It moved slowly, as if St. Pierre was loitering with a purpose and was thinking deeply of what had passed. Carrigan's fingers tightened, and his face grew tense, as he gazed out into the glow of the western sun. Now that the stress of nerve-breaking moments in the cabin was over, he no longer made an effort to preserve the veneer of coolness and decision with which he had encountered the chief of the Boulains. Deep in his soul he was crushed and humiliated. Every nerve in his body was bleeding.

He had heard St. Pierre's big laugh a moment before, but it must have been the laugh of a man who was stabbed to the heart. And he was going back to Marie-Anne like that—drifting scarcely faster than the current that he might steal time to strengthen himself before he looked into her eyes again. David could see him, motionless, his giant shoulders hunched forward a little, his head bowed, and in the stern the Broken Man paddled listlessly, his eyes on the face of his master. Without voice David cursed himself. In his egoism he had told himself that he had made a splendid fight in resisting the temptation of a great love for the wife of St. Pierre. But what was his own struggle compared with this tragedy which St. Pierre was now facing?

He turned from the window and looked about the cabin room again—the woman's room and St. Pierre's—and his face burned in its silent accusation. Like a living thing it painted another picture for him. For a space he lost his own identity. He saw himself in the place of St. Pierre. He was the husband of Marie-Anne, worshipping her even as St. Pierre must worship her, and he came, as St. Pierre had come, to find a stranger in his home, a stranger who had lain in his bed, a stranger whom his wife had nursed back to life, a stranger who had fallen in love with his most inviolable possession, who had told her of his love, who had kissed her, who had held her close, in his arms, whose presence had brought a warmer flush and a brighter glow into eyes and cheeks that until this stranger's coming had belonged only to him. And he heard her, as St. Pierre had heard her, pleading with him to keep this man from harm; he heard her soft voice, telling of the things that had passed between them, and he saw in her eyes—

With almost a cry he swept the thought and the picture from him. It was an atrocious thing to conceive, impossible of reality. And yet the truth would not go. What would he have done in St. Pierre's place?

He went to the window again. Yes, St. Pierre was a bigger man than he. For St. Pierre had come quietly and calmly, offering a hand of friendship, generous, smiling, keeping his hurt to himself, while he, Dave Carrigan, would have come with the murder of man in his heart.

His eyes passed from the canoe to the raft, and from the big raft to the hazy billows of green and golden forest that melted off into interminable miles of distance beyond the river. He knew that on the other side of him lay that same distance, north, east, south, and west, vast spaces in an unpeopled world, the same green and golden forests, ten thousand plains and rivers and lakes, a million hiding-places where romance and tragedy might remain forever undisturbed. The thought came to him that it would not be difficult to slip out into that world and disappear. He almost owed it to St. Pierre. It was the voice of Bateese in a snatch of wild and discordant song that brought him back into grim reality. There was, after all, that embarrassing matter of justice—and the accursed Law!

After a little he observed that the canoe was moving faster, and that Andre's paddle was working steadily and with force. St. Pierre no longer sat hunched in the bow. His head was erect, and he was waving a hand in the direction of the raft. A figure had come from the cabin on the huge mass of floating timber. David caught the shimmer of a woman's dress, something white fluttering over her head, waving back at St. Pierre. It was Marie-Anne, and he moved away from the window.

He wondered what was passing between St. Pierre and his wife in the hour that followed. The *bateau* kept abreast of the raft, moving neither faster nor slower than it did, and twice he surrendered to the desire to scan the deck of the floating timbers through his binoculars. But the cabin held St. Pierre and Marie-Anne, and he saw neither of them again until the sun was setting. Then St. Pierre came out-alone.

Even at that distance over the broad river he heard the booming voice of the chief of the Boulains. Life sprang up where there had been the drowse of inactivity aboard the raft. A dozen more of the great sweeps were swiftly manned by men who appeared suddenly from the shaded places of canvas shelters and striped tents. A murmur of voices rose over the water, and then the murmur was broken by howls and shouts as the rivermen ran to their places at the command of St. Pierre's voice, and as the sweeps began to flash in the setting sun, it gave way entirely to the evening chant of the Paddling Song.

David gripped himself as he listened and watched the slowly drift-ing glory of the world that came down to the shores of the river. He could see St. Pierre clearly, for the *bateau* had worked its way nearer. He could see the bare heads and naked arms of the rivermen at the sweeps. The sweet breath of the forests filled his lungs, as that picture lay before him, and there came into his soul a covetousness and a yearning where before there had been humiliation and the grim urge of duty. He could breathe the air of that world, he could look at its beauty, he could worship it—and yet he knew that he was not a part of it as those others were a part of it. He envied the men at the sweeps; he felt his heart swelling at the exultation and joy in their song.

They were going home—home down the big rivers, home to the heart of God's Country, where wives and sweethearts and happiness were waiting for them, and their visions were his visions as he stared wide-eyed and motionless over the river. And yet he was irrevocably an alien. He was more than that—an enemy, a man-hound sent out on a trail to destroy, an agent of a powerful and merciless force that carried with it punishment and death.

The crew of the *bateau* had joined in the evening song of the riv-ermen on the raft, and over the ridges and hollows of the forest tops, red and green and gold in the last warm glory of the sun, echoed that chanting voice of men. David understood now what St. Pierre's com-mand had been. The huge raft with its tented city of life was preparing to tie up for the night. A quarter of a mile ahead the river widened, so that on the far side was a low, clean shore toward which the efforts of the men at the sweeps were slowly edging the raft. York boats shot out on the shore side and dropped anchors that helped drag the big craft in. Two others tugged at tow-lines fastened to the shoreside bow, and within twenty minutes the first men were plunging up out of the water on the white strip of beach and were whipping the tie-lines about the nearest trees. David unconsciously was smiling in the thrill and triumph of these last moments, and not until they were over did he sense the fact that Bateese and his crew were bringing the *bateau* in to the opposite shore. Before the sun was quite down, both raft and house-boat were anchored for the night.

As the shadows of the distant forests deepened, Carrigan felt impending about him an oppression of emptiness and loneliness which he had not experienced before. He was disappointed that the *bateau* had not tied up with the raft. Already he could see men building fires. Spirals of smoke began to rise from the shore, and he knew that the riverman's happiest of all hours, supper time, was close at hand. He looked at his watch. It was after seven o'clock. Then he watched the fading away of the sun until only the red glow of it remained in the west, and against the still thicker shadows the fires of the rivermen threw up yellow flames.

On his own side, Bateese and the *bateau* crew were preparing their meal. It was eight o'clock when a man he had not seen before brought in his supper. He ate, scarcely sensing the taste of his food, and half an hour later the man reappeared for the dishes.

It was not quite dark when he returned to his window, but the far shore was only an indistinct blur of gloom. The fires were brighter. One of them, built solely because of the rivermen's inherent love of light and cheer, threw the blaze of its flaming logs twenty feet into the air.

He wondered what Marie-Anne was doing in this hour. Last night they had been together. He had marvelled at the witchery of the moonlight in her hair and eyes, he had told her of the beauty of it, she had smiled, she had laughed softly with him—for hours they had sat in the spell of the golden night and the glory of the river. And tonight—now—was she with St. Pierre, waiting as they had waited last night for the rising of the moon? Had she forgotten? COULD she forget? Or was she, as he thought St. Pierre had painfully tried to make him believe, innocent of all the thoughts and desires that had come to him, as he sat worshipping her in their stolen hours? He could think of them only as stolen, for he did not believe Marie-Anne had revealed to her husband all she might have told him.

He was sure he would never see her again as he had seen her then, and something of bitterness rose in him as he thought of that. St. Pierre, could he have seen her face and eyes when he told her that her hair in the moonlight was lovelier than anything he had ever seen, would have throttled him with his naked hands in that meeting in the cabin. For St. Pierre's code would not have had her eyes droop under their long lashes or her cheeks flush so warmly at the words of another man—and he could not take vengeance on the woman herself. No, she had not told St. Pierre all she might have told! There were things which she must have kept to herself, which she dared not reveal even to this great-hearted man who was her husband. Shame, if nothing more, had kept her silent.

Did she feel that shame as he was feeling it? It was inconceivable to think otherwise. And for that reason, more than all others, he knew that she would not meet him face to face again—unless he forced that meeting. And there was little chance of that, for his pledge with St. Pierre had eliminated her from the aftermath of tomorrow's drama, his fight with Bateese. Only when St. Pierre might stand in a court of law would there be a possibility of her eyes meeting his own again, and then they would flame with the hatred that at another time had been in the eyes of Carmin Fanchet.

With the dull stab of a thing that of late had been growing inside him, he wondered what had happened to Carmin Fanchet in the years that had gone since he had brought about the hanging of her brother. Last night and the night before, strange dreams of her had come to him in restless slumber. It was disturbing to him that he should wake up in the middle of the night dreaming of her, when he had gone to his bed with a mind filled to overflowing with the sweet presence of Marie-Anne Boulain. And now his mind reached out poignantly into mysterious darkness and doubt, even as the darkness of night spread itself in a thickening canopy over the river.

Gray clouds had followed the sun of a faultless day, and the stars were veiled overhead. When David turned from the window, it was so dark in the cabin that he could not see. He did not light the lamps, but made his way to St. Pierre's couch and sat down in the silence and gloom.

Through the open windows came to him the cadence of the river and the forests. There was silence of human voice ashore, but under him he heard the lapping murmur of water as it rustled under the stern and side of the *bateau*, and from the deep timber came the never-ceasing whisper of the spruce and cedar tops, and the subdued voice of creatures whose hours of activity had come with the dying out of the sun.

For a long time he sat in this darkness. And then there came to him a sound that was different than the other sounds—a low monotone of voices, the dipping of a paddle—and a canoe passed close under his windows and up the shore. He paid small attention to it until, a little later, the canoe returned, and its occupants boarded the *bateau*. It would have roused little interest in him then had he not heard a voice that was thrillingly like the voice of a woman.

He drew his hunched shoulders erect and stared through the darkness toward the door. A moment more and there was no doubt. It was almost shock that sent the blood leaping suddenly through his veins. The inconceivable had happened. It was Marie-Anne out there, talking in a low voice to Bateese!

Then there came a heavy knock at his door, and he heard the door open. Through it he saw the grayer gloom of the outside night partly shut out a heavy shadow.

"*M'sieu!*" called the voice of Bateese.

"I am here," said David.

"You have not gone to bed, *m'sieu?*"

"No."

The heavy shadow seemed to fade away, and yet there still remained a shadow there. David's heart thumped as he noted the slenderness of it. For a space there was silence. And then,

"Will you light the lamps, M'sieu David?" a soft voice came to him. "I want to come in, and I am afraid of this terrible darkness!"

He rose to his feet, fumbling in his pocket for matches.

18

He did not turn toward Marie-Anne when he had lighted the first of the great brass lamps hanging at the side of the *bateau*. He went to the second, and struck another match, and flooded the cabin with light.

She still stood silhouetted against the darkness beyond the cabin door when he faced her. She was watching him, her eyes intent, her face a little pale, he thought. Then he smiled and nodded. He could not see a great change in her since this afternoon, except that there seemed to be a little more fire in the glow of her eyes. They were looking at him steadily as she smiled and nodded, wide, beautiful eyes in which there was surely no revelation of shame or regret, and no very clear evidence of unhappiness. David stared, and his tongue clove to the roof of his mouth.

"Why is it that you sit in darkness?" she asked, stepping within and closing the door. "Did you not expect me to return and apologize for leaving you so suddenly this afternoon? It was impolite. Afterward I was ashamed. But I was excited, M'sieu David. I—"

"Of course," he hurried to interrupt her. "I understand. St. Pierre is a lucky man. I congratulate you—as well as him. He is splendid, a man in whom you can place great faith and confidence."

"He scolded me for running away from you as I did, M'sieu David. He said I should have shown better courtesy than to leave like that one who was a guest in our—home. So I have returned, like a good child, to make amends."

"It was not necessary."

"But you were lonesome and in darkness!"

He nodded. "Yes."

"And besides," she added, so quietly and calmly that he was amazed, "you know my sleeping apartment is also on the *bateau*. And St. Pierre made me promise to say good night to you."

"It is an imposition," cried David, the blood rushing to his face. "You have given up all this to me! Why not let me go into that little room forward, or sleep on the raft and you and St. Pierre—"

"St. Pierre would not leave the raft," replied Marie-Anne, turning from him toward the table on which were the books and magazines and her work-basket. "And I like my little room forward."

"St. Pierre—"

He stopped himself. He could see a sudden colour deepening in the cheek of St. Pierre's wife as she made pretence of looking for something in her basket. He felt that if he went on he would blunder, if he had not already blundered. He was uncomfortable, for he believed he had guessed the truth. It was not quite reasonable to expect that Marie-Anne would come to him like this on the first night of St. Pierre's homecoming. Something had happened over in the little cabin on the raft, he told himself. Perhaps there had been a quarrel—at least ironical implications on St. Pierre's part. And his sympathy was with St. Pierre.

He caught suddenly a little tremble at the corner of Marie-Anne's mouth as her face was turned partly from him, and he stepped to the opposite side of the table so he could look at her fairly. If there had been unpleasantness in the cabin on the raft, St. Pierre's wife in no way gave evidence of it. The colour had deepened to almost a blush in her cheeks, but it was not on account of embarrassment, for one who is embarrassed is not usually amused, and as she looked up at him her eyes were filled with the flash of laughter which he had caught her lips struggling to restrain. Then, finding a bit of lace work with the needles meshed in it, she seated herself, and again he was looking down on the droop of her long lashes and the seductive glow of her lustrous hair.

Yesterday, in a moment of irresistible impulse, he had told her how lovely it was as she had dressed it, a bewitching crown of interwoven coils, not drawn tightly, but crumpled and soft, as if the mass of tresses were openly rebelling at closer confinement. She had told him the effect was entirely accidental, largely due to carelessness and haste in dressing it. Accidental or otherwise, it was the same tonight, and in the heart of it were the drooping red petals of a flower she had gathered with him early that afternoon.

"St. Pierre brought me over," she said in a calmly matter-of-fact voice, as though she had expected David to know that from the beginning. "He is ashore talking over important matters with Bateese.

I am sure he will drop in and say good night before he returns to the raft. He asked me to wait for him—here." She raised her eyes, so clear and untroubled, so quietly unembarrassed under his gaze, that he would have staked his life she had no suspicion of the confessions which St. Pierre had revealed to him.

"Do you care? Would you rather put out the lights and go to bed?"

He shook his head. "No. I am glad. I was beastly lonesome. I had an idea—"

He was on the point of blundering again when he caught himself. The effect of her so near him was more than ever disturbing, in spite of St. Pierre. Her eyes, clear and steady, yet soft as velvet when they looked at him, made his tongue and his thoughts dangerously uncertain.

"You had an idea, M'sieu David?"

"That you would have no desire to see me again after my talk with St. Pierre," he said. "Did he tell you about it?"

"He said you were very fine, M'sieu David—and that he liked you."

"And he told you it is determined that I shall fight Bateese in the morning?"

"Yes."

The one word was spoken with a quiet lack of excitement, even of interest—it seemed to belie some of the things St. Pierre had told him, and he could scarcely believe, looking at her now, that she had entreated her husband to prevent the encounter, or that she had betrayed any unusual emotion in the matter at all.

"I was afraid you would object," he could not keep from saying. "It does not seem nice to pull off such a thing as that, when there is a lady about—"

"Or LADIES." She caught him up quickly, and he saw a sudden little tightening of her pretty mouth as she turned her eyes to the bit of lace work again. "But I do not object, because what St. Pierre says is right—must be right."

And the softness, he thought, went altogether out of the curve of her lips for an instant. In a flash their momentary betrayal of vexation was gone, and St. Pierre's wife had replaced the work-basket on the table and was on her feet, smiling at him. There was something of wild daring in her eyes, something that made him think of the glory of adventure he had seen flaming in her face the night they had run the rapids of the Holy Ghost.

"Tomorrow will be very unpleasant, M'sieu David," she cried softly. "Bateese will beat you—terribly. Tonight we must think of things more agreeable."

He had never seen her more radiant than when she turned toward the piano. What the deuce did it mean? Had St. Pierre been making a fool of him? She actually appeared unable to restrain her elation at the thought that Bateese would surely beat him up! He stood without moving and made no effort to answer her. Just before they had started on that thrilling adventure into the forest, which had ended with his carrying her in his arms, she had gone to the piano and had played for him. Now her fingers touched softly the same notes. A little humming trill came in her throat, and it seemed to David that she was deliberately recalling his thoughts to the things that had happened before the coming of St. Pierre. He had not lighted the lamp over the piano, and for a flash her dark eyes smiled at him out of the half shadow. After a moment she began to sing.

Her voice was low and without effort, untrained, and subdued as if conscious and afraid of its limitations, yet so exquisitely sweet that to David it was a new and still more wonderful revelation of St. Pierre's wife. He drew nearer, until he stood close at her side, the dark lustre of her hair almost touching his arm, her partly upturned face a bewitching profile in the shadows.

Her voice grew lower, almost a whisper in its melody, as if meant for him alone. Many times he had heard the Canadian Boat Song, but never as its words came now from the lips of Marie-Anne Boulain.

Faintly as tolls the evening chime,
Our voices keep tune, and our oars keep time.
Soon as the woods on shore look dim,
We'll sing at St. Ann's our parting hymn;
Row, brothers, row, the stream runs fast,
The rapids are near, and the daylight's past.

She paused. And David, staring down at her shining head, did not speak. Her fingers trembled over the keys, he could see dimly the shadow of her long lashes, and the spirit-like scent of crushed violets rose to him from the soft lace about her throat and her hair.

"It is your music," he whispered. "I have never heard the Boat Song like that!"

He tried to drag his eyes from her face and hair, sensing that he was a near-criminal, fighting a mighty impulse. The notes under her fingers changed, and again—by chance or design—she was stabbing at him; bringing him face to face with the weakness of his flesh, the iniquity of his desire to reach out his arms and crumple her in them. Yet she did not look up, she did not see him, as she began to sing *Ave Maria*.

Ave, Maria, hear my cry!
O, guide my path where no harm, no harm is nigh—

As she went on, he knew she had forgotten to think of him. With the reverence of a prayer the holy words came from her lips, slowly, softly, trembling with a *pathos* and sweetness that told David they came not alone from the lips, but from the very soul of St. Pierre's wife. And then—

Oh, Mother, hear me where thou art,
And guard and guide my aching heart, my aching heart!

The last words drifted away into a whisper, and David was glad that he was not looking into the face of St. Pierre's wife, for there must have been something there now which it would have been sacrilege for him to stare at, as he was staring at her hair.

No sound of opening door had come from behind them. Yet St. Pierre had opened it and stood there, watching them with a curious humour in eyes that seemed still to hold a glitter of the fire that had leaped from the half-breed's flaming birch logs. His voice was a shock to Carrigan.

"*Peste*, but you are a gloomy pair!" he boomed. "Why no light over there in the corner, and why sing that death-song to chase away the devil when there is no devil near?"

Guilt was in David's heart, but there was no sting of venom in St. Pierre's words, and he was laughing at them now, as though what he saw were a pretty joke and amused him.

"Late hours and shady bowers! I say it should be a love song or something livelier," he cried, closing the door behind him and coming toward them. "Why not *En Roulant ma Boule*, my sweet Jeanne? You know that is my favourite."

He suddenly interrupted himself, and his voice rolled out in a wild chant that rocked the cabin.

The wind is fresh, the wind is free,
En roulant ma boule!
The wind is fresh—my love waits me,

Rouli, roulant, ma boule roulant!
Behind our house a spring you see,
In it three ducks swim merrily,
And hunting, the Prince's son went he,
With a silver gun right fair to see—

David was conscious that St. Pierre's wife had risen to her feet, and now she came out of shadow into light, and he was amazed to see that she was laughing back at St. Pierre, and that her two fore-fingers were thrust in her ears to keep out the bellow of her husband's voice. She was not at all discomfited by his unexpected appearance, but rather seemed to join in the humour of the thing with St. Pierre, though he fancied he could see something in her face that was forced and uneasy. He believed that under the surface of her composure she was suffering a distress which she did not reveal.

St. Pierre advanced and carelessly patted her shoulder with one of his big hands, while he spoke to David.

"Has she not the sweetest voice in the world, *m'sieu*? Did you ever hear a sweeter or as sweet? I say it is enough to get down into the soul of a man, unless he is already half dead! That voice—"

He caught Marie-Anne's eyes. Her cheeks were flaming. Her look, for an instant, flashed lightning as she halted him.

"*Ma foi*, I speak it from the heart," he persisted, with a shrug of his shoulders. "Am I not right, M'sieu Carrigan? Did you ever hear a sweeter voice?"

"It is wonderful," agreed David, wondering if he was hazarding too much.

"Good! It fills me with happiness to know I am right. And now, *cherie*, goodnight! I must return to the raft."

A shadow of vexation crossed Marie-Anne's face. "You seem in great haste."

"Plagues and pests! You are right, Pretty Voice! I am most anxious to get back to my troubles there, and you—"

"Will also bid M'sieu Carrigan goodnight," she quickly interrupted him. "You will at least see me to my room, St. Pierre, and safely put away for the night."

She held out her hand to David. There was not a tremor in it as it lay for an instant soft and warm in his own. She made no effort to withdraw it quickly, nor did her eyes hide their softness as they looked into his own.

Mutely David stood as they went out. He heard St. Pierre's loud voice rumbling about the darkness of the night. He heard them pass along the side of the *bateau* forward, and half a minute later he knew that St. Pierre was getting into his canoe. The dip of a paddle came to him.

For a space there was silence, and then, from far out in the black shadow of the river, rolled back the great voice of St. Pierre Boulain singing the wild river chant, *En Roulant ma Boule.*

At the open window he listened. It seemed to him that from far over the river, where the giant raft lay, there came a faint answer to the words of the song,

19

With the slow approach of the storm which was advancing over the wilderness, Carrigan felt more poignantly the growing unrest that was in him. He heard the last of St. Pierre's voice, and after that the fires on the distant shore died out slowly, giving way to utter blackness. Faintly there came to him the far-away rumbling of thunder. The air grew heavy and thick, and there was no sound of night-bird over the breast of the river, and out of the thick cedar and spruce and balsam there came no cry or whisper of the nocturnal life waiting in silence for the storm to break. In that stillness David put out the lights in the cabin and sat close to the window in darkness.

He was more than sleepless. Every nerve in his body demanded action, and his brain was fired by strange thoughts until their vividness seemed to bring him face to face with a reality that set his blood stirring with an irresistible thrill. He believed he had made a discovery, that St. Pierre had betrayed himself. What he had visioned, the conclusion he had arrived at, seemed inconceivable, yet what his own eyes had seen and his ears had heard pointed to the truth of it all. The least he could say was that St. Pierre's love for Marie-Anne Boulain was a strange sort of love. His attitude toward her seemed more like that of a man in the presence of a child of whom he was fond in a fatherly sort of way. His affection, as he had expressed it, was parental and careless. Not for an instant had there been in it a betrayal of the lover, no suggestion of the husband who cared deeply or who might be made jealous by another man.

Sitting in darkness thickening with the nearer approach of storm, David recalled the stab of pain mingled with humiliation that had come into the eyes of St. Pierre's wife when she had stood facing her husband. He heard again, with a new understanding, the low note of pathos in her voice as in song she had called upon the Mother of

Christ to hear her—and help her. He had not guessed at the tragedy of it then. Now he knew, and he thought of her lying awake in the gloom beyond the bulkhead, her eyes were with tears. And St. Pierre had gone back to his raft, singing in the night! Where before there had been sympathy for him, there rose a sincere revulsion. There had been a reason for St. Pierre's masterly possession of himself, and it had not been, as he had thought, because of his bigness of soul.

It was because he had not cared. He was a splendid hypocrite, playing his game well at the beginning, but betraying the lie at the end. He did not love Marie-Anne as he, Dave Carrigan, loved her. He had spoken of her as a child, and he had treated her as a child, and was serenely dispassionate in the face of a situation which would have roused the spirit in most men. And suddenly, recalling that thrilling hour in the white strip of sand and all that had happened since, it flashed upon David that St. Pierre was using his wife as the vital moving force in a game of his own—that under the masquerade of his apparent faith and bigness of character he was sacrificing her to achieve a certain mysterious something it the scheme of his own affairs.

Yet he could not forget the infinite faith Marie-Anne Boulain had expressed in her husband. There had been no hypocrisy in her waiting and her watching for him, or in her belief that he would straighten out the tangles of the dilemma in which she had become involved. Nor had there been make-believe in the manner she had left him that day in her eagerness to go to St. Pierre. Adding these facts as he had added the others, he fancied he saw the truth staring at him out of the darkness of his cabin room. Marie-Anne loved her husband. And St. Pierre was merely the possessor, careless and indifferent, almost brutally dispassionate in his consideration of her.

A heavy crash of thunder brought Carrigan back to a realization of the impending storm. He rose to his feet in the chaotic gloom, facing the bulkhead beyond which he was certain St. Pierre's wife lay wide awake. He tried to laugh. It was inexcusable, he told himself, to let his thoughts become involved in the family affairs of St. Pierre and Marie-Anne. That was not his business. Marie-Anne, in the final analysis, did not appear to be especially abused, and her mind was not a child's mind. Probably she would not thank him for his interest in the matter. She would tell him, like any other woman with pride, that it was none of his business and that he was presuming upon forbidden ground.

He went to the window. There was scarcely a breath of air, and unfastening the screen, he thrust out his head and shoulders into the night. It was so black that he could not see the shadow of the water almost within reach of his hands, but through the chaos of gloom that lay between him and the opposite shore he made out a single point of yellow light. He was positive the light was in the cabin on the raft. And St. Pierre was probably in that cabin.

A huge drop of rain splashed on his hand, and behind him he heard sweeping over the forest tops the quickening march of the deluge. There was no crash of thunder or flash of lightning when it broke. Straight down, in an inundation, it came out of a sky thick enough to slit with a knife. Carrigan drew in his head and shoulders and sniffed the sweet freshness of it. He tried again to make out the light on the raft, but it was obliterated.

Mechanically he began taking off his clothes, and in a few moments he stood again at the window, naked. Thunder and lightning had caught up with the rain, and in the flashes of fire Carrigan's ghost-white face stared in the direction of the raft. In his veins was at work an insistent and impelling desire. Over there was St. Pierre, he was undoubtedly in the cabin, and something might happen if he, Dave Carrigan, took advantage of storm and gloom to go to the raft.

It was almost a presentiment that drew his bare head and shoulders out through the window, and every hunting instinct in him urged him to the adventure. The stygian darkness was torn again by a flash of fire. In it he saw the river and the vivid silhouette of the distant shore. It would not be a difficult swim, and it would be good training for tomorrow.

Like a badger worming his way out of a hole a bit too small for him, Carrigan drew himself through the window. A lightning flash caught him at the edge of the *bateau*, and he slunk back quickly against the cabin, with the thought that other eyes might be staring out into that same darkness. In the pitch gloom that followed he lowered himself quietly into the river, thrust himself under water, and struck out for the opposite shore.

When he came to the surface again it was in the glare of another lightning flash. He flung the water from his face, chose a point several hundred yards above the raft, and with quick, powerful strokes set out in its direction. For ten minutes he quartered the current without raising his head. Then he paused, floating unresistingly with the slow sweep of the river, and waited for another illumination. When it came, he made out the tented raft scarcely a hundred yards away and a little below him. In the next darkness he found the edge of it and dragged himself up on the mass of timbers.

The thunder had been rolling steadily westward, and David crouched low, hoping for one more flash to illumine the raft. It came at last from a mass of inky cloud far to the west, so indistinct that it made only dim shadows out of the tents and shelters, but it was sufficient to give him direction. Before its faint glare died out, he saw the deeper shadow of the cabin forward.

For many minutes he lay where he had dragged himself, without making a movement in its direction. Nowhere about him could he see a sign of light, nor could he hear any sound of life. St. Pierre's people were evidently deep in slumber.

Carrigan had no very definite idea of the next step in his adventure. He had swum from the *bateau* largely under impulse, with no preconceived scheme of action, urged chiefly by the hope that he would find St. Pierre in the cabin and that something might come of it. As for knocking at the door and rousing the chief of the Boulains from sleep—he had at the present moment no very good excuse for that. No sooner had the thought and its objection come to him than a broad shaft of light shot with startling suddenness athwart the blackness of the raft, darkened in another instant by an obscuring shadow. Swift as the light itself David's eyes turned to the source of the unexpected illumination. The door of St. Pierre's cabin was wide open. The interior was flooded with lamp-glow, and in the doorway stood St. Pierre himself.

The chief of the Boulains seemed to be measuring the weather possibilities of the night. His subdued voice reached David, chuckling with satisfaction, as he spoke to someone who was behind him in the cabin.

"Pitch and brimstone, but it's black!" he cried. "You could carve it with a knife, and stand it on end, *AMANTE*. But it's going west. In a few hours the stars will be out."

He drew back into the cabin, and the door closed. David held his breath in amazement, staring at the blackness where a moment before the light had been. Who was it St. Pierre had called sweetheart? *AMANTE!* He could not have been mistaken. The word had come to him clearly, and there was but one guess to make. Marie-Anne was not on the *bateau*. She had played him for a fool, had completely hoodwinked him in her plot with St. Pierre. They were cleverer than he had supposed, and in darkness she had rejoined her husband on the raft! But why that senseless play of falsehood? What could be their object in wanting him to believe she was still aboard the *bateau*?

He stood up on his feet and mopped the warm rain from his face, while the gloom hid the grim smile that came slowly to his lips. Close upon the thrill of his astonishment he felt a new stir in his blood which added impetus to his determination and his action. He was not disgusted with himself, nor was he embittered by what he had thought of a moment ago as the lying hypocrisy of his captors. To be beaten in his game of man-hunting was sometimes to be expected, and Carrigan always gave proper credit to the winners. It was also "good medicine" to know that Marie-Anne, instead of being an unhappy and neglected wife, had blinded him with an exquisitely clever simulation. Just why she had done it, and why St. Pierre had played his masquerade, it was his duty now to find out.

An hour ago he would have cut off a hand before spying upon St. Pierre's wife or eavesdropping under her window. Now he felt no uneasiness of conscience as he approached the cabin, for Marie-Anne herself had destroyed all reason for any delicate discrimination on his part.

The rain had almost stopped, and in one of the near tents he heard a sleepy voice. But he had no fear of chance discovery. The night would remain dark for a long time, and in his bare feet he made no sound the sharpest ears of a dog ten feet away might have heard. Close to the cabin door, yet in such a way that the sudden opening of it would not reveal him, he paused and listened.

Distinctly he heard St. Pierre's voice, but not the words. A moment later came the soft, joyous laughter of a woman, and for an instant a hand seemed to grip David's heart, filling it with pain. There was no unhappiness in that laughter. It seemed, instead, to tremble in an exultation of gladness.

Suddenly St. Pierre came nearer the door, and his voice was more distinct. "*Chere-coeur*, I tell you it is the greatest joke of my life," he heard him say. "We are safe. If it should come to the worst, we can settle the matter in another way. I cannot but sing and laugh, even in the face of it all. And she, in that very innocence which amuses me so, has no suspicion—"

He turned, and vainly David keyed his ears to catch the final words. The voices in the cabin grew lower. Twice he heard the soft laughter of the woman. St. Pierre's voice, when he spoke, was unintelligible.

The thought that his random adventure was bringing him to an important discovery possessed Carrigan. St. Pierre, he believed, had been on the very edge of disclosing something which he would have given a great deal to know. Surely in this cabin there must be a window, and the window would be open—

Quietly he felt his way through the darkness to the shore side of the cabin. A narrow bar of light at least partly confirmed his judgment. There was a window. But it was almost entirely curtained, and it was closed. Had the curtain been drawn two inches lower, the thin stream of light would have been shut entirely out from the night.

Under this window David crouched for several minutes, hoping that in the calm which was succeeding the storm it might be opened. The voices were still more indistinct inside. He scarcely heard St. Pierre, but twice again he heard the low and musical laughter of the woman. She had laughed differently with HIM—and the grim smile settled on his lips as he looked up at the narrow slit of light over his head. He had an overwhelming desire to look in. After all, it was a matter of professional business—and his duty.

He was glad the curtain was drawn so low. From experiments of his own he knew there was small chance of those inside seeing him through the two-inch slit, and he raised himself boldly until his eyes were on a level with the aperture.

Directly in the line of his vision was St. Pierre's wife. She was seated, and her back was toward him, so he could not see her face. She was partly disrobed, and her hair was streaming loose about her. Once, he remembered, she had spoken of fiery lights that came into her hair under certain illumination. He had seen them in the sun, but never as they revealed themselves now in that cabin lamp glow. He scarcely looked at St. Pierre, who was on his feet, looking down upon her—not until St. Pierre reached out and crumpled the smothering mass of glowing tresses in his big hands, and laughed. It was a laugh filled with the unutterable joy of possession. The woman rose to her feet. Up through her hair went her two white, bare arms, encircling St. Pierre's neck. The giant drew her close. Her slim form seemed to melt in his, and their lips met.

And then the woman threw back her head, laughing, so that her glory of hair fell straight down, and she was out of reach of St. Pierre's lips. They turned. Her face fronted the window, and out in the night Carrigan stifled a cry that almost broke from his lips. For a flash he was looking straight into her eyes. Her parted lips seemed smiling at him; her white throat and bosom were bared to him. He dropped down, his

136

heart choking him as he stumbled through the darkness to the edge of the raft. There, with the lap of the water at his feet, he paused. It was hard for him to get breath. He stared through the gloom in the direction of the *bateau*. Marie-Anne Boulain, the woman he loved, was there! In her little cabin, alone, on the *bateau*, was St. Pierre's wife, her heart crushed.

And in this cabin on the raft, forgetful of her degradation and her grief, was the vilest wretch he had ever known—St. Pierre Boulain. And with him, giving herself into his arms, caressing him with her lips and hair, was the sister of the man he had helped to hang—CARMIN FANCHET!

20

The shock of the amazing discovery which Carrigan had made was as complete as it was unexpected. His eyes had looked upon the last thing in the world he might have guessed at or anticipated when they beheld through the window of St. Pierre's cabin the beautiful face and partly disrobed figure of Carmin Fanchet. The first effect of that shock had been to drive him away. His action had been involuntary, almost without the benefit of reason, as if Carmin had been Marie-Anne herself receiving the caresses which were rightfully hers, and upon which it was both insult and dishonour for him to spy. He realized now that he had made a mistake in leaving the window too quickly.

But he did not move back through the gloom, for there was something too revolting in what he had seen, and with the revulsion of it a swift understanding of the truth which made his hands clench as he sat down on the edge of the raft with his feet and legs submerged in the slow-moving current of the river. The thing was not uncommon. It was the same monstrous story, as old as the river itself, but in this instance it filled him with a sickening sort of horror which gripped him at first even more than the strangeness of the fact that Carmin Fanchet was the other woman. His vision and his soul were reaching out to the *bateau* lying in darkness on the far side of the river, where St. Pierre's wife was alone in her unhappiness.

His first impulse was to fling himself in the river and race to her—his second, to go back to St. Pierre, even in his nakedness, and call him forth to a reckoning. In his profession of man-hunting he had never had the misfortune to kill, but he could kill St. Pierre—now. His fingers dug into the slippery wood of the log under him, his blood ran hot, and in his eyes blazed the fury of an animal as he stared into the wall of gloom between him and Marie-Anne Boulain.

How much did she know? That was the first question which pounded in his brain. He suddenly recalled his reference to the fight, his apology to Marie-Anne that it should happen so near to her presence, and he saw again the queer little twist of her mouth as she let slip the hint that she was not the only one of her sex who would know of tomorrow's fight. He had not noticed the significance of it then. But now it struck home. Marie-Anne was surely aware of Carmin Fanchet's presence on the raft.

But did she know more than that? Did she know the truth, or was her heart filled only with suspicion and fear, aggravated by St. Pierre's neglect and his too-apparent haste to return to the raft that night? Again David's mind flashed back, recalling her defence of Carmin Fanchet when he had first told her his story of the woman whose brother he had brought to the hangman's justice. There could be but one conclusion. Marie-Anne knew Carmin Fanchet, and she also knew she was on the raft with St. Pierre.

As cooler judgment returned to him, Carrigan refused to concede more than that. For any one of a dozen reasons Carmin Fanchet might be on the raft going down the river, and it was also quite within reason that Marie-Anne might have some apprehension of a woman as beautiful as Carmin, and possibly intuition had begun to impinge upon her a disturbing fear of a something that might happen. But until tonight he was confident she had fought against this suspicion, and had overridden it, even though she knew a woman more beautiful than herself was slowly drifting down the stream with her husband. She had betrayed no anxiety to him in the days that had passed; she had waited eagerly for St. Pierre; like a bird she had gone to him when at last he came, and he had seen her crushed close in St. Pierre's arms in their meeting. It was this night, with its gloom and its storm, that had made the shadowings of her unrest a torturing reality. For St. Pierre had brought her back to the *bateau* and had played a pitiably weak part in concealing his desire to return to the raft.

So he told himself Marie-Anne did not know the truth, not as he had seen it through the window of St. Pierre's cabin. She had been hurt, for he had seen the sting of it, and in that same instant he had seen her soul rise up and triumph. He saw again the sudden fire that came into her eyes when St. Pierre urged the necessity of his haste, he saw her slim body grow tense, her red lips curve in a flash of pride and disdain. And as Carrigan thought of her in that way his muscles grew tighter, and he cursed St. Pierre. Marie-Anne might be hurt, she might guess that her husband's eyes and thoughts were too frequently upon another's face—but in the glory of her womanhood it was impossible for her to conceive of a crime such as he had witnessed through the cabin window. Of that he was sure.

And then, suddenly, like a blinding sheet of lightning out of a dark sky, came back to him all that St. Pierre had said about Marie-Anne. He had pitied St. Pierre then; he had pitied this great cool-eyed giant of a man who was fighting gloriously, he had thought, in the face of a situation that would have excited most men. Frankly St. Pierre had told him Marie-Anne cared more for him than she should. With equal frankness he had revealed his wife's confessions to him, that she knew of his love for her, of his kiss upon her hair.

In the blackness Carrigan's face burned hot. If he had in him the desire to kill St. Pierre now, might not St. Pierre have had an equally just desire to kill him? For he had known, even as he kissed her hair, and as his arms held her close to his breast in crossing the creek, that she was the wife of St. Pierre. And Marie-Anne—

His muscles relaxed. Slowly he lowered himself into the cool wash of the river, and struck out toward the *bateau*. He did not breast the current with the same fierce determination with which he had crossed through the storm to the raft, but drifted with it and reached the opposite shore a quarter of a mile below the *bateau*. Here he waited for a time, while the thickness of the clouds broke, and a gray light came through them, revealing dimly the narrow path of pebbly wash along the shore. Silently, a stark naked shadow in the night, he came back to the *bateau* and crawled through his window.

He lighted a lamp, and turned it very low, and in the dim glow of it rubbed his muscles until they burned. He was fit for tomorrow, and the knowledge of that fitness filled him with a savage elation. A good-humoured love of sport had induced him to fling his first half-bantering challenge into the face of Concombre Bateese, but that sentiment was gone. The approaching fight was no longer an incident, a foolish error into which he had unwittingly plunged himself. In this hour it was the biggest physical thing that had ever loomed up in his life, and he yearned for the dawn with the eagerness of a beast that waits for the kill which comes with the break of day. But it was not the half-breed's face he saw under the hammering of his blows. He could not hate the half-breed. He could not even dislike him now. He forced himself to bed, and later he slept. In the dream that came to him it was not Bateese who faced him in battle, but St. Pierre Boulain.

He awoke with that dream a thing of fire in his brain. The sun was not yet up, but the flush of it was painting the east, and he dressed quietly and carefully, listening for some sound of awakening beyond the bulkhead. If Marie-Anne was awake, she was very still. There was noise ashore. Across the river he could hear the singing of men, and through his window saw the white smoke of early fires rising above the tree-tops. It was the Indian who unlocked the door and brought in his breakfast, and it was the Indian who returned for the dishes half an hour later.

After that Carrigan waited, tense with the desire for action to begin. He sensed no premonition of evil about to befall him. Every nerve and sinew in his body was alive for the combat. He thrilled with an overwhelming confidence, a conviction of his ability to win, an almost dangerous, self-conviction of approaching triumph in spite of the odds in weight and brute strength which were pitted against him. A dozen times he listened at the bulkhead between him and Marie-Anne, and still he heard no movement on the other side.

It was eight o'clock when one of the *bateau* men appeared at the door and asked if he was ready. Quickly David joined him. He forgot his taunts to Concombre Bateese, forgot the softly padded gloves in his pack with which he had promised to pommel the half-breed into oblivion. He was thinking only of naked fists.

Into a canoe he followed the *bateau* man, who turned his craft swiftly in the direction of the opposite shore. And as they went, David was sure he caught the slight movement of a curtain at the little window of Marie-Anne's forward cabin. He smiled back and raised his hand, and at that the curtain was drawn back entirely, and he knew that St. Pierre's wife was watching him as he went to the fight.

The raft was deserted, but a little below it, on a wide strip of beach made hard and smooth by flood water, had gathered a crowd of men. It seemed odd to David they should remain so quiet, when he knew the natural instinct of the riverman was to voice his emotion at the top of his lungs. He spoke of this to the *bateau* man, who shrugged his shoulders and grinned.

"Eet ees ze command of St. Pierre," he explained. "St. Pierre say no man make beeg noise at—what you call heem—funeral? An' theese goin' to be wan gran' fun-e-RAL, *m'sieu!*"

"I see," David nodded. He did not grin back at the other's humour.

He was looking at the crowd. A giant figure had appeared out of

141

the centre of it and was coming slowly down to the river. It was St. Pierre. Scarcely had the prow of the canoe touched shore when David leaped out and hurried to meet him. Behind St. Pierre came Bateese, the half-breed. He was stripped to the waist and naked from the knees down. His gorilla-like arms hung huge and loose at his sides, and the muscles of his hulking body stood out like carven mahogany in the glisten of the morning sun. He was like a grizzly, a human beast of monstrous power, something to look at, to back away from, to fear.

Yet, David scarcely noticed him. He met St. Pierre, faced him, and stopped—and he had gone swiftly to this meeting, so that the chief of the Boulains was within earshot of all his men.

St. Pierre was smiling. He held out his hand as he had held it out once before in the *bateau* cabin, and his big voice boomed out a greeting.

Carrigan did not answer, nor did he look at the extended hand. For an instant the eyes of the two men met, and then, swift as lightning, Carrigan's arm shot out, and with the flat of his hand he struck St. Pierre a terrific blow squarely on the cheek. The sound of the blow was like the smash of a paddle on smooth water. Not a riverman but heard it, and as St. Pierre staggered back, flung almost from his feet by its force, a subdued cry of amazement broke from the waiting men. Concombre Bateese stood like one stupefied. And then, in another flash, St. Pierre had caught himself and whirled like a wild beast. Every muscle in his body was drawn for a gigantic, overwhelming leap; his eyes blazed; the fury of a beast was in his face.

Before all his people he had suffered the deadliest insult that could be offered a man of the Three River Country—a blow struck with the flat of another's hand. Anything else one might forgive, but not that. Such a blow, if not avenged, was a brand that passed down into the second and third generations, and even children would call out "Yellow-Back—Yellow-Back," to the one who was coward enough to receive it without resentment. A rumbling growl rose in the throat of Concombre Bateese in that moment when it seemed as though St. Pierre Boulain was about to kill the man who had struck him. He saw the promise of his own fight gone in a flash. For no man in all the northland could now fight David Carrigan ahead of St. Pierre.

David waited, prepared to meet the rush of a madman. And then, for a second time, he saw a mighty struggle in the soul of St. Pierre. The giant held himself back. The fury died out of his face, but his great hands remained clenched as he said, for David alone,

"That was a playful blow, m'sieu? It was—a joke?"

"It was for you, St. Pierre," replied Carrigan, "You are a coward-and a skunk. I swam to the raft last night, looked through your window, and saw what happened there. You are not fit for a decent man to fight, yet I will fight you, if you are not too great a coward—and dare to let our wagers stand as they were made."

St. Pierre's eyes widened, and for a breath or two he stared at Carrigan, as if looking into him and not at him. His big hands relaxed, and slowly the panther-like readiness went out of his body. Those who looked beheld the transformation in amazement, for of all who waited only St. Pierre and the half-breed had heard Carrigan's words, though they had seen and heard the blow of insult.

"You swam to the raft," repeated St. Pierre in a low voice, as if doubting what he had heard. "You looked through the window—and saw—"

David nodded. He could not cover the sneering poison in his voice, his contempt for the man who stood before him.

"Yes, I looked through the window. And I saw you, and the lowest woman on the Three Rivers—the sister of a man I helped to hang, I—"

"STOP!"

St. Pierre's voice broke out of him like the sudden crash of thunder. He came a step nearer, his face livid, his eyes shooting flame. With a mighty effort he controlled himself again. And then, as if he saw something which David could not see, he tried to smile, and in that same instant David caught a grin cutting a great slash across the face of Concombre Bateese. The change that came over St. Pierre now was swift as sunlight coming out from shadowing cloud. A rumble grew in his great chest. It broke in a low note of laughter from his lips, and he faced the *bateau* across the river.

"M'sieu, you are sorry for HER. Is that it? You would fight—"

"For the cleanest, finest little girl who ever lived—your wife!"

"It is funny," said St. Pierre, as if speaking to himself, and still looking at the *bateau*. "Yes, it is very funny, *ma belle* Marie-Anne! He has told you he loves you, and he has kissed your hair and held you in his arms—yet he wants to fight me because he thinks I am steeped in sin, and to make me fight in place of Bateese he has called my Carmin a low woman! So what else can I do? I must fight. I must whip him until he cannot walk. And then I will send him back for you to nurse, *cherie*, and for that blessing I think he will willingly take my punishment! Is it not so, *m'sieu?*"

He was smiling and no longer excited when he turned to David.

"*M'sieu*, I will fight you. And the wagers shall stand. And in this hour let us be honest, like men, and make confession. You love *ma belle* Jeanne—Marie-Anne? Is it not so? And I—I love my Carmin, whose brother you hanged, as I love no other woman in the world. Now, if you will have it so, let us fight!"

He began stripping off his shirt, and with a bellow in his throat Concombre Bateese slouched away like a beaten gorilla to explain to St. Pierre's people the change in the plan of battle. And as that news spread like fire in the fir-tops, there came but a single cry in response—shrill and terrible—and that was from the throat of Andre, the Broken Man.

21

As Carrigan stripped off his shirt, he knew that at least in one way he had met more than his match in St. Pierre Boulain. In the splendid service of which he was a part he had known many men of iron and steel, men whose nerve and coolness not even death could very greatly disturb. Yet St. Pierre, he conceded, was their master—and his own. For a flash he had transformed the chief of the Boulains into a volcano which had threatened to break in savage fury, yet neither the crash nor destruction had come. And now St. Pierre was smiling again, as Carrigan faced him, stripped to the waist. He betrayed no sign of the tempest of passion that had swept him a few minutes before. His cool, steely eyes had in them a look that was positively friendly, as Concombre Bateese marked in the hard sand the line of the circle within which no man might come. And as he did this and St. Pierre's people crowded close about it, St. Pierre himself spoke in a low voice to David.

"*M'sieu*, it seems a shame that we should fight. I like you. I have always loved a man who would fight to protect a woman, and I shall be careful not to hurt you more than is necessary to make you see reason—and to win the wagers. So you need not be afraid of my killing you, as Bateese might have done. And I promise not to destroy your beauty, for the sake of—the lady in the *bateau*. My Carmin, if she knew you spied through her window last night, would say kill you with as little loss of time as possible, for as regards you her sweet disposition was spoiled when you hung her brother, *m'sieu*. Yet to me she is an angel!"

Contempt for the man who spoke of his wife and the infamous Carmin Fanchet in the same breath drew a sneer to Carrigan's lips. He nodded toward the waiting circle of men.

"They are ready for the show, St. Pierre. You talk big. Now let us see if you can fight."

For another moment St. Pierre hesitated. "I am so sorry, m'sieu—

"Are you ready, St. Pierre?"

"It is not fair, and she will never forgive me. You are no match for me. I am half again as heavy."

"And as big a coward as you are a scoundrel, St. Pierre."

"It is like a man fighting a boy."

"Yet it is less dishonourable than betraying the woman who is your wife for another who should have been hanged along with her brother, St. Pierre."

Boulain's face darkened. He drew back half a dozen steps and cried out a word to Bateese. Instantly the circle of waiting men grew tense as the half-breed jerked the big handkerchief from his head and held it out at arm's length. Yet, with that eagerness for the fight there was something else which Carrigan was swift to sense. The attitude of the watchers was not one of uncertainty or of very great expectation, in spite of the staring faces and the muscular tightening of the line. He knew what was passing in their minds and in the low whispers from lip to lip. They were pitying him.

Now that he stood stripped, with only a few paces between him and the giant figure of St. Pierre, the unfairness of the fight struck home even to Concombre Bateese. Only Carrigan himself knew how like tempered steel the sinews of his body were built. But to the eye, in size alone, he stood like a boy before St. Pierre. And St. Pierre's people, their voices stilled by the deadly inequality of it, were waiting for a slaughter and not a fight.

A smile came to Carrigan's lips as he saw Bateese hesitating to drop the handkerchief, and with the swiftness of the trained fighter he made his first plan for the battle before the cloth fell from the half-breed's fingers, As the handkerchief fluttered to the ground, he faced St. Pierre, the smile gone.

"Never smile when you fight," the greatest of all masters of the ring had told him. "Never show anger, Don't betray any emotion at all if you can help it."

Carrigan wondered what the old ring-master would say could he see him now, backing away slowly from St. Pierre as the giant advanced upon him, for he knew his face was betraying to St. Pierre and his people the deadliest of all sins—anxiety and indecision. Very closely, yet with eyes that seemed to shift uneasily, he watched the effect of his trick on Boulain. Twice the huge riverman followed him about the ring of sand, and the steely glitter in his eyes changed to laughter, and the tense faces of the men about them relaxed. A subdued ripple of merriment rose where there had been silence. A third time David manoeuvred his retreat, and his eyes shot furtively to Concombre Bateese and the men at his back. They were grinning.

The half-breed's mouth was wide open, and his grotesque body hung limp and astonished. This was not a fight! It was a comedy— like a rooster following a sparrow around a barnyard! And then a still funnier thing happened, for David began to trot in a circle around St. Pierre, dodging and feinting, and keeping always at a safe distance. A howl of laughter came from Bateese and broke in a roar from the men. St. Pierre stopped in his tracks, a grin on his face, his big arms and shoulders limp and unprepared as Carrigan dodged in close and out again. And then—

A howl broke in the middle of the half-breed's throat. Where there had been laughter, there came a sudden shutting off of sound, a great gasp, as if made by choking men. Swifter than anything they had ever seen in human action Carrigan had leaped in. They saw him strike. They heard the blow. They saw St. Pierre's great head rock back, as if struck from his shoulders by a club, and they saw and heard another blow, and a third—like so many flashes of lightning—and St. Pierre went down as if shot. The man they had laughed at was no longer like a hopping sparrow. He was waiting, bent a little forward, every muscle in his body ready for action. They watched for him to leap upon his fallen enemy, kicking and gouging and choking in the riverman way.

But David waited, and St. Pierre staggered to his feet. His mouth was bleeding and choked with sand, and a great lump was beginning to swell over his eye. A deadly fire blazed in his face, as he rushed like a mad bull at the insignificant opponent who had tricked and humiliated him. This time Carrigan did not retreat, but held his ground, and a yell of joy went up from Bateese as the mighty bulk of the giant descended upon his victim. It was an avalanche of brute-force, crushing in its destructiveness, and Carrigan seemed to reach for it as it came upon him. Then his head went down, swifter than a diving grebe, and as St. Pierre's arm swung like an oaken beam over his shoulder, his own shot in straight for the pit of the other's stomach.

It was a bull's-eye blow with the force of a pile-driver behind it, and the groan that forced its way out of St. Pierre's vitals was heard by every ear in the cordon of watchers. His weight stopped, his arms opened, and through that opening Carrigan's fist went a second time to the other's jaw, and a second time the great St. Pierre Boulain sprawled out upon the sand. And there he lay, and made no effort to rise.

Concombre Bateese, with his great mouth agape, stood for an instant as if the blow had stunned him in place of his master. Then, suddenly he came to life, and leaped to David's side.

"*Diable! Tonnerre!* You have not fight Concombre Bateese yet!" he howled. "*Non*, you have cheat me, you have lie, you have run lak cat from Concombre Bateese, ze stronges' man on all T'ree River! You are wan' gran' coward, wan poltroon, an' you 'fraid to fight ME, who ees greates' fightin' man in all dees countree! *Sapristi!* Why you no hit Concombre Bateese, *m'sieu?* Why you no hit ze greates' fightin' man w'at ees—"

David did not hear the rest. The opportunity was too tempting. He swung, and with a huge grunt the gorilla-like body of Concombre Bateese rolled over that of the chief of the Boulains. This time Carrigan did not wait, but followed up so closely that the half-breed had scarcely gathered the crook out of his knees when another blow on the jaw sent him into the sand again. Three times he tried the experiment of regaining his feet, and three times he was knocked down.

After the last blow he raised himself groggily to a sitting posture, and there he remained, blinking like a stunned pig, with his big hands clutching in the sand. He stared up unseeingly at Carrigan, who waited over him, and then stupidly at the transfixed cordon of men, whose eyes were bulging and who were holding their breath in the astonishment of this miracle which had descended upon them. They heard Bateese muttering something incoherent as his head wobbled, and St. Pierre himself seemed to hear it, for he stirred and raised himself slowly, until he also was sitting in the sand, staring at Bateese.

Carrigan picked up his shirt, and the riverman who had brought him from the *bateau* returned with him to the canoe. There was no demonstration behind them. To David himself the whole thing had been an amazing surprise, and he was not at all reluctant to leave as quickly as his dignity would permit, before some other of St. Pierre's people offered to put a further test upon his prowess. He wanted to laugh. He wanted to thank God at the top of his voice for the absurd run of luck that had made his triumph not only easy but utterly complete. He had expected to win, but he had also expected a terrific fight before the last blow was struck.

And there had been no fight! He was returning to the *bateau* without a scratch, his hair scarcely ruffled, and he had defeated not only St. Pierre, but the giant half-breed as well! It was inconceivable—and yet it had happened; a veritable burlesque, an opera-*bouffe* affair that might turn quickly into a tragedy if either St. Pierre or Concombre Bateese guessed the truth of it. For in that event he might have to face them again, with the god of luck playing fairly, and he was honest enough with himself to confess that the idea no longer held either thrill or desire for him. Now that he had seen both St. Pierre and Bateese stripped for battle, he had no further appetite for fistic discussion with them. After all, there was a merit in caution, and he had several lucky stars to bless just at the present moment!

Inwardly he was a bit suspicious of the ultimate ending of the affair. St. Pierre had almost no cause for complaint, for it was his own carelessness, coupled with his opponent's luck, that had been his undoing—and luck and carelessness are legitimate factors of every fight, Carrigan told himself. But with Bateese it was different. He had held up his big jaw, uncovered and tempting, entreating someone to hit him, and Carrigan had yielded to that temptation. The blow would have stunned an ox. Three others like it had left the huge half-breed sitting weak-mindedly in the sand, and no one of those three blows were exactly according to the rules of the game. They had been mightily efficacious, but the half-breed might demand a rehearing when he came fully into his senses.

Not until they were half-way to the *bateau* did Carrigan dare to glance back over his shoulder at the man who was paddling, to see what effect the fistic travesty had left on him. He was a big-mouthed, clear-eyed, powerfully-muscled fellow, and he was grinning from ear to ear.

"Well, what did you think of it, comrade?"

The other gave his shoulders a joyous shrug.

"*Mon Dieu*! Have you heard of wan *garcon* named Joe Clamart, m'sieu? Non? Well, I am Joe Clamart what was once great fightin' man. Bateese hav' whip' me five times, *m'sieu*—so I say it was wan gr-r-r-a-n' fight! Many years ago I have seen ze same t'ing in Montreal—ze *boxeur de profession*. *Oui*, an' Rene Babin pays me fifteen prime martin against which I put up three scrubby red fox that you would win. They were bad, or I would not have gambled, *m'sieu*. It ees fonny!"

"Yes, it is funny," agreed David. "I think it is a bit too funny. It is a pity they did not stand up on their legs a little longer!" Suddenly an inspiration hit him. "Joe, what do you say—shall you and I return and put up a REAL fight for them?"

Like a sprung trap Joe Clamart's grinning mouth dosed. "*Non, non, non*," he grunted. "Dere has been plenty fight, an' Joe Clamart mus' save hees face tor Antoinette Roland, who hate ze sign of fight lak she hate ze devil, *m'sieu! Non, non!*"

His paddle dug deeper into the water, and David's heart felt lighter. If Joe was an average barometer, and he was a husky and fearless-looking chap, it was probable that neither St. Pierre nor Bateese would demand another chance at him, and St. Pierre would pay his wager.

He could see no one aboard the *bateau* when he climbed from the canoe. Looking back, he saw that two other canoes had started from the opposite shore. Then he went to his cabin door, opened it, and entered, Scarcely had the door closed behind him when he stopped, staring toward the window that opened on the river.

Standing full in the morning glow of it was Marie-Anne Boulain. She was facing him. Her cheeks were flushed. Her red lips were parted. Her eyes were aglow with a fire which she made no effort to hide from him. In her hand she still held the binoculars he had left on the cabin table. He guessed the truth. Through the glasses she had watched the whole miserable fiasco.

He felt creeping over him a sickening shame, and his eyes fell slowly from her to the table. What he saw there caught his breath in the middle. It was the entire surgical outfit of Nepapinas, the old Indian doctor. And there were basins of water, and white strips of linen ready for use, and a pile of medicated cotton, and all sorts of odds and ends that one might apply to ease the agonies of a dying man, And beyond the table, huddled in so small a heap that he was almost hidden by it, was Nepapinas himself, disappointment writ in his mummy-like face as his beady eyes rested on David.

The evidence could not be mistaken. They had expected him to come back more nearly dead than alive, and St. Pierre's wife had prepared for the thing she had thought inevitable. Even his bed was nicely turned down, its fresh white sheets inviting an occupant!

And David, looking at St. Pierre's wife again, felt his heart beating hard in his breast at the look which was in her eyes. It was not the scintillation of laughter, and the flame in her cheeks was not embarrassment. She was not amused. The ludicrousness of her mislaid plans had not struck her as they had struck him. She had placed the binoculars on the table, and slowly she came to him. Her hands reached out, and her fingers rested like the touch of velvet on his arms.

"It was splendid!" she said softly, "It was splendid!"

She was very near, her breast almost touching him, her hands creeping up until the tips of her fingers rested on his shoulders, her scarlet mouth so close he could feel the soft breath of it in his face.

"It was splendid!" she whispered again.

And then, suddenly, she rose up on her tiptoes and kissed him. So swiftly was it done that she was gone before he sensed that wild touch of her lips against his own. Like a swallow she was at the door, and the door opened and closed behind her, and for a moment he heard the quick running of her feet. Then he looked at the old Indian, and the Indian, too, was staring at the door through which St. Pierre's wife had flown.

22

For many seconds that seemed like minutes David stood where she had left him, while Nepapinas rose gruntingly to his feet, and gathered up his belongings, and hobbled sullenly to the *bateau* door and out. He was scarcely conscious of the Indian's movement, for his soul was aflame with a red-hot fire. Deliberately—with that ravishing glory of something in her eyes—St. Pierre's wife had kissed him!

On her tiptoes, her cheeks like crimson flowers, she had given her still redder lips to him! And his own lips burned, and his heart pounded hard, and he stared for a time like one struck dumb at the spot where she had stood by the window. Then suddenly, he turned to the door and flung it wide open, and on his lips was the reckless cry of Marie-Anne's name. But St. Pierre's wife was gone, and Nepapinas was gone, and at the tail of the big sweep sat only Joe Clamart, guarding watchfully.

The two canoes were drawing near, and in one of them were two men, and in the other three, and David knew that—like Joe Clamart-they were watchers set over him by St. Pierre. Then a fourth canoe left the far shore, and when it had reached mid-stream, he recognized the figure in the stern as that of Andre, the Broken Man. The other, he thought, must be St. Pierre.

He went back into the cabin and stood where Marie-Anne had stood—at the window. Nepapinas had not taken away the basins of water, and the bandages were still there, and the pile of medicated cotton, and the suspiciously made-up bed. After all, he was losing something by not occupying the bed—and yet if St. Pierre or Bateese had messed him up badly, and a couple of fellows had lugged him in between them, it was probable that Marie-Anne would not have kissed him. And that kiss of St. Pierre's wife would remain with him until the day he died!

He was thinking of it, the swift, warm thrill of her velvety lips, red as strawberries and twice as sweet, when the door opened and St. Pierre came in. The sight of him, in this richest moment of his life, gave David no sense of humiliation or shame. Between him and St. Pierre rose swiftly what he had seen last night—Carmin Fanchet in all the lure of her dishevelled beauty, crushed close in the arms of the man whose wife only a moment before had pressed her lips close to his; and as the eyes of the two met, there came over him a desire to tell the other what had happened, that he might see him writhe with the sting of the two-edged thing with which he was playing. Then he saw that even that would not hurt St. Pierre, for the chief of the Boulains, standing there with the big lump over his eye, had caught sight of the things on the table and the nicely turned down bed, and his one good eye lit up with sudden laughter, and his white teeth flashed in an understanding smile.

"*Tonnerre*, I said she would nurse you with gentle hands," he rumbled. "See what you have missed, M'sieu Carrigan!"

"I received something which I shall remember longer than a fine nursing," retorted David. "And yet right now I have a greater interest in knowing what you think of the fight, St. Pierre—and if you have come to pay your wager."

St. Pierre was chuckling mysteriously in his throat. "It was splendid—splendid," he said, repeating Marie-Anne's words. "And Joe Clamart says she ran out, blushing like a red rose in August, and that she said no word, but flew like a bird into the white-birch ashore!"

"She was dismayed because I beat you, St. Pierre."

"*Non, non*—she was like a lark filled with joy."

Suddenly his eyes rested on the binoculars.

David nodded. "Yes, she saw it all through the glasses."

St. Pierre seated himself at the table and heaved out a groan as he took one of the bandage strips between his fingers. "She saw my disgrace. And she didn't wait to bandage ME up, did she?"

"Perhaps she thought Carmin Fanchet would do that, St. Pierre."

"And I am ashamed to go to Carmin—with this great lump over my eye, *m'sieu*. And on top of that disgrace—you insist that I pay the wager?"

"I do."

St. Pierre's face hardened.

"*Oui*, I am to pay. I am to tell you all I know about that *bête noir*-Black Roger Audemard. Is it not so?"

153

"That is the wager."

"But after I have told you—what then? Do you recall that I gave you any other guarantee, M'sieu Carrigan? Did I say I would let you go? Did I promise I would not kill you and sink your body to the bottom of the river? If I did, I cannot remember."

"Are you a beast, St. Pierre—a murderer as well as—"

"Stop! Do not tell me again what you saw through the window, for it has nothing to do with this. I am not a beast, but a man. Had I been a beast, I should have killed you the first day I saw you in this cabin. I am not threatening to kill you, and yet it may be necessary if you insist that I pay the wager. You understand, *m'sieu*. To refuse to pay a wager is a greater crime among my people than the killing of a man, if there is a good reason for the killing. I am helpless. I must pay, if you insist. Before I pay it is fair that I give you warning."

"You mean?"

"I mean nothing, as yet. I cannot say what it will be necessary for me to do, after you have heard what I know about Roger Audemard. I am quite settled on a plan just now, *m'sieu*, but the plan might change at any moment. I am only warning you that it is a great hazard, and that you are playing with a fire of which you know nothing, because it has not burned you yet."

Carrigan seated himself slowly in a chair opposite St. Pierre, with the table between them.

"You are wasting time in attempting to frighten me," he said. "I shall insist on the payment of the wager, St Pierre."

For a moment St. Pierre was clearly troubled. Then his lips tightened, and he smiled grimly over the table at David.

"I am sorry, M'sieu David. I like you. You are a fighting man and no coward, and I should like to travel shoulder to shoulder with you in many things. And such a thing might be, for you do not understand. I tell you it would have been many times better for you had I whipped you out there, and it had been you—and not me—to pay the wager!"

"It is Roger Audemard I am interested in, St. Pierre. Why do you hesitate?"

"I? Hesitate? I am not hesitating, *m'sieu*. I am giving you a chance." He leaned forward, his great arms bent on the table. "And you insist, M'sieu David?"

"Yes, I insist."

Slowly the fingers of St. Pierre's hands closed into knotted fists, and he said in a low voice, "Then I will pay, *m'sieu.* *I* AM ROGER AUDEMARD!"

23

The astounding statement of the man who sat opposite him held David speechless. He had guessed at some mysterious relationship between St. Pierre and the criminal he was after, but not this, and Roger Audemard, with his hands unclenching and a slow humour beginning to play about his mouth, waited coolly for him to recover from his amazement. In those moments, when his heart seemed to have stopped beating, Carrigan was staring at the other, but his mind had shot beyond him—to the woman who was his wife. Marie-Anne AUDEMARD—the wife of Black Roger! He wanted to cry out against the possibility of such a fact, yet he sat like one struck dumb, as the monstrous truth took possession of his brain and a whirlwind of understanding swept upon him. He was thinking quickly, and with a terrific lack of sentiment now.

Opposite him sat Black Roger, the wholesale murderer. Marie-Anne was his wife. Carmin Fanchet, sister of a murderer, was simply one of his kind. And Bateese, the man-gorilla, and the Broken Man, and all the dark-skinned pack about them were of Black Roger's breed and kind. Love for a woman had blinded him to the facts which crowded upon him now. Like a lamb he had fallen among wolves, and he had tried to believe in them. No wonder Bateese and the man he had known as St. Pierre had betrayed such merriment at times!

A fighting coolness possessed him as he spoke to Black Roger.

"I will admit this is a surprise. And yet you have cleared up a number of things very quickly. It proves to me again that comedy is not very far removed from tragedy at times."

"I am glad you see the humour of it, M'sieu David." Black Roger was smiling as pleasantly as his swollen eye would permit. "We must not be too serious when we die. If I were to die a-hanging, I would sing as the rope choked me, just to show the world one need not be unhappy because his life is coming to an end."

"I suppose you understand that ultimately I am going to give you that opportunity," said David.

Almost eagerly Black Roger leaned toward him over the table. "You believe you are going to hang me?"

"I am sure of it."

"And you are willing to wager the point, M'sieu David?"

"It is impossible to gamble with a condemned man."

Black Roger chuckled, rubbing his big hands together until they made a rasping sound, and his one good eye glowed at Carrigan.

"Then I will make a wager with myself, M'sieu David. *Ma foi*, I swear that before the leaves fall from the trees, you will be pleading for the friendship of Black Roger Audemard, and you will be as much in love with Carmin Fanchet as I am! And as for Marie-Anne—"

He thrust back his chair and rose to his feet, the old note of subdued laughter rumbling in his chest. "And because I make this wager with myself, I cannot kill you, M'sieu David—though that might be the best thing to do. I am going to take you to the Chateau Boulain, which is in the forests of the Yellowknife, beyond the Great Slave. Nothing will happen to you if you make no effort to escape. If you do that, you will surely die. And that would hurt me, M'sieu David, because I love you like a brother, and in the end I know you are going to grip the hand of Black Roger Audemard, and get down on your knees to Carmin Fanchet. And as for Marie-Anne—" Again he interrupted himself, and went out of the cabin, laughing. And there was no mistake in the metallic click of the lock outside the door.

For a time David did not move from his seat near the table. He had not let Roger Audemard see how completely the confession had upset his inner balance, but he made no pretence of concealing the thing from himself now. He was in the power of a cut-throat, who in turn had an army of cut-throats at his back, and both Marie-Anne and Carmin Fanchet were a part of this ring. And he was not only a prisoner. It was probable, under the circumstances, that Black Roger would make an end of him when a convenient moment came. It was even more than a probability. It was a grim necessity. To let him live and escape would be fatal to Black Roger.

From back of these convictions, riding over them as if to demoralize any coherence and logic that might go with the evidence he was building up, came question after question, pounding at him one after the other, until his mind became more than ever a whirling chaos of uncertainty. If St. Pierre was Black Roger, why would he confess to that fact simply to pay a wager? What reason could he have for letting him live at all? Why had not Bateese killed him? Why had Marie-Anne nursed him back to life? His mind shot to the white strip of sand in which he had nearly died. That, at least, was convincing. Learning in some way that he was after Black Roger, they had attempted to do away with him there. But if that were so, why was it Bateese and Black Roger's wife and the Indian Nepapinas had risked so much to make him live, when if they had left him where he had fallen he would have died and caused them no trouble?

There was something exasperatingly uncertain and illogical about it all. Was it possible that St. Pierre Boulain was playing a huge joke on him? Even that was inconceivable. For there was Carmin Fanchet, a fitting companion for a man like Black Roger, and there was Marie-Anne, who, if it had been a joke, would not have played her part so well.

Suddenly his mind was filled only with her. Had she been his friend, using all her influence to protect him, because her heart was sick of the environment of which she was a part? His own heart jumped at the thought. It was easy to believe. In Marie-Anne he had faith, and that faith refused to be destroyed, but persisted—even clearer and stronger as he thought again of Carmin Fanchet and Black Roger. In his heart grew the conviction it was sacrilege to believe the kiss she had given him that morning was a lie. It was something else—a spontaneous gladness, a joyous exultation that he had returned unharmed, a thing unplanned in the soul of the woman, leaping from her before she could stop it. Then had come shame, and she had run away from him so swiftly he had not seen her face again after the touch of her lips. If it had been a subterfuge, a lie, she would not have done that.

He rose to his feet and paced restlessly back and forth as he tried to bring together a few tangled bits of the puzzle. He heard voices outside, and very soon felt the movement of the *bateau* under his feet, and through one of the shoreward windows he saw trees and sandy beach slowly drifting away. On that shore, as far as his eyes could travel up and down, he saw no sign of Marie-Anne, but there remained a canoe, and near the canoe stood Black Roger Audemard, and beyond him, huddled like a charred stump in the sand, was Andre, the Broken Man. On the opposite shore the raft was getting under way.

During the next half-hour several things happened which told him there was no longer a sugar-coating to his imprisonment. On each side of the *bateau* two men worked at his windows, and when they had finished, no one of them could be opened more than a few inches. Then came the rattle of the lock at the door, the grating of a key, and somewhat to Carrigan's surprise it was Bateese who came in.

The half-reed bore no facial evidence of the paralyzing blows which had knocked him out a short time before. His jaw, on which they had landed, was as aggressive as ever, yet in his face and his attitude, as he stared curiously at Carrigan, there was no sign of resentment or unfriendliness. Nor did he seem to be ashamed. He merely stared, with the curious and rather puzzled eyes of a small boy gazing at an inexplicable oddity. Carrigan, standing before him, knew what was passing in the other's mind, and the humour of it brought a smile to his lips.

Instantly Concombre's face split into a wide grin. "*Mon dieu*, w'at if you was on'y brother to Concombre Bateese, *m'sieu*. T'ink of zat—you—me—*frere d'armes! ventre saint gris*, but we mak' all fightin' men in nort' countree run lak rabbits ahead of ze fox! *Oui*, we mak' gr-r-r-eat pair, *m'sieu*—you, w'at knock down Bateese—an' Bateese, w'at keel polar bear wit hees naked hands, w'at pull down trees, w'at chew flint w'en hees tobacco gone."

His voice had risen, and suddenly there came a laugh from outside the door, and Concombre cut himself short and his mouth closed with a snap. It was Joe Clamart who had laughed.

"I w'ip heem five time, an' now I w'ip heem seex!" hissed Bateese in an undertone. "Two time each year I w'ip zat gargon Joe Clamart so he understan' w'at good fightin' man ees. An' you will w'ip heem, eh, *m'sieu*? *Oui*? An' I will breeng odder good fightin' mans for you to w'ip—all w'at Concombre Bateese has w'ipped—ten, dozen, forty—an' you w'ip se gran' bunch, m'sieu. Eh, shall we mak' ze bargain?"

"You are planning a pleasant time for me, Bateese," said Carrigan, "but I am afraid it will be impossible. You see, this captain of yours, Black Roger Audemard—"

"W'at!" Bateese jumped as if stung. "W'at you say, m'sieu?"

"I said that Roger Audemard, Black Roger, the man I thought was St. Pierre Boulain—"

Carrigan said no more. What he had started to say was unimportant compared with the effect of Roger Audernard's name on Concombre Bateese. A deadly light glittered in the half-breed's eyes, and for the first time David realized that in the grotesque head of the riverman was a brain quick to grip at the significance of things. The fact was evident that Black Roger had not confided in Bateese as to the price of the wager and the confession of his identity, and for a moment after the repetition of Audemard's name came from David's lips the half-breed stood as if something had stunned him. Then slowly, as if forcing the words in the face of a terrific desire that had transformed his body into a hulk of quivering steel, he said:

"*M'sieu*—I come with message—from St. Pierre. You see windows—closed. Outside door—she locked. On bot' sides de *bateau*, all de time, we watch. You try get away, an' we keel you. Zat ees all. We shoot. We five mans on ze *bateau*, all ze day, *toute la nuit*. You unnerstan'?"

He turned sullenly, waiting for no reply, and the door opened and closed after him—and again came the snap of the lock outside.

Steadily the *bateau* swept down the big river that day. There was no let-up in the steady creaking of the long sweep. Even in the swifter currents David could hear the working of it, and he knew he had seen the last of the more slowly moving raft. Near one of the partly open windows he heard two men talking just before the *bateau* shot into the Brule Point rapids. They were strange voices. He learned that Audemard's huge raft was made up of thirty-five cribs, seven abreast, and that nine times between the Point Brule and the Yellowknife the raft would be split up, so that each crib could be run through dangerous rapids by itself.

That would be a big job, David assured himself. It would be slow work as well as hazardous, and as his own life was in no immediate jeopardy, he would have ample time in which to formulate some plan of action for himself. At the present moment, it seemed, the one thing for him to do was to wait—and behave himself, according to the half-breed's instructions. There was, when he came to think about it, a saving element of humour about it all. He had always wanted to make a trip down the Three Rivers in a *bateau*. And now—he was making it!

At noon a guard brought in his dinner. He could not recall that he had ever seen this man before, a tall, lithe fellow built to run like a hound, and who wore a murderous-looking knife at his belt. As the door opened, David caught a glimpse of two others. They were business-like looking individuals, with muscles built for work or fight; one sitting cross-legged on the *bateau* deck with a rifle over his knees, and the other standing with a rifle in his hand.

The man who brought his dinner wasted no time or words. He merely nodded, murmured a curt *bonjour*, and went out. And Carrigan, as he began to eat, did not have to tell himself twice that Audemard had been particular in his selection of the *bateau's* crew, and that the eyes of the men he had seen could be as keen as a hawk's when levelled over the tip of a rifle barrel. They meant business, and he felt no desire to smile in the face of them, as he had smiled at Concombre Bateese.

It was another man, and a stranger, who brought in his supper. And for two hours after that, until the sun went down and gloom began to fall, the *bateau* sped down the river. It had made forty miles that day, he figured.

It was still light when the *bateau* was run ashore and tied up, but tonight there were no singing voices or wild laughter of men whose hours of play-time and rest had come. To Carrigan, looking through his window, there was an oppressive menace about it all. The shadowy figures ashore were more like a death-watch than a guard, and to dispel the gloom of it he lighted two of the lamps in the cabin, whistled, drummed a simple chord he knew on the piano, and finally settled down to smoking his pipe. He would have welcomed the company of Bateese, or Joe Clamart, or one of the guards, and as his loneliness grew upon him there was something of companionship even in the subdued voices he heard occasionally outside. He tried to read, but the printed words jumbled themselves and meant nothing.

It was ten o'clock, and clouds had darkened the night, when through his open windows he heard a shout coming from the river. Twice it came before it was answered from the *bateau*, and the second time Carrigan recognized it as the voice of Roger Audemard. A brief interval passed between that and the scraping of a canoe alongside, and then there was a low conversation in which even Audemard's great voice was subdued, and after that the grating of a key in the lock, and the opening of the door, and Black Roger came in, bearing an Indian reed basket under his arm. Carrigan did not rise to meet him.

It was not like the coming of the old St. Pierre, and on Black Roger's lips there was no twist of a smile, nor in his eyes the flash of good-natured greeting. His face was darkly stern, as if he had travelled far and hard on an unpleasant mission, but in it there was no shadow of menace, as there had been in that of Concombre Bateese. It was rather the face of a tired man, and yet David knew what he saw was not physical exhaustion. Black Roger guessed something of his thought, and his mouth for an instant repressed a smile.

"Yes, I have been having a rough time," he nodded, "This is for

161

you!"

He placed the basket on the table. It held half a bushel, and was filled to the curve of the handle. What lay in it was hidden under a cloth securely tied about it.

"And you are responsible," he added, stretching himself in a chair with a gesture of weariness. "I should kill you, Carrigan. And instead of that I bring you good things to eat! Half the day she has been fussing with the things in the basket, and then insisted that I bring them to you. And I have brought them simply to tell you another thing. I am sorry for her. I think, M'sieu Carrigan, you will find as many tears in the basket as anything else, for her heart is crushed and sick because of the humiliation she brought upon herself this morning."

He was twisting his big, rough hands, and David's own heart went sick as he saw the furrowed lines that had deepened in the other's face. Black Roger did not look at him as he went on.

"Of course, she told me. She tells me everything. And if she knew I was telling you this, I think she would kill herself. But I want you to understand. She is not what you might think she is. That kiss came from the lips of the best woman God ever made, M'sieu Carrigan!"

David, with the blood in him running like fire, heard himself answering, "I know it. She was excited, glad you had not stained your hands with my life—"

This time Audemard smiled, but it was the smile of a man ten years older than he had appeared yesterday. "Don't try to answer, *m'sieu*. I only want you to know she is as pure as the stars. It was unfortunate, but to follow the impulse of one's heart cannot be a sin. Everything has been unfortunate since you came. But I blame no one, except—"

"Carmin Fanchet?"

Audemard nodded. "Yes. I have sent her away. Marie-Anne is in the cabin on the raft now. But even Carmin I cannot blame very greatly, *m'sieu*, for it is impossible to hold anything against one you love. Tell me if I am right? You must know. You love my Marie-Anne. Do you hold anything against her?"

"It is unfair," protested David. "She is your wife, Audemard, is it possible you don't love her?"

"Yes, I love her."

"And Carmin Fanchet?"

"I love her, too. They are so different. Yet I love them both. Is it not possible for a big heart like mine to do that, *m'sieu*?"

With almost a snort David rose to his feet and stared through one of the windows into the darkness of the river. "Black Roger," he said without turning his head, "the evidence at Headquarters condemns you as one of the blackest-hearted murderers that ever lived. But that crime, to me, is less atrocious than the one you are committing against your own wife. I am not ashamed to confess I love her, because to deny it would be a lie. I love her so much that I would sacrifice myself—soul and body—if that sacrifice could give you back to her, clean and undefiled and with your hand unstained by the crime for which you must hang!"

He did not hear Roger Audemard as he rose from his chair. For a moment the riverman stared at the back of David's head, and in that moment he was fighting to keep back what wanted to come from his lips in words. He turned before David faced him again, and did not pause until he stood at the cabin door with his hand at the latch. There he was partly in shadow.

"I shall not see you again until you reach the Yellowknife," he said. "Not until then will you know—or will I know—what is going to happen. I think you will understand strange things then, but that is for the hour to tell. Bateese has explained to you that you must not make an effort to escape. You would regret it, and so would I. If you have red blood in you, *m'sieu*—if you would understand all that you cannot understand now—wait as patiently as you can. *Bonne nuit,* M'sieu Carrigan!"

"Goodnight!" nodded David.

In the pale shadows he thought a mysterious light of gladness illumined Black Roger's face before the door opened and closed, leaving him alone again.

24

With the going of Black Roger also went the oppressive loneliness which had gripped Carrigan, and as he stood listening to the low voices outside, the undeniable truth came to him that he did not hate this man as he wanted to hate him. He was a murderer, and a scoundrel in another way, but he felt irresistibly the impulse to like him and to feel sorry for him. He made an effort to shake off the feeling, but a small voice which he could not quiet persisted in telling him that more than one good man had committed what the law called murder, and that perhaps he didn't fully understand what he had seen through the cabin window on the raft. And yet, when unstirred by this impulse, he knew the evidence was damning.

But his loneliness was gone. With Audemard's visit had come an unexpected thrill, the revival of an almost feverish anticipation, the promise of impending things that stirred his blood as he thought of them. "You will understand strange things then," Roger Audemard had said, and something in his voice had been like a key unlocking mysterious doors for the first time. And then, "Wait, as patiently as you can!" Out of the basket on the table seemed to come to him a whispering echo of that same word—wait! He laid his hands upon it, and a pulse of life came with the imagined whispering. It was from Marie-Anne. It seemed as though the warmth of her hands were still there, and as he removed the cloth the sweet breath of her came to him. And then, in the next instant, he was trying to laugh at himself and trying equally hard to call himself a fool, for it was the breath of newly-baked things which her fingers had made.

Yet never had he felt the warmth of her presence more strangely in his heart. He did not try to explain to himself why Roger Audemard's visit had broken down things which had seemed insurmountable an hour ago. Analysis was impossible, because he knew the transformation within himself was without a shred of reason. But it had come, and with it his imprisonment took on another form. Where before there had been thought of escape and a scheming to jail Black Roger, there filled him now an intense desire to reach the Yellowknife and the Château Boulain.

It was after midnight when he went to bed, and he was up with the early dawn. With the first break of day the *bateau* men were preparing their breakfast. David was glad. He was eager for the day's work to begin, and in that eagerness he pounded on the door and called out to Joe Clamart that he was ready for his breakfast with the rest of them, but that he wanted only hot coffee to go with what Black Roger had brought to him in the basket.

That afternoon the *bateau* passed Fort McMurray, and before the sun was well down in the west Carrigan saw the green slopes of Thickwood Hills and the rising peaks of Birch Mountains. He laughed outright as he thought of Corporal Anderson and Constable Frazer at Fort McMurray, whose chief duty was to watch the big waterway. How their eyes would pop if they could see through the padlocked door of his prison! But he had no inclination to be discovered now. He wanted to go on, and with a growing exultation he saw there was no intention on the part of the *bateau*'s crew to loiter on the way. There was no stop at noon, and the tie-up did not come until the last glow of day was darkening into the gloom of night in the sky. For sixteen hours the *bateau* had travelled steadily, and it could not have made less than sixty miles as the river ran. The raft, David figured, had not travelled a third of the distance.

The fact that the *bateau*'s progress would bring him to Chateau Boulain many days, and perhaps weeks, before Black Roger and Marie-Anne could arrive on the raft did not check his enthusiasm. It was this interval between their arrivals which held a great speculative promise for him. In that time, if his efficiency had not entirely deserted him, he would surely make discoveries of importance.

Day after day the journey continued without rest. On the fourth day after leaving Fort McMurray it was Joe Clamart who brought in David's supper, and he grunted a protest at his long hours of muscle-breaking labour at the sweeps. When David questioned him he shrugged his shoulders, and his mouth closed tight as a clam. On the fifth, the *bateau* crossed the narrow western neck of Lake Athabasca, slipping past Chipewyan in the night, and on the sixth it entered the Slave River. It was the fourteenth day when the *bateau* entered Great

Slave Lake, and the second night after that, as dusk gathered thickly between the forest walls of the Yellowknife, David knew that at last they had reached the mouth of the dark and mysterious stream which led to the still more mysterious domain of Black Roger Audemard.

That night the rejoicing of the *bateau* men ashore was that of men who had come out from under a strain and were throwing off its tension for the first time in many days. A great fire was built, and the men sang and laughed and shouted as they piled wood upon it. In the flare of this fire a smaller one was built, and kettles and pans were soon bubbling and sizzling over it, and a great coffee pot that held two gallons sent out its steam laden with an aroma that mingled joyously with the balsam and cedar smells in the air.

David could see the whole thing from his window, and when Joe Clamart came in with supper, he found the meat they were cooking over the fire was fresh moose steak. As there had been no trading or firing of guns coming down, he was puzzled and when he asked where the meat had come from Joe Clamart only shrugged his shoulders and winked an eye, and went out singing about the *allouette* bird that had everything plucked from it, one by one. But David noticed there were never more than four men ashore at the same time. At least one was always aboard the *bateau*, watching his door and windows.

And he, too, felt the thrill of an excitement working subtly within him, and this thrill pounded in swifter running blood when he saw the men about the fire jump to their feet suddenly and go to meet new and shadowy figures that came up indistinctly just in the edge of the forest gloom. There they mingled and were lost in identity for a long time, and David wondered if the newcomers were of the people of Château Boulain. After that, Bateese and Joe Clamart and two others stamped out the fires and came over the plank to the *bateau* to sleep. David followed their example and went to bed.

The cook fires were burning again before the gray dawn was broken by a tint of the sun, and when the voices of many men roused David, he went to his window and saw a dozen figures where last night there had been only four. When it grew lighter he recognized none of them. All were strangers. Then he realized the significance of their presence. The *bateau* had been travelling north, but downstream. Now it would still travel north, but the water of the Yellow-knife flowed south into Great Slave Lake, and the *bateau* must be towed. He caught a glimpse of the two big York boats a little later, and six rowers to a boat, and after that the *bateau* set out slowly but steadily upstream.

For hours David was at one window or the other, with something of awe working inside him as he saw what they were passing through—and between. He fancied the water trail was like an entrance into a forbidden land, a region of vast and unbroken mystery, a country of enchantment, possibly of death, shut out from the world he had known. For the stream narrowed, and the forest along the shores was so dense he could not see into it. The tree-tops hung in a tangled canopy overhead, and a gloom of twilight filled the channel below, so that where the sun shot through, it was like filtered moonlight shining on black oil. There was no sound except the dull, steady beat of the rowers' oars, and the ripple of water along the sides of the *bateau*. The men did not sing or laugh, and if they talked it must have been in whispers. There was no cry of birds from ashore. And once David saw Joe Clamart's face as he passed the window, and it was set and hard and filled with the superstition of a man who was passing through a devil-country.

And then suddenly the end of it came. A flood of sunlight burst in at the windows, and all at once voices came from ahead, a laugh, a shout, and a yell of rejoicing from the *bateau*, and Joe Clamart started again the everlasting song of the *allouette* bird that was plucked of everything it had. Carrigan found himself grinning. They were a queer people, these bred-in-the-blood northerners—still moved by the superstitions of children. Yet he conceded that the awesome deadness of the forest passage had put strange thoughts into his own heart.

Before nightfall Bateese and Joe Clamart came in and tied his arms behind him, and he was taken ashore with the rumble of a waterfall in his ears. For two hours he watched the labours of the men as they beached the *bateau* on long rollers of smooth birch and rolled it foot by foot over a cleared trail until it was launched again above the waterfall. Then he was led back into the cabin and his arms freed. That night he went to sleep with the music of the waterfall in his ears.

The second day the Yellowknife seemed to be no longer a river, but a narrow lake, and the third day the rowers came into the Nine Lake country at noon, and until another dusk the *bateau* threaded its way through twisting channels and impenetrable forests, and beached at last at the edge of a great open where the timber had been cut. There was more excitement here, but it was too dark for David to understand the meaning of it. There were many voices; dogs barked. Then voices were at his door, a key rattled in the lock, and it opened.

David saw Bateese and Joe Clamart first. And then, to his amazement, Black Roger Audemard stood there, smiling at him and nodding good-evening.

It was impossible for David to repress his astonishment.

"Welcome to Château Boulain," greeted Black Roger. "You are surprised? Well, I beat you out by half a dozen hours—in a canoe, *m'sieu*. It is only courtesy that I should be here to give you welcome!"

Behind him Bateese and Joe Clamart were grinning widely, and then both came in, and Joe Clamart picked up his dunnage-sack and threw it over his shoulder.

"If you will come with us, *m'sieu*—"

David followed, and when he stepped ashore there were Bateese, and Joe Clamart and one other behind him, and three or four shadowy figures ahead, with Black Roger walking at his side. There were no more voices, and the dog had ceased barking. Ahead was a wall of darkness, which was the deep black forest beyond the clearing, and into it led a trail which they followed. It was a path worn smooth by the travel of many feet, and for a mile not a star broke through the tree-tops overhead, nor did a flash of light break the utter chaos of the way but once, when Joe Clamart lighted his pipe. No one spoke. Even Black Roger was silent, and David found no word to say.

At the end of the mile the trees began to open above their heads, and they soon came to the edge of the timber. In the darkness David caught his breath. Dead ahead, not a rifle shot away, was the Château Boulain. He knew it before Black Roger had said a word. He guessed it by the lighted windows, full a score of them, without a curtain drawn to shut out their illumination from the night. He could see nothing but these lights, yet they measured off a mighty place to be built of logs in the heart of a wilderness, and at his side he heard Black Roger chuckling in low exultation.

"Our home, *m'sieu*," he said. "Tomorrow, when you see it in the light of day, you will say it is the finest *château* in the north—all built of sweet cedar where birch is not used, so that even in the deep snows it gives us the perfume of springtime and flowers."

David did not answer, and in a moment Audemard said:

"Only on Christmas and New Year and at birthdays and wedding feasts is it lighted up like that. Tonight it is in your honour, M'sieu David." Again he laughed softly, and under his breath he added, "And there is someone waiting for you there whom you will be surprised to see!"

David's heart gave a jump. There was meaning in Black Roger's words and no double twist to what he meant. Marie-Anne had come ahead with her husband!

Now, as they passed on to the brilliantly lighted chateau, David made out the indistinct outlines of other buildings almost hidden in the out-creeping shadows of the forest-edges, with now and then a ray of light to show people were in them. But there was a brooding silence over it all which made him wonder, for there was no voice, no bark of dog, not even the opening or closing of a door. As they drew nearer, he saw a great veranda reaching the length of the chateau, with screening to keep out the summer pests of mosquitoes and flies and the night prowling insects attracted by light. Into this they went, up wide birch steps, and ahead of them was a door so heavy it looked like the postern gate of a castle. Black Roger opened it, and in a moment David stood beside him in a dimly lighted hall where the mounted heads of wild beasts looked down like startled things from the gloom of the walls. And then David heard the low, sweet notes of a piano coming to them very faintly.

He looked at Black Roger. A smile was on the lips of the chateau master; his head was up, and his eyes glowed with pride and joy as the music came to him. He spoke no word, but laid a hand on David's arm and led him toward it, while Bateese and Joe Clamart remained standing at the entrance to the hall. David's feet trod in thick rugs of fur; he saw the dim lustre of polished birch and cedar in the walls, and over his head the ceiling was rich and matched, as in the *bateau* cabin. They drew nearer to the music and came to a closed door. This Black Roger opened very quietly, as if anxious not to disturb the one who was playing.

They entered, and David held his breath. It was a great room he stood in, thirty feet or more from end to end, and scarcely less in width—a room brilliant with light, sumptuous in its comfort, sweet with the perfume of wild-flowers, and with a great black fireplace at the end of it, from over which there stared at him the glass eyes of a monster moose. Then he saw the figure at the piano, and something rose up quickly and choked him when his eyes told him it was not Marie-Anne. It was a slim, beautiful figure in a soft and shimmering white gown, and its head was glowing gold in the lamplight.

Roger Audemard spoke, "Carmin!"

The woman at the piano turned about, a little startled at the unexpectedness of the voice, and then rose quickly to her feet—and David

Carrigan found himself looking into the eyes of Carmin Fanchet!

Never had he seen her more beautiful than in this moment, like an angel in her shimmering dress of white, her hair a radiant glory, her eyes wide and glowing—and, as she looked at him, a smile coming to her red lips. Yes, SHE WAS SMILING AT HIM—this woman whose brother he had brought to the hangman, this woman who had stolen Black Roger from another! She knew him—he was sure of that; she knew him as the man who had believed her a criminal along with her brother, and who had fought to the last against her freedom. Yet from her lips and her eyes and her face the old hatred was gone. She was coming toward him slowly; she was reaching out her hand, and half blindly his own went out, and he felt the warmth of her fingers for a moment, and he heard her voice saying softly,

"Welcome to Chateau Boulain, M'sieu Carrigan."

He bowed and mumbled something, and Black Roger gently pressed his arm, drawing him back to the door. As he went he saw again that Carmin Fanchet was very beautiful as she stood there, and that her lips were very red—but her face was white, whiter than he had ever seen the face of a woman before.

As they went up a winding stair to the second floor, Roger Audemard said, "I am proud of my Carmin, M'sieu David. Would any other woman in the world have given her hand like that to the man who had helped to kill her brother?"

They stopped at another door. Black Roger opened it. There were lights within, and David knew it was to be his room. Audemard did not follow him inside, but there was a flashing humour in his eyes.

"I say, is there another woman like her in the world, *m'sieu*?"

"What have you done to Marie-Anne—your wife?" asked David.

It was hard for him to get the words out. A terrible thing was gripping at his throat, and the clutch of it grew tighter as he saw the wild light in Black Roger's eyes.

"Tomorrow you will know, *m'sieu*. But not tonight. You must wait until tomorrow."

He nodded and stepped back, and the door closed—and in the same instant came the harsh grating of a key in the lock.

25

Carrigan turned slowly and looked about his room. There was no other door except one opening into a closet, and but two windows. Curtains were drawn at these windows, and he raised them. A grim smile came to his lips when he saw the white bars of tough birch nailed across each of them, outside the glass. He could see the birch had been freshly stripped of bark and had probably been nailed there that day. Carmin Fanchet and Black Roger had welcomed him to Château Boulain, but they were evidently taking no chances with their prisoner. And where was Marie-Anne?

The question was insistent, and with it remained that cold grip of something in his heart that had come with the sight of Carmin Fanchet below. Was it possible that Carmin's hatred still lived, deadlier than ever, and that with Black Roger she had plotted to bring him here so that her vengeance might be more complete—and a greater torture to him? Were they smiling and offering him their hands, even as they knew he was about to die? And if that was conceivable, what had they done with Marie-Anne?

He looked about the room. It was singularly bare, in an unusual sort of way, he thought. There were rich rugs on the floor—three magnificent black bearskins, and two wolf. The heads of two bucks and a splendid caribou hung against the walls. He could see, from marks on the floor, where a bed had stood, but this bed was now replaced by a couch made up comfortably for one inclined to sleep. The significance of the thing was clear—nowhere in the room could he lay his hand upon an object that might be used as a weapon!

His eyes again sought the white-birch bars of his prison, and he raised the two windows so that the cool, sweet breath of the forests reached in to him. It was then that he noticed the mosquito-proof screening nailed outside the bars. It was rather odd, this thinking of his comfort even as they planned to kill him!

If there was truth to this new suspicion that Black Roger and his mistress were plotting both vengeance and murder, their plans must also involve Marie-Anne. Suddenly his mind shot back to the raft. Had Black Roger turned a clever *coup* by leaving his wife there, while he came on ahead of the *bateau* with Carmin Fanchet? It would be several weeks before the raft reached the Yellowknife, and in that time many things might happen. The thought worried him. He was not afraid for himself. Danger, the combating of physical forces, was his business. His fear was for Marie-Anne. He had seen enough to know that Black Roger was hopelessly infatuated with Carmin Fanchet. And several things might happen aboard the raft, planned by agents as black-souled as himself. If they killed Marie-Anne—

His hand gripped the knob of the door, and for a moment he was filled with the impulse to shout for Black Roger and face him with what was in his mind. And as he stood there, every muscle in his body ready to fight, there came to him faintly the sound of music. He heard the piano first, and then a woman's voice singing. Soon a man's voice joined the woman's, and he knew it was Black Roger, singing with Carmin Fanchet.

Suddenly the mad impulse in his heart went out, and he leaned his head nearer to the crack of the door, and strained his ears to hear. He could make out no word of the song, yet the singing came to him with a thrill that set his lips apart and brought a staring wonder into his eyes. In the room below him, fifteen hundred miles from civilization, Black Roger and Carmin Fanchet were singing "Home, Sweet Home!"

An hour later David looked through one of the barred windows upon a world lighted by a splendid moon. He could see the dark edge of the distant forest that rimmed in the *château*, and about him seemed to be a level meadow, with here and there the shadow of a building in which the lights were out. Stars were thick in the sky, and a strange quietness hovered over the world he looked upon. From below him floated up now and then a perfume of tobacco smoke. The guard under his window was awake, but he made no sound.

A little later he undressed, put out the two lights in his room, and stretched himself between the cool, white sheets on the couch. After a time he slept, but it was a restless slumber filled with troubled dreams. Twice he was half awake, and the second time it seemed to him his nostrils sensed a sharper tang of smoke than that of burning tobacco, yet he did not fully rouse himself, and the hours passed, and new sounds and smells that rose in the night impinged themselves upon him only as a part of the troublous fabric of his dreams. But at last there came a shock, something which beat over these things which chained him, and seized upon his consciousness, demanding that he rouse himself, open his eyes, and get up.

He obeyed the command, and before he was fully awake, found himself on his feet. It was still dark, but he heard voices, voices no longer subdued, but filled with a wild note of excitement and command. And what he smelled was not the smell of tobacco smoke! It was heavy in his room. It filled his lungs. His eyes were smarting with the sting of it.

Then came vision, and with a startled cry he leaped to a window. To the north and east he looked out upon a flaming world!

With his fist he rubbed his smarting eyes. The moon was gone. The gray he saw outside must be the coming of dawn, ghostly with that mist of smoke that had come into his room. He could see shadowy figures of men running swiftly in and out and disappearing, and he could hear the voices of women and children, and from beyond the edge of the forest to the west came the howling of many dogs. One voice rose above the others. It was Black Roger's, and at its commands little groups of figures shot out into the gray smoke-gloom and did not appear again.

North and east the sky was flaming sullen red, and a breath of air blowing gently in David's face told him the direction of the wind. The chateau lay almost in the centre of the growing line of conflagration.

He dressed himself and went again to the window. Quite distinctly now, he could make out Joe Clamart under his window, running toward the edge of the forest at the head of half a dozen men and boys who carried axes and cross-cut saws over their shoulders. It was the last of Black Roger's people that he saw for some time in the open meadow, but from the front of the *château* he could hear many voices, chiefly of women and children, and guessed it was from there that the final operations against the fire were being directed. The wind was blowing stronger in his face. With it came a sharper tang of smoke, and the widening light of day was fighting to hold its own against the deepening pall of flame-lit gloom advancing with the wind.

There seemed to come a low and distant sound with that wind, so indistinct that to David's ears it was like a murmur a thousand miles away. He strained his ears to hear, and as he listened, there came another sound—a moaning, sobbing voice below his window! It was grief he heard now, something that went to his heart and held him cold and still. The voice was sobbing like that of a child, yet he knew it was not a child's. Nor was it a woman's.

A figure came out slowly in his view, humped over, twisted in its shape, and he recognized Andre, the Broken Man. David could see that he was crying like a child, and he was facing the flaming forests, with his arms reaching out to them in his moaning. Then, of a sudden, he gave a strange cry, as if defiance had taken the place of grief, and he hurried across the meadow and disappeared into the timber where a great lightning-riven spruce gleamed dully white through the settling veil of smoke-mist.

For a space David looked after him, a strange beating in his heart. It was as if he had seen a little child going into the face of a deadly peril, and at last he shouted out for someone to bring back the Broken Man. But there was no answer from under his window. The guard was gone. Nothing lay between him and escape—if he could force the white birch bars from the window.

He thrust himself against them, using his shoulder as a battering-ram. Not the thousandth part of an inch could he feel them give, yet he worked until his shoulder was sore. Then he paused and studied the bars more carefully. Only one thing would avail him, and that was some object which he might use as a lever.

He looked about him, and not a thing was there in the room to answer the purpose. Then his eyes fell on the splendid horns of the caribou head. Black Roger's discretion had failed him there, and eagerly David pulled the head down from the wall. He knew the woodsman's trick of breaking off a horn from the skull, yet in this room, without log or root to help him, the task was difficult, and it was a quarter of an hour after he had last seen the Broken Man before he stood again at the window with the caribou horn in his hands. He no longer had to hold his breath to hear the low moaning in the wind, and where there had been smoke-gloom before there were now black clouds rolling and twisting up over the tops of the north and eastern forests, as if mighty breaths were playing with them from behind.

David thrust the big end of the caribou horn between two of the white-birch bars, but before he had put his weight to the lever he heard a great voice coming round the end of the *château*, and it was calling for Andre, the Broken Man. In a moment it was followed by Black Roger Audemard, who ran under the window and faced the lightning-struck spruce as he shouted Andre's name again.

Suddenly David called down to him, and Black Roger turned and looked up through the smoke-gloom, his head bare, his arms naked, and his eyes gleaming wildly as he listened.

"He went that way twenty minutes ago," David shouted. "He disappeared into the forest where you see the dead spruce yonder. And he was crying, Black Roger—he was crying like a child."

If there had been other words to finish, Black Roger would not have heard them. He was running toward the old spruce, and David saw him disappear where the Broken Man had gone. Then he put his weight on the horn, and one of the tough birch bars gave way slowly, and after that a second was wrenched loose, and a third, until the lower half of the window was free of them entirely. He thrust out his head and found no one within the range of his vision. Then he worked his way through the window, feet first, and hanging the length of arms and body from the lower sill, dropped to the ground.

Instantly he faced the direction taken by Roger Audemard, it was HIS turn now, and he felt a savage thrill in his blood. For an instant he hesitated, held by the impulse to rush to Carmin Fanchet and with his fingers at her throat, demand what she and her paramour had done with Marie-Anne. But the mighty determination to settle it all with Black Roger himself overwhelmed that impulse like an inundation. Black Roger had gone into the forest. He was separated from his people, and the opportunity was at hand.

Positive that Marie-Anne had been left with the raft, the thought that the Château Boulain might be devoured by the onrushing conflagration did not appal David. The *château* held little interest for him now. It was Black Roger he wanted. As he ran toward the old spruce, he picked up a club that lay in the path.

This path was a faintly-worn trail where it entered the forest beyond the spruce, very narrow, and with brush hanging close to the sides of it, so that David knew it was not in general use and that but few feet had ever used it. He followed swiftly, and in five minutes came suddenly out into a great open thick with smoke, and here he saw why Château Boulain would not burn. The break in the forest was a clearing a rifle-shot in width, free of brush and grass, and partly tilled; and it ran in a semi-circle as far as he could see through the smoke in both directions. Thus had Black Roger safeguarded his wilderness castle, while providing tillable fields for his people; and as David followed the faintly beaten path, he saw green stuffs growing on both sides of him, and through the centre of the clearing a long strip of wheat, green and very thick. Up and down through the fog of smoke he could hear voices, and he knew it was this great, circular fire-clearing the people of Château Boulain were watching and guarding.

But he saw no one as he trailed across the open. In soft patches of the earth he found footprints deeply made and wide apart, the footprints of hurrying men, telling him Black Roger and the Broken Man were both ahead of him, and that Black Roger was running when he crossed the clearing.

The footprints led him to a still more indistinct trail in the farther forest, a trail which went straight into the face of the fire ahead. He followed it. The distant murmur had grown into a low moaning over the tree-tops, and with it the wind was coming stronger, and the smoke thicker. For a mile he continued along the path, and then he stopped, knowing he had come to the dead-line. Over him was a swirling chaos. The fire-wind had grown into a roar before which the tree-tops bent as if struck by a gale, and in the air he breathed he could feel a swiftly growing heat. For a space he stood there, breathing quickly in the face of a mighty peril. Where had Black Roger and the Broken Man gone? What mad impulse could it be that dragged them still farther into the path of death? Or had they struck aside from the trail? Was he alone in danger?

As if in answer to the questions there came from far ahead of him a loud cry. It was Black Roger's voice, and as he listened, it called over and over again the Broken Man's name,

"Andre—Andre—Andre—"

Something in the cry held Carrigan. There was a note of terror in it, a wild entreaty that was almost drowned in the trembling wind and the moaning that was in the air. David was ready to turn back. He had already approached too near to the red line of death, yet that cry of Black Roger urged him on like the lash of a whip. He plunged ahead into the chaos of smoke, no longer able to distinguish a trail under his feet. Twice again in as many minutes he heard Black Roger's voice, and ran straight toward it. The blood of the hunter rushed over all other things in his veins. The man he wanted was ahead of him and the moment had passed when danger or fear of death could drive him back. Where Black Roger lived, he could live, and he gripped his club and ran through the low brush that whipped in stinging lashes against his face and hands.

He came to the foot of a ridge, and from the top of this he knew

Black Roger had called. It was a huge hog's-back, rising a hundred feet up out of the forest, and when he reached the top of it, he was panting for breath. It was as if he had come suddenly within the blast of a hot furnace. North and east the forest lay under him, and only the smoke obstructed his vision. But through this smoke he could make out a thing that made him rub his eyes in a fierce desire to see more clearly. A mile away, perhaps two, the conflagration seemed to be splitting itself against the tip of a mighty wedge. He could hear the roar of it to the right of him and to the left, but dead ahead there was only a moaning whirlpool of fire-heated wind and smoke. And out of this, as he looked, came again the cry,

"Andre—Andre—Andre!"

Again he stared north and south through the smoke-gloom. Mountains of resinous clouds, black as ink, were swirling skyward along the two sides of the giant wedge. Under that death-pall the flames were sweeping through the spruce and cedar tops like race-horses, hidden from his eyes. If they closed in there could be no escape; in fifteen minutes they would inundate him, and it would take him half an hour to reach the safety of the clearing.

His heart thumped against his ribs as he hurried down the ridge in the direction of Black Roger's voice. The giant wedge of the forest was not burning—yet, and Audemard was hurrying like mad toward the tip of that wedge, crying out now and then the name of the Broken Man. And always he kept ahead, until at last—a mile from the ridge—David came to the edge of a wide stream and saw what it was that made the wedge of forest. For under his eyes the stream split, and two arms of it widened out, and along each shore of the two streams was a wide fire-clearing made by the axes of Black Roger's people, who had foreseen this day when fire might sweep their world.

Carrigan dashed water into his eyes, and it was warm. Then he looked across. The fire had passed, the pall of smoke was clearing away, and what he saw was the black corpse of a world that had been green. It was smouldering; the deep mould was afire. Little tongues of flame still licked at ten thousand stubs charred by the fire-death—and there was no wind here, and only the whisper of a distant moaning sweeping farther and farther away.

And then, out of that waste across the river, David heard a terrible cry. It was Black Roger, still calling—even in that place of hopeless death—for Andre, the Broken Man!

26

Into the stream Carrigan plunged and found it only waist-deep in crossing. He saw where Black Roger had come out of the water and where his feet had plowed deep in the ash and char and smouldering debris ahead. This trail he followed. The air he breathed was hot and filled with stifling clouds of ash and char-dust and smoke. His feet struck red-hot embers under the ash, and he smelled burning leather. A forest of spruce and cedar skeletons still crackled and snapped and burst out into sudden tongues of flame about him, and the air he breathed grew hotter, and his face burned, and into his eyes came a smarting pain—when ahead of him he saw Black Roger. He was no longer calling out the Broken Man's name, but was crashing through the smoking chaos like a great beast that had gone both blind and mad.

Twice David turned aside where Black Roger had rushed through burning debris, and a third time, following where Audemard had gone, his feet felt the sudden stab of living coals. In another moment he would have shouted Black Roger's name, but even as the words were on his lips, mingled with a gasp of pain, the giant river-man stopped where the forest seemed suddenly to end in a ghostly, smoke-filled space, and when David came up behind him, he was standing at the black edge of a cliff which leaped off into a smouldering valley below.

Out of this narrow valley between two ridges, an hour ago choked with living spruce and cedar, rose up a swirling, terrifying heat. Down into this pit of death Black Roger stood looking, and David heard a strange moaning coming in his breath. His great, bare arms were black and scarred with heat; his hair was burned; his shirt was torn from his shoulders. When David spoke—and Black Roger turned at the sound—his eyes glared wildly out of a face that was like a black mask. And when he saw it was David who had spoken, his great body seemed to sag, and with an unintelligible cry he pointed down.

David, staring, saw nothing with his half-blind eyes, but under his feet he felt a sudden giving way, and the fire-eaten tangle of earth and roots broke off like a rotten ledge, and with it both he and Black Roger went crashing into the depths below, smothered in an avalanche of ash and sizzling earth. At the bottom David lay for a moment, partly stunned. Then his fingers clutched a bit of living fire, and with a savage cry he staggered to his feet and looked to see Black Roger. For a space his eyes were blinded, and when at last he could see, he made out Black Roger, fifty feet away, dragging himself on his hands and knees through the blistering muck of the fire. And then, as he stared, the stricken giant came to the charred remnant of a stump and crumpled over it with a great cry, moaning again that name—

"Andre—Andre—"

David hurried to him, and as he put his hands under Black Roger's arms to help him to his feet, he saw that the charred stump was not a stump, but the fire-shrivelled corpse of Andre, the Broken Man!

Horror choked back speech on his own lips. Black Roger looked up at him, and a great breath came in a sob out of his body. Then, suddenly, he seemed to get grip of himself, and his burned and bleeding fingers closed about David's hand at his shoulder.

"I knew he was coming here," he said, the words forcing themselves with an effort through his swollen lips. "He came home—to die."

"Home—?"

"Yes. His mother and father were buried here nearly thirty years ago, and he worshiped them. Look at him, Carrigan. Look at him closely. For he is the man you have wanted all these years, the finest man God ever made, Roger Audemard! When he saw the fire, he came to shield their graves from the flames. And now he is dead!"

A moan came to his lips, and the weight of his body grew so heavy that David had to exert his strength to keep him from falling.

"And YOU?" he cried. "For God's sake, Audemard—tell me—"

"I, m'sieu? Why, I am only St. Pierre Audemard, his brother."

And with that his head dropped heavily, and he was like a dead man in David's arms.

How at last David came to the edge of the stream again, with the weight of St. Pierre Audemard on his shoulders, was a torturing nightmare which would never be quite clear in his brain. The details were obliterated in the vast agony of the thing. He knew that he fought as he had never fought before; that he stumbled again and again in the fire-muck; that he was burned, and blinded, and his brain was sick. But he held to St. Pierre, with his twisted, broken leg, knowing that he would die if he dropped him into the flesh-devouring heat of the smouldering debris under his feet. Toward the end he was conscious of St. Pierre's moaning, and then of his voice speaking to him. After that he came to the water and fell down in the edge of it with St. Pierre, and inside his head everything went as black as the world over which the fire had swept.

He did not know how terribly he was hurt. He did not feel pain after the darkness came. Yet he sensed certain things. He knew that over him St. Pierre was shouting. For days, it seemed, he could hear nothing but that great voice bellowing away in the interminable distance. And then came other voices, now near and now far, and after that he seemed to rise up and float among the clouds, and for a long time he heard no other sound and felt no movement, but was like one dead.

Something soft and gentle and comforting roused him out of darkness. He did not move, he did not open his eyes for a time, while reason came to him. He heard a voice, and it was a woman's voice, speaking softly, and another voice replied to it. Then he heard gentle movement, and someone went away from him, and he heard the almost noiseless opening and closing of a door. A very little he began to see. He was in a room, with a patch of sunlight on the wall. Also, he was in a bed. And that gentle, comforting hand was still stroking his forehead and hair, light as thistledown. He opened his eyes wider and looked up. His heart gave a great throb. Over him was a glorious, tender face smiling like an angel into his widening eyes. And it was the face of Carmin Fanchet!

He made an effort, as if to speak.

"Hush," she whispered, and he saw something shining in her eyes, and something wet fell upon his face. "She is returning—and I will go. For three days and nights she has not slept, and she must be the first to see you open your eyes."

She bent over him. Her soft lips touched his forehead, and he heard her sobbing breath.

"God bless you, David Carrigan!"

Then she was going to the door, and his eyes dropped shut again. He began to experience pain now, a hot, consuming pain all over him, and he remembered the fight through the path of the fire. Then the door opened very softly once more, and someone came in, and knelt down at his side, and was so quiet that she scarcely seemed to breathe. He wanted to open his eyes, to cry out a name, but he waited, and lips soft as velvet touched his own. They lay there for a moment, then moved to his closed eyes, his forehead, his hair—and after that something rested gently against him.

His eyes shot open. It was Marie-Anne, with her head nestled in the crook of his arm as she knelt there beside him on the floor. He could see only a bit of her face, but her hair was very near, crumpled gloriously on his breast, and he could see the tips of her long lashes as she remained very still, seeming not to breathe. She did not know he had roused from his sleep—the first sleep of those three days of torture which he could not remember now; and he, looking at her, made no movement to tell her he was awake. One of his hands lay over the edge of the bed, and so lightly he could scarce feel the weight of her fingers she laid one of her own upon it, and a little at a time drew it to her, until the bandaged thing was against her lips. It was strange she did not hear his heart, which seemed all at once to beat like a drum inside him!

Suddenly he sensed the fact that his other hand was not bandaged. He was lying on his side, with his right arm partly under him, and against that hand he felt the softness of Marie-Anne's cheek, the velvety crush of her hair!

And then he whispered, "Marie-Anne—"

She still lay, for a moment, utterly motionless. Then, slowly, as if believing he had spoken her name in his sleep, she raised her head and looked into his wide-open eyes. There was no word between them in that breath or two. His bandaged hand and his well hand went to her face and hair, and then a sobbing cry came from Marie-Anne, and swiftly she crushed her face down to his, holding him close with both her arms for a moment. And after that, as on that other day when she kissed him after the fight, she was up and gone so quickly that her name had scarcely left his lips when the door closed behind her, and he heard her running down the hall.

He called after her, "Marie-Anne! Marie-Anne!"

He heard another door, and voices, and quick footsteps again, coming his way, and he was waiting eagerly, half on his elbow, when into his room came Nepapinas and Carmin Fanchet. And again he saw the glory of something in the woman's face.

His eyes must have burned strangely as he stared at her, but it did not change that light in her own, and her hands were wonderfully gentle as she helped Nepapinas raise him so that he was sitting up straight, with pillows at his back.

"It doesn't hurt so much now, does it?" she asked, her voice low with a mothering tenderness.

He shook his head. "No. What is the matter?"

"You were burned—terribly. For two days and nights you were in great pain, but for many hours you have been sleeping, and Nepapinas says the burns will not hurt any more. If it had not been for you—"

She bent over him. Her hand touched his face, and now he began to understand the meaning of that glory shining in her eyes.

"If it hadn't been for you—he would have died!"

She drew back, turning to the door. "He is coming to see you-alone," she said, a little broken note in her throat. "And I pray God you will see with clear understanding, David Carrigan—and forgive me—as I have forgiven you—for a thing that happened long ago."

He waited. His head was in a jumble, and his thoughts were tumbling over one another in an effort to evolve some sort of coherence out of things amazing and unexpected. One thing was impressed upon him—he had saved St. Pierre's life, and because he had done this Carmin Fanchet was very tender to him. She had kissed him, and Marie-Anne had kissed him, and—

A strange dawning was coming to him, thrilling him to his fingertips. He listened. A new sound was approaching from the hall. His door was opened, and a wheel-chair was rolled in by old Nepapinas. In the chair was St. Pierre Audemard. Feet and hands and arms were wrapped in bandages, but his face was uncovered and wreathed in smiling happiness when he saw David propped up against his pillows. Nepapinas rolled him close to the bed and then shuffled out, and as he closed the door, David was sure he heard the subdued whispering of feminine voices down the hall.

"How are you, David?" asked St. Pierre.

"Fine," nodded Carrigan. "And you?"

"A bit scorched, and a broken leg." He held up his padded hands. "Would be dead if you hadn't carried me to the river. Carmin says she owes you her life for having saved mine."

"And Marie-Anne?"

"That's what I've come to tell you about," said St. Pierre. "The instant they knew you were able to listen, both Carmin and Marie-

Anne insisted that I come and tell you things. But if you don't feel well enough to hear me now—"

"Go on!" almost threatened David.

The look of cheer which had illumined St. Pierre's face faded away, and David saw in its place the lines of sorrow which had settled there. He turned his gaze toward a window through which the afternoon sun was coming, and nodded slowly.

"You saw—out there. He's dead. They buried him in a casket made of sweet cedar. He loved the smell of that. He was like a little child. And once—a long time ago—he was a splendid man, a greater and better man than St. Pierre, his brother, will ever be. What he did was right and just, M'sieu David. He was the oldest—sixteen—when the thing happened. I was only nine, and didn't fully understand. But he saw it all—the death of our father because a powerful factor wanted my mother. And after that he knew how and why our mother died, but not a word of it did he tell us until years later—after the day of vengeance was past.

"You understand, David? He didn't want me in that. He did it alone, with good friends from the upper north. He killed the murderers of our mother and father, and then he buried himself deeper into the forests with us, and we took our mother's family names which was Boulain, and settled here on the Yellowknife. Roger—Black Roger, as you know him—brought the bones of our father and mother and buried them over in the edge of that plain where he died and where our first cabin stood. Five years ago a falling tree crushed him out of shape, and his mind went at the same time, so that he has been like a little child, and was always seeking for Roger Audemard—the man he once was. That was the man your law wanted. Roger Audemard. Our brother."

"OUR brother," cried David. "Who is the other?"

"My sister."

"Yes?"

"Marie-Anne."

"Good God!" choked David. "St. Pierre, do you lie? Is this another bit of trickery?"

"It is the truth," said St. Pierre. "Marie-Anne is my sister, and Carmin—whom you saw in my arms through the cabin window—"

He paused, smiling into David's staring eyes, taking full measure of recompense in the other's heart-breaking attitude as he waited. "—Is my wife, M'sieu David."

A great gasp of breath came out of Carrigan.

"Yes, my wife, and the greatest-hearted woman that ever lived, without one exception in all the world!" cried St. Pierre, a fierce pride in his voice. "It was she, and not Marie-Anne, who shot you on that strip of sand, David Carrigan! *Mon Dieu*, I tell you not one woman in a million would have done what she did—let you live! Why? Listen, *m'sieu*, and you will understand at last. She had a brother, years younger than she, and to that brother she was mother, sister, everything, because they had no parents almost from babyhood. She worshiped him. And he was bad.

"Yet the worse he became, the more she loved him and prayed for him. Years ago she became my wife, and I fought with her to save the brother. But he belonged to the devil hand and foot, and at last he left us and went south, and became what he was when you were sent out to get him, Sergeant Carrigan. It was then that my wife went down to make a last fight to save him, to bring him back, and you know how she made that fight, *m'sieu*—until the day you hanged him!"

St. Pierre was leaning from his chair, his face ablaze. "Tell me, did she not fight?" he cried. "And YOU, until the last—did you not fight to have her put behind prison bars with her brother?"

"Yes, it is so," murmured Carrigan.

"She hated you," went on St. Pierre. "You hanged her brother, who was almost a part of her flesh and body. He was bad, but he had been hers from babyhood, and a mother will love her son if he is a devil. And then—I won't take long to tell the rest of it! Through friends she learned that you, who had hanged her brother, were on your way to run down Roger Audemard. And Roger Audemard, mind you, was the same as myself, for I had sworn to take my brother's place if it became necessary. She was on the *bateau* with Marie-Anne when the messenger came. She had but one desire—to save me—to kill you. If it had been some other man, but it was you, who had hanged her brother! She disappeared from the *bateau* that day with a rifle.

"You know, M'sieu David, what happened. Marie-Anne heard the shooting and came—alone—just as you rolled out in the sand as if dead. It was she who ran out to you first, while my Carmin crouched there with her rifle, ready to send another bullet into you if you moved. It was Marie-Anne you saw standing over you, it was she who knelt down at your side, and then—"

St. Pierre paused, and he smiled, and then grimaced as he tried to rub his two bandaged hands together. "David, fate mixes things up in a funny way. My Carmin came out and stood over you, hating you; and Marie-Anne knelt down there at your side, loving you. Yes, it is true. And over you they fought for life or death, and love won, because it is always stronger than hate. Besides, as you lay there bleeding and helpless, you looked different to my Carmin than as you did when you hanged her brother. So they dragged you up under a tree, and after that they plotted together and planned, while I was away up the river on the raft.

"The feminine mind works strangely, M'sieu David, and perhaps it was that thing we call intuition which made them do what they did. Marie-Anne knew it would never do for you to see and recognize my Carmin, so in their scheming of things she insisted on passing herself off as my wife, while my Carmin came back in a canoe to meet me. They were frightened, and when I came, the whole thing had gone too far for me to mend, and I knew the false game must be played out to the end. When I saw what was happening—that you loved Marie-Anne so well that you were willing to fight for her honour even when you thought she was my wife—I was sure it would all end well. But I could take no chances until I knew. And so there were bars at your windows, and—"

St. Pierre shrugged his shoulders, and the lines of grief came into his face again, and in his voice was a little break as he continued: "If Roger had not gone out there to fight back the flames from the graves of his dead, I had planned to tell you as much as I dared, M'sieu David, and I had faith that your love for our sister would win. I did not tell you on the river because I wanted you to see with your own eyes our paradise up here, and I knew you would not destroy it once you were a part of it. And so I could not tell you Carmin was my wife, for that would have betrayed us—and—besides—that fight of yours against a love which you thought was dishonest interested me very much, for I saw in it a wonderful test of the man who might become my brother if he chose wisely between love and what he thought was duty. I loved you for it, even when you sat me there on the sand like a silly loon. And now, even my Carmin loves you for bringing me out of the fire—But you are not listening!"

David was looking past him toward the door, and St. Pierre smiled when he saw the look that was in his face.

"Nepapinas!" he called loudly. "Nepapinas!"

In a moment there was shuffling of feet outside, and Nepapinas came in. St. Pierre held out his two great, bandaged hands, and David met them with his own, one bandaged and one free. Not a word was spoken between them, but their eyes were the eyes of men between whom had suddenly come the faith and understanding of a brotherhood as strong as life itself.

Then Nepapinas wheeled St. Pierre from the room and David straightened himself against his pillows, and waited, and listened, until it seemed two hearts were thumping inside him in the place of one.

It was an interminable time, he thought, before Marie-Anne stood in the doorway. For a breath she paused there, looking at him as he stretched out his bandaged arm to her, moved by every yearning impulse in her soul to come in, yet ready as a bird to fly away. And then, as he called her name, she ran to him and dropped upon her knees at his side, and his arms went about her, insensible to their hurt—and her hot face was against his neck, and his lips crushed in the smothering sweetness of her hair. He made no effort to speak, beyond that first calling of her name. He could feel her heart throbbing against him, and her hands tightened at his shoulders, and at last she raised her glorious face so near that the breath of it was on his lips. Then, seeing what was in his eyes, her soft mouth quivered in a little smile, and with a broken throb in her throat she whispered,

"Has it all ended—right—David?"

He drew the red mouth to his own, and with a glad cry which was no word in itself he buried his face in the lustrous tresses he loved. Afterward he could not remember all it was that he said, but at the end Marie-Anne had drawn a little away so that she was looking at him, her eyes shining gloriously and her cheeks beautiful as the petals of a wild rose. And he could see the throbbing in her white throat, like the beating of a tiny heart.

"And you'll take me with you?" she whispered joyously.

"Yes; and when I show you to the old man—Superintendent McVane, you know—and tell him you're my wife, he can't go back on his promise. He said if I settled this Roger Audemard affair, I could have anything I might ask for. And I'll ask for my discharge, I ought to have it in September, and that will give us time to return before the snow flies. You see—"

He held out his arms again. "You see," he cried, his face smothered in her hair again, "I've found the place of my dreams up here, and I want to stay—always. Are you a little glad, Marie-Anne?"

In a great room at the end of the hall, with windows opening in three directions upon the wilderness, St. Pierre waited in his wheel-chair, grunting uneasily now and then at the long time it was taking Carmin to discover certain things out in the hall. Finally he heard her coming, tiptoeing very quietly from the direction of David Carrigan's door, and St. Pierre chuckled and tried to rub his bandaged hands when she came in, her face pink and her eyes shining with the greatest thrill that can stir a feminine heart.

"If we'd only known," he tried to whisper, "I would have had the keyhole made larger, Cherie! He deserves it for having spied on us at the cabin window. But—tell me!—Could you see? Did you hear? What—"

Carmin's soft hand went over his mouth. "In another moment you'll be shouting," she warned. "Maybe I didn't see, and maybe I didn't hear, Big Bear—but I know there are four very happy people in Chateau Boulain. And now, if you want to guess who is the happiest—"

"I am, *chere-coeur.*"

"No."

"Well, then, if you insist—YOU are."

"Yes. And the next?"

St. Pierre chuckled. "David Carrigan," he said.

"No, no, no! If you mean that—"

"I mean—always—that I am second, unless you will ever let me be first," corrected St. Pierre, kissing the hand that was gently stroking his cheek.

And then he leaned his great head back against her where she stood behind him, and Carmin's fingers ran where his hair was crisp with the singe of fire, and for a long time they said no other word, but let their eyes rest upon the dim length of the hall at the far end of which was David Carrigan's room.

The Fiddling Man

Breault's cough was not pleasant to hear. A cough possesses mani-fold and almost unclassifiable diversities. But there is only one cough when a man has a bullet through his lungs and is measuring his life by minutes, perhaps seconds. Yet Breault, even as he coughed the red stain from his lips, was not afraid. Many times he had found himself in the presence of death, and long ago it had ceased to frighten him. Some day he had expected to come under the black shadow of it himself—not in a quiet and peaceful way, but all at once, with a shock. And the time had come. He knew that he was dying; and he was calm. More than that—in dying he was achieving a triumph. The red-hot death-sting in his lung had given birth to a frightful thought in his sickening brain. The day of his great opportunity was at hand. The hour—the minute.

A last flush of the pale afternoon sun lighted up his black-bearded face as his eyes turned, with their new inspiration, to his sledge. It was a face that one would remember—not pleasantly, perhaps, but as a fixture in a shifting memory of things; a face strong with a brute strength, implacable in its hard lines, emotionless almost, and beyond that, a mystery.

It was the best known face in all that part of the northland which reaches up from Fort McMurray to Lake Athabasca and westward to Fond du Lac and the Wholdais country. For ten years Breault had made that trip twice a year with the northern mails. In all its reaches there was not a cabin he did not know, a face he had not seen, or a name he could not speak; yet there was not a man, woman, or child who welcomed him except for what he brought. But the government had found its faith in him justified. The police at their lonely outposts had come to regard his comings and goings as dependable as day and night. They blessed him for his punctuality, and not one of them missed him when he was gone. A strange man was Breault.

With his back against a tree, where he had propped himself after the first shock of the bullet in his lung, he took a last look at life with a passionless imperturbability. If there was any emotion at all in his face it was one of vindictiveness—an emotion roused by an intense and terrible hatred that in this hour saw the fulfilment of its vengeance. Few men nursed a hatred as Breault had nursed his. And it gave him strength now, when another man would have died.

He measured the distance between himself and the sledge. It was, perhaps, a dozen paces. The dogs were still standing, tangled a little in their traces,—eight of them,—wide-chested, thin at the groins, a wolfish horde, built for endurance and speed. On the sledge was a quarter of a ton of his Majesty's mail. Toward this Breault began to creep slowly and with great pain. A hand inside of him seemed crushing the fibre of his lung, so that the blood oozed out of his mouth. When he reached the sledge there were many red patches in the snow behind him. He opened with considerable difficulty a small dunnage sack, and after fumbling a bit took there-from a pencil attached to a long red string, and a soiled envelope.

For the first time a change came upon his countenance—a ghastly smile. And above his hissing breath, that gushed between his lips with the sound of air pumped through the fine mesh of a colander, there rose a still more ghastly croak of exultation and of triumph. Laboriously he wrote. A few words, and the pencil dropped from his stiffening fingers into the snow. Around his neck he wore a long red scarf held together by a big brass pin, and to this pin he fastened securely the envelope.

This much done,—the mystery of his death solved for those who might someday find him,—the ordinary man would have contented himself by yielding up life's struggle with as little more physical difficulty as possible. Breault was not ordinary. He was, in his one way, efficiency incarnate. He made space for himself on the sledge, and laid himself out in that space with great care, first taking pains to fasten about his thighs two *babiche* thongs that were employed at times to steady his freight. Then he ran his left arm through one of the loops of the stout mail-chest. By taking these precautions he was fairly secure in the belief that after he was dead and frozen stiff no amount of rough trailing by the dogs could roll him from the sledge.

In this conjecture he was right. When the starved and exhausted malamutes dragged their silent burden into the Northwest Mounted

Police outpost barracks at Crooked Bow twenty-four hours later, an axe and a sapling bar were required to pry Francois Breault from his bier. Previous to this process, however, Sergeant Fitzgerald, in charge at the outpost, took possession of the soiled envelope pinned to Breault's red scarf. The information it bore was simple, and yet exceedingly definite. Few men in dying as Breault had died could have made the matter easier for the police.

On the envelope he had written:

Jan Thoreau shot me and left me for dead. Have just strength to write this—no more.
                    Francois Breault.

It was epic—a colossal monument to this man, thought Sergeant Fitzgerald, as they pried the frozen body loose.

To Corporal Blake fell the unpleasant task of going after Jan Thoreau. Unpleasant, because Breault's starved huskies and frozen body brought with them the worst storm of the winter. In the face of this storm Blake set out, with the sergeant's last admonition in his ears:

"Don't come back, Blake, until you've got him, dead or alive."

That is a simple and efficacious formula in the rank and file of the Royal Northwest Mounted Police. It has made volumes of stirring history, because it means a great deal and has been lived up to. Twice before, the words had been uttered to Blake—in extreme cases. The first time they had taken him for six months into the Barren Lands between Hudson's Bay and the Great Slave—and he came back with his man; the second time he was gone for nearly a year along the rim of the Arctic—and from there also he came back with his man. Blake was of that sort. A bull-dog, a Nemesis when he was once on the trail, and—like most men of that kind—without a conscience. In the Blue Books of the service he was credited with arduous patrols and unusual exploits. "Put Blake on the trail" meant something, and "He is one of our best men" was a firmly established conviction at departmental headquarters.

Only one man knew Blake as Blake actually lived under his skin—and that was Blake himself. He hunted men and ran them down without mercy—not because he loved the law, but for the reason that he had in him the inherited instincts of the hound. This comparison, if quite true, is none the less unfair to the hound. A hound is a good dog at heart.

In the January storm it may be that the vengeful spirit of François Breault set out in company with Corporal Blake to witness the consummation of his vengeance. That first night, as he sat close to his fire in the shelter of a thick spruce timber, Blake felt the unusual and disturbing sensation of a presence somewhere near him. The storm was at its height. He had passed through many storms, but tonight there seemed to be an uncannily concentrated fury in its beating and wailing over the roofs of the forests.

He was physically comfortable. The spruce trees were so dense that the storm did not reach him, and fortune favoured him with a good fire and plenty of fuel. But the sensation oppressed him. He could not keep away from him his mental vision of Breault as he had helped to pry him from the sledge—his frozen features, the stiffened fingers, the curious twist of the icy lips that had been almost a grin.

Blake was not superstitious. He was too much a man of iron for that. His soul had lost the plasticity of imagination. But he could not forget Breault's lips as they had seemed to grin up at him. There was a reason for it. On his last trip down, Breault had said to him, with that same half-grin on his face:

"*M'sieu*, some day you may go after my murderer, and when you do, François Breault will go with you."

That was three months ago. Blake measured the time back as he sucked at his pipe, and at the same time he looked at the shadowy and half-lost forms of his dogs, curled up for the night in the outer rim of firelight.

Over the treetops a sudden blast of wind howled. It was like a monster voice. Blake rose to his feet and rolled upon the fire the big night log he had dragged in, and to this he added, with the woodman's craft of long experience, lengths of green timber, so arranged that they would hold fire until morning. Then he went into his silk service tent and buried himself in his sleeping-bag.

For a long time he did not sleep. He listened to the crackle of the fire. Again and again he heard that monster voice moaning and shrieking over the forest. Never had the rage of storm filled him with the uneasiness of tonight. At last the mystery of it was solved for him. The wind came and went each time in a great moaning, half shrieking sound: B-r-r-r—e-e-e-e—aw-w-w-w!

It was like a shock to him; and yet, he was not a superstitious man. No, he was not that. He would have staked his life on it. But it was not pleasant to hear a dead man's name shrieked over one's head by the wind. Under the cover of his sleeping-bag flap Corporal Blake laughed. Funny things were always happening, he tried to tell himself. And this was a mighty good joke. Breault wasn't so slow, after all. He had given his promise, and he was keeping it; for, if it wasn't really Breault's voice up there in the wind, multiplied a thousand times, it was a good imitation of it. Again Corporal Blake laughed—a laugh as unpleasant as the cough that had come from Breault's bullet-punctured lung. He fell asleep after a time; but even sleep could not drive from him the clinging obsession of the thought that strange things were to happen in this taking of Jan Thoreau.

With the gray dawn there was nothing to mark the passing of the storm except freshly fallen snow, and Blake was on the trail before it was light enough to see a hundred yards ahead. There was a defiance and a contempt of last night in the crack of his long caribou-gut whip and the halloo of his voice as he urged on his dogs. Breault's voice in the wind? Bah! Only a fool would have thought that. Therefore he was a fool. And Jan Thoreau—it would be like taking a child. There would be no happenings to report—merely an arrest, a quick return journey, an affair altogether too ordinary to be interesting. Perhaps it was all on account of the hearty supper of caribou liver he had eaten. He was fond of liver, and once or twice before it had played him tricks.

He began to wonder if he would find Jan Thoreau at home. He remembered Jan quite vividly. The Indians called him *Kitoochikun* because he played a fiddle. Blake, the Iron Man, disliked him because of that fiddle. Jan was never without it, on the trail or off. The Fiddling Man, he called him contemptuously—a baby, a woman; not fit for the big north. Tall and slim, with blond hair in spite of his French blood and name, a quiet and unexcitable face, and an air that Blake called "damned superiority." He wondered how the Fiddling Man had ever screwed up nerve enough to kill Breault. Undoubtedly there had been no fight. A quick and treacherous shot, no doubt. That was like a man who played a fiddle. POOF! He had no more respect for him than if he dressed in woman's clothing.

And he DID have a wife, this Jan Thoreau. They lived a good twenty miles off the north-and-south trail, on an island in the middle of Black Bear Lake. He had never seen the wife. A poor sort of woman, he made up his mind, that would marry a fiddler. Probably a half-breed; maybe an Indian. Anyway, he had no sympathy for her. Without a doubt, it was the woman who did the trapping and cut the wood. Any man who would tote a fiddle around on his back—

Corporal Blake travelled fast, and it was afternoon of the second day when he came to the dense spruce forest that shut in Black Bear Lake. Here something happened to change his plans somewhat. He met an Indian he knew—an Indian who, for two or three good reasons that stuck in the back of his head, dared not lie to him; and this tribesman, coming straight from the Thoreau cabin, told him that Jan was not at home, but had gone on a three-day trip to see the French missioner who lived on one of the lower Wholdaia waterways.

Blake was keen on stratagem. With him, man-hunting was like a game of chess; and after he had questioned the Indian for a quarter of an hour he saw his opportunity. Pastamoo, the Cree, was made a part of his Majesty's service on the spot, with the promise of torture and speedy execution if he proved himself a traitor.

Blake turned over to him his dogs and sledge, his provisions, and his tent, and commanded him to camp in the heart of a cedar swamp a few miles back, with the information that he would return for his outfit at some time in the indefinite future. He might be gone a day or a week. When he had seen Pastamoo off, he continued his journey toward the cabin, in the hope that Jan Thoreau's wife was either an Indian or a fool. He was too old a hand at his game to be taken in by the story that had been told to the Cree.

Jan had not gone to the French missioner's. A murderer's trail would not be given away like that. Of course the wife knew. And Corporal Blake desired no better string to a criminal than the faith of a wife. Wives were easy if handled right, and they had put the finishing touch to more than one of his great successes.

At the edge of the lake he fell back on his old trick—hunger, exhaustion, a sprained leg. It was not more than a quarter of a mile across the snow-covered ice of the lake to the thin spiral of smoke that he saw rising above the thick balsams on the island. Five times in that distance he fell upon his face; he crawled like a man about to die. He performed an arduous task, a devilish task, and when at last he reached the balsams he cursed his luck until he was red in the face. No one had seen him. That quarter-mile of labour was lost, its finesse a failure. But he kept up the play, and staggered weakly through the sheltering balsams to the cabin. His artifice had no shame, even when played on women; and he fell heavily against the door, beat upon it with his fist; and slipped down into the snow, where he lay with his head bowed, as if his last strength was gone.

He heard movement inside, quick steps—and then the door opened. He did not look up for a moment. That would have been crude. When he did raise his head, it was very slowly, with a look of anguish in his face. And then—he stared. His body all at once grew tense, and the counterfeit pain in his eyes died out like a flash in this most astounding moment of his life. Man of iron though he was, steeled to the core against the weaknesses of sudden emotions, it was impossible for him to restrain the gasp of amazement that rose to his lips.

In that stifled cry Jan Thoreau's wife heard the supplication of a dying man. She did not catch, back of it, the note of a startled beast. She was herself startled, frightened for a moment by the unexpectedness of it all.

And Blake stared. This—the fiddler's wife! She was clutching in her hand a brush with which she had been arranging her hair. The hair, jet black, was wonderful. Her eyes were still more wonderful to Blake. She was not an Indian—not a half-breed—and beautiful. The loveliest face he had ever visioned, sleeping or awake, was looking down at him.

With a second gasp, he remembered himself, and his body sagged, and the amazed stare went out of his eyes as he allowed his head to fall a little. In this movement his cap fell off. In another moment she was at his side, kneeling in the snow and bending over him.

"You are hurt, *m'sieu!*"

Her hair fell upon him, smothering his neck and shoulders. The perfume of it was like the delicate scent of a rare flower in his nostrils. A strange thrill swept through him. He did not try to analyze it in those few astonishing moments. It was beyond his comprehension, even had he tried. He was ignorant of the finer fundamentals of life, and of the great truth that the case-hardened nature of a man, like the body of an athlete, crumbles fastest under sudden and unexpected change and strain.

He regained his feet slowly and stupidly, assisted by Marie. They climbed the one step to the door. As he sank back heavily on the cot, in the room they entered, a thick tress of her hair fell softly upon his face. He closed his eyes for a space. When he opened them, Marie was bending over the stove.

And SHE was Thoreau's wife! The instant he had looked up into her face, he had forgotten the fiddler; but he remembered him now as he watched the woman, who stood with her back toward him. She was as slim as a reed. Her hair fell to her hips. He drew a deep breath.

Unconsciously he clenched his hands. SHE—the fiddler's wife! The thought repeated itself again and again. Jan Thoreau, MURDERER, and this woman—HIS WIFE.

She returned in a moment with hot tea, and he drank with subtle hypocrisy from the cup she held to his lips.

"Sprained my leg," he said then, remembering his old part, and replying to the questioning anxiety in her eyes. "Dogs ran away and left me, and I got here just by chance. A little more and—"

He smiled grimly, and as he sank back he gave a sharp cry. He had practised that cry in more than one cabin, and along with it a convulsion of his features to emphasize the impression he laboured to make.

"I'm afraid—I'll be a trouble to you," he apologized. "It's not broken; but it's bad, and I won't be able to move—soon. Is Jan at home?"

"No, m'sieu; he is away."

"Away," repeated Blake disappointedly. "Perhaps sometime he has told you about me," he added with sudden hopefulness. "I am John Duval."

"M'sieu—DUVAL!"

Marie's eyes, looking down at him, became all at once great pools of glowing light. Her lips parted. She leaned toward him, her slim hands clasped suddenly to her breast.

"M'sieu Duval—who nursed him through the smallpox?" she cried, her voice trembling. "M'sieu Duval—who saved my Jan's life!"

Blake had looked up his facts at headquarters. He knew what Duval, the Barren Land trapper, had once upon a time done for Jan.

"Yes; I am John Duval," said. "And so—you see—I am sorry that Jan is away."

"But he is coming back soon—in a few days," exclaimed Marie. "You shall stay, m'sieu! You will wait for him? Yes?"

"This leg—" began Blake. He cut himself short with a grimace. "Yes, I'll stay. I guess I'll have to."

Marie had changed at the mention of Duval's name. With the glow in her eyes had come a flush into her cheeks, and Blake could see the strange little quiver at her throat as she looked at him. But she did not see Blake so much as what lay beyond him—Duval's lonely cabin away up on the edge of the Great Barren, the hours of darkness and agony through which Jan had passed, and the magnificent comradeship of this man who had now dragged himself to their own cabin, half dead.

Many times Jan had told her the story of that terrible winter when Duval had nursed him like a woman, and had almost given up his life as a sacrifice. And this—THIS—was Duval? She bent over him again as he lay on the cot, her eyes shining like stars in the growing dusk. In that dusk she was unconscious of the fact that his fingers had found a long tress of her hair and were clutching it passionately. Remembering Duval as Jan had enshrined him in her heart, she said:

"I have prayed many times that the great God might thank you, *m'sieu.*"

He raised a hand. For an instant it touched her soft, warm cheek and caressed her hair. Marie did not shrink—yes, that would have been an insult. Even Jan would have said that. For was not this Duval, to whom she owed all the happiness in her life—Duval, more than brother to Jan Thoreau, her husband?

"And you—are Marie?" said Blake.

"Yes, *m'sieu*, I am Marie."

A joyous note trembled in her voice as she drew back from the cot. He could hear her swiftly braiding her hair before she struck a match to light the oil lamp hanging from the ceiling. After that, through partly closed eyes, he watched her as she prepared their supper. Occasionally, when she turned toward him as if to speak, he feigned a desire to sleep. It was a catlike watchfulness, filled with his old cunning. In his face there was no sign to betray its hideous significance. Outwardly he had regained his iron-like impassiveness; but in his body and his brain every nerve and fibre was consumed by a monstrous desire—a desire for this woman, the murderer's wife. It was as strange and as sudden as the death that had come to Francois Breault.

The moment he had looked up into her face in the doorway, it had overwhelmed him. And now even the sound of her footsteps on the floor filled him with an exquisite exultation. It was more than exultation. It was a feeling of POSSESSION.

In the hollow of his hand he—Blake, the man-hunter—held the fate of this woman. She was the Fiddler's wife—and the Fiddler was a murderer.

Marie heard the sudden deep breath that forced itself from his lips, a gasp that would have been a cry of triumph if he had given it voice.

"You are in pain, *m'sieu*," she exclaimed, turning toward him quickly.

"A little," he said, smiling at her. "Will you help me to sit up,

196

Marie?"

He saw ahead of him another and more thrilling game than the manhunt now. And Marie, unsuspicious, put her arms about the shoulders of the Pharisee and helped him to rise. They ate their supper with a narrow table between them. If there had been a doubt in Blake's mind before that, the half hour in which she sat facing him dispelled it utterly. At first the amazing beauty of Thoreau's wife had impinged itself upon his senses with something of a shock. But he was cool now. He was again master of his old cunning. Pitilessly and without conscience, he was marshalling the crafty forces of his brute nature for this new and more thrilling fight—the fight for a woman.

That in representing the Law he was pledged to virtue as well as order had never entered into his code of life. To him the Law was force—power. It had exalted him. It had forged an iron mask over the face of his savagery. And it was the savage that was dominant in him now. He saw in Marie's dark eyes a great love—love for a murderer.

It was not his thought that he might alienate that. For that look, turned upon himself, he would have sacrificed his whole world as it had previously existed. He was scheming beyond that impossibility, measuring her even as he called himself Duval, counting—not his chances of success, but the length of time it would take him to succeed.

He had never failed. A man had never beaten him. A woman had never tricked him. And he granted no possibility of failure now. But—HOW? That was the question that writhed and twisted itself in his brain even as he smiled at her over the table and told her of the black days of Jan's sickness up on the edge of the Barren.

And then it came to him—all at once. Marie did not see. She did not FEEL. She had no suspicion of this loyal friend of her husband's.

Blake's heart pounded triumphant. He hobbled back to the cot, leaning on Marie slim shoulder; and as he hobbled he told her how he had helped Jan into his cabin in just this same way, and how at the end Jan had collapsed—just as he collapsed when he came to the cot. He pulled Marie down with him—accidentally. His lips touched her head. He laughed.

For a few moments he was like a drunken man in his new joy. Willingly he would have gambled his life on his chance of winning. But confidence displaced none of his cunning. He rubbed his hands and said:

"Gawd, but won't it be a surprise for Jan? I told him that someday

I'd come. I told him!"

It would be a tremendous joke—this surprise he had in store for Jan. He chuckled over it again and again as Marie went about her work; and Marie's face flushed and her eyes were bright and she laughed softly at this great love which Duval betrayed for her husband. No; even the loss of his dogs and his outfit couldn't spoil his pleasure! Why should it? He could get other dogs and another outfit—but it had been three years since he had seen Jan Thoreau! When Marie had finished her work he put his hand suddenly to his eyes and said:

"*Peste!* but last night's storm must have hurt my eyes. The light blinds them, *ma cheri.* Will you put it out, and sit down near me, so that I can see you as you talk, and tell me all that has happened to Jan Thoreau since that winter three years ago?"

She put out the light, and threw open the door of the box-stove. In the dim firelight she sat on a stool beside Blake's cot. Her faith in him was like that of a child. She was twenty-two. Blake was fifteen years older. She felt the immense superiority of his age.

This man, you must understand, had been more than a brother to Jan. He had been a father. He had risked his life. He had saved him from death. And Marie, as she sat at his side, did not think of him as a young man—thirty-seven. She talked to him as she might have talked to an elder brother of Jan's, and with something like the same reverence in her voice.

It was unfortunate—for her—that Jan had loved Duval, and that he had never tired of telling her about him. And now, when Blake's caution warned him to lie no more about the days of plague in Duval's cabin, she told him—as he had asked her—about herself and Jan; how they had lived during the last three years, the important things that had happened to them, and what they were looking forward to. He caught the low note of happiness that ran through her voice; and with a laugh, a laugh that sounded real and wholesome, he put out his hand in the darkness—for the fire had burned itself low—and stroked her hair. She did not shrink from the caress. He was happy because THEY were happy. That was her thought! And Blake did not go too far.

She went on, telling Jan's life away, betraying him In her happiness, crucifying him in her faith. Blake knew that she was telling the truth. She did not know that Jan had killed Francois Breault, and she believed that he would surely return—in three days. And the way he had left her that morning! Yes, she confided even that to this big brother of Jan, her cheeks flushing hotly in the darkness—how he had hated to go, and held her a long time in his arms before he tore himself away.

Had he taken his fiddle along with him? Yes—always that. Next to herself he loved his violin. Oo-oo—no, no—she was not jealous of the violin! Blake laughed—such a big, healthy, happy laugh, with an odd tremble in it. He stroked her hair again, and his fingers lay for an instant against her warm cheek.

And then, quite casually, he played his second big card.

"A man was found dead on the trail yesterday," he said. "Someone killed him. He had a bullet through his lung. He was the mail-runner, Francois Breault."

It was then, when he said that Breault had been murdered, that Blake's hand touched Marie's cheek and fell to her shoulder. It was too dark in the cabin to see. But under his hand he felt her grow suddenly rigid, and for a moment or two she seemed to stop breathing. In the gloom Blake's lips were smiling. He had struck, and he needed no light to see the effect.

"Francois—Breault!" he heard her breathe at last, as if she was fighting to keep something from choking her. "Francois Breault—dead—killed by someone—"

She rose slowly. His eyes followed her, a shadow in the gloom as she moved toward the stove. He heard her strike a match, and when she turned toward him again in the light of the oil-lamp, her face was pale and her eyes were big and staring. He swung himself to the edge of the cot, his pulse beating with the savage thrill of the inquisitor. Yet he knew that it was not quite time for him to disclose himself—not quite. He did not dread the moment when he would rise and tell her that he was not injured, and that he was not M'sieu Duval, but Corporal Blake of the Royal Mounted Police. He was eager for that moment. But he waited—discreetly. When the trap was sprung there would be no escape.

"You are sure—it was Francois Breault?" she said at last.

He nodded.

"Yes, the mail-runner. You knew him?"

She had moved to the table, and her hand was gripping the edge of it. For a space she did not answer him, but seemed to be looking somewhere through the cabin walls—a long way off. Ferret-like, he was watching her, and saw his opportunity. How splendidly fate was playing his way!

He rose to his feet and hobbled painfully to her, a splendid hypocrite, a magnificent dissembler. He seized her hand and held it in both his own. It was small and soft, but strangely cold.

"*Ma cheri*—my dear child—what makes you look like that? What has the death of Francois Breault to do with you—you and Jan?"

It was the voice of a friend, a brother, low, sympathetic, filled just enough with anxiety. Only last winter, in just that way, it had won the confidence and roused the hope of Pierrot's wife, over on the Athabasca. In the summer that followed they hanged Pierrot. Gently Blake spoke the words again. Marie's lips trembled. Her great eyes were looking at him—straight into his soul, it seemed.

"You may tell me, *ma cheri*," he encouraged, barely above a whisper. "I am Duval. And Jan—I love Jan."

He drew her back toward the cot, dragging his limb painfully, and seated her again upon the stool. He sat beside her, still holding her hand, patting it, encouraging her. The colour was coming back into Marie's cheeks. Her lips were growing full and red again, and suddenly she gave a trembling little laugh as she looked up into Blake's face. His presence began to dispel the terror that had possessed her all at once.

"Tell me, Marie."

He saw the shudder that passed through her slim shoulders.

"They had a fight—here—in this cabin—three days ago," she confessed. "It must have been—the day—he was killed."

Blake knew the wild thought that was in her heart as she watched him. The muscles of his jaws tightened. His shoulders grew tense. He looked over her head as if he, too, saw something beyond the cabin walls. It was Marie's hand that gripped his now, and her voice, panting almost, was filled with an agonized protest.

"No, no, no—it was not Jan," she moaned. "It was not Jan who killed him!"

"Hush!" said Blake.

He looked about him as if there was a chance that someone might hear the fatal words she had spoken. It was a splendid bit of acting, almost unconscious, and tremendously effective. The expression in his face stabbed to her heart like a cold knife. Convulsively her fingers clutched more tightly at his hands. He might as well have spoken the words: "It was Jan, then, who killed Francois Breault!"

Instead of that he said:

"You must tell me everything, Marie. How did it happen? Why did they fight? And why has Jan gone away so soon after the killing? For Jan's sake, you must tell me—everything."

He waited. It seemed to him that he could hear the fighting struggle in Marie's breast. Then she began, brokenly, a little at a time, now and then barely whispering the story. It was a woman's story, and she told it like a woman, from the beginning. Perhaps at one time the rivalry between Jan Thoreau and Francois Breault, and their struggle for her love, had made her heart beat faster and her cheeks flush warm with a woman's pride of conquest, even though she had loved one and had hated the other. None of that pride was in her voice now, except when she spoke of Jan.

"Yes—like that—children together—we grew up," she confided. "It was down there at Wollaston Post, in the heart of the big forests, and when I was a baby it was Jan who carried me about on his shoulders. *Oui*, even then he played the violin. I loved it. I loved Jan—always. Later, when I was seventeen, Francois Breault came."

She was trembling.

"Jan has told me a little about those days," lied Blake. "Tell me the rest, Marie."

"I—I knew I was going to be Jan's wife," she went on, the hands she had withdrawn from his twisting nervously in her lap. "We both knew. And yet—he had not spoken—he had not been definite. Oo-oo, do you understand, M'sieu Duval? It was my fault at the beginning! Francois Breault loved me. And so—I played with him—only a little, *m'sieu!*—to frighten Jan into the thought that he might lose me. I did not know what I was doing. No—no; I didn't understand.

"Jan and I were married, and on the day Jan saw the missioner—a week before we were made man and wife—Francois Beault came in from the trail to see me, and I confessed to him, and asked his forgiveness. We were alone. And he—Francois Breault—was like a madman."

She was panting. Her hands were clenched. "If Jan hadn't heard my cries, and come just in time—" she breathed.

Her blazing eyes looked up into Blake's face. He understood, and nodded.

"And it was like that—again—three days ago," she continued. "I hadn't seen Breault in two years—two years ago down at Wollaston Post. And he was mad. Yes, he must have been mad when he came three days ago. I don't know that he came so much for me as it was to kill Jan, He said it was Jan. Ugh, and it was here—in the cabin—that they fought!"

"And Jan—punished him," said Blake in a low voice.

Again the convulsive shudder swept through Marie's shoulders.

"It was strange—what happened, *m'sieu*. I was going to shoot. Yes, I would have shot him when the chance came. But all at once Francois Breault sprang back to the door, and he cried: 'Jan Thoreau, I am mad—mad! Great God, what have I done?' Yes, he said that, *m'sieu*, those very words—and then he was gone."

"And that same day—a little later—Jan went away from the cabin, and was gone a long time," whispered Blake. "Was it not so, Marie?"

"Yes; he went to his trap-line, *m'sieu*."

For the first time Blake made a movement. He took her face boldly between his two hands, and turned it so that her staring eyes were looking straight into his own. Every fibre in his body was trembling with the thrill of his monstrous triumph. "My dear little girl, I must tell you the truth," he said. "Your husband, Jan, did not go to his trap-line three days ago. He followed Francois Breault, and killed him. And I am not John Duval. I am Corporal Blake of the Mounted Police, and I have come to get Jan, that he may be hanged by the neck until he is dead for his crime. I came for that. But I have changed my mind. I have seen you, and for you I would give even a murderer his life. Do you understand? For YOU—YOU—YOU—"

And then came the grand finale, just as he had planned it. His words had stupefied her. She made no movement, no sound—only her great eyes seemed alive. And suddenly he swept her into his arms with the wild passion of a beast. How long she lay against his breast, his arms crushing her, his hot lips on her face, she did not know.

The world had grown suddenly dark. But in that darkness she heard his voice; and what it was saying roused her at last from the deadliness of her stupor. She strained against him, and with a wild cry broke from his arms, and staggered across the cabin floor to the door of her bedroom. Blake did not pursue her. He let the darkness of that room shut her in. He had told her—and she understood.

He shrugged his shoulders as he rose to his feet. Quite calmly, in spite of the wild rush of blood through his body, he went to the cabin door, opened it, and looked out into the night. It was full of stars, and quiet.

It was quiet in that inner room, too—so quiet that one might fancy he could hear the beating of a heart. Marie had flung herself in the farthest corner, beyond the bed. And there her hand had touched something. It was cold—the chill of steel. She could almost have screamed, in the mighty reaction that swept through her like an electric shock. But her lips were dumb and her hand clutched tighter at the cold thing.

She drew it toward her inch by inch, and levelled it across the bed. It was Jan's goose-gun, loaded with buck-shot. There was a single metallic click as she drew the hammer back. In the doorway, looking at the stars, Blake did not hear.

Marie waited. She was not reasoning things now, except that in the outer room there was a serpent that she must kill. She would kill him as he came between her and the light; then she would follow over Jan's trail, overtake him somewhere, and they would flee together. Of that much she thought ahead. But chiefly her mind, her eyes, her brain, her whole being, were concentrated on the twelve-inch opening between the bedroom door and the outer room. The serpent would soon appear there. And then—

She heard the cabin door close, and Blake's footsteps approaching. Her body did not tremble now. Her forefinger was steady on the trigger. She held her breath—and waited. Blake came to the deadline and stopped. She could see one arm and a part of his shoulder. But that was not enough. Another half step—six inches—four even, and she would fire. Her heart pounded like a tiny hammer in her breast.

And then the very life in her body seemed to stand still. The cabin door had opened suddenly, and someone had entered. In that moment she would have fired, for she knew that it must be Jan who had returned. But Blake had moved. And now, with her finger on the trigger, she heard his cry of amazement:

"Sergeant Fitzgerald!"

"Yes. Put up your gun, Corporal. Have you got Jan Thoreau?"

"He—is gone."

"That is lucky for us." It was the stranger's voice, filled with a great relief. "I have travelled fast to overtake you. Matao, the half-breed, was stabbed in a quarrel soon after you left; and before he died he confessed to killing Breault. The evidence is conclusive. Ugh, but this fire is good! Anybody at home?"

"Yes," said Blake slowly. "Mrs. Thoreau—is—at home."

The Match

Sergeant Brokaw was hatchet-faced, with shifting pale blue eyes that had a glint of cruelty in them. He was tall, and thin, and lithe as a cat. He belonged to the Royal Northwest Mounted Police, and was one of the best men on the trail that had ever gone into the North. His business was man hunting. Ten years of seeking after human prey had given to him many of the characteristics of a fox. For six of those ten years he had represented law north of fifty-three. Now he had come to the end of his last hunt, close up to the Arctic Circle. For one hundred and eighty-seven days he had been following a man. The hunt had begun in midsummer, and it was now midwinter. Billy Loring, who was wanted for murder, had been a hard man to find. But he was caught at last, and Brokaw was keenly exultant. It was his greatest achievement. It would mean a great deal for him down at headquarters.

In the rough and dimly lighted cabin his man sat opposite him, on a bench, his manacled hands crossed over his knees. He was a younger man than Brokaw—thirty, or a little better. His hair was long, reddish, and untrimmed. A stubble of reddish beard covered his face. His eyes, too, were blue—of the deep, honest blue that one remembers, and most frequently trusts. He did not look like a criminal. There was something almost boyish in his face, a little hollowed by long privation. He was the sort of man that other men liked. Even Brokaw, who had a heart like flint in the face of crime, had melted a little.

"Ugh!" he shivered. "Listen to that beastly wind! It means three days of storm." Outside a gale was blowing straight down from the Arctic. They could hear the steady moaning of it in the spruce tops over the cabin, and now and then there came one of those raging blasts that filled the night with strange shrieking sounds. Volleys of fine, hard snow beat against the one window with a rattle like shot. In the cabin it was comfortable. It was Billy's cabin. He had built it deep in a swamp, where there were lynx and fisher cat to trap, and where he had thought that no one could find him. The sheet-iron stove was glowing hot. An oil lamp hung from the ceiling. Billy was sitting so that the glow of this fell in his face. It scintillated on the rings of steel about his wrists. Brokaw was a cautious man, as well as a clever one, and he took no chances.

"I like storms—when you're inside, an' close to a stove," replied Billy. "Makes me feel sort of—safe." He smiled a little grimly. Even at that it was not an unpleasant smile.

Brokaw's snow-reddened eyes gazed at the other.

"There's something in that," he said. "This storm will give you at least three days more of life."

"Won't you drop that?" asked the prisoner, turning his face a little, so that it was shaded from the light.

"You've got me now, an' I know what's coming as well as you do." His voice was low and quiet, with the faintest trace of a broken note in it, deep down in his throat. "We're alone, old man, and a long way from anyone. I ain't blaming you for catching me. I haven't got anything against you. So let's drop this other thing—what I'm going down to—and talk something pleasant. I know I'm going to hang. That's the law. It'll be pleasant enough when it comes, don't you think? Let's talk about—about—home. Got any kids?"

Brokaw shook his head, and took his pipe from his mouth.

"Never married," he said shortly.

"Never married," mused Billy, regarding him with a curious softening of his blue eyes. "You don't know what you've missed, Brokaw. Of course, it's none of my business, but you've got a home—somewhere—" Brokaw shook his head again.

"Been in the service ten years," he said. "I've got a mother living with my brother somewhere down in York State. I've sort of lost track of them. Haven't seen 'em in five years."

Billy was looking at him steadily. Slowly he rose to his feet, lifted his manacled hands, and turned down the light.

"Hurts my eyes," he said, and he laughed frankly as he caught the suspicious glint in Brokaw's eyes. He seated himself again, and leaned over toward the other. "I haven't talked to a white man for three months," he added, a little hesitatingly. "I've been hiding—close. I had a dog for a time, and he died, an' I didn't dare go hunting for another. I knew you fellows were pretty close after me. But I wanted to get enough fur to take me to South America. Had it all planned, an' SHE was going to join me there—with the kid. Understand? If you'd kept away another month—"

There was a husky break in his voice, and he coughed to clear it.

"You don't mind if I talk, do you—about her, an' the kid? I've got to do it, or bust, or go mad. I've got to because—today—she was twenty-four—at ten o'clock in the morning—an' it's our wedding day—"

The half gloom hid from Brokaw what was in the other's face. And then Billy laughed almost joyously. "Say, but she's been a true little pardner," he whispered proudly, as there came a lull in the storm. "She was just born for me, an' everything seemed to happen on her birthday, an' that's why I can't be downhearted even NOW. It's her birthday? you see, an' this morning, before you came, I was just that happy that I set a plate for her at the table, an' put her picture and a curl of her hair beside it—set the picture up so it was looking at me—an' we had breakfast together. Look here—"

He moved to the table, with Brokaw watching him like a cat, and brought something back with him, wrapped in a soft piece of buckskin. He unfolded the buckskin tenderly, and drew forth a long curl that rippled a dull red and gold in the lamp-glow, and then he handed a photograph to Brokaw.

"That's her!" he whispered.

Brokaw turned so that the light fell on the picture. A sweet, girlish face smiled at him from out of a wealth of flowing, dishevelled curls.

"She had it taken that way just for me," explained Billy, with the enthusiasm of a boy in his voice. "She's always wore her hair in curls—an' a braid—for me, when we're home. I love it that way. Guess I may be silly but I'll tell you why. THAT was down in York State, too. She lived in a cottage, all grown over with honeysuckle an' morning glory, with green hills and valleys all about it—and the old apple orchard just behind. That day we were in the orchard, all red an' white with bloom, and she dared me to a race. I let her beat me, and when I came up she stood under one of the trees, her cheeks like the pink blossoms, and her hair all tumbled about her like an armful of gold, shaking the loose apple blossoms down on her head. I forgot everything then, and I didn't stop until I had her in my arms, an'—an' she's been my little pardner ever since. After the baby came we moved up into Canada, where I had a good chance in a new mining town. An' then—" A furious blast of the storm sent the overhanging spruce tops smashing against the top of the cabin. Straight overhead the wind shrieked almost like human voices, and the one window rattled as though it were shaken by human hands. The lamp had been burning lower and lower. It began to flicker now, the quick sputter of the wick lost in the noise of the gale. Then it went out. Brokaw leaned over and opened the door of the big box stove, and the red glow of the fire took the place of the lamplight. He leaned back and relighted his pipe, eyeing Billy. The sudden blast, the going out of the light, the opening of the stove door, had all happened in a minute, but the interval was long enough to bring a change in Billy's voice. It was cold and hard when he continued. He leaned over toward Brokaw, and the boyishness had gone from his face.

"Of course, I can't expect you to have any sympathy for this other business, Brokaw," he went on. "Sympathy isn't in your line, an' you wouldn't be the big man you are in the service if you had it. But I'd like to know what YOU would have done. We were up there six months, and we'd both grown to love the big woods, and she was growing prettier and happier every day—when Thorne, the new superintendent, came up. One day she told me that she didn't like Thorne, but I didn't pay much attention to that, and laughed at her, and said he was a good fellow. After that I could see that something was worrying her, and pretty soon I couldn't help from seeing what it was, and everything came out. It was Thorne. He was persecuting her. She hadn't told me, because she knew it would make trouble and I'd lose my job. One afternoon I came home earlier than usual, and found her crying. She put her arms round my neck, and just cried it all out, with her face snuggled in my neck, and kissin' me—"

Brokaw could see the cords in Billy's neck. His manacled hands were clenched.

"What would you have done, Brokaw?" he asked huskily. "What if you had a wife, an' she told you that another man had insulted her, and was forcing his attentions on her, and she asked you to give up your job and take her away? Would you have done it, Brokaw? No, you wouldn't. You'd have hunted up the man. That's what I did. He had been drinking—just enough to make him devilish, and he laughed at me—I didn't mean to strike so hard.—But it happened. I killed him. I got away. She and the baby are down in the little cottage again—down in York State—an' I know she's awake this minute—our wedding day—thinking of me, an' praying for me, and counting the days between now and spring. We were going to South America then."

Brokaw rose to his feet, and put fresh wood into the stove.

"I guess it must be pretty hard," he said, straightening himself. "But the law up here doesn't take them things into account—not very much. It may let you off with manslaughter—ten or fifteen years. I hope it does. Let's turn in."

Billy stood up beside him. He went with Brokaw to a bunk built against the wall, and the sergeant drew a fine steel chain from his pocket. Billy lay down, his hands crossed over his breast, and Brokaw deftly fastened the chain about his ankles.

"And I suppose you think THIS is hard, too," he added. "But I guess you'd do it if you were me. Ten years of this sort of work learns you not to take chances. If you want anything in the night just whistle."

It had been a hard day with Brokaw, and he slept soundly. For an hour Billy lay awake, thinking of home, and listening to the wail of the storm. Then he, too, fell into sleep—a restless, uneasy slumber filled with troubled visions. For a time there had come a lull in the storm, but now it broke over the cabin with increased fury. A hand seemed slapping at the window, threatening to break it. The spruce boughs moaned and twisted overhead, and a volley of wind and snow shot suddenly down the chimney, forcing open the stove door, so that a shaft of ruddy light cut like a red knife through the dense gloom of the cabin. In varying ways the sounds played a part in Billy's dreams. In all those dreams, and segments of dreams, the girl—his wife—was present. Once they had gone for wild flowers and had been caught in a thunderstorm, and had run to an old and disused barn in the middle of a field for shelter. He was back in that barn again, with HER—and he could feel her trembling against him, and he was stroking her hair, as the thunder crashed over them and the lightning filled her eyes with fear.

After that there came to him a vision of the early autumn nights when they had gone corn roasting, with other young people. He had always been afflicted with a slight nasal trouble, and smoke irritated him. It set him sneezing, and kept him dodging about the fire, and she had always laughed when the smoke persisted in following him about, like a young scamp of a boy bent on tormenting him. The smoke was unusually persistent tonight. He tossed in his bunk, and buried his face in the blanket that answered for a pillow. The smoke reached him even there, and he sneezed chokingly. In that instant the girl's face disappeared. He sneezed again—and awoke.

A startled gasp broke from his lips, and the handcuffs about his wrists clanked as he raised his hands to his face. In that moment his dazed senses adjusted themselves. The cabin was full of smoke. It partly blinded him, but through it he could see tongues of fire shooting toward the ceiling. He could hear the crackling of burning pitch, and he yelled wildly to Brokaw. In an instant the sergeant was on his feet. He rushed to the table, where he had placed a pail of water the evening before, and Billy heard the hissing of the water as it struck the flaming wall.

"Never mind that," he shouted. "The shack's built of pitch cedar. We've got to get out!" Brokaw groped his way to him through the smoke and began fumbling at the chain about his ankles.

"I can't—find—the key—" he gasped chokingly. "Here grab hold of me!"

He caught Billy under the arms and dragged him to the door. As he opened it the wind came in with a rush and behind them the whole cabin burst into a furnace of flame. Twenty yards from the cabin he dropped Billy in the snow, and ran back. In that seething room of smoke and fire was everything on which their lives depended, food, blankets, even their coats and caps and snowshoes. But he could go no farther than the door. He returned to Billy, found the key in his pocket, and freed him from the chain about his ankles. Billy stood up. As he looked at Brokaw the glass in the window broke and a sea of flame sprouted through. It lighted up their faces. The sergeant's jaw was set hard. His leathery face was curiously white. He could not keep from shivering. There was a strange smile on Billy's face, and a strange look in his eyes. Neither of the two men had undressed for sleep, but their coats, and caps, and heavy mittens were in the flames.

Billy rattled his handcuffs. Brokaw looked him squarely in the eyes.

"You ought to know this country," he said. "What'll we do?"

"The nearest post is sixty miles from here," said Billy.

"I know that," replied Brokaw. "And I know that Thoreau's cabin is only twenty miles from here. There must be some trapper or Indian shack nearer than that. Is there?" In the red glare of the fire Billy smiled. His teeth gleamed at Brokaw. It was a lull of the wind, and he went close to Brokaw, and spoke quietly, his eyes shining more and more with that strange light that had come into them.

"This is going to be a big sight easier than hanging, or going to jail for half my life, Brokaw—an' you don't think I'm going to be fool enough to miss the chance, do you? It ain't hard to die of cold. I've almost been there once or twice. I told you last night why I couldn't give up hope—that something good for me always came on her birthday, or near to it. An' it's come. It's forty below, an' we won't live the day out. We ain't got a mouthful of grub. We ain't got clothes enough on to keep us from freezing inside the shanty, unless we had a fire. Last night I saw you fill your match bottle and put it in your coat pocket. Why, man, WE AIN'T EVEN GOT A MATCH!"

In his voice there was a thrill of triumph. Brokaw's hands were clenched, as if someone had threatened to strike him.

"You mean—" he gasped.

"Just this," interrupted Billy, and his voice was harder than Brokaw's now. "The God you used to pray to when you was a kid has given me a choice, Brokaw, an' I'm going to take it. If we stay by this fire, an' keep it up, we won't die of cold, but of starvation. We'll be dead before we get half way to Thoreau's. There's an Indian shack that we could make, but you'll never find it—not unless you unlock these irons and give me that revolver at your belt. Then I'll take you over there as my prisoner. That'll give me another chance for South America—an' the kid an' home." Brokaw was buttoning the thick collar of his shirt close up about his neck. On his face, too, there came for a moment a grim and determined smile.

"Come on," he said, "we'll make Thoreau's or die."

"Sure," said Billy, stepping quickly to his side. "I suppose I might lie down in the snow, an' refuse to budge. I'd win my game then, wouldn't I? But we'll play it—on the square. It's Thoreau's, or die. And it's up to you to find Thoreau's."

He looked back over his shoulder at the burning cabin as they entered the edge of the forest, and in the gray darkness that was preceding dawn he smiled to himself. Two miles to the south, in a thick swamp, was Indian Joe's cabin. They could have made it easily. On their way to Thoreau's they would pass within a mile of it. But Brokaw would never know. And they would never reach Thoreau's. Billy knew that. He looked at the man hunter as he broke trail ahead of him—at the pugnacious hunch of his shoulders, his long stride, the determined clench of his hands, and wondered what the soul and the heart of a man like this must be, who in such an hour would not trade life for life. For almost three-quarters of an hour Brokaw did not utter a word.

The storm had broke. Above the spruce tops the sky began to

clear. Day came slowly. And it was growing steadily colder. The swing of Brokaw'a arms and shoulders kept the blood in them circulating, while Billy's manacled wrists held a part of his body almost rigid. He knew that his hands were already frozen. His arms were numb, and when at last Brokaw paused for a moment on the edge of a frozen stream Billy thrust out his hands, and clanked the steel rings.

"It must be getting colder," he said. "Look at that."

The cold steel had seared his wrists like hot iron, and had pulled off patches of skin and flesh. Brokaw looked, and hunched his shoulders. His lips were blue. His cheeks, ears, and nose were frost-bitten. There was a curious thickness in his voice when he spoke.

"Thoreau lives on this creek," he said. "How much farther is it?"

"Fifteen or sixteen miles," replied Billy. "You'll last just about five, Brokaw. I won't last that long unless you take these things off and give me the use of my arms."

"To knock out my brains when I ain't looking," growled Brokaw. "I guess—before long—you'll be willing to tell where the Indian's shack is." He kicked his way through a drift of snow to the smoother surface of the stream. There was a breath of wind in their faces, and Billy bowed his head to it. In the hours of his greatest loneliness and despair Billy had kept up his fighting spirit by thinking of pleasant things, and now, as he followed in Brokaw's trail, he began to think of home. It was not hard for him to bring up visions of the girl wife who would probably never know how he had died.

He forgot Brokaw. He followed in the trail mechanically, failing to notice that his captor's pace was growing steadily slower, and that his own feet were dragging more and more like leaden weights. He was back among the old hills again, and the sun was shining, and he heard laughter and song. He saw Jeanne standing at the gate in front of the little white cottage, smiling at him, and waving Baby Jeanne's tiny hand at him as he looked back over his shoulder from down the dusty road. His mind did not often travel as far as the mining camp, and he had completely forgotten it now. He no longer felt the sting and pain of the intense cold.

It was Brokaw who brought him back into the reality of things. The sergeant stumbled and fell in a drift, and Billy fell over him. For a moment the two men sat half buried in the snow, looking at each other without speaking. Brokaw moved first. He rose to his feet with an effort. Billy made an attempt to follow him. After three efforts he gave it up, and blinked up into Brokaw's face with a queer laugh. The laugh was almost soundless. There had come a change in Brokaw's face. Its determination and confidence were gone.

At last the iron mask of the Law was broken, and there shone through it something of the emotions and the brotherhood of man. He was fumbling in one of his pockets, and drew out the key to the handcuffs. It was a small key, and he held it between his stiffened fingers with difficulty. He knelt down beside Billy. The keyhole was filled with snow. It took a long time—ten minutes—before the key was fitted in and the lock clicked. He helped to tear off the cuffs. Billy felt no sensation as bits of skin and flesh came "with them. Brokaw gave him a hand, and assisted him to rise. For the first time he spoke.

"Guess you've got me beat, Billy," he said.

"Where's the Indian's?"

He drew his revolver from its holster and tossed it in the snowdrift. The shadow of a smile passed grimly over his face. Billy looked about him. They had stopped where the frozen path of a smaller stream joined the creek. He raised one of his stiffened arms and pointed to it.

"Follow that creek—four miles—and you'll come to Indian Joe's shack," he said.

"And a mile is just about our limit"

"Just about—your's," replied Billy. "I can't make another half. If we had a fire—"

"IF—" wheezed Brokaw.

"If we had a fire," continued Billy. "We could warm ourselves, an' make the Indian's shack easy, couldn't we?"

Brokaw did not answer. He had turned toward the creek when one of Billy's pulseless hands fell heavily on his arm.

"Look here, Brokaw."

Brokaw turned. They looked into each other's eyes.

"I guess mebby you're a man, Brokaw," said Billy quietly. "You've done what you thought was your duty. You've kept your word to th' law, an' I believe you'll keep your word with me. If I say the word that'll save us now will you go back to headquarters an' report me dead?" For a full half minute their eyes did not waver.

Then Brokaw said:

"No."

Billy dropped his hand. It was Brokaw's hand that fell on his arm now.

"I can't do that," he said. "In ten years I ain't run out the white flag once. It's something that ain't known in the service. There ain't a coward in it, or a man who's afraid to die. But I'll play you square. I'll wait until we're both on our feet, again, and then I'll give you twenty-four hours the start of me."

Billy was smiling now. His hand reached out. Brokaw's met it, and the two joined in a grip that their numb fingers scarcely felt.

"Do you know," said Billy softly, "there's been somethin' runnin' in my head ever since we left the burning cabin. It's something my mother taught me: *Do unto others as you'd have others do unto you.*' I'm a d—— fool, ain't I? But I'm goin' to try the experiment, Brokaw, an' see what comes of it. I could drop in a snowdrift an' let you go on—to die. Then I could save myself. But I'm going to take your word—an' do the other thing. I'VE GOT A MATCH."

"A MATCH!"

"Just one. I remember dropping it in my pants pocket yesterday when I was out on the trail. It's in THIS pocket. Your hand is in better shape than mine. Get it."

Life had leaped into Brokaw's face. He thrust his hand into Billy's pocket, staring at him as he fumbled, as if fearing that he had lied. When he drew his hand out the match was between his fingers.

"Ah!" he whispered excitedly.

"Don't get nervous," warned Billy. "It's the only one."

Brokaw's eyes were searching the low timber along the shore. "There's a birch tree," he cried. "Hold it—while I gather a pile of bark!"

He gave the match to Billy, and staggered through the snow to the bank. Strip after strip of the loose bark he tore from the tree. Then he gathered it in a heap in the shelter of a low-hanging spruce, and added dry sticks, and still more bark, to it. When it was ready he stood with his hands in his pockets, and looked at Billy.

"If we had a stone, an' a piece of paper—" he began.

Billy thrust a hand that felt like lifeless lead inside his shirt, and fumbled in a pocket he had made there. Brokaw watched him with red, eager eyes. The hand reappeared, and in it was the buckskin wrapped photograph he had seen the night before, Billy took off the buckskin. About the picture there was a bit of tissue paper. He gave this and the match to Brokaw.

"There's a little gun-file in the pocket the match came from," he said. "I had it mending a trapchain. You can scratch the match on that."

He turned so that Brokaw could reach into the pocket, and the manhunter thrust in his hand. When he brought it forth he held the file. There was a smile on Billy's frostbitten face as he held the picture for a moment under Brokaw's eyes. Billy's own hands had ruffled up the girl's shining curls an instant before the picture was taken, and she was laughing at him when the camera clicked.

"It's all up to her, Brokaw," Billy said gently. "I told you that last night. It was she who woke me up before the fire got us. If you ever prayed—pray a little now. FOR SHE'S GOING TO STRIKE THAT MATCH!"

He still looked at the picture as Brokaw knelt beside the pile he had made. He heard the scratch of the match on the file, but his eyes did not turn. The living, breathing face of the most beautiful thing in the world was speaking to him from out of that picture. His mind was dazed. He swayed a little. He heard a voice, low and sweet, and so distant that it came to him like the faintest whisper. "I am coming—I am coming, Billy—coming—coming—coming—" A joyous cry surged up from his soul, but it died on his lips in a strange gasp. A louder cry brought him back to himself for a moment. It was from Brokaw. The sergeant's face was terrible to behold. He rose to his feet, swaying, his hands clutched at his breast. His voice was thick—hopeless.

"The match—went—out—" He staggered up to Billy, his eyes like a madman's. Billy swayed dizzily. He laughed, even as he crumpled down in the snow. As if in a dream he saw Brokaw stagger off on the frozen trail. He saw him disappear in his hopeless effort to reach the Indian's shack. And then a strange darkness closed him in, and in that darkness he heard still the sweet voice of his wife. It spoke his name again and again, and it urged him to wake up—wake up—WAKE UP! It seemed a long time before he could respond to it. But at last he opened his eyes. He dragged himself to his knees, and looked first to find Brokaw. But the manhunter had gone—forever. The picture was still in his hand. Less distinctly than before he saw the girl smiling at him. And then—at his back—he heard a strange and new sound. With an effort he turned to discover what it was.

The match had hidden an unseen spark from Brokaw's eyes. From out of the pile of fuel was rising a pillar of smoke and flame.

The Yellow-Back

Above God's Lake, where the Bent Arrow runs red as pale blood under its crust of ice, Reese Beaudin heard of the dog auction that was to take place at Post Lac Bain three days later. It was in the cabin of Joe Delesse, a trapper, who lived at Lac Bain during the summer, and trapped the fox and the lynx sixty miles farther north in this month of February.

"Diantre, but I tell you it is to be the greatest sale of dogs that has ever happened at Lac Bain!" said Delesse. "To this *wakao* they are coming from all the four directions. There will be a hundred dogs, huskies, and malamutes, and Mackenzie hounds, and mongrels from the south, and I should not wonder if some of the little Eskimo devils were brought from the north to be sold as breeders. Surely you will not miss it, my friend?"

"I am going by way of Post Lac Bain," replied Reese Beaudin equivocally.

But his mind was not on the sale of dogs. From his pipe he puffed out thick clouds of smoke, and his eyes narrowed until they seemed like coals peering out of cracks; and he said, in his quiet, soft voice:

"Do you know of a man named Jacques Dupont, *m'sieu?*"

Joe Delesse tried to peer through the cloud of smoke at Reese Beaudin's face.

"Yes, I know him. Does he happen to be a friend of yours?"

Reese laughed softly.

"I have heard of him. They say that he is a devil. To the west I was told that he can whip any man between Hudson's Bay and the Great Bear, that he is a beast in man-shape, and that he will surely be at the big sale at Lac Bain."

On his knees the huge hands of Joe Delesse clenched slowly, gripping in their imaginary clutch a hated thing.

"*Oui*, I know him," he said. "I know also—Elise—his wife. See!"

He thrust suddenly his two huge knotted hands through the smoke that drifted between him and the stranger who had sought the shelter of his cabin that night.

"See—I am a man full-grown, *m'sieu*—a man—and yet I am afraid of him! That is how much of a devil and a beast in man-shape he is."

Again Reese Beaudin laughed in his low, soft voice.

"And his wife, *mon ami*? Is she afraid of him?"

He had stopped smoking. Joe Delesse saw his face. The stranger's eyes made him look twice and think twice.

"You have known her—sometime?"

"Yes, a long time ago. "We were children together. And I have heard all has not gone well with her. Is it so?"

"Does it go well when a dove is mated to a vulture, *m'sieu*?"

"I have also heard that she grew up to be very beautiful," said Reese Beaudin, "and that Jacques Dupont killed a man for her. If that is so—"

"It is not so," interrupted Delesse. "He drove another man away—no, not a man, but a yellow-livered coward who had no more fight in him than a porcupine without quills! And yet she says he was not a coward. She has always said, even to Dupont, that it was the way *le Bon Dieu* made him, and that because he was made that way he was greater than all other men in the North Country. How do I know? Because, *m'sieu*, I am Elise Dupont's cousin."

Delesse wondered why Reese Beaudin's eyes were glowing like living coals.

"And yet—again, it is only rumour I have heard—they say this man, whoever he was, did actually run away, like a dog that had been whipped and was afraid to return to its kennel."

"Pst!" Joe Delesse flung his great arms wide. "Like that—he was gone. And no one ever saw him again, or heard of him again. But I know that she knew—my cousin, Elise. What word it was he left for her at the last she has always kept in her own heart, *mon Dieu*, and what a wonderful thing he had to fight for! You knew the child. But the woman—*non*? She was like an angel. Her eyes, when you looked into them—what can I say, *m'sieu*? They made you forget. And I have seen her hair, unbound, black and glossy as the velvet side of a sable, covering her to the hips. And two years ago I saw Jacques Dupont's hands in that hair, and he was dragging her by it—"

Something snapped. It was a muscle in Reese Beaudin's arm. He had stiffened like iron.

"And you let him do that!"

Joe Delesse shrugged his shoulders. It was a shrug of hopelessness, of disgust.

"For the third time I interfered, and for the third time Jacques Dupont beat me until I was nearer dead than alive. And since then I have made it none of my business. It was, after all, the fault of the man who ran away. You see, *m'sieu*, it was like this: Dupont was mad for her, and this man who ran away—the Yellow-back—wanted her, and Elise loved the Yellow-back. This Yellow-back was twenty-three or four, and he read books, and played a fiddle and drew strange pictures—and was weak in the heart when it came to a fight. But Elise loved him. She loved him for those very things that made him a fool and a weakling, *m'sieu*, the books and the fiddle and the pictures; and she stood up with the courage for them both.

And she would have married him, too, and would have fought for him with a club if it had come to that, when the thing happened that made him run away. It was at the midsummer carnival, when all the trappers and their wives and children were at Lac Bain. And Dupont followed the Yellow-back about like a dog. He taunted him, he insulted him, he got down on his knees and offered to fight him without getting on his feet; and there, before the very eyes of Elise, he washed the Yellow-back's face in the grease of one of the roasted caribou! And the Yellow-back was a man! Yes, a grown man! And it was then that Jacques Dupont shouted out his challenge to all that crowd. He would fight the Yellow-back. He would fight him with his right arm tied behind his back!

And before Elise and the Yellow-back, and all that crowd, friends tied his arm so that it was like a piece of wood behind him, and it was his right arm, his fighting arm, the better half of him that was gone. And even then the Yellow-back was as white as the paper he drew pictures on. *Ventre saint gris*, but then was his chance to have killed Jacques Dupont! Half a man could have done it. Did he, *m'sieu*? No, he did not. With his one arm and his one hand Jacques Dupont whipped that Yellow-back, and he would have killed him if Elise had not rushed in to save the Yellow-back's purple face from going dead black. And that night the Yellow-back slunk away. Shame? Yes. From that night he was ashamed to show his face ever again at Lac Bain. And no one knows where he went. No one—except Elise. And her secret is in her own breast."

"And after that?" questioned Reese Beaudin, in a voice that was scarcely above a whisper.

"I cannot understand," said Joe Delesse. "It was strange, *m'sieu*, very strange. I know that Elise, even after that coward ran away, still loved him. And yet—well, something happened. I overheard a terrible quarrel one day between Jan Thiebout, father of Elise, and Jacques Dupont. After that Thiebout was very much afraid of Dupont. I have my own suspicion. Now that Thiebout is dead it is not wrong for me to say what it is. I think Thiebout killed the halfbreed Bedore who was found dead on his trap-line five years ago. There was a feud between them. And Dupont, discovering Thiebout's secret—well, you can understand how easy it would be after that, *m'sieu*. Thiebout's winter trapping was in that Burntwood country, fifty miles from neighbour to neighbour, and very soon after Bedore's death Jacques Dupont became Thiebout's partner. I know that Elise was forced to marry him. That was four years ago. The next year old Thiebout died, and in all that time not once has Elise been to Post Lac Bain!"

"Like the Yellow-back—she never returned," breathed Reese Beaudin.

"Never. And now—it is strange—"

"What is strange, Joe Delesse?"

"That for the first time in all these years she is going to Lac Bain—to the dog sale."

Reese Beaudin's face was again hidden in the smoke of his pipe. Through it his voice came.

"It is a cold night, M'sieu Delesse. Hear the wind howl!"

"Yes, it is cold—so cold the foxes will not run. My traps and poison-baits will need no tending tomorrow."

"Unless you dig them out of the drifts."

"I will stay in the cabin."

"What! You are not going to Lac Bain!"

"I doubt it."

"Even though Elise, your cousin, is to be there?"

"I have no stomach for it, *m'sieu*. Nor would you were you in my boots, and did you know why he is going. *Par les mille cornes d'u diable*, I cannot whip him but I can kill him—and if I went—and the thing happens which I guess is going to happen—"

"*Qui?* Surely you will tell me—"

"Yes, I will tell you. Jacques Dupont knows that Elise has never stopped loving the Yellow-back. I do not believe she has ever tried to

218

hide it from him. Why should she? And there is a rumour, *m'sieu*, that the Yellow-back will be at the Lac Bain dog sale."

Reese Beaudin rose slowly to his feet, and yawned in that smoke-filled cabin.

"And if the Yellow-back should turn the tables, Joe Delesse, think of what a fine thing you will miss," he said.

Joe Delesse also rose, with a contemptuous laugh.

"That fiddler, that picture-drawer, that book-reader—Pouff! You are tired, *m'sieu*, that is your bunk."

Reese Beaudin held out a hand. The bulk of the two stood out in the lamp-glow, and Joe Delesse was so much the bigger man that his hand was half again the size of Reese Beaudin's. They gripped. And then a strange look went over the face of Joe Delesse. A cry came from out of his beard. His mouth grew twisted. His knees doubled slowly under him, and in the space of ten seconds his huge bulk was kneeling on the floor, while Reese Beaudin looked at him, smiling.

"Has Jacques Dupont a greater grip than that, Joe Delesse?" he asked in a voice that was so soft it was almost a woman's.

"*Mon Dieu!*" gasped Delesse. He staggered to his feet, clutching his crushed hand. "*M'sieu*—"

Reese Beaudin put his hands to the other's shoulders, smiling, friendly.

"I will apologize, I will explain, *mon ami*," he said. "But first, you must tell me the name of that Yellow-back who ran away years ago. Do you remember it?"

"*Oui*, but what has that to do with my crushed hand? The Yellow-back's name was Reese Beaudin—"

"And I am Reese Beaudin," laughed the other gently.

On that day—the day of *wakoa*, the dog sale—seven fat caribou were roasting on great spits at Post Lac Bain, and under them were seven fires burning red and hot of seasoned birch, and around the seven fires were seven groups of men who slowly turned the roasting carcasses.

It was the Big Day of the mid-winter festival, and Post Lac Bain, with a population of twenty in times of quiet, was a seething wilderness metropolis of two hundred excited souls and twice as many dogs. From all directions they had come, from north and south and east and west; from near and from far, from the Barrens, from the swamps, from the farther forests, from river and lake and hidden trail—a few white men, mostly French; half-breeds and breeds, Chippewans, and

Crees, and here and there a strange, dark-visaged little interloper from the north with his strain of Eskimo blood. Foregathered were all the breeds and creeds and fashions of the wilderness.

Over all this, pervading the air like an incense, stirring the desire of man and beast, floated the aroma of the roasting caribou. The feast-hour was at hand. With cries that rose above the last words of a wild song the seven groups of men rushed to seven pairs of props and tore them away. The great carcasses swayed in mid-air, bent slowly over their spits, and then crashed into the snow fifteen feet from the fire. About each carcass five men with razor-sharp knives ripped off hunks of the roasted flesh and passed them into eager hands of the hungry multitude. First came the women and children, and last the men.

On this there peered forth from a window in the factor's house the darkly bearded, smiling face of Reese Beaudin.

"I have seen him three times, wandering about in the crowd, seeking someone," he said. "*Bien*, he shall find that someone very soon!"

In the face of McDougall, the factor, was a strange look. For he had listened to a strange story, and there was still something of shock and amazement and disbelief in his eyes.

"Reese Beaudin, it is hard for me to believe."

"And yet you shall find that it is true," smiled Reese.

"He will kill you. He is a monster—a giant!"

"I shall die hard," replied Reese.

He turned from the window again, and took from the table a violin wrapped in buckskin, and softly he played one of their old love songs. It was not much more than a whisper, and yet it was filled with a joyous exultation. He laid the violin down when he was finished, and laughed, and filled his pipe, and lighted it.

"It is good for a man's soul to know that a woman loves him, and has been true," he said. "*Mon père,* will you tell me again what she said? It is strength for me—and I must soon be going."

McDougall repeated, as if under a strain from which he could not free himself:

"She came to me late last night, unknown to Dupont. She had received your message, and knew you were coming. And I tell you again that I saw something in her eyes which makes me afraid! She told me, then, that her father killed Bedore in a quarrel, and that she married Dupont to save him from the law—and kneeling there, with her hand on the cross at her breast, she swore that each day of her life she has let Dupont know that she hates him, and that she loves you, and that someday Reese Beaudin would return to avenge her. Yes, she told him that—I know it by what I saw in her eyes. With that cross clutched in her fingers she swore that she had suffered torture and shame, and that never a word of it had she whispered to a living soul, that she might turn the passion of Jacques Dupont's black heart into a great hatred. And today—Jacques Dupont will kill you!"

"I shall die hard," Reese repeated again.

He tucked the violin in its buckskin covering under his arm. From the table he took his cap and placed it on his head.

In a last effort McDougall sprang from his chair and caught the other's arm.

"Reese Beaudin—you are going to your death! As factor of Lac Bain—agent of justice under power of the Police—I forbid it!"

"So-o-o-o," spoke Reese Beaudin gently. "*Mon père*—"

He unbuttoned his coat, which had remained buttoned. Under the coat was a heavy shirt; and the shirt he opened, smiling into the factor's eyes, and McDougall's face froze, and the breath was cut short on his lips.

"That!" he gasped.

Reese Beaudin nodded.

Then he opened the door and went out.

Joe Delesse had been watching the factor's house, and he worked his way slowly along the edge of the feasters so that he might casually come into the path of Reese Beaudin. And there was one other man who also had watched, and who came in the same direction. He was a stranger, tall, closely hooded, his moustached face an Indian bronze. No one had ever seen him at Lac Bain before, yet in the excitement of the carnival the fact passed without conjecture or significance. And from the cabin of Henri Paquette another pair of eyes saw Reese Beaudin, and Mother Paquette heard a sob that in itself was a prayer.

In and out among the devourers of caribou-flesh, scanning the groups and the ones and the twos and the threes, passed Jacques Dupont, and with him walked his friend, one-eyed Layonne. Layonne was a big man, but Dupont was taller by half a head. The brutishness of his face was hidden under a coarse red beard; but the devil in him glowered from his deep-set, inhuman eyes; it walked in his gait, in the hulk of his great shoulders, in the gorilla-like slouch of his hips. His huge hands hung partly clenched at his sides. His breath was heavy with whisky that Layonne himself had smuggled in, and in his heart was black murder.

"He has not come!" he cried for the twentieth time. "He has not come!"

He moved on, and Reese Beaudin—ten feet away—turned and smiled at Joe Delesse with triumph in his eyes. He moved nearer.

"Did I not tell you he would not find in me that narrow-shouldered, smooth-faced stripling of five years ago?" he asked. "*N'est-ce pas*, friend Delesse?"

The face of Joe Delesse was heavy with a sombre fear.

"His fist is like a wood-sledge, m'sieu."

"So it was years ago."

"His forearm is as big as the calf of your leg."

"*Oui*, friend Delesse, it is the forearm of a giant."

"He is half again your weight."

"Or more, friend Delesse."

"He will kill you! As the great God lives, he will kill you!"

"I shall die hard," repeated Reese Beaudin for the third time that day.

Joe Delesse turned slowly, doggedly. His voice rumbled.

"The sale is about to begin, *m'sieu*. See!"

A man had mounted the log platform raised to the height of a man's shoulders at the far end of the clearing. It was Henri Paquette, master of the day's ceremonies, and appointed auctioneer of the great *wakao*. A man of many tongues was Paquette. To his lips he raised a great megaphone of birchbark, and sonorously his call rang out in French, in Cree, in Chippewan, and the packed throng about the caribou-fires heaved like a living billow, and to a man and a woman and a child it moved toward the appointed place.

"The time has come," said Reese Beaudin. "And all Lac Bain shall see!"

Behind them—watching, always watching—followed the bronze-faced stranger in his close-drawn hood.

For an hour the men of Lac Bain gathered close-wedged about the log platform on which stood Henri Paquette and his Indian helper. Behind the men were the women and children, and through the cordon there ran a *babiche*-roped pathway along which the dogs were brought.

The platform was twenty feet square, with the floor side of the logs hewn flat, and there was no lack of space for the gesticulation and wild pantomime of Paquette. In one hand he held a notebook, and in the other a pencil. In the notebook the sales of twenty dogs were already tabulated, and the prices paid.

Anxiously, Reese Beaudin was waiting. Each time that a new dog came up he looked at Joe Delesse, but, as yet Joe had failed to give the signal.

On the platform the Indian was holding two malamutes in leash now and Paquette was crying, in a well simulated fit of great fury:

"What, you cheap *kimootisks*, will you let this pair of malamutes go for seven mink and a cross fox. Are you men? Are you poverty-stricken? Are you blind? A breed dog and a male giant for seven mink and a cross fox? Non, I will buy them myself first, and kill them, and use their flesh for dog-feed, and their hides for fools' caps! I will—"

"Twelve mink and a Number Two Cross," came a voice out of the crowd.

"Twelve mink and a Number One," shouted another.

"A little better—a little better!" wailed Paquette. "You are waking up, but slowly—*mon Dieu*, so slowly! Twelve mink and—"

A voice rose in Cree:

"*Nesi-tu-now-unisk!*"

Paquette gave a triumphant yell.

"The Indian beats you! The Indian from Little Neck Lake—an Indian beats the white man! He offers twenty beaver—prime skins! And beaver are wanted in Paris now. They're wanted in London. Beaver and gold—they are the same! But they are the price of one dog alone. Shall they both go at that? Shall the Indian have them for twenty beaver—twenty beaver that may be taken from a single house in a day—while it has taken these malamutes two and a half years to grow? I say, you cheap *kimootisks*—"

And then an amazing thing happened. It was like a bomb falling in that crowded throng of wondering and amazed forest people.

It was the closely hooded stranger who spoke.

"I will give a hundred dollars cash," he said.

A look of annoyance crossed Reese Beaudin's face.

He was close to the bronze-faced stranger, and edged nearer.

"Let the Indian have them," he said in a low voice. "It is Meewe. I knew him years ago. He has carried me on his back. He taught me first to draw pictures."

"But they are powerful dogs," objected the stranger. "My team needs them."

The Cree had risen higher out of the crowd. One arm rose above his head. He was an Indian who had seen fifty years of the forests, and his face was the face of an Egyptian.

"*Nesi-tu-now Nesoo-sap umisk!*" he proclaimed.

Henri Paquette hopped excitedly, and faced the stranger.

"Twenty-two beaver," he challenged. "Twenty-two—"

"Let Meewe have them," replied the hooded stranger.

Three minutes later a single dog was pulled up on the log platform. He was a magnificent beast, and a rumble of approval ran through the crowd.

The face of Joe Delesse was gray. He wet his lips. Reese Beaudin, watching him, knew that the time had come. And Joe Delesse, seeing no way of escape, whispered:

"It is her dog, *m'sieu*. It is Parka—and Dupont sells him today to show her that he is master."

Already Paquette was advertising the virtues of Parka when Reese Beaudin, in a single leap, mounted the log platform, and stood beside him.

"Wait!" he cried.

There fell a silence, and Reese said, loud enough for all to hear:

"M'sieu Paquette, I ask the privilege of examining this dog that I want to buy."

At last he straightened, and all who faced him saw the smiling sneer on his lips.

"Who is it that offers this worthless cur for sale?" Lac Bain heard him say. "P-s-s-st—it is a woman's dog! It is not worth bidding for!"

"You lie!" Dupont's voice rose in a savage roar. His huge shoulders bulked over those about him. He crowded to the edge of the platform. "You lie!"

"He is a woman's dog," repeated Reese Beaudin without excitement, yet so clearly that every ear heard. "He is a woman's pet, and M'sieu Dupont most surely does lie if he denies it!"

So far as memory went back no man at Lac Bain that day had ever heard another man give Jacques Dupont the lie. A thrill swept those who heard and understood. There was a great silence, in that silence men near him heard the choking rage in Dupont's great chest. He was staring up—straight up into the smiling face of Reese Beaudin; and in that moment he saw beyond the glossy black beard, and amazement and unbelief held him still. In the next, Reese Beaudin had the violin in his hands. He flung off the buckskin, and in a flash the instrument was at his shoulder.

"See! I will play, and the woman's pet shall sing!"

And once more, after five years, Lac Bain listened to the magic of Reese Beaudin's violin. And it was Elise's old love song that he played. He played it, smiling down into the eyes of a monster whose face was turning from red to black; yet he did not play it to the end, nor a quarter of it, for suddenly a voice shouted:

"It is Reese Beaudin—come back!"

Joe Delesse, paralyzed, speechless, could have sworn it was the hooded stranger who shouted; and then he remembered, and flung up his great arms, and bellowed:

"*Oui*—by the Saints, it is Reese Beaudin—Reese Beaudin come back!"

Suddenly as it had begun the playing ceased, and Henri Paquette found himself with the violin in his hands. Reese Beaudin turned, facing them all, the wintry sun glowing in his beard, his eyes smiling, his head high—unafraid now, more fearless than any other man that had ever set foot in Lac Bain. And McDougall, with his arm touching Elise's hair, felt the wild and throbbing pulse of her body. This day-this hour—this minute in which she stood still, inbreathing—had confirmed her belief in Reese Beaudin. As she had dreamed, so had he risen. First of all the men in the world he stood there now, just as he had been first in the days when she had loved his dreams, his music, and his pictures. To her he was the old god, more splendid,—for he had risen above fear, and he was facing Dupont now with that strange quiet smile on his lips. And then, all at once, her soul broke its fetters, and over the women's heads she reached out her arms, and all there heard her voice in its triumph, its joy, its fear.

"Reese! Reese—my *sakeakun!*"

Over the heads of all the forest people she called him beloved! Like the fang of an adder the word stung Dupont's brain. And like fire touched to powder, swiftly as lightning illumines the sky, the glory of it blazed in Reese Beaudin's face. And all that were there heard him clearly:

"I am Reese Beaudin. I am the Yellow-back. I have returned to meet a man you all know—Jacques Dupont. He is a monkey-man—a whipper of boys, a stealer of women, a cheat, a coward, a thing so foul the crows will not touch him when he dies—"

There was a roar. It was not the roar of a man, but of a beast—and Jacques Dupont was on the platform!

Quick as Dupont's movement had been it was no swifter than that of the closely-hooded stranger. He was as tall as Dupont, and about him there was an air of authority and command.

"Wait," he said, and placed a hand on Dupont's heaving chest. His smile was cold as ice. Never had Dupont seen eyes so like the pale blue of steel.

"M'sieu Dupont, you are about to avenge a great insult. It must be done fairly. If you have weapons, throw them away. I will search this—this Reese Beaudin, as he calls himself! And if there is to be a fight, let it be a good one. Strip yourself to that great garment you have on, friend Dupont. See, our friend—this Reese Beaudin—is already stripping!"

He was unbuttoning the giant's heavy Hudson's Bay coat. He pulled it off, and drew Dupont's knife from its sheath. Paquette, like a stunned cat that had recovered its ninth life, was scrambling from the platform. The Indian was already gone. And Reese Beaudin had tossed his coat to Joe Delesse, and with it his cap. His heavy shirt was closely buttoned; and not only was it buttoned, Delesse observed, but also was it carefully pinned. And even now, facing that monster who would soon be at him, Reese Beaudin was smiling.

For a moment the closely hooded stranger stood between them, and Jacques Dupont crouched himself for his vengeance. Never to the people of Lac Bain had he looked more terrible. He was the gorilla-fighter, the beast fighter, the fighter who fights as the wolf, the bear and the cat—crushing out life, breaking bones, twisting, snapping, inundating and destroying with his great weight and his monstrous strength. He was a hundred pounds heavier than Reese Beaudin. On his stooping shoulders he could carry a tree. With his giant hands he could snap a two-inch sapling. With one hand alone he had set a bear-trap. And with that mighty strength he fought as the cave-man fought. It was his boast there was no trick of the Chippewan, the Cree, the Eskimo or the forest man that he did not know. And yet Reese Beaudin stood calmly, waiting for him, and smiling!

In another moment the hooded stranger was gone, and there was none between them.

"A long time I have waited for this, *m'sieu*," said Reese, for Dupont's ears alone. "Five years is a long time. And my Elise still loves me."

Still more like a gorilla Jacques Dupont crept upon him. His face was twisted by a rage to which he could no longer give voice. Hatred and jealousy robbed his eyes of the last spark of the thing that was human. His great hands were hooked, like an eagle's talons. His lips were drawn back, like a beast's. Through his red beard yellow fangs were bared.

And Reese Beaudin no longer smiled. He laughed!

"Until I went away and met real men, I never knew what a pig of a man you were, M'sieu Dupont," he taunted amiably, as though speaking in jest to a friend. "You remind me of an aged and over-fat porcupine with his big paunch and crooked arms. What horror must it have been for my Elise to have lived in sight of such a beast as you!"

With a bellow Dupont was at him. And swifter than eyes had ever seen man move at Lac Bain before, Reese Beaudin was out of his way, and behind him; and then, as the giant caught himself at the edge of the platform, and turned, he received a blow that sounded like the broadside of a paddle striking water. Reese Beaudin had struck him with the flat of his unclenched hand!

A murmur of incredulity rose out of the crowd. To the forest man such a blow was the deadliest of insults. It was calling him an *Iskwao*—a woman—a weakling—a thing too contemptible to harden one's fist against. But the murmur died in an instant. For Reese Beaudin, making as if to step back, shot suddenly forward—straight through the giant's crooked arms—and it was his fist this time that landed squarely between the eyes of Dupont. The monster's head went back, his great body wavered, and then suddenly he plunged backward off the platform and fell with a crash to the ground.

A yell went up from the hooded stranger. Joe Delesse split his throat. The crowd drowned Reese Beaudin's voice. But above it all rose a woman's voice shrieking forth a name.

And then Jacques Dupont was on the platform again. In the moments that followed one could almost hear his neighbour's heart beat. Nearer and still nearer to each other drew the two men. And now Dupont crouched still more, and Joe Delesse held his breath. He noticed that Reese Beaudin was standing almost on the tips of his toes—that each instant he seemed prepared, like a runner, for sudden flight. Five feet—four—and Dupont leapt in, his huge arms swinging like the limb of a tree, and his weight following with crushing force behind his blow.

For an instant it seemed as though Reese Beaudin had stood to meet that fatal rush, but in that same instant—so swiftly that only the hooded stranger knew what had happened—he was out of the way, and his left arm seemed to shoot downward, and then up, and then his right straight out, and then again his left arm downward, and up—and it was the third blow, all swift as lightning, that brought a yell from the hooded stranger. For though none but the stranger had seen it, Jacques Dupont's head snapped back—and all saw the fourth blow that sent him reeling like a man struck by a club.

There was no sound now. A mental and a vocal paralysis seized upon the inhabitants of Lac Bain. Never had they seen fighting like this fighting of Reese Beaudin. Until now had they lived to see the science of the sawdust ring pitted against the brute force of Brob-dingnagian, of Antaeus and Goliath. For Reese Beaudin's fighting was a fighting without tricks that they could see. He used his fists, and his fists alone. He was like a dancing man. And suddenly, in the midst of the miracle, they saw Jacques Dupont go down. And the second mira-cle was that Reese Beaudin did not leap on him when he had fallen. He stood back a little, balancing himself in that queer fashion on the balls and toes of his feet. But no sooner was Dupont up than Reese Beaudin was in again, with the swiftness of a cat, and they could hear the blows, like solid shots, and Dupont's arms waved like tree-tops, and a second time he was off the platform.

He was staggering when he rose. The blood ran in streams from his mouth and nose. His beard dripped with it. His yellow teeth were caved in.

This time he did not leap upon the platform—he clambered back to it, and the hooded stranger gave him a lift which a few minutes before Dupont would have resented as an insult.

"Ah, it has come," said the stranger to Delesse.

"He is the best close-in fighter in all—"

He did not finish.

"I could kill you now—kill you with a single blow," said Reese Beaudin in a moment when the giant stood swaying. "But there is a greater punishment in store for you, and so I shall let you live!"

And now Reese Beaudin was facing that part of the crowd where the woman he loved was standing. He was breathing deeply. But he was not winded. His eyes were black as night, his hair wind-blown. He looked straight over the heads between him and she whom Dupont had stolen from him.

Reese Beaudin raised his arms, and where there had been a mur-mur of voices there was now silence.

For the first time the stranger threw back his hood. He was unbut-toning his heavy coat.

And Joe Delesse, looking up, saw that Reese Beaudin was making a mighty effort to quiet a strange excitement within his breast. And then there was a rending of cloth and of buttons and of pins as in one swift movement he tore the shirt from his own breast—exposing to the eyes of Lac Bain blood-red in the glow of the winter sun, the crimson badge of the Royal Northwest Mounted Police!

And above the gasp that swept the multitude, above the strange cry of the woman, his voice rose:

"I am Reese Beaudin, the Yellow-back. I am Reese Beaudin, who ran away. I am Reese Beaudin,—Sergeant in His Majesty's Royal Northwest Mounted Police, and in the name of the law I arrest Jacques Dupont for the murder of Francois Bedore, who was killed on his trap-line five years ago! Fitzgerald—"

The hooded stranger leaped upon the platform. His heavy coat fell off. Tall and grim he stood in the scarlet jacket of the Police. Steel clinked in his hands. And Jacques Dupont, terror in his heart, was trying to see as he groped to his knees. The steel snapped over his wrists.

And then he heard a voice close over him. It was the voice of Reese Beaudin.

"And this is your final punishment, Jacques Dupont—to be hanged by the neck until you are dead. For Bedore was not dead when Elise's father left him after their fight on the trap-line. It was you who saw the fight, and finished the killing, and laid the crime on Elise's father. Mukoki, the Indian, saw you. It is my day, Dupont, and I have waited long—"

The rest Dupont did not hear. For up from the crowd there went a mighty roar. And through it a woman was making her way with out-reaching arms—and behind her followed the factor of Lac Bain.

The Case of Beauvais

Madness? Perhaps. And yet if it was madness. . . .

But strange things happen up there, gentlemen. I have found it sometimes hard to define that word. There are so many kinds of madness, so many ways in which the human brain may go wrong; and so often it happens that what we call madness is both reasonable and just. It is so. Yes. A little reason is good for us, a little more makes wise men of some of us—but when our reason over-grows us and we reach too far, something breaks and we go insane.

But I will tell you the story. That is what you want to hear, and you expect that it will be prejudiced—that I will either deliberately attempt to protect and prolong a human life, or shorten and destroy it. I shall do neither, gentlemen of the Royal Mounted Police. I have a faith in you that is in its way an unbounded as my faith in God. I have looked up to you in all my life in the wilderness as the heart of chivalry and the soul of honour and fairness to all men. Pathfinders, men of iron, guardians of people and spaces of which civilization knows but little, I have taught my children of the forests to honour, obey and to trust you. And so I shall tell you the story without prejudice, with the gratitude of a missioner who has lived his life for forty years in the wilderness, gentlemen.

I am a Catholic. It is four hundred miles straight north by dog-sledge or snowshoe to my cabin, and this is the first time in nineteen years that I have been down to the edge of the big world which I remember now as little more than a dream. But up there I knew that my duty lay, just at the edge of the Big Barren. See! My hands are knotted like the snarl of a tree. The glare of your lights hurts my eyes. I travelled today in the middle of your street because my moccasined feet stumbled on the smoothness of your walks. People stared, and some of them laughed.

Forty years I have lived in another world. You—and especially you gentlemen who have trailed in the Patrols of the north—know what that world is. As it shapes different hands, as it trains different feet, as it gives to us different eyes, so also it has bred into my forest children hearts and souls that may be a little different, and a code of right and wrong that too frequently has had no court of law to guide it. So judge fairly, gentlemen of the Royal Mounted Police! Understand, if you can.

It was a terrible winter—that winter of Le Mort Rouge. So far down as men and children now living will remember, it will be called by my people the winter of Famine and Red Death. Starvation, gentlemen—and the smallpox. People died like—what shall I say? It is not easy to describe a thing like that. They died in *tepees*. They died in shacks. They died on the trail. From late December until March I said my prayers over the dead. You are wondering what all this has to do with my story; why it matters that the caribou had migrated in vast herds to the westward, and there was no food; why it matters that there were famine and plague in the great unknown land, and that people were dying and our world going through a cataclysm.

My backwoods eyes can see your thought. What has all this to do with Joseph Brecht? What has it to do with Andre Beauvais? Why does this little forest priest take up so much time in telling so little? you ask. And because it has its place—because it has its meaning—I ask you for permission to tell my story in my own way. For these sufferings, this hunger and pestilence and death, had a strange and terrible effect on many human creatures that were left alive when spring came. It was like a great storm that had swept through a forest of tall trees. A storm of suffering that left heads bowed, shoulders bent, and minds gone. Yes, GONE!

Since that winter of Le Mort Rouge I know of eyes into which the life of laughter will never come again; I know of strong men who became as little children; I have seen faces that were fair with youth shrivel into age—and my people call it *noot' akutawin keskwawin*—the cold and hungry madness. May God help Andre Beauvais!

I will tell the story now.

It was in June. The last of the mush-snows had gone early, nearly a fortnight before, and the waters were free from ice, when word was brought to me that Father Boget was dying at Old Fort Reliance. Father Boget was twenty years older than I, and I called him *mon père*. He was a father to me in our earlier years. I made haste to reach him that I might hold his hand before he died, if that was possible. And you, Sergeant McVeigh, who have spent years in that country of the Great Slave, know what a race with death from Christie Bay to Old Fort Reliance would be. To follow the broken and twisted waters of the Great Slave would mean two hundred miles, while to cut straight across the land by smaller streams and lakelets meant less than seventy. But on your maps that space of seventy miles is a blank. You have in it no streams and no larger waters. You know little of it. But I can tell you, for I have been through it.

It is a Lost Hell. It is a vast country in which berry bushes grow abundantly, but on which there are no berries, where there are forests and swamps, but not a living creature to inhabit them; a country of water in which there are no fish, of air in which there are no birds, of plants without flowers—a reeking, stinking country of brimstone, a hell. In your Blue Books you have called it the Sulphur Country. And this country, as you draw a line from Christie Bay to Old Fort Reliance, is straight between. *Mon père* was dying, and my time was short. I decided to venture it—cut across that Sulphur Country, and I sought for a man to accompany me. I could find none.

To the Indian it was the land of *Wetikoo*—the Devil Country; to the Breeds it was filled with horror. Forty miles distant there was a man I knew would go, a white man. But to reach him would lose me three days, and I was about to set out alone when the stranger came. He was, indeed, a strange man. When he came to what I called my chateau, from nowhere, going nowhere, I hardly knew whether to call him young or old. But I made my guess. That terrible winter had branded him. When I asked him his name, he said:

"I am a wanderer, and in wandering I have lost my name. Call me *M'sieu.*"

I found this was a long speech for him, that his tongue was tied by a horrible silence. When I told him where I was going, and described the country I was going through, and that I wanted a man, he merely nodded that he would accompany me.

We started in a canoe, and I placed him ahead of me so that I could make out, if I could, something of what he was. His hair was dark. His beard was dark. His eyes were sunken but strangely clear. They puzzled me. They were always questing. Always seeking. And always expecting, it seemed to me. A man of unfathomable mystery, of unutterable tragedy, of a silence that was almost inhuman. Was he mad? I ask you, gentlemen—was he mad? And I leave the answer to you. To me he was good. When I told him what *mon père* had been to me, and that I wanted to reach him before he died, he spoke no word of hope or sympathy—but worked until his muscles cracked. We ate together, we drank together, we slept side by side—and it was like eating and drinking and sleeping with a sphinx which some strange miracle had endowed with life.

The second day we entered the Sulphur Country. The stink of it was in our nostrils that second night we camped. The moon rose, and we saw it as if through the fumes of a yellow smoke. Far behind us we heard a wolf howl, and it was the last sound of life. With the dawn we went on. We passed through broad, low morasses out of which rose the sulphurous fogs. In many places the water we touched with our hands was hot; in other places the forests we paddled through were so dense they were almost tropical. And lifeless. Still, with the stillness of death for thousands and perhaps tens of thousands of years. The food we ate seemed saturated with the vileness of sulphur; it seeped into our water-bags; it turned us to the colour of saffron; it was terrible, frightening, inconceivable. And still we went on by compass, and *M'sieu* showed no fear—even less, gentlemen, than did I.

And then, on the third day—in the heart of this diseased and horrible region—we made a discovery that drew a strange cry even from those mysteriously silent lips of *M'sieu*.

It was the print of a naked human foot in a bar of mud.

How it came there, why it was there, and why if was a naked foot I suppose were the first thoughts that leaped into our startled minds. What man could live in these infernal regions? WAS it a man, or was it the footprint of some primeval ape, a monstrous survival of the centuries?

The trail led through a steaming slough in which the mud and water were tepid and which grew rank with yellow reeds and thick grasses—grasses that were almost flesh-like, it seemed to me, as if swollen and about to burst from some dreadful disease, Perhaps your scientists can tell why sulphur has this effect on vegetation. It is so; there was sulphur in the very wood we burned. Through those reeds and grasses we soon found where a narrow trail was beaten, and then we came to a rise of land sheltered in timber, a sort of hill in that flat world, and on the crest of this hill we found a cabin.

Yes, a cabin; a cabin built roughly of logs, and it was yellow with sulphur, as if painted. We went inside and we found there the man whom you know as Joseph Brecht. I did not look at *M'sieu* when he first rose before us, but I heard a great gasp from his throat behind me. And I think I stood as if life had suddenly gone out of me. Joseph Brecht was half naked. His feet were bare. He looked like a wild man, with his uncut hair—a wild man except that his face was smooth. Curious that a man would shave there! And not so odd, perhaps, when one knows how a beard gathers sulphur. He had risen from a cot on which there was a bed of boughs, and in the light that came in through the open door he looked terribly emaciated, with the skin drawn tightly over his cheek bones. It was he who spoke first.

"I am glad you have come," he said, his eyes staring wildly. "I guess I am dying. Some water, please. There is a spring back of the cabin."

Quite sanely he spoke, and yet the words were scarcely out of his mouth when he fell back upon the cot, his eyes rolling in the top of his head, his mouth agape, his breath coming in great panting gasps. It was a strange sickness. I will not trouble you with all the details. You are anxious for the story—the tragedy—which alone will count with you gentlemen of the law. It came out in his fever, and in the fits of sanity into which he at times succeeded in rousing himself. His name, he said, was Joseph Brecht. For two years he had lived in that sulphur hell. He had, by accident, found the spring of fresh, sweet water trickling out of the hill—another miracle for which I have not tried to account; he built his cabin; for two years he had gone with his canoe to the shore of the great Slave, forty miles distant, for the food he ate.

But WHY was he here? That was the story that came bit by bit, half in his fever, half in his sanity. I will tell it in my own words. He was a Government man, mapping out the last timber lines along the edge of the Great Barren, when he first met Andre Beauvais and his wife, Marie. An accident took him to their cabin, a sprained leg. Andre was a fox-hunter, and it was when he was coming home from one of his trips that he found Joseph Brecht helpless in the deep snow, and carried him on his shoulders to his cabin.

Ah, gentlemen, it was the old story—the story old as time. In his sanity he told us about Marie, I hovering over him closely, *M'sieu* sitting back in the shadows. She was like some wonderful wildflower, French, a little Indian. He told us how her long black hair would stream in a shining cascade, soft as the breast of a swan, to her knees and below; how it would hang again in two great, lustrous braids, and how her eyes were limpid pools that set his soul afire, and how her slim, beautiful body filled him with a monstrous desire. She must have been beautiful. And her husband, Andre Beauvais, worshipped her, and the ground she trod on. And he had the faith in her that a mother has in her child.

It was a sublime love, and Joseph Brecht told us about it as he lay there, dying, as he supposed. In that faith of his Andre went unsuspectingly to his trap-lines and his poison-trails, and Marie and Joseph were for many hours at a time alone, sometimes for a day, sometimes for two days, and occasionally for three, for even after his limb had regained its strength Joseph feigned that it was bad. It was a hard fight, he said—a hard fight for him to win her; but win her he did, utterly, absolutely, heart, body and soul. Remember, he was from the South, with all its power of language, all its tricks of love, all its furtiveness of argument, a strong man with a strong mind—and she had lived all her life in the wilderness. She was no match for him. She surrendered. He told us how, after that, he would unbind her wonderful hair and pillow his face in it; how he lived in a heaven of transport, how utterly she gave herself to him in those times when Andre, was away.

Did he love her?

Yes, in that mad passion of the brute. But not as you and I might love a woman, gentlemen. Not as Andre loved her. Whether she had a heart or a soul it did not matter. His eyes were blind with an insensate joy when he shrouded himself in her wonderful hair. To see the wild colour painting her face like a flower filled his veins with fire. The beauty of her, the touch of her, the mad beat of her heart against him made him like a drunken man in his triumph. Love? Yes, the love of the brute! He prolonged his stay. He had no idea of taking her with him. When the time came, he would go. Day after day, week after week he put it off, feigning that the bone of his leg was affected, and Andre Beauvais treated him like a brother. He told us all this as he lay there in his cabin in that sulphur hell. I am a man of God, and I do not lie.

Is there need to tell you that Andre discovered them? Yes, he found them—and with that wonderful hair of hers so closely about them that he was still bound in the tresses when the discovery came.

Andre had come in exhausted, and unexpectedly. There was a terrible fight, and in spite of his exhaustion he would have killed Joseph Brecht if at the last moment the latter had not drawn his revolver. After all is said and done, gentlemen, can a woman love but once? Joseph Brecht fired. In that infinitesimal moment between the levelling of the gun and the firing of the shot Marie Beauvais found answer to that question. Who was it she loved? She sprang to her husband's breast, sheltering him with the body that had been disloyal to its soul, and she died there—with a bullet through her heart.

Joseph Brecht told us how, in the horror of his work—and possessed now by a terrible fear—he ran from the cabin and fled for his life. And Andre Beauvais must have remained with his dead. For it was many hours later before he took up the trail of the man whom he made solemn oath to his God to kill. Like a hunted hare, Joseph Brecht eluded him, and it was weeks before the fox-trapper came upon him. Andre Beauvais scorned to kill him from ambush. He wanted to choke his life out slowly, with his two hands, and he attacked him openly and fairly.

And in that cabin—gasping for breath, dying as he thought, Joseph Brecht said to us: "It was one or the other. He had the best of me. I drew my revolver again—and killed him, killed Andre Beauvais, as I had killed his wife, Marie!"

Here in the South Joseph Brecht might not have been a bad man, gentlemen. In every man's heart there is a devil, but we do not know the man as bad until the devil is roused. And passion, the mad passion for a woman, had roused him. Now that it had made twice a murderer of him the devil slunk back into his hiding, and the man who had once been the clean-living, red-blooded Joseph Brecht was only a husk without a heart, slinking from place to place in the evasion of justice. For you men of the Royal Mounted Police were on his trail. You would have caught him, but you did not think of seeking for him in the Sulphur Hell. For two years he had lived there, and when he finished his story he was sitting on the edge of the cot, quite sane, gentlemen.

And for the first time *M'sieu*, my comrade, spoke.

"Let us bring up the dunnage from the canoe, *mon père*."

He led the way out of the cabin, and I followed. We were fifty steps away when he stopped suddenly.

"Ah," he said, "I have forgotten something. I will overtake you."

He turned back to the cabin, and I went on to the canoe.

He did not join me. When I returned with my burden, *M'sieu* appeared at the door. He amazed me, startled me, I will say, gentlemen. I could not imagine such a change as I saw in him—that man of horrible silence, of grim, dark mystery. He was smiling; his white teeth shone; his voice was the voice of another man. He seemed to me ten years younger as he stood there, and as I dropped my load and went in he was laughing, and his hand was laid pleasantly on my shoulder.

Across the cot, with his head stretched down to the floor, his eyes bulging and his jaws agape, lay Joseph Brecht. I sprang to him. He was dead. And then I SAW Gentlemen, he had been choked to death!

"He made one leetle meestake, *mon père*. Andre Beauvais did not die. I am Andre Beauvais."

That is all, gentlemen of the Royal Mounted. May the Law have mercy!

The Mouse

"Why, you ornery little cuss," said Falkner, pausing with a forkful of beans half way to his mouth. "Where in God A'mighty's name did YOU come from?"

It was against all of Jim's crude but honest ethics of the big wilderness to take the Lord's name in vain, and the words he uttered were filled more with the softness of a prayer than the harshness of profanity. He was big, and his hands were hard and knotted, and his face was covered with a coarse red scrub of beard. But his hair was blond, and his eyes were blue, and just now they were filled with unbounded amazement. Slowly the fork loaded with beans descended to his plate, and he said again, barely above a whisper:

"Where in God A'mighty's name DID you come from?"

There was nothing human in the one room of his wilderness cabin to speak of. At the first glance there was nothing alive in the room, with the exception of Jim Falkner himself. There was not even a dog, for Jim had lost his one dog weeks before. And yet he spoke, and his eyes glistened, and for a full minute after that he sat as motionless as a rock. Then something moved—at the farther end of the rough board table. It was a mouse—a soft, brown, bright-eyed little mouse, not as large as his thumb. It was not like the mice Jim had been accustomed to see in the North woods, the larger, sharp-nosed, rat-like creatures which sprung his traps now and then, and he gave a sort of gasp through his beard.

"I'm as crazy as a loon if it isn't a sure-enough down-home mouse, just like we used to catch in the kitchen down in Ohio," he told himself. And for the third time he asked. "Now where in God A'mighty's name DID YOU come from?"

The mouse made no answer. It had humped itself up into a little ball, and was eyeing Jim with the keenest of suspicion.

"You're a thousand miles from home, old man," Falkner addressed it, still without a movement. "You're a clean thousand miles straight north of the kind o' civilization you was born in, and I want to know how you got here. By George—is it possible—you got mixed up in that box of stuff SHE sent up? Did you come from HER?"

He made a sudden movement, as if he expected an answer, and in a flash the mouse had scurried off the table and had disappeared under his bunk.

"The little cuss!" said Falkner. "He's sure got his nerve!"

He went on eating his beans, and when he had done he lighted a lamp, for the half Arctic darkness was falling early, and began to clear away the dishes. When he had done he put a scrap of bannock and a few beans on the corner of the table.

"I'll bet he's hungry, the little cuss," he said. "A thousand miles—in that box!"

He sat down close to the sheet-iron box stove, which was glowing red-hot, and filled his pipe. Kerosene was a precious commodity, and he had turned down the lamp wick until he was mostly in gloom. Outside a storm was wailing down across the Barrens from the North. He could hear the swish of the spruce-boughs overhead, and those moaning, half-shrieking sounds that always came with storm from out of the North, and sometimes fooled even him into thinking they were human cries. They had seemed more and more human to him during the past three days, and he was growing afraid. Once or twice strange thoughts had come into his head, and he had tried to fight them down. He had known of men whom loneliness had driven mad—and he was terribly lonely. He shivered as a piercing blast of wind filled with a mourning wail swept over the cabin.

And that day, too, he had been taken with a touch of fever. It burned more hotly in his blood tonight, and he knew that it was the loneliness—the emptiness of the world about him, the despair and black foreboding that came to him with the first early twilights of the Long Night. For he was in the edge of that Long Night. For weeks he would only now and then catch a glimpse of the sun. He shuddered.

A hundred and fifty miles to the south and east there was a Hudson's Bay post. Eighty miles south was the nearest trapper's cabin he knew of. Two months before he had gone down to the post, with a thick beard to cover his face, and had brought back supplies—and the box. His wife had sent up the box to him, only it had come to him as "John Blake" instead of Jim Falkner, his right name. There were things in it for him to wear, and pictures of the sweet-faced wife who was still filled with prayer and hope for him, and of the kid, their boy. "He is walking now," she had written to him, "and a dozen times a day he goes to your picture and says 'Pa-pa—Pa-pa'—and every night we talk about you before we go to bed, and pray God to send you back to us soon."

"God bless 'em!" breathed Jim.

He had not lighted his pipe, and there was something in his eyes that shimmered and glistened in the dull light. And then, as he sat silent, his eyes clearing, he saw that the little mouse had climbed back to the edge of the table. It did not eat the food he had placed there for it, but humped itself up in a tiny ball again, and its tiny shining eyes looked in his direction.

"You're not hungry," said Jim, and he spoke aloud. "YOU'RE lonely, too—that's it!"

A strange thrill shot through him at the thought, and he wondered again if he was mad at the longing that filled him—the desire to reach out and snuggle the little creature in his hand, and hold it close up to his bearded face, and TALK TO IT! He laughed, and drew his stool a little more into the light. The mouse did not run. He edged nearer and nearer, until his elbows rested on the table, and a curious feeling of pleasure took the place of his loneliness when he saw that the mouse was looking at him, and yet seemed unafraid.

"Don't be scairt," he said softly, speaking directly to it. "I won't hurt you. No, siree, I'd—I'd cut off a hand before I'd do that. I ain't had any company but you for two months. I ain't seen a human face, or heard a human voice—nothing—nothing but them shrieks 'n' wails 'n' baby-cryings out there in the wind. I won't hurt you—" His voice was almost pleading in its gentleness. And for the tenth time that day he felt, with his fever, a sickening dizziness in his head. For a moment or two his vision was blurred, but he could still see the mouse—farther away, it seemed to him.

"I don't s'pose you've killed anyone—or anything," he said, and his voice seemed thick and distant to him. "Mice don't kill, do they? They live on—cheese. But I have—I've killed. I killed a man. That's why I'm here."

His dizziness almost overcame him, and he leaned heavily against the table. Still the little mouse did not move. Still he could see it through the strange gauze veil before his eyes.

"I killed—a man," he repeated, and now he was wondering why the mouse did not say something at that remarkable confession. "I killed him, old man, an' you'd have done the same if you'd been in my place. I didn't mean to. I struck too hard. But I found 'im in my cabin, an' SHE was fighting—fighting him until her face was scratched an' her clothes torn,—God bless her dear heart!—fighting him to the last breath, an' I come just in time! He didn't think I'd be back for a day—a black-hearted devil we'd fed when he came to our door hungry. I killed him. And they've hunted me ever since. They'll put a rope round my neck, an' choke me to death if they catch me—because I came in time to save her! That's law!

"But they won't find me. I've been up here a year now, and in the spring I'm going down there—where you come from—back to the Girl and the Kid. The policemen won't be looking for me then. An' we're going to some other part of the world, an' live happy. She's waitin' for me, she an' the kid, an' they know I'm coming in the spring. Yessir, I killed a man. An' they want to kill me for it. That's the law–Canadian law—the law that wants an eye for an eye and a tooth for a tooth, an' where there ain't no extenuatin' circumstance. They call it murder. But it wasn't—was it?"

He waited for an answer. The mouse seemed going farther and farther away from him. He leaned more heavily on the table.

"It wasn't—was it?" he persisted.

His arms reached out; his head dropped forward, and the little mouse scurried to the floor. But Falkner did not know that it had gone.

"I killed him, an' I guess I'd do it again," he said, and his words were only a whisper. "An' tonight they're prayin' for me down there—she ' the kid—an' he's sayin', 'Pa-pa—Pa-pa'; an' they sent you up—to keep me comp'ny—"

His head dropped wearily upon his arms. The red stove crackled, and turned slowly black. In the cabin it grew darker, except where the dim light burned on the table. Outside the storm wailed and screeched down across the Barren. And after a time the mouse came back. It looked at Jim Falkner. It came nearer, until it touched the unconscious man's sleeve. More daringly it ran over his arm. It smelled of his fingers.

Then the mouse returned to the corner of the table, and began eating the food that Falkner had placed there for it.

The wick of the lamp had burned low when Falkner raised his head. The stove was black and cold. Outside, the storm still raged, and it was the shivering shriek of it over the cabin that Falkner first heard. He felt terribly dizzy, and there was a sharp, knife-like pain just back of his eyes. By the gray light that came through the one window he knew that what was left of Arctic day had come. He rose to his feet, and staggered about like a drunken man as he rebuilt the fire, and he tried to laugh as the truth dawned upon him that he had been sick, and that he had rested for hours with his head on the table. His back seemed broken. His legs were numb, and hurt when he stepped on them. He swung his arms a little to bring back circulation, and rubbed his hands over the fire that began to crackle in the stove.

It was the sickness that had overcome him—he knew that. But the thought of it did not appal him as it had yesterday, and the day before. There seemed to be something in the cabin now that comforted and soothed him, something that took away a part of the loneliness that was driving him mad. Even as he searched about him, peering into the dark corners and at the bare walls, a word formed on his lips, and he half smiled. It was a woman's name—Hester. And a warmth entered into him. The pain left his head. For the first time in weeks he felt DIFFERENT. And slowly he began to realize what had wrought the change. He was not alone. A message had come to him from the one who was waiting for him miles away; something that lived, and breathed, and was as lonely as himself. It was the little mouse.

He looked about eagerly, his eyes brightening, but the mouse was gone. He could not hear it. There seemed nothing unusual to him in the words he spoke aloud to himself.

"I'm going to call it after the Kid," he chuckled, "I'm goin' to call it Little Jim. I wonder if it's a girl mouse—or a boy mouse?"

He placed a pan of snow-water on the stove and began making his simple preparations for breakfast. For the first time in many days he felt actually hungry. And then all at once he stopped, and a low cry that was half joy and half wonder broke from his lips. With tensely gripped hands and eyes that shone with a strange light he stared straight at the blank surface of the log wall—through it—and a thousand miles away. He remembered THAT day—years ago—the scenes of which came to him now as though they had been but yesterday. It was afternoon, in the glorious summer, and he had gone to Hester's home. Only the day before Hester had promised to be his wife, and he remembered how fidgety and uneasy and yet wondrously happy he was as he sat out on the big white veranda, waiting for her to put on her pink muslin dress, which went go well with the gold of her hair and the blue of her eyes. And as he sat there, Hester's Maltese pet came up the steps, bringing in its jaws a tiny, quivering brown mouse. It was playing with the almost lifeless little creature when Hester came through the door.

He heard again the low cry that came from her lips then. In an instant she had snatched the tiny, limp thing from between the cat's paws, and had faced him. He was laughing at her, but the glow in her blue eyes sobered him. "I didn't think you—would take pleasure in that, Jim," she said. "It's only a mouse, but it's alive, and I can feel its poor little heart beating!"

They had saved it, and he, a little ashamed at the smallness of the act, had gone with Hester to the barn and made a nest for it in the hay. But the wonderful words that he remembered were these: "Perhaps some day a little mouse will help you, Jim!" Hester had spoken laughingly. And her words had come true!

All the time that Falkner was preparing and eating his breakfast he watched for the mouse, but it did not appear. Then he went to the door. It swung outward, and it took all his weight to force it open. On one side of the cabin the snow was drifted almost to the roof. Ahead of him he could barely make out the dark shadow of the scrub spruce forest beyond the little clearing he had made. He could hear the spruce-tops wailing and twisting in the storm, and the snow and wind stung his face, and half blinded him.

It was dark—dark with that gray and maddening gloom that yesterday would have driven him still nearer to the merge of madness. But this morning he laughed as he listened to the wailings in the air and stared out into the ghostly chaos. It was not the thought of his loneliness that come to him now, but the thought that he was safe. The Law could not reach him now, even if it knew where he was. And before it began its hunt for him again in the spring he would be hiking southward, to the Girl and the Baby, and it would still be hunting for him when they three would be making a new home for themselves in some other part of the world. For the first time in months he was almost happy. He closed and bolted the door, and began to WHISTLE. He was amazed at the change in himself, and wonderingly he stared at his reflection in the cracked bit of mirror against the wall. He grinned, and addressed himself aloud.

"You need a shave," he told himself. "You'd scare fits out of anything alive! Now that we've got company we've got to spruce up, an' look civilized."

It took him an hour to get rid of his heavy beard. His face looked almost boyish again. He was inspecting himself in the mirror when he heard a sound that turned him slowly toward the table. The little mouse was nosing about his tin plate. For a few moments Falkner watched it, fearing to move. Then he cautiously began to approach the table. "Hello there, old chap," he said, trying to make his voice soft and ingratiating. "Pretty late for breakfast, ain't you?"

At his approach the mouse humped itself into a motionless ball and watched him. To Falkner's delight it did not run away when he reached the table and sat down. He laughed softly.

"You ain't afraid, are you?" he asked. "We're goin' to be chums, ain't we? Yessir, we're goin' to be chums!"

For a full minute the mouse and the man looked steadily at each other. Then the mouse moved deliberately to a crumb of bannock and began nibbling at its breakfast.

For ten days there was only an occasional lull in the storm that came from out of the North. Before those ten days were half over, Jim and the mouse understood each other. The little mouse itself solved the problem of their nearer acquaintance by running up Falkner's leg one morning while he was at breakfast, and coolly investigating him

243

from the strings of his *moccasin* to the collar of his blue shirt. After that it showed no fear of him, and a few days later would nestle in the hollow of his big hand and nibble fearlessly at the bannock which Falkner would offer it. Then Jim took to carrying it about with him in his coat pocket. That seemed to suit the mouse immensely, and when Jim went to bed nights, or it grew too warm for him in the cabin, he would hang the coat over his bunk, with the mouse still in it, so that it was not long before the little creature made up its mind to take full possession of the pocket. It intimated as much to Falkner on the tenth and last day of the storm, when it began very business-like operations of building a nest of paper and rabbits' fur in the coat pocket. Jim's heart gave a big and sudden jump of delight when he saw the work going on.

"Bless my soul, I wonder if it's a girl mouse an' we're goin' to have BABIES!" he gasped.

After that he did not wear the coat, through fear of disturbing the nest. The two became more and more friendly, until finally the mouse would sit on Jim's shoulder at meal time, and nibble at bannock. What little trouble the mouse caused only added to Falkner's love for it.

"He's a human little cuss," he told himself one day, as he watched the mouse busy at work caching away scraps of food, which it carried through a crack in the sapling floor. "He's that human I've got to put all my grub in the tin cans or we'll go short before spring!" His chief trouble was to keep his snowshoes out of his tiny companion's reach. The mouse had developed an unholy passion for *babiche*, the caribou skin thongs used in the webs of his shoes, and one of the webs was half eaten away before Falkner discovered what was going on. At last he was compelled to suspend the shoes from a nail driven in one of the roof-beams.

In the evening, when the stove glowed hot, and a cotton wick sputtered in a pan of caribou grease on the table, Falkner's chief diversion was to tell the mouse all about his plans, and hopes, and what had happened in the past. He took an almost boyish pleasure in these one-sided entertainments—and yet, after all, they were not entirely one-sided, for the mouse would keep its bright, serious-looking little eyes on Falkner's face; it seemed to understand, if it could not talk.

Falkner loved to tell the little fellow of the wonderful days of four or five years ago away down in the sunny Ohio valley where he had courted the Girl and where they lived before they moved to the farm in Canada. He tried to impress upon Little Jim's mind what it meant for a great big, unhandsome fellow like himself to be loved by a tender slip of a girl whose hair was like gold and whose eyes were as blue as the wood-violets. One evening he fumbled for a minute under his bunk and came back to the table with a worn and finger-marked manila envelope, from which he drew tenderly and with almost trembling care a long, shining tress of golden hair.

"That HERS," he said proudly, placing it on the table close to the mouse. "An' she's got so much of it you can't see her to the hips when she takes it down; an' out in the sun it shines like—like—glory!"

The stove door crashed open, and a number of coals fell out upon the floor. For a few minutes Falkner was busy, and when he returned to the table he gave a gasp of astonishment. The curl and the mouse were gone! Little Jim had almost reached its nest with its lovely burden when Falkner captured it.

"You little cuss!" he breathed revently. "Now I know you come from her! I know it!"

In the weeks that followed the storm Falkner again followed his trap-lines, and scattered poison-baits for the white foxes on the Barren. Early in January the second great storm of that year came from out of the North. It gave no warning, and Falkner was caught ten miles from camp. He was making a struggle for life before he reached the shack. He was exhausted, and half blinded. He could hardly stand on his feet when he staggered up against his own door. He could see nothing when he entered. He stumbled over a stool, and fell to the floor. Before he could rise a strange weight was upon him. He made no resistance, for the storm had driven the last ounce of strength from his body.

"It's been a long chase, but I've got you now, Falkner," he heard a triumphant voice say. And then came the dreaded formula, feared to the uttermost limits of the great Northern wilderness: "I warn you! You are my prisoner, in the name of His Majesty, the King!"

Corporal Carr, of the Royal Mounted of the Northwest, was a man without human sympathies. He was thin faced, with a square, bony jaw, and lips that formed a straight line. His eyes were greenish, like a cat's, and were constantly shifting. He was a beast of prey, as much as the wolf, the lynx, or the fox—and his prey was men. Only such a man as Carr, alone would have braved the treacherous snows and the intense cold of the Arctic winter to run him down. Falkner knew that, as an hour later he looked over the roaring stove at his captor. About Carr there was something of the unpleasant quickness, the sinuous movement, of the little white ermine—the outlaw of the wilderness. His eyes were as merciless. At times Falkner caught the same red glint in them. And above his despair, the utter hopelessness of his situation, there rose in him an intense hatred and loathing of the man.

Falkner's hands were then securely tied behind him.

"I'd put the irons on you," Carr had explained a hard, emotionless voice, "only I lost them somewhere back there."

Beyond that he had not said a dozen words. He had built up the fire, thawed himself out, and helped himself to food. Now, for the first time, he loosened up a bit.

"I've had a devil of a chase," he said bitterly, a cold glitter in his eyes as he looked at Falkner. "I've been after you three months, and now that I've got you this accursed storm is going to hold me up! And I left my dogs and outfit a mile back in the scrub."

"Better go after 'em," replied Falkner. "If you don't there won't be any dogs an' outfit by morning."

Corporal Carr rose to his feet and went to the window. In a moment he turned.

"I'll do that," he said. "Stretch yourself out on the bunk. I'll have to lace you down pretty tight to keep you from playing a trick on me."

There was something so merciless and brutal in his eyes and voice that Falkner felt like leaping upon him, even with his hands tied behind his back.

He was glad, however, that Carr had decided to go. He was, filled with an overwhelming desire to be rid of him, if only for an hour.

He went to the bunk and lay down. Corporal Carr approached, pulling a roll of *babiche* cord from his pocket.

"If you don't mind you might tie my hands in front instead of behind," suggested Falkner. "It's goin' to be mighty unpleasant to have 'em under me, if I've got to lay here for an hour or two."

"Not on your life I won't tie 'em in front!" snapped Carr, his little eyes glittering. And then he gave a cackling laugh, and his eyes were as green as a cat's. "An' it won't be half so unpleasant as having something 'round your NECK!" he joked.

"I wish I was free," breathed Falkner, his chest heaving. "I wish we could fight, man t' man. I'd be willing to hang then, just to have the chance to break your neck. You ain't a man of the Law. You're a devil."

Carr laughed the sort of laugh that sends a chill up one's back, and drew the caribou-skin cord tight about Falkner's ankles.

"Can't blame me for being a little careful," he said in his revolting way. "By your hanging I become a Sergeant. That's my reward for running you down."

He lighted the lamp and filled the stove before he left the cabin. From the door he looked back at Falkner, and his face was not like a man's, but like that of some terrible death-spirit, ghostly, and thin, and exultant in the dim glow of the lamp. As he opened the door the roar of the blizzard and a gust of snow filled the cabin. Then it closed, and a groaning curse fell from Falkner's lips. He strained fiercely at the thongs that bound him, but after the first few minutes he lay still breathing hard, knowing that every effort he made only tightened the caribou-skin cord that bound him.

On his back, he listened to the storm. It was filled with the same strange cries and moaning sound that had almost driven him to madness, and now they sent through him a shivering chill that he had not felt before, even in the darkest and most hopeless hours of his loneliness and despair. A breath that was almost a sob broke from his lips as a vision of the Girl and the Kid came to shut out from his ears the moaning tumult of the wind. A few hours before he had been filled with hope—almost happiness, and now he was lost. From such a man as Carr there was no hope for mercy, or of escape. Flat on his back, he closed his eyes, and tried to think—to scheme something that might happen in his favour, to foresee an opportunity that might give him one last chance. And then, suddenly, he heard a sound. It travelled over the blanket that formed a pillow for his head. A cool, soft little nose touched his ear, and then tiny feet ran swiftly over his shoulder, and halted on his breast. He opened his eyes, and stared.

"You little cuss!" he breathed. A hundred times he had spoken those words, and each time they were of increasing wonder and adoration. "You little cuss!" he whispered again, and he chuckled aloud.

The mouse was humped on his breast in that curious little ball that it made of itself, and was eyeing him, Jim thought, in a questioning sort of way, "What's the matter with you?" it seemed to ask. "Where are your hands?"

And Jim answered:

"They've got me, old man. Now what the dickens are we going to do?"

The mouse began investigating. It examined his shoulder, the end of his chin, and ran along his arm, as far as it could go.

"Now what do you think of that!" Falkner exclaimed softly. "The little cuss is wondering where my hands are!" Gently he rolled over on his side.

"There they are," he said, "hitched tighter 'n bark to a tree!"

He wiggled his fingers, and in a moment he felt the mouse. The little creature ran across the opened palm of his hand to his wrist, and then every muscle in Falkner's body grew tense, and one of the strangest cries that ever fell from human lips came from his. The mouse had found once more the dried hide-flesh of which the snowshoe webs were made. It had found *babiche*. And it had begun TO GNAW!

In the minutes that followed Falkner scarcely breathed. He could feel the mouse when it worked. Above the stifled beating of his heart he could hear its tiny jaws. In those moments he knew that his last hope of life hung in the balance. Five, ten minutes passed, and not until then did he strain at the thongs that bound his wrists. Was that the bed that had snapped? Or was it the breaking of one of the *babiche* cords? He strained harder. The thongs were loosening; his wrists were freer; with a cry that sent the mouse scurrying to the floor he doubled himself half erect, and fought like a madman. Five minutes later and he was free.

He staggered to his feet, and looked at his wrists. They were torn and bleeding. His second thought was of Corporal Carr—and a weapon. The man-hunter had taken the precaution to empty the chambers of Falkner's revolver and rifle and throw his cartridges out in the snow. But his skinning-knife was still in its sheath and belt, and he buckled it about his waist. He had no thought of killing Carr, though he hated the man almost to the point of murder. But his lips set in a grim smile as he thought of what he WOULD do.

He knew that when Carr returned he would not enter at once into the cabin. He was the sort of man who would never take an unnecessary chance. He would go first to the little window—and look in. Falkner turned the lamp-wick lower, and placed the lamp on the table directly between the window and the bunk. Then he rolled his blankets into something like a human form, and went to the window to see the effect. The bunk was in deep shadow. From the window Corporal Carr could not see beyond the lamp. Then Falkner waited, out of range of the window, and close to the door.

It was not long before he heard something above the wailing of the storm. It was the whine of a dog, and he knew that a moment later the Corporal's ghostly face was peering in at the window. Then there came the sudden, swift opening of the door, and Carr sprang in like a cat, his hand on the butt of his revolver, still obeying that first governing law of his merciless life—caution, Falkner was so near that he could reach out and touch Carr, and in an instant he was at his enemy's throat. Not a cry fell from Carr's lips. There was death in the terrible grip of Falkner's hands, and like one whose neck had been broken Carr sank to the floor. Falkner's grip tightened, and he did not loosen it until Carr was black in the face and his jaw fell open. Then Falkner bound him hand and foot with the *babiche* thongs, and dragged him to the bunk.

Through the open door one of the sledge-dogs had thrust his head and shoulders. It was a Barracks team, accustomed to warmth and shelter, and Falkner had no difficulty in getting the leader and his three mates inside. To make friends with them he fed them chunks of raw caribou meat, and when Carr opened his eyes he was busy packing. He laughed joyously when he saw that the man-hunter had regained consciousness, and was staring at him with evident malice.

"Hello, Carr," he greeted affably. "Feeling better? Tables sort of turned, ain't they?"

Carr made no answer. His white lips were set like thin bands of steel.

"I'm getting ready to leave you," Falkner explained, as he rolled up a blanket and shoved it into his rubber pack-pouch. "And you're going to stay here—until spring. Do you get onto that? You've GOT to stay. I'm going to leave you marooned, so to speak. You couldn't travel a hundred yards out there without snowshoes, and I'm goin' to take your snowshoes. And I'm goin' to take your guns, and burn your pack, your coat, mittens, cap, an' *moccasins*. Catch on? I'm not goin' to kill you, and I'm going to leave you enough grub to last until spring, but you won't dare risk yourself out in the cold and snow. If you do, you'll freeze off your tootsies, and make your lungs sick. Don't you feel sort of pleasant—you—you—devil!"

Six hours later Falkner stood outside the cabin. The dogs were in their traces, and the sledge was packed. The storm had blown itself out, and a warmer temperature had followed in the path of the blizzard. He wore his coat now, and gently he felt of the bulging pocket, and laughed joyously as he faced the South.

"It's goin' to be a long hike, you little cuss," he said softly. "It's goin' to be a darned long hike. But we'll make it. Yessir, we'll make it. And won't they be s'prised when we fall in on 'em, six months ahead of time?"

He examined the pocket carefully, making sure that he had buttoned down the flap.

"I wouldn't want to lose you," he chuckled. "Next to her, an' the kid, I wouldn't want to lose you!"

Then, slowly, a strange smile passed over his face, and he gazed questioningly for a moment at the pocket which he held in his hand.

"You nervy little cuss!" he grinned. "I wonder if you're a girl mouse, an' if we're goin' to have a fam'ly on the way home! An'—an'—what the dickens do you feed baby mice?"

He lowered the pocket, and with a sharp command to the waiting dogs turned his face into the South.

LEONAUR

ALSO FROM LEONAUR
AVAILABLE IN SOFTCOVER OR HARDCOVER WITH DUST JACKET

THE PRISONER OF ZENDA & ITS SEQUEL RUPERT OF HENTZAU *by Anthony Hope*—Two famous novels of high adventure in one volume.

THE GLADIATORS *by G. J. Whyte Melville*—A Classic Novel of Ancient Rome—Three Volumes in One Special Edition.

THE COMPLETE CAPTAIN DANGEROUS *by George Augustus Sala*—The Adventures of a Soldier, Sailor, Merchant, Spy, Slave and Bashaw of the Grand Turk.

ORTHERIS, LEAROYD & MULVANEY *by Rudyard Kipling*—The Complete Soldiers Three stories.

SIR NIGEL & THE WHITE COMPANY *by Arthur Conan Doyle*—Two Classic Novels of the 100 Years' War.

THE ILLUSTRATED & COMPLETE BRIGADIER GERARD *by Arthur Conan Doyle*—All 18 Stories with the Original Strand Magazine Illustrations by Wollen and Paget.

THE OHIO RIVER TRILOGY 1: BETTY ZANE *by Zane Grey*—The land along the Ohio River is newly settled. Indomitable men and women—Col. Zane and his family, the McCollochs, Wetzel, the "Death Wind" Indian killer, among them—have hewn a life out of the frontier wilderness.

THE OHIO RIVER TRILOGY 2: THE SPIRIT OF THE BORDER *by Zane Grey*—Fort Henry still stands as a bastion for the settlers on the frontier along the Ohio River. More pioneers are now moving west to carve new lives out of the wilderness.

THE OHIO RIVER TRILOGY 3: THE LAST TRAIL *by Zane Grey*—This final volume of Zane Grey's Ohio River Trilogy is a gripping finale to a great series—another thrilling story of life and death on the early American frontier and a classic in the tradition of Drums Along the Mohawk.

THE NAPOLEONIC NOVELS: VOLUME 1 *by Erckmann-Chatrian*—This book comprises two linked novels—*The Conscript & Waterloo*—about the adventures a young conscript in the French Army. during the Napoleonic wars.

THE NAPOLEONIC NOVELS: VOLUME 2 *by Erckmann-Chatrian*—*The Blockade of Phalsburg & The Invasion of France in 1814*—the events portrayed in these two novels of the Napoleonic period properly fit in time between those of the first volume. They appear together here since each—unlike the other two in this series—is a stand alone work.

LEONAUR

ALSO FROM LEONAUR
AVAILABLE IN SOFTCOVER OR HARDCOVER WITH DUST JACKET

THE CIVIL WAR NOVELS: 1 *by Joseph A. Altsheler*—*The Guns of Bull Run &
The Guns of Shiloh*—the first and second novels of a series of eight adventures which
follow the momentous events, campaigns and battles of the great American Civil War
between the Northern and Southern states.

THE CIVIL WAR NOVELS: 2 *by Joseph A. Altsheler*—*The Scouts of Stonewall
& The Sword of Antietam*—the third and fourth novels of a series of nine adventures
which follow the momentous events, campaigns and battles of the great American
Civil War between the Northern and Southern states.

THE CIVIL WAR NOVELS: 3 *by Joseph A. Altsheler*—*The Star of Gettysburg
& The Rock of Chickamauga*—the fifth and sixth novels of a series of nine adventures
which follow the momentous events, campaigns and battles of the great American
Civil War between the Northern and Southern states.

THE CIVIL WAR NOVELS: 4 *by Joseph A. Altsheler*—*The Shades of the Wilderness & The Tree of Appomattox*—the seventh and eighth novels of a series of nine
adventures which follow the momentous events, campaigns and battles of the great
American Civil War between the Northern and Southern states.

THE CIVIL WAR NOVELS: 5 *by Joseph A. Altsheler*—*Before the Dawn: a Story
of the Fall of Richmond*—the last of a series of nine adventures which follow the momentous events, campaigns and battles of the great American Civil War between the
Northern and Southern states.

THE FRENCH & INDIAN WAR NOVELS: 1 *by Joseph A. Altsheler*—*The
Hunters of the Hills & The Shadow of the North*—In this three volume, six novel set the
story of the war, with many of its real life characters, is told through the adventures
of its principal characters, Robert Lennox, the hunter Willet and his Indian companion Tayoga.

THE FRENCH & INDIAN WAR NOVELS: 2 *by Joseph A. Altsheler*—*The
Rulers of the Lakes & The Masters of the Peaks*—In this three volume, six novel set the
story of the war, with many of its real life characters, is told through the adventures
of its principal characters, Robert Lennox, the hunter Willet and his Indian companion Tayoga.

THE FRENCH & INDIAN WAR NOVELS: 1 *by Joseph A. Altsheler*—*The Lords
of the Wild & The Sun of Quebec*—In this three volume, six novel set the story of the
war, with many of its real life characters, is told through the adventures of its principal
characters, Robert Lennox, the hunter Willet and his Indian companion Tayoga.

LEONAUR

ALSO FROM LEONAUR

AVAILABLE IN SOFTCOVER OR HARDCOVER WITH DUST JACKET

MR MUKERJI'S GHOSTS *by S. Mukerji*—Supernatural tales from the British Raj period by India's Ghost story collector.

KIPLINGS GHOSTS *by Rudyard Kipling*—Twelve stories of Ghosts, Hauntings, Curses, Werewolves & Magic.